THE ABRAXAS PROPHECY

A Minos Industries Novel

H.F. Payne

Copyright © 2024 S M Payne

All rights reserved

The characters and events portrayed in this book are fictitious. Any similarity to real persons, living or dead, is coincidental and not intended by the author.

No part of this book may be reproduced, or stored in a retrieval system, or transmitted in any form or by any means, electronic, mechanical, photocopying, recording, or otherwise, without express written permission of the author.

To my mum, for always being my biggest supporter.

BY H.F. PAYNE

Minos Industries Novels
The Abraxas Prophecy
The Abraxas Prophecy Explored
The Abraxas Prophecy Reborn

CHAPTER 1

The door clicked shut behind Parker. She locked it, threw herself onto her sofa and released a sigh of relief. She loved her family, but after a whole day with them, she was exhausted. Spending time with any of them separately was fine. However, with her parents, sister, brother-in-law and their four young boys, she could sometimes feel mentally and physically overwhelmed.

She looked around her living room, appreciating her safe space and the peace and quiet it brought. The only sound filtering through was the fridge whirring in the kitchen. It wasn't the biggest home, but it was perfect for her. She had made a few little changes since she moved in to make it feel like home, the one-bedroom house didn't allow for a large amount of furniture or many decorations.

Parker considered tidying up the mess strewn around from earlier in the day but decided that it could wait until the following morning. After settling down with a cup of tea, she unwound by watching a rerun of a murder mystery.

Luckily it was a Friday night, so she didn't have work in the morning. Message notifications had been pinging on her phone all day, from a group chat with her friends. After a quick scan, she had ascertained that they were updates on her friend's children, swimming lesson anecdotes and general grumbles about parent life. Once again, she struggled to relate and added an obligatory response which consisted of "lol", a laughing emoji and a heart.

Parker started her bedtime routine; she showered, pulled her long wavy hair up into a ponytail, removed her makeup and brushed her teeth. She grimaced whilst looking in the mirror, her brown roots were starting to get a little long. Parker would need to re-dye her hair soon, to maintain her preferred red colour. She had always thought that the red was more complimentary for her fair complexion and dusky blue eyes.

After climbing into bed and snuggling under the sheets, Parker could still hear her phone pinging messages. She muted the notifications and started to consider her predicament. Parker had turned twenty-eight the previous month and was feeling frustrated with her life's current trajectory. As she stared out of her skylight at the stars, she made a choice; she was going to start making changes.

Parker was considering her options and chuckled at the thought of the more outrageous ones. Starting a hobby was a good idea, but she was never going to attend a Zumba class or go scuba diving. Any sort of highly physical activity was excluded from the list of potentials. Parker enjoyed a nice leisurely walk as much as the next woman, but at her own pace, so there weren't many options available. Her lack of interest in high-octane pastimes was evident in her slightly rounded, hourglass figure. Parker went to sleep with the hope that she would come up with a fantastic idea by the morning.

When Parker woke, she took the next logical step, she began to search online for clubs or classes in her area. A few weren't considered due to the meeting time, location or lack of parking. The shortlist included a book club that met on Saturday afternoons, a pottery class on Sunday mornings or a jewellery design workshop on Wednesday evenings.

She was known for her impatience and hatred of waiting once her mind had been made up, so Parker emailed the book club secretary asking if she could attend. That way, if it didn't work out, she had two other classes to try. As she waited for an email response, Parker reluctantly decided that she should make an effort to clean up the previous day's mess.

It was slow work as Parker kept checking her phone

every five minutes for a response. Luckily, it wasn't too long until the email reply was in her inbox. They would welcome her attendance at the meeting and provided the salient details regarding the time and location.

Her plan was to mostly observe during the first meeting, as she wouldn't have time to read this week's book. Parker loved to read urban fantasy and was hoping that the book was one of the hundreds she had already read.

She checked her outfit to ensure that it was suitable, she wanted to give a good impression after all. Parker was happy, there were no erroneous stains from her cleaning frenzy on her jeans or green shirt. Parker brushed and re-straightened her hair, as it had turned frizzy from the exertion of cleaning. She slipped on her slightly scuffed Converse and headed out, feeling optimistic about the possibilities of the afternoon.

Pulling up outside the historical brick building in her old silver compact, Parker checked the time. She hated being late and always chose to arrive early, unless unavoidable. Whilst waiting she surveyed the building, admiring the beauty of the architecture. Parker had always admired the history and character associated with older buildings, as opposed to the new builds popping up everywhere. It was a warm, sunny day with a clear blue sky and all of the features of the building were showcased in all their glory.

Parker spent the next fifteen minutes on her phone, reading through the latest messages on her friend's group chat, checking emails and browsing entertainment news. She ensured that she was kept busy and her thoughts occupied whilst she waited, to prevent the inevitable anxiety associated with new situations and meeting new people.

A few minutes before the meeting time, Parker saw a group of elderly women entering the building. They were laughing and joking with each other. She climbed out of her car and followed them up the stairs.

As she walked through the large, wooden front door, she identified the building as a church community centre. There was a sign to the left, indicating the room where the book club was being held.

Parker entered the room and saw a circle of mismatched folding chairs, which had clearly had a lot of use over the years. Almost all of the seats were occupied by the ladies she had observed entering, most with a hot drink in one hand and a large book in the other. An overwhelming scent of lavender tickled her nose.

A few turned and smiled warmly at her as she took a seat, whilst the others were too engrossed in their own conversations to notice her entrance. "Hello, I'm Gladys." a lady to Parker's right whispered. Before Parker could respond she continued swiftly, "You must be Parker. Annabeth mentioned that we should be expecting a new member."

"Yes." Parker replied smiling, "I've always loved reading and thought it would be fun to attend a book club."

By then she could see that everyone else's conversations had come to a halt, as all eyes turned to the new attendee. Parker smiled nervously around the room, she hated to be the centre of attention. She had hoped to blend in at first until she was more comfortable.

All at once, several of the women started to ask questions, whether she was single, married, had a lovely man (or woman, one lady noted) waiting at home, what she did for a career etc. A woman stood up abruptly and announced that it was time for the book club to commence. Parker felt a surge of relief at the end of the interrogation.

When the woman in charge read out the title of this week's book, Parker realised too late that the type of book they would be discussing wouldn't be anything she typically enjoyed. Once again, acting without thought and on impulse had put her in a bit of a predicament.

Her face turned crimson as they all discussed at length, how the lead character had her wildest sensual desires fulfilled by the handsome brute. Surprisingly for Parker, the discussion became quite heated.

Joyce was dubious about the practicalities of having "nookie" in a cow shed. Betty was adamant that as long as there were no cows in there at the time, the characters could still enjoy a titillating experience. However, she did concede that any smells from cow excrement would be a definite mood killer, regardless of the levels of passion.

Parker tried her hardest to keep a straight face and not chuckle at the discussion unfolding. She wasn't typically prudish and quite enjoyed reading books with passionate intercourse. However, she hadn't prepared herself for this very unabashed discussion with a group of elderly ladies on a Saturday afternoon.

Parker scolded herself for her childish embarrassment and continued to find humour in the situation. This would be a fantastic story to regale to her best friend Julia later on that evening. Julia could tell her about whatever birthday party the kids had attended that day and Parker could tell her all about her new X-rated book club!

She would love to be as enthusiastic and carefree as these ladies when she reached her eighties, but it probably wasn't the right club for her to expand her social circle. On leaving the meeting, Parker was non-committal about whether she would attend the following Saturday but did tell the group how much she had enjoyed participating in their discussion. The book for the following week sounded even raunchier than the last.

Parker drove home with a smile on her face. Even though it had not been what she expected and it didn't fulfil the goal she'd set herself, it had been a fun afternoon. She kicked off her shoes as she entered her home and then proceeded to reheat leftover Chinese takeaway for dinner.

As she lived alone, there was no need for formalities like sitting at the tiny dining table. She swung her feet under her on the sofa and browsed the TV guide. Finally, she settled on a TV movie about a mystery-solving antique store owner, chosen for its easy-watching.

Parker fired off a quick message to Julia, sending her a

teasing line guaranteed to get her intrigued about her day: *Just wondering if it's weird to discuss sexual desires with a feisty eighty-year-old lady called Joyce x.*

Within two minutes her phone rang and Julia's picture popped up on the screen. Parker laughed as she answered, "Hello?" she enquired innocently.

"OK, spill. I've asked Jeremy to put the kids to bed because I literally cannot wait for this explanation!" Julia responded, desperate to hear what had ensued.

"Alright," Parker said whilst laughing, "strangely my message was completely true." She then proceeded to regale the events of the afternoon, Julia muffling her laughs to ensure she didn't miss any of the details. Once Parker had finished her recollection, Julia happily indulged in laughing loudly with Parker joining her in her elation.

This was followed by Julia's insistence that if she didn't have to ferry around the kids on Saturdays to ballet and the inevitable birthday parties, she would definitely attend the book club meetings going forward as they sounded thrilling. Parker found it amusing that her friend sounded genuinely disappointed.

After Julia had been updated on her plan to find new friends, she seemed quieter and less vocal. Parker sensed that she was worried about losing their friendship, so she quickly reassured her, "Of course, you know that it won't change anything between us. You won't be able to get rid of me that easily. I'm just hoping to expand my friendship group so that I have company when you're busy."

Julia sounded livelier after hearing the assurance, "I would love to be able to accompany you to the pottery and jewellery-making class, but on Wednesday evenings Sophia and Edith do ballet and on Sunday mornings we all attend Church." Parker was warmed by her friend's support and promised that she would keep her updated with any adventures, although, she wasn't expecting the same excitement as today.

Julia then confided in Parker her own update, advising of

the frustration she had been feeling towards a coworker, who spent the entire time making hot drinks and chatting with the male workers. Once Julia had finished her rant and Parker had provided a sympathetic ear, they ended the call with promises to keep each other abreast of further updates as they occurred.

It was getting late for Parker, but as it was a Saturday night, she climbed into bed after her usual nighttime routine and started a book she had been desperate to read for the last month. Just before starting, Parker re-read the email she had received from the pottery class, she wanted to confirm the time and location. Parker set an alarm on her phone, as she didn't want to be late the following morning.

Sunday arrived and Parker felt groggy; once she started reading a book, she couldn't put it down until she finished it. She loved a good read and always promised herself 'one more page', completely ignoring the following day's plans. Her eyes looked a little bloodshot and more tired than she would have liked. She would have usually slept in, but she had a class to attend.

Parker added concealer to her morning makeup ritual and promised herself some much-needed caffeine. She was eager to attend her first pottery class, loving the idea of making things and unleashing her creative side. She pulled on another pair of jeans, the same pair she usually wore on weekends, but this pair were starting to look well-worn. The Scooby-Doo T-shirt she wore had also seen better days, fading from frequent wear, but she didn't want to risk ruining any of her newer clothes. It was usually only worn around the house but felt appropriate.

The pottery class was within walking distance from her house but there was a chill in the air, so Parker pulled on her Converse and a light coat. Fortunately, it was dry with no rain forecast, so she didn't require an umbrella or raincoat. She set off with plenty of time, walking through the park instead of along the busy roads.

Parker smiled as she passed a group of giggling teenage girls enjoying the sunshine, and across the pond, she could see a father feeding the ducks with his toddler. It was a great way to start the day and she tilted her head back to embrace the warm rays. This positive mood wasn't even dampened when she stumbled over a small branch and almost fell.

She quickly scoured the faces of those she had seen, to check that they hadn't witnessed her clumsiness. Parker chuckled at her awkwardness and continued along the path, unable to afford any further trips due to her inattentiveness.

Her destination was one of the local colleges. It was eerie seeing a school with no students milling about and it made Parker feel slightly out of kilter.

Parker was looking for the Leach building on their sign and she spotted it, second from the bottom. It directed her to a building at the rear of the campus. It looked friendly and welcoming, with the exterior painted in bright orange and yellow hues, with a large purple swirl running through it.

The door as she approached looked shut. She rattled the handle but it was locked. She promptly pressed the doorbell located to the right of the doorway. Parker heard a harsh buzz from somewhere inside the building, followed shortly after by swift footsteps.

A lady appeared and Parker observed her as she approached. She looked to be in her early forties, of Spanish origin and had thick black, curly hair partially wrapped in a teal head scarf. She had already donned an apron over the top of a floral, knee-length dress. She was muttering to herself as she opened the door and said with a smile, "Hello, are you here for the pottery class?"

"Hi, yes. I emailed you yesterday, enquiring about joining your class. My name's Parker."

"Of course, you are slightly early, so I haven't had a chance to open up yet. You are more than welcome to come in and get yourself seated. I'm Judy."

Parker entered as Judy held the door open for her. She paused to allow Judy to take the lead. The room they entered was large and bright, with windows along two of the walls. There were seven tables spread around the room, with a potter's wheel next to each. Parker had watched a pottery show and had picked up the basics, so could identify most of the equipment provided.

Judy suggested that she choose one of the tables to set up on as they weren't pre-assigned. Parker chose a table next to one of the windows, which had the benefit of fresh air and good lighting. The walls were covered with various ceramic items, ornaments, clocks and a selection of ornate plates. They had been created by the students of the college, names were included under each piece of art.

Whilst Parker had been observing the room, Judy had been busy setting out lumps of clay and sheets of paper with ideas. A few seconds later, Parker heard voices from the hallway outside and three individuals entered the room. There was a tall young male, she guessed early twenties. He was pale, wore an all-black outfit and had blond spiky hair.

Following him in was an older lady with a tanned glow to her face, she appeared to be in her forties. This lady was wearing a red shirt with a black and white polka dot skirt, she had mousy brown hair which had been scraped back into a hair clip.

The third individual was another lady in her forties, with dark brown skin and gorgeous black curly hair that framed her face. She was wearing a pink vest top and fitted dark blue jeans. They started talking to Judy who promptly introduced them to Parker as Andy, Isabelle and Sandra. Greetings were exchanged, which allowed Parker to introduce herself to the group.

All of a sudden, there was a commotion at the door and another individual burst in. The woman said breathlessly, "Sorry I'm late, I got sidetracked... again." And grinned at the four individuals. Parker unashamedly stared at the newest arrival; she was by far the most interesting. She was wearing a bright yellow fitted top that had a picture of a dodo in the centre and a forest green, knee-length flowing skirt. The bag hanging off her shoulder appeared to be a fluffy racoon. Her spiked pixie cut was jet black with a green tint. The tint complimented her emerald green eyes and her tanned, freckled complexion. This lady was in her mid-twenties, slim-figured and very tall.

Parker finally caught herself staring and mused that there couldn't possibly be a dull moment in her company. Judy must have mentioned to the newcomer that they had a new attendee, as she turned with an infectious smile towards Parker.

Parker immediately returned a genuine and unabashed grin. Before she could introduce herself properly, this whirlwind of colours, flamboyance and energy bounded straight up to Parker and plonked her bag down on the table next to hers.

"Hi, I'm Ellie. Well actually, my full name is Eileithyia but no one calls me that as it's such a mouthful, so I always go by Ellie. Only my parents use my full name. You must be Parker. I hope you don't mind if I take the table next to you. I always prefer sitting next to the window, I just feel better when I can see the outdoors."

Ellie barely stopped to catch a breath, but in the briefest of pauses, Parker responded in the same upbeat tone. She was trying to appear friendly and sociable, "No, of course I don't mind. I hope you don't mind that I may need to rely on you for help. It's been a long time since I made thumb pots in a pottery class at school."

"Ooh, of course I'll help you. You'll love it, it's great getting to make anything you can imagine."

Parker thought that 'anything' might be slightly optimistic, as she was sure her skill level would be the limiter on her imagination. Before she could continue the conversation, Judy started talking about what they were going to make in today's class.

They were going to be using the potter's wheels and trying to throw vases, the complexity varying in line with the skill of the individual. The clay had been handed out and Parker was directed to where the aprons were hung.

Judy demonstrated one of the more basic designs, making it seem so simple, followed by a more complex style with a bulbous base and an elegantly flared lip. Parker had already decided that it was better to do simple well, as opposed to spectacularly failing the more elaborate vase.

She sat at the wheel and glimpsed over to what the others were doing. Ellie must have noticed her reticence and immediately started chatting to her, to put her at ease. "Don't worry, just try and centralise it as much as you can and go slowly. You can always try again until it works, but I think that you'll do fine."

Parker smiled at her and took a breath, before committing to smacking the clay onto the centre of the wheel. She placed her hands on either side and pressed firmly, before pushing the pedal to cause the wheel to spin. Parker had impressed herself and believed she was doing incredibly well on her first try; it was even starting to look a bit like a vase.

Her confidence grew and she pressed down on the pedal harder. It began to spin faster and faster, which in turn caused her to panic. Instead of releasing the pedal, she ended up pushing it down further. Under the strain from the increased speed, the clay vase flopped and was flung violently in all directions.

Parker gave a little yelp and raised her hands to shield her face from the chaos she was causing. She felt herself being splattered until she finally took her foot off the pedal completely. She wasn't ready to lower her hands and see the inevitable devastation.

There was a brief pause before Ellie burst out laughing. Parker took the laughter as a safe enough sign that she could come out of hiding and survey the scene. She saw the mess she'd caused and observed clay covering her entire area, along with big chunks on Ellie's apron and work area. The rest of the class were trying to politely conceal their laughter from Parker. She grinned, to reassure them that she was fine and also found it comical.

Judy checked that she was alright, then returned to her own project. Ellie walked over grinning. Parker could see small pieces of clay on her face and in her hair, so she was dreading looking at her own reflection. She was really glad that she hadn't worn anything nicer.

"That was brilliant!" Ellie beamed, "I've never seen such a spectacular pottery explosion."

"I'm so sorry, Ellie." Parker exclaimed whilst laughing into her hands, "I guess I should go back to making thumb pots!"

Ellie started pulling chunks of clay out of Parker's hair whilst failing to hide her grimace. "I hope you weren't planning on going out anywhere after this class. You may need to wash your hair first." The grimace soon turned back into a toothy grin.

"Luckily, I have no immediate plans following this, but I feel like I should confess that you may have one or two teeny tiny bits of clay in your own hair."

Ellie feigned shock and disgust before reverting to grinning, "Oh well, I guess neither of us should be seen in public after this impressive mess." They both proceeded to clean up the clay. Parker was grateful for Ellie's help and thought she should thank her in some way.

Parker apologetically said as they finished, "Thank you so much for helping me clean up this disaster. I know that we said we shouldn't be seen out in public, but as a thank you, can I take you out for a frappe or coffee? Hopefully, people will be less likely to think I usually look like this if you come with me!"

Ellie didn't hesitate, "You don't need to thank me, I'm sure you would have helped me too. However, I absolutely love frappes! I am actually starting to worry I've become addicted. I think that's a problem for another day though."

There were still twenty minutes left of class, so Parker decided to give it another go. This time she stayed slow and steady. The outcome was a very stubby and wide-walled vase, which probably wouldn't survive the kiln, but it was infinitely better than the first attempt. She optimistically thought that she wasn't a complete lost cause and promised herself that she would return to the pottery class.

Ellie and Parker walked out of the building together. Parker was secretly hopeful about the possibility of adding Ellie as a new friend. Her plan to widen her social group could be working. Ellie enquired, "Did you drive here?"

"No. I don't live far from here."

"I'll drive us, I know a great local coffee house."

Parker followed Ellie to her car, it was a bright orange Volkswagen Beetle. "Of course, it is," thought Parker aloud with a grin. She carefully climbed in, trying to not get clay on the seats. Ellie pulled up at a small building a couple of minutes later.

Ellie grabbed a table whilst Parker went up to the counter. She ordered their drinks, indulging in a chocolate brownie for herself and a millionaire shortbread for Ellie. They started chatting as soon as Parker's butt hit the seat.

"So, it doesn't look like we are getting too many funny looks, that's a definite bonus," Parker said.

"Nope, people are definitely used to seeing weirder. So, tell me, what caused you to come to the pottery class?"

"To be completely honest with you, I was just hoping to find something new to bring a little bit of interest into my currently boring life! All of my friends have settled down, so holidays away with them have dwindled and I've found that small children are not conducive to frequent evenings out." Parker replied, double-guessing her honesty and hoping she hadn't appeared too needy.

"Yes, I get that. I live in a big community, with lots of people taking an interest in my life and keeping me busy. It's a double-edged sword, lots of support but also lots of people with opinions about my life." Ellie looked contemplative for a minute, then exclaimed with excitement, "I know! I'm going to a neighbourhood street party tonight, lots of people going. It will help to kick off your new social life."

Parker hesitated briefly; she was nervous about meeting such a large number of strangers. She was also used to being in bed by half past nine, but she wanted this. Parker knew that she needed to put herself out there, so before she could change her mind, she confirmed her attendance and they exchanged phone numbers.

"I'll message you the details. It's casual, food and drinks

will be provided. Of course, you may want to wash your hair first." Ellie teased. They parted ways and Parker walked home after politely refusing a lift. She was nervous but excited and spent the time walking home thinking about what to wear for the party.

CHAPTER 2

Parker grabbed a bite to eat from the kitchen, as she didn't want to arrive at the party grumpy from hunger. She showered, blow dried and straightened her hair, once again bemoaning her roots. Makeup application was never one of her strongest skills, so she did her best with the basics, foundation, blusher, eyeshadow and mascara. She didn't worry about it being perfect, as the light would be starting to dim when she arrived.

Makeup done, she rifled through her wardrobe and looked at her jeans with longing. She had already shaved her legs, pre-empting a dress or skirt. Parker selected several different options and laid them out on the bed.

She settled on a black, skater-style dress, which fell just above her knees. It had elbow-length sleeves and a moderately low neckline. Parker wanted to make the most of her assets without being too risqué. She added a silver pendant necklace with matching earrings and a tennis bracelet.

Parker reviewed her reflection in the mirror and was happy with the look. The final part of the outfit was a pair of low-heeled, knee-high, black leather boots. They were her favourites and made her feel confident.

This was one occasion where she didn't want to arrive early. She waited until half-past nine before setting off. Parker double-checked that the essentials were in her black and silver purse, phone, keys, ID and money.

Ellie had provided her home address for Parker to leave her car outside. She promised that she would be waiting for her, so that she wouldn't have to arrive at the party alone. Parker appreciated Ellie's thoughtfulness and consideration, reaffirming her thoughts that she could be a great friend.

Ellie's house was in a neighbourhood that she hadn't visited before. The houses all looked to be recently built, of a similar design, with well-kept front gardens. The only variant seemed to be the size of the properties, some quite modest and others looking like they would fit an entire football team comfortably.

Parker expected Ellie's home to be colourful and quirky, maybe a peacock statue in the middle of the lawn. She started smiling to herself imagining it. However, Ellie's house was modest and quaint. Ivy was growing up and around her front door, which had been painted an electric shade of blue. There was also a vast array of plants in her garden. Parker would have loved to have a similar garden, but she wasn't willing to put in the work to make it happen.

Just as Parker lifted her hand to ring the bell, the door opened and Ellie stood there eagerly. Ellie had chosen to wear a brightly coloured rainbow jumpsuit, combined with a flamingo print bag, chunky plastic fuchsia jewellery and hot pink heels. They couldn't have looked more opposite in their attire if they tried, not that either of them cared.

Ellie grabbed her hand and steered Parker down the street, "I'm so glad that you chose to come tonight. There are lots of people that I want you to meet that I think you'll get on well with." Parker wasn't feeling anxious, as she was planning on sticking by Ellie's side the entire evening.

She could hear the chatter and music before she could see the party. They had only walked a short distance before Parker saw it. There were more people than she had expected, she guessed between sixty and eighty. Parker was surprised that there were this many people at a party on a Sunday night, she was not looking forward to going to work tomorrow.

She briefly considered calling in sick but knew that she wouldn't, as she would feel too guilty. It wasn't that she was instrumental at work or that things would fall apart without her, but she hated lying and always tried to choose honesty unless a little white lie was the better option.

Ellie called out, "Thalia!" A female turned her head and offered a friendly smile at Ellie, before looking towards Parker and frowning. Parker had always been self-conscious, so tried to ignore her feelings of insecurity and just dismissed them as her own paranoia. Thalia looked similar to Ellie in height and build, but slightly older. She had dark hair which had a blue tint in the evening light.

She was wearing a floor-length, halter-neck dress in sage green. Ellie explained, "This is Thalia, one of my sisters. She's always worrying about me, one of those people I mentioned who always want to have a say in my life choices." And rolled her eyes. As they reached where Thalia was standing, she had replaced the frown with the original friendly smile. It convinced Parker that she had been imagining it.

"Hey little sis, glad you could make the party. I thought you weren't coming." Thalia welcomed her.

Ellie replied, "I wasn't sure if I could make it, but after receiving all of your messages I decided to come. I also made a new friend today, who I thought would enjoy the fun. This is Parker."

Thalia turned her gaze towards Parker, "It's nice to meet you, help yourself to food and drink. Everyone who attends brings a selection, so we always have lots to go around." She noticed that Parker looked uncomfortable and correctly guessed the cause. "Don't worry about not bringing anything, there's more than enough food. Besides, you're a guest and therefore automatically exempt."

Parker breathed a sigh of relief but could see that Thalia was correct. It looked like there was enough food to feed hundreds of people and it all looked amazing. Ellie and Thalia guided her towards the food table and Thalia handed her a plate.

Thalia turned towards Ellie, "Could you do me a favour? I need your help bringing some plates and cups from my house. It won't take more than a couple of minutes." Ellie glanced at Parker who nodded, silently confirming that she was alright to be left alone.

The two sisters walked into the crowd and whilst Parker added food to her plate, she looked around at the other neighbours. People were gathered in small groups, laughing and chatting. They seemed to be a friendly and lively group of people, varying in age and ethnicity.

She had noticed people looking at her, who then quickly looked away when she made eye contact. An uneasy feeling started to fester in her stomach and it was growing. Those who were avoiding her eye contact also seemed to be having whispered conversations with other individuals within their groups.

Parker checked that her dress wasn't tucked into her knickers, having flashbacks to an embarrassing moment on a night out, and looked in her reflective phone case to ensure that she hadn't got anything stuck on her face. Parker decided to ignore it because she couldn't think of a reason as to why they would be focusing on her.

After spending several minutes trying to spot the sisters, she finally saw them walking back towards the group. Parker was relieved to see them return and belatedly thought that she should have offered to help carry the plates. When she could clearly see their expressions, Ellie no longer looked happy and lively, she looked dismayed and Thalia looked regretful. Parker wondered what had happened whilst they were away, but felt that it wasn't her business or place to ask.

Before Ellie rejoined Parker, arguing began a few houses down between a couple of people, which was getting louder by the minute. She couldn't yet hear what they were saying. The arguing appeared to stop suddenly when a bang pierced the silence. Everyone had turned to face the disturbance, but no one appeared to be concerned.

Subconsciously, Parker moved gradually towards the argument she was clearly too intrigued by to ignore. She navigated a large group of people and noticed a man and woman in the middle of the street. Most of the commotion came from the woman yelling at the man.

Parker was shocked to see that the house they were next to had its front door lying in the middle of the lawn. Baffled as to what could cause a door to fly off its hinges, she fixated on the couple.

All of a sudden, the woman's skin turned pale blue and her hair looked like it was moving underwater, in a slow wave. Parker couldn't look away, but she also couldn't believe what she was seeing.

"Astris! Calm down!" a voice boomed from behind her and a tall male rushed past. He looked well over six feet tall, in his early thirties and had a swimmer's physique; with broad shoulders and a tapered waist. The male had surfer-style blond hair, what appeared to be blue eyes and a tan that he had clearly been working on for a while.

He was wearing a tightly fitted white T-shirt which showcased his muscles and a pair of navy jeans, "What do you think you are doing?" The woman looked his way and paused slightly, but didn't seem to heed his order to calm down. She looked middle-aged with blonde hair and was wearing a floor-length blue summer dress.

She screamed deafeningly and pointed her finger at the male opposite her, who seemed unaffected by her anger. This clearly wasn't the first time that he had been on the receiving end of her wrath.

"How dare he? How dare he come back into my home after months of being away with no contact. No messages, calls or even an email to let me know he was alright. I thought something had happened to him, but no. He was shacked up with a bimbo off the coast of Jamaica!"

As she finished her last word, a hose pipe placed on a nearby lawn unravelled and a jet of water gushed towards the shameless male. It hit him straight in the centre of his chest and knocked him off his feet. Parker stood silently in amazement, wondering what unexplainable thing was going to happen next.

The man who had initially told Astris to calm down

walked over and spoke reprovingly to the male sprawled on the floor, "Jason! What on earth were you thinking? You know Astris has a temper and who can blame her this time? I think you need to leave for a while so she can cool off."

Jason started grumbling and cautiously made his way to his feet. He was a middle-aged man with receding red hair and a pale complexion. "Sorry Gregorios, I honestly didn't think that she would find out. It was just a bit of a fling. Astris has been nagging me to settle down and to be honest, it's just not my thing."

"Not your thing?" Astris fumed, "I've put up with your wandering ways for far too long. Leave now or you will regret ever being born you slimy toad!"

Jason wisely hurried off and Parker watched him until he left her view. Everyone else seemed to busy themselves with their own conversations, acting like nothing had happened. Clearly, this type of disturbance was a regular occurrence, but Parker had found the entire scene captivating. Not least because of the unexplainable things she had just witnessed. She knew that she had to find Ellie and quiz her on what she had witnessed.

A few minutes later, Parker had tracked Ellie and Thalia down. They had all been searching for each other. Parker excitedly whispered, "Did you see that?" Ellie and Thalia exchanged a look, which Parker couldn't decipher.

Ellie spoke first, "What exactly did you see? Or think you saw?"

"There was a woman arguing with a man. She said that he had been cheating on her with someone. That was intriguing, but then something really weird happened. She turned blue! I don't mean she was holding her breath and her face turned blue through lack of oxygen, but as in, her skin turned blue. Also, her hair suddenly went all light and wavy like she was underwater, but that's impossible. Right?"

Thalia laughed nervously, "How much have you had to drink? You probably just saw one of the coloured lights we have around reflected on her."

"Well, I'm only drinking sparkling water."

"Tell her Ellie. After all, we all know that people don't change colour, right?" but Parker thought that Thalia was starting to sound desperate. She was sure that there was something that the two sisters were hiding. Maybe it was a joke that everyone was playing on her, but either way, she was upset to think that Ellie wasn't who she had hoped she was.

After a moment of reflection, Parker remembered the way her hair moved and the hose that fired water at the man with no human interference. She was confident that she hadn't been imagining things and responded stubbornly, "Well, I know what I saw, I know that it was real. But if you two don't believe me, then I think I'll just go home now. Thanks for the invite."

Parker knew that she sounded snippy, but she hated not being believed and wanted to leave. Thalia and Ellie exchanged a few hastily whispered words and Ellie announced, "OK, you're right. You did see something. If you come back to my house, I'll explain everything."

Parker looked at Ellie dubiously but agreed as the curiosity was starting the get the better of her.

Ellie and Parker walked back to her house in silence. Thalia had promised that she would catch up but wanted to say her goodbyes to some of the neighbours. The walk home was significantly quieter than the walk to the party. Parker wasn't in a rush to fill the silence, believing that it was Ellie's turn to do the talking.

Ellie opened the door and Parker stormed inside. Even through her anger, Parker couldn't help but notice that the décor reflected Ellie's personality. The walls were pale blue and covered in paintings containing seascapes and woodland scenery, with wooden flooring throughout. The furniture seemed eclectic but comfortable, with a small seating area to the left and the kitchen diner to the right.

Across the room she could see the stairs, leading up to what she assumed were bedrooms. Ellie politely offered her a seat. Parker sat in a dark green armchair and sank comfily into the cushions.

Ellie took a breath, gave a quick smile and started to talk, "I know you've been waiting to hear an explanation, but I would rather wait for Thalia so that I don't explain it badly."

"It's ok, I'm happy to wait for Thalia if that's easier. Although, I'm starting to get nervous if I'm honest." Sending an anxious smile to Ellie.

Ellie laughed, "Don't worry, it isn't anything sordid and you have nothing to worry about."

The door opened and Thalia arrived with the blond-haired gentleman from earlier. Thalia introduced him, "This is Gregorios, but everyone just calls him Greg." Greg gave a curt nod at Parker, it didn't help to ease her anxiety.

Suddenly, she realised the predicament that she had placed herself in. She was in a house with two strangers and a person she had met that day, although that seemed a long time ago now. Parker hadn't even updated Julia on her evening's plans. There was no one who knew where she was. Cats may have nine lives, but Parker was acutely aware that she only had the one.

Whilst she sat there, running all of the dangers through her mind, she could hear the other three arguing. They didn't seem concerned that she could hear everything they were saying. Greg began questioning the two sisters, "Why did you bring her here? Do you know who she is or if she has any ulterior motives? This was a very foolish decision to make and one that could cost all of us."

Ellie jumped in with her response, "Don't blame Thalia, she didn't know that I had invited Parker. I met her this morning. She is really nice. You just need to give her a chance."

"But why did you bring her here? You know the dangers. What do you truly know about her?" Greg snapped back. Parker was feeling slightly irked that people could think so little of her. She still didn't have a clue what they were talking about. She thought that the smartest thing to do was to keep quiet and learn all she could from their interactions.

Thalia tried to calm the situation, "I'm sure she had a reason for bringing her, didn't you Ellie?"

Ellie looked sheepish, then it morphed into defiance, "Yes, actually. I did have a reason for inviting her, but I didn't want to get you or Damon involved. You still see me as a child and wouldn't have believed me."

Parker was listening with bated breath; this was all fascinating. She didn't know who Damon was yet but assumed that it would be made clear later. Greg let out a frustrated sigh and ran his hand through his now tousled hair, "You complain that you're treated like a child, but then you pull a stunt like this. How do you expect us to treat you when we can't trust you?"

Ellie's eyes welled up with tears and she furiously wiped them away, "I had a vision a few days ago. I couldn't see a lot, but I saw her face at one of our parties. I didn't know who she was but then when I met her at my pottery class, I realised that it was my responsibility to get her here. I couldn't trust you or the others to not interfere. I was afraid that you wouldn't believe me."

Parker, Greg and Thalia looked at Ellie in surprise. Thalia sounded hesitant, as she clearly didn't want to upset Ellie but responded gently, "But Ellie, no one has had a true vision in decades. Are you sure it was a vision? Maybe you saw her somewhere and remembered her face in a dream?"

"This is exactly why I didn't tell you. I know what I saw. It wasn't a memory or dream. It was a vision. The fact that no one has had a vision in decades is exactly why I knew you wouldn't believe me."

Greg looked sceptical but had come to a decision, "I'll contact Damon and ask him what he wants to do." Parker didn't like the sound of that, as she still didn't know who Damon was. She also felt like it was time for her to make her own voice heard. Greg went back outside and pulled his phone out of his pocket.

"Look, I don't know who Damon is, why his opinion matters or why a vision is important. What I do know is that

I'm tired, it's getting late and I have work in the morning. I'm going home and we can deal with this later, Ellie has my phone number." Parker's tone was assertive, her leaving was not up for discussion.

Parker rose from the chair and made her way to the door; she was going to leave. Ellie smiled sadly and said, "I'm really sorry Parker, please don't hate me. I really do want to be your friend and I thought you'd have fun tonight. I never thought that it would cause all of this drama. Please just sit for a few more minutes and have a cup of tea with me."

Parker wanted to believe her and decided that she would sleep on it before making any decisions. She knew that she hadn't actually received any answers, but they were less important than getting home and away from the situation. Parker could worry about answers later and started towards the door, "I'll speak to you tomorrow, Ellie. It's late and I want to go home and sleep, so I'm not a zombie at work tomorrow."

Greg addressed her statement as he walked back through the door, "Let's all sit down with a hot drink first. I have a few things that I want to discuss with everyone." Ellie quickly made a round of hot drinks and handed Parker a cup of floral-scented tea. It wasn't her usual choice, but she decided to try it. It tasted slightly fruity and quite pleasant, so she continued to drink as she sat back down.

Parker immediately felt a sense of calm wash over her and was suddenly far less worried about the strangers in the room. Greg continued, "I've spoken to Damon; he thinks that it would be a good idea for Parker to spend the night here. He's out of town on business at the minute, but will be back tomorrow morning and would like to meet her then."

Parker raised her eyebrows, but she didn't seem to be as concerned as she normally would have been, "As I just said, I can't stay here as I have work tomorrow. Besides, I want to go home."

"You'll have to call in sick tomorrow, there's a lot that you need to be told and we can't risk you telling anyone what you have seen." Greg gently took her phone from her hand and continued, "You'll be perfectly safe here. I can't watch over you forever, but I can promise you true safety for one night. I always keep my promises. We don't want to keep you here, but a lot of people's safety is at risk, including Thalia and Ellie's."

Parker looked across at Ellie, so far no one had actually threatened or harmed her. She felt strangely calm about the whole thing and considered whether she should give these people the benefit of the doubt.

Parker thought back to what she had seen earlier and her curiosity was bubbling up again. She wasn't stupid and agreed with a compromise, "I will agree to stay here tonight and tomorrow morning on one condition, that I can send a message to my friend, letting her know exactly where I am. I won't alert her to anything being wrong, but I would feel more comfortable with her knowing." Parker had given away her vulnerable position, but this would be a good indicator of their intentions.

Greg thought for a second, "I can't see there being a problem with that." He handed Parker back her phone and she wrote out a quick message: *Sorry it's late, but I did promise an update. Made a new friend and staying at hers tonight, 4 Chatsworth Road near Kingfisher Lake. Will update you tomorrow x*

Greg watched her write the message and let her press send before confiscating her phone again. Ellie took Parker's arm in hers; she stood up and was steered towards the bar stools at the kitchen counter, "I will try to make this as painless as possible; we can just pretend it's a sleepover. I didn't ever get to have sleepovers as a child, my parents were always super protective and didn't want me to stay anywhere else. Also, I have nine siblings. We didn't really have any extra space for visitors to stay over."

Parker momentarily forgot her situation, "Nine siblings?! That is a lot of brothers and sisters. I only have the one, my sister, but we're close."

"I'm the middlest child," Ellie joked, "I'm also the black sheep. My parents are always nagging me about my career choice. I wanted to work in the city, to experience the hustle and bustle. I work for a big company in the admin department, not particularly exciting but it's a start. My siblings all went into outdoorsy professions, landscaper, environmental scientist, marine biologist. Hell, one is currently studying monkeys in Borneo! I have to tell you, if I have to hear Cleo talk about Silvered Langur and Western Tarsier monkeys one more time I may scream! What do you do?"

Parker laughed at her obvious frustration, "I work in a call centre, not very exciting I know. I went to university, worked hard and obtained a degree, only to find out that no one wanted to hire me due to lack of experience. The job is boring. It pays the bills for now, but I'm looking for something new."

"Do you know what you would like to do for a career? Any specific route you would like to pursue?"

"Nope, I'm open to opportunities. After all, there are thousands of jobs out there that I haven't even heard of yet."

Ellie nodded in earnest agreement; Parker continued to relax. She knew she should be feeling a lot more concerned about her predicament, but couldn't experience the feeling of worry at the minute. She felt comfortable around Ellie and felt that she could trust her, for now.

"You said you were tired Parker. I think that I have a spare pair of pyjamas that would fit you." Ellie offered, clearly trying to continue in the pleasant pretence that this was a sleepover instead of confinement.

During the discussion, Greg and Thalia had left. Parker was under no illusion that the house was going to be watched, to ensure that she didn't leave at any point during the night. When Ellie started to walk upstairs, Parker followed her. Ellie pointed to a room on her right, "That's my guest room, that's where you'll be sleeping. I hope it's comfortable enough for you. There's a small ensuite bathroom attached with toiletries. Help yourself to anything you find in there. This is my room," And she pointed to a room at the end of the hall.

"Wow, an ensuite in your guest room is fancy. I can only

just about fit one tiny bathroom in my house."

"Yes, I am lucky. They tried to consider all requirements when building these homes. I really am sorry about all of this Parker; I know that this isn't what you expected. But I believe that there is a purpose behind all of this. I'm hoping that it becomes clear to all of us. I also know that you are a good person and will listen tomorrow without judgement. I'll bring your pyjamas across in a minute." Parker gave a noncommittal smile, still relaxed but not sure how to take the mystic undertones of Ellie's speech.

Upon opening the wooden door to her temporary accommodation, she couldn't help but smile. The walls were teal green and there were plants everywhere, on every surface. There was a wooden double bed to the left, the floor was also wooden but it was adorned with a soft, white rug.

The bedding had a green leafy pattern and the whole room felt surprisingly tranquil. She located the bathroom through a door on the opposite side. She stepped through into a simple bathroom, with the same colour scheme as the bedroom. Parker opened the medicine cabinet and found a brand-new toothbrush and toothpaste, along with necessities like a hairbrush.

There was a knock on the door before it opened and in walked Ellie, holding out a pair of bright yellow pyjamas with embroidered birds all over them. "Here, I'm hoping these should fit you. They are cropped trousers on me, so should fit you perfectly," Ellie teased.

"Ha, ha, ha. I'm actually taller than average for a woman, it's not my fault that you know it's raining before anyone else does." It wasn't Parker's best comeback, but it still made them both chuckle.

"I think comedian needs to be ruled out of your list of career options." Ellie grinned. Parker thrust out her bottom lip and feigned disappointment before laughing. She started to yawn. "I'll leave you to get some sleep. Please do try to rest and don't worry too much about tomorrow. I will be by your side the whole time."

"Night Ellie, I'll try."

Ellie left the room, shutting the door gently behind her. Parker changed into the pyjamas, they were very snug, but she wasn't worried as no one was going to see her in them. She climbed into the bed and sunk into a heavenly mattress. It felt amazing. Parker would have to ask Ellie where she bought it from in the morning.

It felt strange not having her mobile phone; she was used to browsing the internet each night before going to sleep. Sometimes giving into the temptation of online shopping, other times just keeping up-to-date with the latest entertainment news. Parker limited the time spent reading about current affairs. She liked to know what was going on in the world, but the majority of the articles were too depressing or upsetting.

Even with her brain revisiting the events of the day, she still couldn't summon the energy to worry about her future. Parker closed her eyes and, between the comfortable bed and an eventful day, was asleep in seconds.

CHAPTER 3

Voices radiating from downstairs woke Parker and light spilled through the gaps in the wooden blinds. Parker bolted upright as she remembered yesterday's events and proceeded to jump out of bed. She visited the bathroom and rushed through only the most essential of the morning tasks. Parker paused and looked into the medicine cabinet mirror; she was surprised at how well-rested she looked.

Without a phone, she had no idea how long she had been asleep. After psyching herself up, she decided that it was time to make her way downstairs. She could hear muffled voices, which stopped when she was halfway down the stairs.

In the living room sat Ellie and Greg, they silently watched her enter the room. Ellie asked, "Did you sleep well?"

"Yes, thank you. I must have been more tired than I realised. I love your plants, the only thing I seem to be able to keep alive is ivy and that's practically a weed. Also, your bed is amazing."

Greg sat forward in his seat and addressed Parker, "Thank you for staying here last night, I appreciate that it must be disconcerting. Damon should be here within the next hour and you will finally get your answers." Parker nodded at Greg, her stomach made an embarrassingly loud rumble.

Ellie jumped up, "Sorry, I should have asked you what you wanted for breakfast. Tea, coffee, milk, juice, water? I also have a selection of cereals or toast?"

"Tea and toast would be perfect, thank you."

"Great, butter or jam?"

"Just butter, milk and two sugars in my tea please."

Ellie started to work on preparing her breakfast. Greg was engrossed in his mobile phone. Parker turned towards him, "I don't suppose that I can get my phone back yet?"

Greg smiled, "Sorry but no, not quite yet. It won't be long though." Parker thought that if it wasn't for the circumstances of their meeting, she would have probably found Greg quite attractive. He wasn't her typical type, she preferred the cliché of tall, dark and handsome.

Buttered toast was placed in front of Parker and Ellie slid across a cup of tea. Parker grasped the tea in both hands and took a sip. She wasn't particular about the amount of milk or strength of tea; the only item of importance was the sugar. It tasted like heaven and she sighed happily. She took a few more sips before starting on the toast.

There was an easy silence throughout the room as Parker ate her breakfast. Ellie sat next to her at the breakfast bar, with her own cup of tea. Seconds after breakfast finished there was a knock on the door, which Greg opened.

Parker nervously held her breath. She didn't know who Damon was or why he was important, but she knew that he was a person of authority in this group. Parker knew that he would be making decisions which would affect her future.

A large male walked through the door, he filled the doorway. He was slightly taller than Greg and looked to be in his early thirties. She judged him to be about six and a half feet tall. He was well-built and exuded a powerful aura. He had dark brown, wavy hair that was cut shorter on the back and sides.

Damon was wearing a white shirt with the sleeves rolled up to his elbows, the top button was undone and he wore dark blue fitted jeans. He looked too imposing for Parker to even consider his attractiveness. He had piercing blue eyes, that appeared to be scrutinising her. She felt like a deer caught in headlights and didn't move for fear of his reaction.

It felt like he had been observing her for hours. In reality, it couldn't have been longer than thirty seconds. Parker glimpsed at Ellie for reassurance, but she was busy making herself scarce by clearing the breakfast plates away. Parker squared her shoulders and met his gaze defiantly. After all, she hadn't done anything wrong.

One side of his mouth rose slightly in amusement, but it was gone so quickly that she convinced herself she had imagined it, "So, you must be Parker," he said in a confident tone, his voice was strong but pleasant.

It wasn't a question so Parker responded in kind, "So, you must be Damon." He raised one eyebrow, and there was a pause where everyone appeared to stop breathing. Parker started to reconsider her response. Thinking about whether giving attitude was a good idea or a mistake, reminding herself that she still didn't have nine lives. It was too late now though, so she waited for Damon to take the lead.

"Take a seat." He finally said, gesturing towards one of the armchairs. Parker considered responding with, 'Take a seat, please,' but decided that would be pushing him too far and she wanted to stay on his good side.

She didn't rush to sit down but made her way there slowly. Greg went to sit with Ellie in the kitchen. Parker raised an eyebrow at Ellie who had promised to be by her side, Ellie responded with a sheepish smile and Parker rolled her eyes.

Damon was used to people giving him their undivided attention and cleared his throat. Parker turned her head back towards him and waited expectantly. The silence was deafening and seemed to last forever, but Parker wasn't going to be the one to break it, regardless of how desperate she was to have answers.

Moments before Parker gave in, Damon started to talk, "Eileithyia, please also come and take a seat." Ellie swiftly moved to sit in the chair next to Parker, across from Damon. "I want you to explain what happened yesterday." He sounded disapproving, but Ellie didn't refuse his request.

"I'm not sure how much Greg has told you, but I want to explain fully." She began, "It all started about a week ago when I had a vision. I saw an unfamiliar face, followed by people laughing and joking at a neighbourhood party. I recognised those faces as my own neighbours. I felt a heavy sense of importance and urgency, but it wasn't clear as to what that was. I knew that it was important that they attended the party. I knew that there hadn't been a true vision in years, so I didn't think that anyone would listen. Also, what was I going to say? That I saw a person I didn't know at a party?"

Damon clasped his hands together and remained silent, he hadn't shown any reaction to her story so far. Ellie continued, "I didn't know what to do, so I decided to continue on with my original plans for the week. On Sunday I attended my usual pottery class. That was when I saw her, I had found the person that the face belonged to, Parker. I honestly didn't know what to do at first but we started talking to each other, she was really nice and I liked her."

Ellie took a breath before continuing, "After chatting for a while, I did the only thing I could think of. I invited her to the neighbourhood party. I honestly didn't think that it could hurt, as they are usually quite uneventful. I was afraid that I would tell you or one of my family members about the vision and you would stop me, I was right. Thalia didn't believe me when I told her, she just thought it was a dream. Anyway, Jason and Astris ended up having a fight, he had been cheating on her. She was so angry; you can imagine what happened next and Parker saw it all. Thalia tried to convince her that she had imagined it, but that obviously didn't work."

Ellie was studying Damon's face, trying to decipher his reaction and continued nervously, "Parker is really nice and she has also been very patient with us. She stayed here last night with me and didn't try to escape, even though Greg confiscated her phone. She is trusting us and we promised to give her answers."

Everyone looked at Damon who seemed pensive. He hadn't moved and was thinking through Ellie's story. After a couple of minutes, he had a resolved look on his face and started giving orders, "Firstly, Ellie? You need to learn to trust us. I'm not sure what decision would have been made had you come to us when you had a vision, but we could have prepared. We would also not have been put in this predicament."

Ellie turned red and nodded at Damon in acceptance. Damon turned his head towards Parker, "I have a proposition for you, but you must make your decision before you are allowed to leave here. If you wish to be told the truth about yesterday and everything else associated with it, then you will leave your job and come to work for my company, so that we can keep an eye on you.

"You will leave your home and relocate to one of my company's properties. The alternative is that you go back to your old job and home, but we won't tell you anything. You won't ever see or speak to Ellie again. If you try and tell anyone about what you saw, we will ensure that you are never believed."

Parker considered her options and quickly concluded that there was only one she could live with, but needed to clarify a few points first. "What about my friends and family? In your first option would I still be able to speak to them and see them regularly?"

"Yes, there's no reason that you can't see them as before. However, if you tell them anything you shouldn't, there will be repercussions that you do not want."

"Will I be a prisoner at your company or property? Am I able to move about freely?"

"You can continue to live your life as you would normally, there are no restrictions as to where you decide to go. However, you will be working at my company and you must reside in one of my properties."

"Would I have an entire property to myself or would I be forced to live with other people?"

Damon gave a subtle smile, exposing that he liked that she was considering all aspects before committing and not rushing in foolishly. "I infer from your phrasing that you would dislike living with others, so you would of course have your own property. It would likely be similar to Ellie's."

"Can I have a little time to think this through?"

"As I said, we will need an answer before you are allowed to leave. Do you have any more questions at this time?"

"Not that I can think of. I would like to go upstairs and think this through before giving you an answer."

Damon nodded in confirmation, "I have business to attend to, so let Greg know your decision". He stood, nodded towards Greg and walked out the door without looking back.

Parker didn't speak to Greg or Ellie and instead walked straight up to the guest room. She shut the door and sat on the bed. Parker started weighing up the pros and cons. In the 'cons' column, she listed that these people were practically strangers and she didn't know if she could trust them.

She would be starting a job at this person's company; she didn't know what the job would be or what the company does. However, she wasn't happy at her current job so it wasn't really a 'con' to have to leave. In the 'pro's' column, she would get answers and be introduced to what appeared to be a secret supernatural society.

Parker had been looking to add excitement to her life, would she ever get this opportunity again if she let it pass her by? She wouldn't have to stop contact with her family or friends, which would have been a deal breaker.

Parker flopped back on the bed with an audible huff. She thought that she had made up her mind, but didn't want to make an impulsive decision that she would later regret. And as she'd surmised earlier, there really weren't that many options available.

She started thinking back to what she saw and tried to rationalise it herself, what did she know of that could turn blue? Parker could only think of two instances, but she didn't believe the woman was a Smurf. The other blue woman was in a movie she'd seen, where she could change her appearance, that was quite cool.

A gentle knock sounded at the door, followed by Ellie poking her head through the gap, "Can I please come in? I just wanted to check that you're alright." It was only when Ellie was halfway through the door, that Parker noticed what she was wearing. The pyjamas were yellow and covered in Gnomes riding dinosaurs, and on her feet were fluffy bunny rabbit slippers.

Parker was briefly distracted, thinking who even sold pyjamas like that? Ellie took advantage of the momentary distraction and lay on the bed next to Parker. They lay in companionable silence for a while. Ellie finally asked her initial question again. She sounded concerned, "Are you alright?"

Parker thought it through. She had been fed, had a great night's sleep and had been offered an exciting opportunity to expand her world. All at once she was sure of her answer and sat up on the bed, "Yes. I am actually. Surprisingly."

Ellie wasn't entirely convinced and sat up next to her, trying to read her face for any signs of hysteria. "Honestly." Parker smiled, attempting to look reassuring.

"Are you ready to give Greg your answer? Have you made your decision?" Ellie knew what she wanted Parker to decide, but didn't want to influence her.

"Yes, I know what I want to do. Let's go downstairs."

Ellie followed Parker out of the room and down the stairs. Greg had made himself at home. He had a laptop out on the kitchen counter and was looking at it intently. Parker looked over his shoulder and saw her own smiling face looking back at her.

Greg was looking through her social media accounts. Parker wasn't exactly sure what he was looking for, but it was clear that he didn't trust her. She wasn't concerned as she had nothing to hide. She had ensured that her accounts were all family-friendly when she started to get serious about wanting a career. She had removed any of the embarrassing photos from her younger years.

Without turning around Greg spoke, "Have you come to a decision?" He had obviously heard her coming and wasn't concerned that he had been caught researching her.

"If you wanted to know something about me, you could

have just asked," Parker informed him.

"Yes, but would you have told me the truth?" Greg replied.

Parker instead of being offended started laughing, "I feel like you're trying to find my deepest, darkest secrets. So, I give up, I might as well tell you the truth. When I was eight, I ate my sister's last Easter egg and lied about it. When I was applying for university, I made up my hobbies to make myself sound more exciting. I also regularly go over the speed limit, not by too much but it's still illegal.

"My first job was working in a shop and I would sometimes read magazines, without buying them. I'm not sure if there's anything else important that I've missed, but if I think of it, I will definitely let you know. Would you prefer an email or text?" She asked sarcastically. Parker heard Ellie giggling behind her and Greg sighed wearily.

"Have you made your decision Parker?" Greg asked, ignoring her previous statement.

"Yes, I have. I have chosen the first option, I want answers." Greg nodded as if he hadn't expected any other response.

He pulled his phone out of his pocket and sent three text messages, "I'm just getting the balls rolling." He said in explanation, "Take a seat, I'm going to give you a brief overview now and you will learn more over the coming weeks and months as you become more immersed in our world."

Parker walked straight over and sat on the edge of the chair in anticipation. She still had a small fear in the back of her mind, that this was all going to be a joke. "Not Smurf's, right?" Parker said only half-jokingly. For the first time, she saw an emotion other than annoyance from Greg, as he threw his head back and laughed.

He had a striking smile, with perfect white teeth and it transformed his whole face. It suited him more than his frown. Clearly, this whole situation had been causing him stress, "No, we aren't Smurf's." He said still smiling, "What do you know about the Greek myths?"

Parker considered his question, it wasn't the way she thought that this conversation would go. "Do you mean like Zeus and Olympus, with all of the gods and heroes?"

"Yes, but the part I'll focus on is more about the monsters. Satyrs, nymphs, gorgons, harpies and the like. There is a whole world that you are unaware of. We all look human, so you wouldn't know if you passed one of us on the high street. The woman you saw turn blue is a descendant of a nymph from the Greek myths, her ancestor was a water nymph. The man she was arguing with is a satyr.

"Some of the mythological creatures you will have heard of really existed and are our ancestors. Of course, the myths weren't exactly accurate. The people of the time saw unexplainable things and their imaginations went wild. Gorgons had an extremely persuasive charm, which they frequently used to their own benefit. They chose to wear their hair in long braids.

"Wives started spreading the rumours of snakes for hair, to cause fear and hatred because of their jealousy. There's too much for me to explain everything to you now, but working in Damon's company and living in one of our neighbourhoods you will learn fast. Do you have any questions?" Greg asked whilst trying to decipher if Parker was about to jump up and run away screaming.

Parker was absolutely fascinated. She had always loved the Greek myths and couldn't believe that they were based on reality. She couldn't wait to find out more, about the truth behind these mythological creatures. Were they all real? Were the Gods real? Was there really a golden fleece? There were numerous questions flying through her mind, but she settled on one that she found she was most interested in. "Are you and Damon descended from the same ancestor? What are you? Who exactly is Damon?"

"You will find that out soon enough. I have given your house key to one of our employees and they have organised for all of your possessions to be moved to your new home. You can choose what to do with your old property, rent or sell. I can arrange for someone to manage this for you should you wish.

"A portion of your pay will be deducted each month to pay towards your new home. Don't worry, it is a very small amount and below market value. I should probably explain further about that part. Damon's company has several branches and one owns property. Entire neighbourhoods are owned to enable Supernaturals to live with others of their own kind safely, we all look after each other.

"You are currently in one of our neighbourhoods, you will of course be one of only a handful of humans. We have assigned you a home nearby, as Ellie will be able to answer some of your questions and support you through the transition to your new life."

Parker was busy taking it all in. Instead of being afraid, she was excited and looked towards Ellie who also looked excited by this information, "We have contacted your workplace, handed in your notice effective immediately and provided a forwarding address. If you can spend some more time here today, your property will be ready from four o'clock. I will text Ellie your new address so she knows where to take you, which reminds me." And he handed her back her phone, "I have programmed my number into your phone." Greg instructed, "Only contact me if there is an emergency."

Parker was curious how he had managed to do that when she had a PIN code locking the phone, but it seemed unimportant compared to the other information being processed. "Ellie, Damon has made it known that you will not be attending work today due to other, more pertinent duties. Please keep an eye on Parker, keep her out of trouble and show her to her new home this afternoon. I have sent her address to you. Contact me if you need me. Next time, if you believe you've had a vision, don't keep it to yourself."

With that final statement, Greg stood up, walked over to Ellie and gave her a quick hug before leaving. Parker was impressed with their efficiency and was trying to think if they had forgotten anything. She wasn't happy with the idea that someone would be packing her granny pants and was praying that she hadn't left anything embarrassing in a drawer. However, it was too late now, it was already underway. She put it to the back of her mind to worry about another day. She also wasn't amused that he had tasked Ellie with, 'keeping her out of trouble', but she would make sure to pay him back for that another time.

Parker sat back in the chair, digesting all of this new information. Ellie came over with a cup of tea and a cookie. She then flopped into the other armchair and smiled, "Looks like I get a day off work. Want to get some fresh air?"

Parker nodded, "Yes, that would be great. First, I need to send some text messages to let people know I'm alright. If I don't message my mum regularly, she worries."

She sent a couple of short messages to her mum and Julia. Advising that she was fine, had a busy weekend and would see them soon. Ellie walked to the back door and flung it wide open. The sky was cloudy but luckily it was dry. Her garden was gorgeous, filled with a wide variety of beautiful flowers and a couple of apple trees. They walked to the bottom of the garden and sat on a bench, perfectly positioned underneath a rose arch. It all smelled heavenly. "I guess that it's time that I asked you, Ellie, what are you?" And peered up at her friend.

Ellie looked quite excited to be able to share her secret with Parker. "I'm a nymph. Somewhere along the line two different ancestral lines crossed and I am a descendant of both water and forest nymphs. It means that I'm not as strong as some of those with only one line, but I can access two different types of magic. As you may have now guessed, I have a slight advantage with my garden."

"You mentioned something about a vision, does that mean that you can see the future? Can all nymphs see the future?"

Ellie became more serious, "Well, that's where things get interesting. Our ancestors had frequent visions. Most visions foretold events like a storm on the horizon, the engagement of royalty, or a plague spreading. Then there were the prophecies. Visions that wouldn't make sense at the time, but they were the most important of all.

"Once a prophecy was announced, wise men of the time would gather to try and decipher it. The danger was always that by trying to cause or prevent a prophecy, the resulting actions could directly cause the unwanted event to transpire. However, as more and more of the supernatural world mated with humans instead of other supernaturals, the bloodlines began to dilute.

"Our scientists believe that this is the reason some of us are losing our abilities. Some are able to access more of our powers than others. About a hundred years ago the visions began to dry up and about seventy years ago they stopped completely, after one final prophecy. That is why I didn't think that anyone would believe me about my vision."

Parker was listening intently and trying to remember as much as possible, "What was the final prophecy about?"

"I don't know. When the prophecy was foretold, it was written down and placed in a vault. Those in control were too afraid to let the prophecy be widely known, as they didn't want our actions to influence the outcome negatively."

"Who makes those decisions? Do you have a government or governing body?"

"That's complicated, most of us follow Damon and his senior team. He's really strict but fair and ensures that all supernaturals under him are looked after. There are others who don't agree with him and who want the supernatural world to no longer be a secret. They seem to forget all the problems that happened the first time around, the jealousy and hatred. It's why we let ourselves become myths, tales to be told to children. We started to hide ourselves away in plain sight."

Ellie suddenly looked hesitant, like she wanted to tell Parker something. She made a decision, "I have a confession, but I want you to know that I would never hurt you, ever. Last night,

I used a little bit of my magic in your tea, I just altered it enough to enhance the calming properties. I didn't want you to worry and I knew Greg wouldn't let you leave. I didn't want you to be scared and I so badly need answers. I promise that it wouldn't have caused you to do anything dangerous, it also has no lasting effects."

Parker felt hurt, she knew that her feelings last night seemed off, "I will be honest with you, I'm not sure I can fully trust you again. Never ever do that to me again, promise me, Ellie."

"Of course, I promise. I couldn't keep this from you, I have been agonising about it all night. Greg thought that it was the safest option for you. I'm not blaming it on him as I had a choice, but he didn't force me."

After another half an hour of discussing and setting boundaries, they decided to have a break and go out for a frappe. Parker and Ellie went back to the same coffee shop that they visited the day before. Instead of being covered in clay, she was now slightly overdressed as she didn't have a change of clothes with her.

Ellie had chosen a blue jumpsuit, covered in bright yellow sunflowers. They spent the next couple of hours enjoying their drinks and chatting about everything from TV shows to old boyfriends. Eventually, Ellie glimpsed at the time and noticed that it was half past four, "Did you want to go and explore your new home? They should have finished preparing it all by now."

Parker was quite excited to see it, so they gathered their belongings and set off to her new home. Ellie parked outside of her own house and they walked to Parker's home so that she would know where Ellie lived in relation to her. It was only a five-minute walk, past where the neighbourhood party had been held the previous night. There were no signs of the party and the door was no longer in the middle of the lawn. It had been placed back on its hinges, looking no worse for wear.

Ellie stopped outside a house that looked almost identical to hers. There were no plants in the front garden, just a neatly mowed lawn. The door was painted in forest green. Ellie opened it and guided her inside.

It was eerie seeing all of her own furniture placed around the home. The layout was the same as Ellie's, but the colour scheme was neutral, with beige walls and blinds. Due to it being larger than her own one-bedroom house, her furniture didn't fill it and it still looked quite sparse. "I'm not sure what the rules are with this house, can I change it to my own taste? Am I allowed to paint it?" Parker asked.

"Of course, it's yours. The payments that are taken out of your pay are to purchase the home, not rent. If you chose to move in the future to another supernatural neighbourhood, the funds you have paid would be transferred to another home." Parker felt better about that, she had always hated the idea of renting. It felt like throwing money away, as you had nothing at the end.

"There is an information pack on the table. I'll leave you alone now to get settled in. I had better go and visit my mum. If she finds out about you from Thalia and I don't update her, I will never hear the end of it." Parker thanked Ellie for being by her side and they hugged before Ellie left.

Parker took a deep breath and began exploring; opening the kitchen cabinets to see where her items had been placed. Venturing upstairs to explore her rooms, she saw that all of the furniture and clothing had been placed in the room Ellie indicated as her own. However, she hadn't actually been in Ellie's room so she wasn't sure what to expect. It was a large room looking out onto her new back garden. The garden had a couple of small trees, but was mostly just lawn and a wooden fence separated her property from her neighbours.

Parker took a moment to feel sad about leaving her old home, she had become emotionally attached to her house and the memories created there. She locked away those thoughts to deal with later and continued exploring. The beige paint continued throughout the home.

There was a large bathroom attached to her room, with

a bath and shower. Her towels and toiletries had been placed in the bathroom; they had thought of everything. The wooden flooring flowed through the home, she made a mental note to buy some rugs to break it up.

She glimpsed in the wardrobes and drawers so that she knew where they had placed her various items. Then Parker headed over to the spare room, expecting to find it empty. When she walked through the door, she saw a fully furnished spare room. It had a sturdy wooden bed against the wall to the left, with intricately carved patterns on the headboard and footboard.

When she looked closer, the carvings were of flowers, vines and trees. The bedding looked to be of a high quality, super soft and thick sheets. The ensuite also housed the basic guest essentials.

Parker went back downstairs and made herself a cheese salad sandwich. Someone had considerately filled her fridge with the essentials, which she knew hadn't been in her fridge at home. She sat down at the kitchen breakfast bar and pulled the information pack towards her, she read it as she ate.

It contained a page of emergency contacts, a plumber, an electrician and a handyman. The next page contained her new internet login details, which had already been set up for her. Following those details was information about the house, who the gas and electricity providers were, along with their contact details.

There was a page containing information about the local facilities, pharmacy, doctor, school, library, shops etc. Lastly was a section on local areas of interest which included public parks, caverns, a conservation centre, a botanical garden and a memorial park.

A text message from Ellie came through, advising that she would pick her up for work at eight o'clock the following morning and to dress smart-casual. It was nine o'clock by the time she had finished the information pack and retreated upstairs. Parker had been wanting to dye her hair for a couple of weeks due to her roots getting a little long, fortunately, she had bought a home-dye kit a week before and it had been placed in her bathroom.

Parker's plan was to dye her hair, get changed into her own nightwear and settle in for the night. She completed her tasks and climbed into bed. Parker placed a towel underneath her head, in case her newly dyed hair marked the pillowcase. She grabbed her phone and began refreshing her knowledge of the Greek myths. She quickly realised that there were too many stories for a bit of nighttime reading, so she decided to settle on the ones she now knew were real.

The gorgons and nymphs, for each there were a number of different stories and versions. Parker was worried that she wouldn't be able to wind down, so she downloaded the sequel to the book she finished on Friday night and started reading. She fell asleep a couple of hours later.

CHAPTER 4

The following day arrived earlier than she would have liked. Parker had never been a morning person and had always hated the sound of her alarm. She had tried changing it to various tunes but it didn't make a difference, she hated the new tone within a week. The alarm had been set earlier than required so that she could fully prepare for the day ahead.

She looked at her newly dyed red hair in the mirror, she had been extra careful not to get it on her skin. Parker was happy with the refreshed colour and was glad that she had thought to dye it ready for her first day. She wondered what she would be doing; working one-on-one with the various supernaturals, helping to make important decisions, assisting with research or contributing to human relations.

The usual pangs of anxiety started in her stomach. Starting a new job was nerve-wracking enough, without the supernatural element being thrown in. Parker finished getting dressed. She chose a knee-length, navy skater dress, with a black lace trim and her black boots.

Parker moved on to breakfast, settling on a bowl of porridge instead of toast. Toast never seemed to fill her for long and she had no idea what the lunch plans were. She was extra careful whilst eating to ensure it didn't spill on her dress. She didn't want to have to change, already having spent ages agonising over first impressions. Unfortunately, she had a habit of spilling food on her chest.

Parker turned on the news for some background noise as the silence in the house was unsettling and alien. She glanced around the room and concluded that she really needed to do some shopping. However, she would probably have to wait for her next payday in order to be able to afford it.

A horn beeped outside, she grabbed her phone and purse before exiting. Ellie was sitting in her car, waving enthusiastically at her. Parker locked the front door, double-checked it, as was her usual habit and hurried across to Ellie.

"How was your first night in your new home?" Ellie asked.

"Good actually. I spent a lot of time familiarising myself with the house and I read through the information pack. I was surprised to find that my guest room is fully furnished, the furniture is nicer than my own."

"I'm glad you like it. I think that they want to make sure you're happy. We all know that it must be hard to be uprooted so suddenly."

"One thing I will need to do at some point is to buy some extra furniture, rugs and other decorations. It's a lot bigger than my house. Sorry, I mean my old house. Also, I would love to have your help with buying some plants. I don't want anything difficult though, I'm not nearly as green-fingered as you are!"

"Plants are one area where I can definitely be of help," Ellie smiled, "I can also accompany you shopping for other stuff if you want me to."

"Thanks, I'll let you know when I plan on going," Parker promised.

They continued chatting about the house, how she wanted to decorate and what type of plants she liked. It was about ten minutes later that Ellie pulled into a huge car park. Parker saw a large office building at one end, with a large sign on the front, 'Minos Industries'.

The building was an imposing, modern glass cube, over twenty storeys high. They exited the car and walked towards the entrance with the other employees starting their shifts. They passed a large fountain and entered through two sliding glass doors.

Security was abundant in the foyer. Guards were stationed on either side of the doors and at the security checkpoint, located next to the elevators. The reception was placed in a central location with a desk the length of a bus, three individuals were working.

Ellie strode to the reception desk and provided Parker's full name, 'Parker Marie Porter'. She then requested her employee ID. Parker hadn't realised that Ellie knew her full name, as she hadn't told her. Then realised that Greg must have known it from the beginning, in order to research her properly and organise everything. Begrudgingly, she was impressed by his efficiency.

Ellie took the ID on a lanyard from reception and handed it to Parker. Ellie advised that whilst she was on the premises, it must be worn at all times. If she ever loses it, she must report it immediately so that the access can be revoked. Parker inspected the card, it was fairly standard and had a picture of her on the front, along with a barcode. Greg must have taken the picture from her social media and she was grateful that he had chosen one of the more flattering ones.

They walked towards the security checkpoint and Ellie showed her ID, it was scanned by a stern-looking gentleman in a security uniform. Parker copied her actions and they were allowed through. Ellie explained that she would need to have a meeting with Human Resources first, which was scheduled for nine o'clock.

Ellie directed Parker around a corner and bustled her into an elevator. Pressing the necessary buttons, Ellie dextrously guided her towards the HR department on the fourth floor and left her on one of the comfy chairs in the foyer, before informing a staff member that she had arrived. Parker sat patiently, watching the clock. At one minute past nine she was starting to get annoyed, lateness always frustrated her. At eight minutes past nine a lady walked over and with a beaming smile, introduced herself as Catherine before inviting her into her office.

Parker observed the woman's appearance as she followed behind, she seemed to be late thirties with blonde curly hair that fell slightly below her shoulders. Her black suit looked immaculate and of high quality, twinned with black stilettos of equal class. Parker was envious. She had never been adept at walking in stilettos or high heels and had to make do with a wedge or chunky heel.

Catherine led her into an office and gestured for her to take a seat. She then moved behind her desk, smoothing her suit as she sat. "Hello Parker, welcome to Minos Industries. We hope that this will be the beginning of a long and successful career with our company. We value all of our employees and want you to feel like part of the team. Our aim is to help you reach your full potential and we anticipate great things from you. If you have concerns at any time, please don't hesitate to speak to me or one of the Human Resources team."

She then scanned the mountain of paper on her desk, "We will need you to complete a few forms before you are able to start. It will cover items like your medical information, next of kin should an accident occur and your past experience. The documents will also include the company benefits, some of which I believe you are already aware of. It details the expected working hours. We try to be flexible but do have core hours when you must be in the office. Once we are finished here, I will transfer you to your new manager. He will oversee your work and ensure you settle in successfully. Do you have any questions?"

"Yes, I have one question at the moment. What exactly will my role in the company be?" She asked eagerly.

"You have been assigned to our administration department. Your day-to-day tasks will be assigned by your manager based on your skills."

Parker's excitement deflated. She was leaving a boring job in administration and starting a brand-new exciting job - in administration. She tried to hide her disappointment, which wasn't too difficult as Catherine was too busy gathering her tomes of paperwork to notice. She pulled herself together. Just because she was starting in administration, didn't mean that she would stay there forever. It just wasn't her dream career.

Parker recalled that Ellie worked in the admin department, so that was one positive. She also understood that a lot of admin teams kept their companies running, dealing with all departments. She would take this opportunity to truly understand the company and the supernatural beings within it.

They walked through the building to the elevators and rode down to the third floor. They exited the elevator and the floor was separated into offices on one side and partially open cubicles on the other. Catherine led her to one of the offices, where she was introduced to a gentleman in his forties. He had short mousy brown hair, a rounded figure and a slightly ruffled brown suit, his name was Jaxon.

The paperwork was handed over to Parker. Catherine said her goodbyes and left swiftly. Jaxon guided Parker over to a cubicle that was assigned to her. It was basic with a curved desk, laptop, second computer screen and a landline phone. There was a desk tidy full of stationery supplies on the left-hand side of the computer.

"I will leave you to work through your paperwork. Once it is complete, please let me know and I will arrange for it to be sent to Human Resources." Jaxon informed her. "After the paperwork is complete, I will arrange for a list of tasks to be assigned to you so that we can assess your strengths."

Parker leaned back in her seat as Jaxon left. She pulled off the post-it note stuck to the laptop detailing her login details. It advised her to change the password on the first login. Before she could start working on the paperwork provided, a familiar face peeked over her cubicle wall. "How's it going?" Ellie said with a grin, "This is great, I'm so glad you'll be working in my department."

Parker smiled in response, "I'm happy to be working with you too."

"I will leave you to your work, Jaxon is really cool actually. He is fairly relaxed as long as the job gets done, he doesn't mind us socialising with each other." And Ellie's head disappeared from view as quickly as it had shot up.

Parker was pleased to hear that Jaxon was relaxed. Not being able to speak to Ellie or any of her other colleagues during the working day would get boring fast. She spent the next hour working through her myriad of forms and when the ordeal was finally complete, she informed Jaxon that it was ready to be collected.

After logging into the laptop and changing her password, she checked her emails. There was one from Ellie which made her smile. There was also a meeting request from Damon, for three o'clock in his office. She began to get nervous, what would he want to speak to her about? Surely, he had minions that would cover any important topics. Before she could dwell on it for too long, Jaxon called her into his office and asked her to bring her laptop.

Parker was asked to complete a series of tasks, testing her typing speed and accuracy, her attention to detail, along with her verbal and written communication skills. Other tasks covered logical reasoning and evaluated her numerical abilities. She felt quite confident once the test had ended as she had plenty of experience in those areas.

The next few hours passed quite pleasantly. She had lunch with Ellie in the canteen, the food was delicious. Jaxon informed her that he was more than happy with the results from her tests and started assigning tasks. She was trying to concentrate on a data entry job but was acutely aware that it was getting closer and closer to three o'clock.

She kept glimpsing at the time and at two forty-five she rose from her desk and knocked on the door to Jaxon's office. "Can I help?" He asked as he looked up from his computer.

"I have a meeting with Damon at three o'clock. I wanted to ensure that you knew where I had disappeared off to. Can you please let me know how I get to his office?"

Jaxon looked surprised that this new starter was having a meeting with the boss on her first day. He obliged by informing her that his office was on the top floor and to ride the elevator all the way to the top. She'd have to scan her I.D. in the elevator to be admitted to the top floor.

Parker set off and she pressed the button for the elevators, waiting patiently. It was half-full when she stepped on and pressed the top floor button, which turned out to be the twenty-second floor. As she scanned her ID, she noticed that there were also three subfloors.

As the elevator rose, more and more people exited until she was the only one remaining. The other occupants had been giving her side glances after seeing her intended destination. Her stomach had been doing somersaults, she was so nervous.

The elevator pinged and the doors opened. She walked out into an open space foyer, with a personal assistant situated in a large round command station in the centre. There were doors to seven offices around the perimeter of the room.

This floor had a higher ceiling than the others, was decorated in shades of light grey and the cabinetry appeared to be made of exquisite solid walnut. There were large green plants positioned tastefully to enhance the room. The whole floor gave off a whiff of significantly more upmarket than her cubical down on the admin level, Parker couldn't help but notice.

Next to the elevator was a grouping of leather chairs. She realised that she hadn't moved forward since stepping foot on the floor, so she started towards the bemused-looking lady. "I have a meeting with Damon at three o'clock," Parker informed her politely.

"Of course, let me just check that for you." The lady pushed her tortoise-shell glasses further up her nose and started typing on her computer.

This lady looked like someone's grandma; she was quite possibly eligible for her pension, with greying hair and a kindly grandparent demeanour. Her aura was very calming and immediately put Parker at ease. "If you would like to take a seat, he will be out in a minute." She gestured towards the leather chairs.

Parker sat facing the offices, waiting for a door to open.

At exactly three o'clock, the door furthest away opened and Damon strode out. His attire was smarter than at her last encounter with him. He was wearing a perfectly fitted black suit, with a white shirt and blood-red tie. As he was walking towards her, she was appreciating how attractive he looked and that his entire ensemble screamed that he meant business. Her daydream ended abruptly as he spoke, "Parker."

"Damon." She still couldn't help but respond with the same brusque tone.

"Thank you for being prompt. Follow me." And he turned without waiting for her to follow.

Parker stood and walked after him at her own pace, she hated bossy people and always responded better to a polite request. She was tempted to perform a mimic of him as she traipsed after him but didn't want to stoop that low and also, she felt like she would have disappointed the kindly PA somehow. He left the door open and requested that she shut it after entering.

He sat in a leather chair behind his desk and gestured to an empty chair across from him. There was already someone sitting in a chair next to hers, "Parker, Nicola." He said shortly.

Parker decided to get one up on Damon and display the manners that he was clearly lacking, "Hello Nicola, I'm Parker. It's very nice to meet you," and held out her hand, which Nicola shook whilst smiling widely.

Nicola had a beautiful smile, dark brown skin and long braided hair. Parker couldn't see the ends of her hair, so assumed that the braids went all the way to the base of her spine. Her red dress radiated against her skin tone and Parker self-consciously smoothed down her own dress. "Parker, stand up and drink the entire glass of water on the desk," Nicola said calmly.

Parker frowned, raised one eyebrow and then looked at Nicola inquisitively. Why would she want to do that? "Thank you, but I don't actually want any water right now." And looked towards Damon.

Nicola calmly repeated the request again. This time Parker felt a strange tingle in her forehead. However, she ignored it and again declined, "No, thank you."

She was starting to feel uncomfortable, as they were both staring at her intently. She began to worry that she had spilt her lunch down herself again. Nicola stood after a brief pause, held a hand out towards Parker and said, "It was nice to meet you, Parker." They shook hands and Nicola exited the room.

Parker watched her leave, then looked at Damon, setting her face into what she hoped said 'What the hell was all that about?' without having to actually state it out loud. He sat back in his chair and clasped his hands in front of him.

She took this opportunity to look around his office, it was painted in a combination of light and dark greys. The floor was covered in a slate grey, thick luxurious carpet. The desk was made out of chunky mahogany wood and displayed minimal adornments. The room gave no hint whatsoever as to who the man behind the suit might be.

There was a seating area next to a set of windows; a three-seater sofa and two individual armchairs in black leather, with a coffee table in between. Parker had always preferred fabric, as she found that leather was cold in winter and she stuck to it in the summer.

There were two slightly ajar doors at the far end of the room, wide enough to ascertain that they were a bathroom and bedroom. She wasn't sure why someone would have a bedroom in their office but rationalised that it was probably due to working long hours. It was good to be in charge she thought, you can indulge all of your whims.

When she returned to rest her gaze upon Damon, it was clear he had been watching her. She decided to start the conversation, "You wanted to see me? Also, what was that all about?" And gestured back towards the door that Nicola had exited through.

"I thought that it important for us to have a conversation, there are still unanswered questions."

Parker suddenly recalled when she had heard about women with long braids in their hair. She thought back to what Greg had told her about gorgons. He mentioned something about a persuasive charm, could Nicola have been a gorgon? It seemed to make sense.

"Is Nicola a gorgon?" Parker asked directly.

Damon raised one eyebrow and Parker detected the faintest hint of a smile at the corners of his lips, "What makes you think that she is a gorgon?" Parker decided that his lack of denial was confirmation that she was right, but then what were they trying to achieve? She narrowed her eyes at him.

"Alright, yes Nicola is a gorgon. We are still trying to figure out how you fit into our world and I wanted to assess your strength of will. I'm not sure if you are aware, but not everyone can be charmed by a gorgon. Only those of moderate or weak will can be charmed. Also, if you are prepared and know what is happening, you can resist it. I wonder which category you fit into."

Parker wasn't sure whether she should be flattered that she was considered strong-willed, or insulted that he thought she could be weak-willed but prepared, so retorted "Well I hardly could have prepared for her presence, could I?"

"Touché," Damon acknowledged, "Do you have any ancestors that were born in Greece or the surrounding countries?"

"I don't believe so. My ancestors as far back as I know were Latvian and English."

"Are you sure? We couldn't find anything, but we need to double-check."

Parker wasn't surprised that they had researched her that thoroughly. She was considering asking what they had found out about her family tree, it would be interesting information, "Nope, no one from Greece."

He was still staring intently at her face as if he would find an answer there. "Is there anything special about you? Ever done anything extraordinary?"

"I'm assuming that you aren't asking about when I won the backwards race at school?" Parker replied in a mock-serious tone.

Damon didn't seem amused and continued, "Of course, there is the possibility that Ellie was mistaken. It wasn't actually you that she saw, but someone similar." He didn't look convinced by this latest theory.

"I feel like I should remind you of something, I attended a pottery class and got invited to a party. Since then, my life has been turned upside down. I have been held against my will, drugged and accused of ulterior motives. As far as I am aware, I have yet to do anything suspicious or warranting of your distrust." Parker finished her tirade and crossed her arms in defiance.

Damon sighed. He knew that everything she had said was true, so decided to ease up on his suspicions. "You are right, but you need to know that I am responsible for a lot of people. I cannot afford to make silly mistakes and you are currently an unknown factor. Let's move to a more comfortable area to finish this chat." He walked across to the sofa and sat at one end.

She felt like she had made progress with Damon and so strode over with more confidence than she was actually feeling, sitting on the other end of the sofa. "Would you like a drink? I promise I won't try and make you drink a whole glass of water." He said with a deadpan expression but had a glint in his eye.

"I'm still fine for now thank you, but will let you know should I get thirsty."

"I know that Gregorios has given you a brief overview, that today's supernaturals are descendants of the original Greek myths. As far as we are aware, the only descendants that exist are from the 'monsters' or 'creatures'. The myths that are known today are exactly that, and far from accurate.

"With all of the stories told there was definitely a fear effect. People feared the unexplainable and made supernaturals into monsters, things to scare their children into behaving. Each line of descendants has its own truth. I know that you were asking about what Greg is, what we are, so I shall begin there."

Damon relaxed further and continued, "It all started with

a King called Minos, he was the King of Crete. Villainized by the Athenians, he was portrayed as a cruel tyrant. However, these were lies created by those in power. They didn't want their own citizens moving to the more prosperous Crete. The truth was that he was a benevolent ruler and legislator.

"During his reign the original 'minotaur' came into existence. No one knows where or how he was born, as the tale has changed many times over the centuries. Some believe that he appeared fully grown one day, others say that he was born from a beautiful woman who was never seen again.

"This man possessed powers that people had never seen. He had unmeasurable strength, moved faster than mere mortals and had heightened senses like hearing, smell and vision. In addition to his physical attributes, he also possessed superior intelligence and awareness.

"The only time that he visibly changed was when angered. He grew in size and his eyes glowed an ominous red. The name 'minotaur' was originally an affectionate nickname provided by King Minos, due to the man having strength he likened to a bull. Unfortunately, the man's original name has become lost over time.

"The King grew fond of him and valued him as a friend. The Athenians were afraid of the power this man gave to King Minos, through his wisdom and strength. They sent assassins to try and murder him. One of their attempts almost succeeded and the King ordered the creation of the Labyrinth. It was supposed to provide the minotaur a fortress of protection, that only the King and the minotaur could navigate safely.

"The Athenians started spreading rumours of a minotaur in a maze. They used his affectionate nickname against him and demonised him. Spreading lies about a man with the head of a bull, people feared this beast and they continued sending people to try and kill him. Blaming the unreturned Athenians on the crazy demands of King Minos.

"Ariadne, King Minos' daughter would visit the minotaur. She spent many hours in his company, bringing him games and food. Eventually, the minotaur and Ariadne fell in love and, with the King's blessing, they left the Labyrinth and went into hiding. Their descendants are the minotaurs in existence today. As time went on, Ariadne and the minotaur's descendants chose surnames. My lineage chose the surname 'Minos' out of respect for the King.

"Luckily for me, he didn't have the head of a bull. He was just a slightly hairy, well-built, dark-haired man. When the Athenians discovered that the minotaur had left the Labyrinth, they created the story of Theseus slaying the minotaur after gaining help from King Minos' own daughter. They knew that Ariadne could not dispute this, for fear of exposing the two of them to danger."

Damon paused, allowing the information to sink in. Parker was enraptured. This would mean that the man in front of her was actually a minotaur. She momentarily stared at him open-mouthed in awe. Parker then snapped herself out of it in embarrassment and blushed. "Do you need that drink now? I promise I won't tell your boss." He said with amusement.

Without waiting for an answer, Damon walked over to a discreet bar hidden behind an array of plants. He poured her a generous measure of an amber-coloured liquid out of a decanter. He then handed it to Parker who eagerly took a large gulp, before coughing in surprise as her throat burned from what she identified as brandy.

After she had finished coughing, she gathered herself together and set the glass on the table. Damon assessed her reaction and was happy that she had not been too overwhelmed with his revelation, "Do you have any immediate questions?"

"Honestly, I think I need to process this all first. If I have a question for you, should I just email you? Or would you prefer I direct my questions to someone else?" Parker enquired. She didn't think that she could just pop into his office at her convenience.

"An email is fine. I believe that Ellie is waiting to take you home if you are ready to go. If anything out of the ordinary occurs, please inform me or one of my senior team immediately." Parker nodded and finished her drink in one gulp, she had prepared herself for the burn this time. Damon stood up and opened the door, officially signalling the end of their meeting.

Parker smiled at the personal assistant as she entered the elevator and stopped by her desk on the third floor, to search for Ellie. She was sitting in her cubicle on her personal phone, her shift had finished half an hour before. They collected their belongings and exited the building together.

Ellie waited until they were in the car before asking what had happened in her meeting with Damon. Parker updated her, along with her thoughts and feelings about the latest revelation. The traffic was minimal and Ellie dropped Parker off at home, as Ellie had plans to babysit that evening for one of her sisters. At some point during the day, Parker's car had been dropped off at her new home.

That evening, after she had returned from food shopping and had eaten dinner, there was a knock at the door. Outside was a neighbour, with a 'welcome to the neighbourhood' gift basket. It contained a small plant, along with a selection of the biggest fruit she had ever seen.

From the size of the fruit on display, she guessed that her neighbour had an affinity with plants. Probably a satyr based on her limited knowledge, but she thought that it was rude to ask. Her neighbour was an older gentleman, with grey hair and a long beard. His clothes were well worn, with the knees ingrained with mud.

It was apparent that he had been working in his garden, "It's so nice to meet you, my name's Thomas. I didn't want to disturb you when you first moved in, as I wanted to let you settle." He saw the lack of greenery indoors and assumed correctly that she wasn't great at gardening. "If you would like some help with your garden, just let me know. I enjoy working outside and it keeps me busy in my retirement."

Parker thanked him for his kindness and started trying to

think of a way to repay him after he left. She would ask Ellie her opinion when she next saw her. Parker once again settled in for the evening and sat quietly for a period of time in order to think through all of the information received on her first day at her new job.

It didn't surprise her that Damon was a minotaur. It was fascinating how the truth of the minotaur varied from the myth. She couldn't wait to find out what other myths had a basis in truth.

CHAPTER 5

The following week dragged by very slowly. She realised that she hadn't updated her family or Julia about her change in job or address. It had all happened so quickly; it was only when she had a bit of breathing time, that she felt awful for not keeping people informed.

Parker started to worry that they would hear it from someone else, one of her old nosey neighbours or a friend who noticed the moving vans. She immediately drove to her parent's house. She didn't think that this was a conversation that should be had over text messages.

Her mum was a young-looking fifty-eight and on Parker's arrival, was wearing her usual attire of a floral blouse and a below-knee floaty skirt. Her dad had just turned sixty, he lived in a T-shirt and jeans. The T-shirt always had a classic car on the front.

She didn't broach the subject straight away, instead talking about the weather and her nephews. They were always getting up to something. Having four boys meant that there was always some drama unfolding or a trip to the emergency room, they were all very adventurous.

Eventually, she built up the courage to tell her parents, "By the way, I've been meaning to tell you. I have some great news. I have a new job in a company called 'Minos Industries', I'm not sure if you have heard of them. The job is great, with better pay and lots of potential. One of the best perks is that it comes with the option of buying a company property, for less than market value. So, I went for it and have moved already."

Parker was trying to sound as positive as she could, trying

to get all of the information out in one quick spurt. Her mum was shocked, "Wow, that was fast. You didn't even tell us that you had applied for a new job. The interview process must have been quick."

"Yes, it was pretty quick, but it was such a fantastic opportunity that I didn't want to wait. I also didn't tell you because I wasn't sure that I was going to get it." Parker told a little white lie, thinking it was the better option.

"What are you going to do with your house? I thought that you loved that place. Are you sure that you're making the right decision?" Her mum rattled off several quick-fire questions in concern.

"I haven't made my final decision, but I will either rent it out or sell it. I do love that house, but this one is easily double the size and is in a really good and safe neighbourhood. It isn't far away from where I lived before, maybe a ten-minute drive. You will love it." Parker was trying to reassure her; she didn't want her mum worrying.

"What did you say the company was called again? Minos Industries? I think your cousin tried applying there and kept getting rejected, she was really quite upset about it. They must be highly selective. I can't wait to tell your aunt that you got in. I'm so proud of you." Her dad hadn't said much, he normally let her mum do most of the talking. He had barely looked up from his car magazine during her visit.

Parker's sister Cassie popped by with her boys to borrow a food processor for the latest recipe fad that she had seen online, so Parker took the opportunity to update her also. She was excited for her. Cassie had made the decision to be a stay-at-home mum. While a rewarding job, and one that meant she could spend quality time with her four boys, she did sometimes miss getting to mingle with adults.

The next hour was spent playing ball with the boys outside. She didn't get to see them as much as she'd like. After Cassie left, Parker stayed for dinner and departed shortly after. They had one of her personal favourites, lasagna with garlic bread and a salad.

Parker decided that it was easier to call Julia, as it was difficult to just drop by with the kid's schedules. Julia was concerned at first, worried that Parker had joined a cult and also the speedy timeframe. Parker secretly thought that if she was worried about the possibility of a cult, how would she react if she told her the truth?

She wasn't tempted to spill the secret to either her family or Julia, as she didn't want to face the consequences. Parker was also smart enough to realise there would be mass panic if their secret was exposed. After all, the stories told of these people weren't fairytales of cute harmless creatures.

On Wednesday she carpooled with Ellie again, they lived so close that it made sense. She had to finish the data entry task assigned the previous day, which took her until mid-afternoon. The rest of the day was filled with filing and photocopying.

Parker was slowly getting to know everyone and felt like she was beginning to settle in. She found herself hoping for a meeting request to appear in her inbox from a grumpy boss, anything to add a little excitement to her day.

Thursday was slightly more eventful as there was a small argument between two colleagues about a missing lunch. It was resolved fairly swiftly as the lunch hadn't been stolen, just misplaced. Parker completed more filing work and started a task proof-reading some documents of no real sensitivity or interest.

Her tasks sometimes required her to visit other departments; she still couldn't tell who was human and who was supernatural. She had assumed that there were other humans working there, but she could be the only one.

Parker started to understand more about Minos Industries' business. They seemed to have branches in property, maintenance, research and engineering. She didn't fully understand what each one consisted of.

Property made sense due to the number of properties they had to own, in excess of those they provided to their employees.

She was curious about the research they invested in, but no one could or would tell her. This piqued her interest further, but knew she would have to watch and wait to find out answers.

On Friday, the tasks assigned didn't get any more interesting and the day passed slowly. Parker was starting to feel more and more like this was not the job of her dreams. An admin department was the same whether it was in a regular or supernatural company. Paperwork still needed filing and bills needed to be paid.

Parker had been invited out that evening for a few drinks with her colleagues in the admin department, which she happily accepted. It gave her something to look forward to and helped the day drag less. She found that she spent her time at work counting down the minutes to the next break, lunch or home time.

The plan was to go home and get changed before meeting later for snacks and drinks in a local bar. Parker offered to drive. After throwing on a pair of tight black jeans and a low-cut, dark green top, she jumped in her car and drove to Ellie's house.

After giving the horn a quick beep, Ellie walked to the car wearing a floor-length strappy dress with a vibrant peacock feather pattern. She had in her hand an orange fluffy purse and paired it with orange chunky earrings, "Thanks for picking me up, I'm really looking forward to this. We have been trying to arrange work drinks for ages but someone is always busy." Ellie said appreciatively.

"No problem, it's the least I can do. You have been giving me lifts to and from work all week."

"It's really no inconvenience, you're on my way and I like the company on the drive. How was your first week?" Ellie enquired.

"I honestly thought it would be more exciting, but admin is admin." Parker laughed but continued as she didn't want to insult Ellie's job. "I don't mean any offence; I just want something different."

"I can't say it's exciting for me either, but I'm not staying in that department forever. It just works for me for now." Ellie explained.

Ellie directed Parker to the bar, there was a newly empty parking space a short distance away. They entered the bar together; it had an Americana theme with a jukebox playing in the corner. License plates from the various states covered one wall and there were neon signs decorating the other walls.

They spotted the rest of their party at the far end; they had already secured a table. Drinks were ordered and Parker also requested cheese and bacon-topped fries, she was starving and had to stop herself from over-ordering. Their entire team had turned up, Pam, Stephen, Charlie and Rachel.

From their conversations during the week, she knew that Pam had two small children at home. She wore an off-the-shoulder, knee-length jumper, with a thick belt around her waist. Stephen was single, but Parker knew that it wouldn't last long as he always had a new love interest. He was tall and slim, wearing a navy polo shirt and chinos.

Charlie was an older widow; her husband had died years before. From her stories, it had been a happy marriage. She wore a baby blue high-necked blouse and black trousers. Rachel was sitting next to Parker. The music was loud enough that it was too difficult to talk to the entire group, so she chatted with Rachel. Her chestnut brown hair was styled into a long bob and she wore a cream-coloured jacket over a tank top and jeans.

Parker hadn't been able to find out who these individuals really were, it didn't feel appropriate to ask them directly. Luckily Rachel broached the subject, "So how are you getting on? I hear that the supernatural world is really new to you. You seem to be handling it really well."

"Yes, it's definitely new. I only found out about it a few days ago. I'm still really curious and there is a lot I don't know. Is it rude to ask someone their story?" Parker asked.

"It depends, some people are open, but others don't like to discuss it with non-supers. I really don't mind and I am happy to answer your questions." Rachel didn't seem concerned that they would be overheard by anyone. The music provided a good cover.

"I've heard the stories of the gorgons and the nymphs, are you a nymph or gorgon? If you aren't, can I ask what you are?"

Rachel smiled, reassuring her that she was happy to answer, "No, I'm not a nymph or gorgon. I'm actually a harpy. Have you heard of them?"

"Yes, but as you don't have wings or birds' legs I'm assuming that once again the myth isn't quite accurate?"

"No, my ancestors didn't have wings," Rachel laughed. "However, they did have a special relationship with all birds. They could also command the wind, sometimes using it to move at superhuman speeds. Fear caused rumours and stories to spread, they merged elements of the truth. The harpies often chose to have birds near due to their affinity and combined with the speed, people told stories of monsters with wings and claws.

"One of my ancestors did have a strong sense of justice and believed that people should be punished for wrongs. One day she came across a man beating his wife. She used her abilities to rush in and prevent the man from harming his wife further, distracting him by commanding numerous birds to attack him.

"She then also carried him away and caused him to disappear. The wife was grateful, but it started a new story as there were several people nearby. Of course, they hadn't lifted a finger to help. Back then men were allowed to discipline their wives. It spread that the harpies were commanded by Zeus to snatch people from Earth if they committed any wrongs. People had extremely vivid imaginations back then.

"Anyone that disappeared over the years was blamed on the harpies. Of course, the positive was that it caused a lot of men to straighten themselves out. But it also caused a lot of animosity towards those labelled as harpies and we, like the others, decided to go into hiding."

Parker listened intently to the story. It amazed her how the truth had been twisted. "Thank you for sharing that with me. I'm really eager to learn, but don't want to upset anyone with an ignorant question."

"That's understandable. I'm not sure if you are aware, but there are some supernaturals that hate humans. They call humans, outsiders. They blame you for us having to go into hiding. It's not logical as it was your ancestors' ignorant beliefs and not yours. You yourself have clearly embraced working with us. I'm just telling you so that you are pre-warned." Parker nodded her thanks for the heads-up.

The others had been engaged in their own conversations. Pam, Stephen and Ellie rose and began dancing to a lively tune. Parker decided to join in, long ago discovering she didn't need alcohol to enjoy getting up with her friends on a dancefloor.

They were dancing to their second song when a man came up behind Ellie and started dancing too closely for her comfort. He placed his hands on her waist and was being overly familiar. He wore fitted black jeans, a black shirt with the top three buttons undone and had slicked-back brown hair. Ellie politely took his hands and removed them from her sides, subtly stepping away and closer to Parker.

Parker took Ellie's hand and swung her around. She swapped places and had her back to the gentleman instead, hoping that this would be a big enough hint that they weren't interested. They had all experienced this situation numerous times. Some accept the rejection, others persevere.

Parker found that there was a direct correlation between perseverance and the amount of alcohol consumed. "Get lost, I'm just trying to dance with your friend." He said in a gruff tone to Parker.

"Sorry, I don't think she's interested." Parker could smell the stench of alcohol on his breath and could tell that ignoring him and hoping he disappeared back to his bar stool was wishful thinking. So, they decided that leaving the dancefloor was the better option and they all sat back down at their table.

The gentleman clearly hadn't taken the rejection well and began to shout slurs at the group as he sat at the bar. Pam leant towards Parker and said, "Watch this." Nothing happened at first until the water nozzle behind the bar burst. Strangely, it only covered the vile man with water. Several expletives later he stumbled out of the bar soaking wet. Weirdly, the water ceased spraying after a minute and the whole bar was laughing.

Pam told Parker, "We try to avoid using our powers in public, but I don't think this will be a problem. We have learnt to disguise it as accidents," she chuckled. They continued with their drinks and it began to get late. One by one they left, leaving Ellie, Parker and Rachel at the bar.

The trio left together and as Rachel had parked a little further away, they all walked to her car to ensure safety in numbers. She had parked in the middle of a dimly lit car park. It wasn't the safest place to park, but there weren't many options. As they approached the vehicle, a man stepped out of the shadows behind them.

Parker recognised him as the man from the bar. He was a little drier than when they saw him leave. "You thought that was funny, did you?" He said menacingly, "I'm thinking I should teach you three a lesson."

Parker froze, she was petrified. Her first thought was to be selfishly grateful that she wasn't facing him alone. Then almost immediately, her instincts had her trying to pull Ellie and Rachel behind her to protect them. They were both younger and without conscious thought she wanted to shield them. She said whilst shaking, in the most confident tone she could muster, "Run. Go. Get help."

He was about the same height as Ellie and thus several inches taller than Parker. He made a wild lunge for Parker and before she could react, Rachel intercepted his hand with one of hers and forced her other against his elbow. A snap echoed through the car park.

He screamed and Rachel followed it up by kicking him in the knee and hitting him in the face as he fell. He was unconscious before he hit the floor. Parker immediately threw her arms around Rachel, she was shaking and felt immense gratitude.

Parker heard Ellie speaking to someone and it took her a few minutes to realise she had her phone out. She suddenly felt very cold and realised that she was shivering. Ellie finished the call and saw Parker's condition, "It's alright, I've called for help. We are fine, no one is hurt. Apart from him obviously." And gestured at the man on the floor.

A few minutes later, a black van turned into the car park at speed and screeched to a halt by the women. Out climbed a large male in a long-sleeved fitted black T-shirt and jogging bottoms. Parker took a couple of steps back hesitantly and breathed a sigh of relief when she saw Greg follow him out.

The male that had exited first was enormous. He looked nearly seven feet tall and like he would struggle to fit widthways through most doorways. His mass was all power, minimal fat. She was glad he was on their side, or at least she hoped that he was. His face displayed concern, he had short brown hair and dark eyes. She couldn't see their colour due to the dim lighting. He quickly scanned the three women and assessed the situation.

Greg introduced this Leviathan as Leo, short for Leonidas. He was another of Damon's team. Leo nodded in greeting, clearly not big on small talk. Not that she minded, she wasn't in the mood for pleasantries. He then gave a disgusted glance towards the unconscious man, and in one deft movement, grabbed him by his belt and threw him in the back of the van, like he weighed nothing.

When Parker finally felt like she could speak without screaming hysterically, she approached Rachel. She was slightly embarrassed that it was hitting her so hard when Ellie and Rachel appeared to take it in their stride.

Ellie turned to Rachel and said, "That was amazing." Before turning to Parker and continuing, "Thank you for trying to protect us." And she hugged Parker, "But why on earth would you put yourself in front of us, Parker? You know we have powers to protect ourselves, we should have been protecting you!"

Parker blushed whilst replying, "I didn't even think. I was

much too scared to have any rational thought. I just wanted to protect you two." And she started crying.

Ellie spent the next few minutes holding Parker whilst she cried. Eventually, Parker got a grip, composed herself and wiped away the tears. Parker hated crying in front of people and Ellie appeared to read that in her face, so, she continued talking to Rachel, "When did you learn how to do that? You were kick-ass!"

Rachel looked towards Leo and Greg, "The short version is that they taught me. A while back I became involved with a man who appeared caring and loving. The perfect man, at first. Then he started to get physically abusive when I did something he didn't like, or I disagreed with him. After the first time he actually hit me, I walked out. Somehow Greg took one look at me and knew what had happened.

"He demanded to know the details. I explained what had happened and he offered to have it dealt with. I didn't want to get them involved, but my ex wouldn't leave me alone. He would turn up outside my house and leave me notes apologising. I'm used to dealing with things myself. So, after talking it through with Greg, we decided that the best option was for me to learn self-defence.

"He also helped me to move into one of the supernatural neighbourhoods for protection. I didn't want anyone else at the company to know, I was embarrassed. Leo and the others all wanted to help, so they each spent time with me. I will always be grateful." She sent Leo and Greg an appreciative smile.

"I hope that you realise that there was nothing to be embarrassed about, it was clearly his problem. I am thankful to you though for being here and saving us. We won't say anything to anyone else, it's not their business." Parker said and then gave her another hug.

Greg walked over, "We are getting the CCTV camera footage wiped. I'm assuming you didn't use any powers, but we don't want the police asking questions. Leo will sort out this scumbag and take him to a hospital anonymously. I will drive Rachel home if you two are alright to go home together?"

Parker responded, "I'm not sure, I still feel shaky." She was nervous as she would be the one driving.

"It's fine. Greg, you drive them home. I have my cousin staying with me at the minute, so he will be there when I get home." Rachel offered.

Greg counteroffered, "How about I drive you all home in one car and arrange for someone to collect Parker's car later? That way I will know that you are all home safe."

Parker was relieved by this suggestion. She didn't think that she could drive and Ellie had consumed too much alcohol. However, her conscience wouldn't allow Rachel to go home alone. So, they all piled into Rachel's car. It was a four-seater convertible, so the seats in the back were a squeeze, but she wasn't going to complain. Parker had wanted more excitement in her life but was now considering whether she needed to dial this back a bit.

They drove in silence the entire journey home. Parker was dropped off first and she thanked them before exiting. They waited until she was inside with the door locked, before pulling away. She immediately made herself a cup of tea. She should have asked Ellie to make her one of her calming blends. They were lucky that Rachel knew how to protect herself.

Parker always liked the idea of learning self-defence but believed that she was too clumsy and uncoordinated. As she sat on her sofa and looked around, she wanted to feel productive and in control. She messaged Ellie: *Home furnishing shopping tomorrow? No worries if you're busy x.*

A few minutes later Ellie sent a response: *Definitely! I would love to. I know a place that will give us a good price. Just let me know when you're ready tomorrow x.*

Parker needed to distract herself and there was no cleaning to be done, the house was still spotless. She settled on some late-night TV before going to bed. The events of the night flashed through her head. It was a shame that such a good night with friends was marred by a drunken idiot. Now that she was alone, she allowed herself to cry as much as she wanted.

She kept thinking of what could have happened. What if he'd had a knife? What if one of them had been hurt or killed? Eventually, she stopped crying. Parker had always felt better after having a good cry. Her last thought before drifting off was that maybe she should research some self-defence classes.

It was the first time in a long time that Parker had slept beyond ten o'clock. She was clearly exhausted and her mind needed time to process. She messaged Ellie, letting her know that she was awake: *Hey, I'm up. Want to go out for lunch, then go shopping? x.*

About ten minutes later she received a response: *Sorry, I was just in the shower. I'm always up for food, there is a great diner near here unless you fancy something else. x.*

They finalised details over a few more texts and Parker dressed for the day. She wanted to wear something comfortable, so chose her jeans, a baggy sweatshirt and Converse. Parker's car had been returned at some point in the night, so she drove to collect Ellie. Ellie walked out wearing a 'Save the Turtles' T-shirt and yellow crop trousers, with a white cat print.

Ellie acted as chief navigator in the passenger seat and when they arrived at the diner, Ellie didn't wait for Parker and flounced inside, grabbing a booth. Parker locked the car and followed her friend inside. Ellie handed Parker a menu.

The trauma of the previous night seemed like weeks ago, replaced by the promise of good conversation and better food. "I don't need the menu. I always order the same, American-style pancakes with bacon and maple syrup," Ellie said grinning.

Parker browsed the menu and ordered chicken strips and fries, with a chocolate milkshake when the waitress sidled up to their table. As Parker perused the diner, she couldn't help but feel a supernatural vibe. She couldn't explain it but knew that this place was special. "Is this a supernatural hangout?" Parker whispered.

Ellie smiled and nodded, "They do the best food; they do have an advantage as the owner's wife is a nymph. A little bit of her particular brand of magic and the fresh produce grown is extra delicious."

Parker began wondering how many times she had walked into a supernatural hangout and hadn't realised. The food was exactly as Ellie had described, everything tasted amazing. She would definitely be returning but may have to cut back on the chocolate milkshakes.

In between large bites of food, they spent their time discussing what Parker was shopping for. Luckily, her first payday from Minos Industries and her last payday from her old company had simultaneously arrived in her bank account the previous day, so she could afford to have a little fun. She had been pleasantly surprised with her salary increase.

They walked into a large homeware superstore. Parker decided that she would have to be slightly sensible, as there was so much choice. She wanted to eat more than toast that month. They went to the seating section first and she picked out two, dark grey, armchairs. They looked nice, but the clinching factor was when she sat in them, they felt like heaven.

They then spent the next two hours picking out little touches and decorations, along with new bedding for her room. As Ellie had promised, she received a fantastic discount from the store manager and they even arranged free next day delivery for her. Once they had finished at that store, Ellie directed her to a beautiful home covered in flowering plants.

Ellie explained that this was the best place to get plants for her home. A lady answered the door, with frizzy, curly, grey hair and a warm smile. She was wearing denim dungarees with patches on the knees. Ellie introduced her as Khloris and they were welcomed inside. She invited Parker to sit at her kitchen table and asked her questions. She wanted to know her likes and dislikes, as well as what her house was like.

Once she had finished her list of questions, she promised that her son-in-law would drop off a plant selection later that day which would be perfect for her. Parker was amused that Khloris would know what she liked from those questions but thought that it wouldn't hurt to go along with it. They said their goodbyes and headed home, Parker was looking forward to getting home and relaxing.

Ellie stopped in for a coffee before heading off. She was only half way through her drink when Khloris' son-in-law delivered a large selection of plants. Parker was shocked but conceded that she probably had the space to house them all. Ellie looked over the selection of foliage and confirmed that Khloris had selected low-maintenance plants for Parker, which she was grateful for.

Ellie finished up her coffee and bid farewell, leaving Parker to worry about placing and caring for her newly acquired jungle. Parker felt like the house was beginning to feel like a home and like she was finally embracing her new life.

CHAPTER 6

Monday morning arrived and with it a sense of misery. Weekends always ended far too soon for Parker. She dragged herself out of bed and hoped that work would offer some excitement. She considered enquiring about other positions available in the company, however, she didn't think that Damon would be keen, as she knew that he still didn't trust her. Parker decided that she was still going to enquire, it couldn't hurt. The worst-case scenario was that they said no.

After dressing in a navy pencil skirt and cream, fitted shirt, she slipped on a pair of ballet pumps. She pulled her hair back into a high ponytail and wore her gold teardrop earrings with a matching necklace.

Ellie came by to pick her up, uncharacteristically leaving plenty of time to get to the office. Typically, they got caught in a traffic jam caused by an accident earlier that morning. They just managed to arrive on time and Parker and Ellie rushed to their desks. Parker had brought in a couple of items from home to make it feel cosy, a picture of her nephews and a small plant.

She noticed that a small clay pot had been added to her desk, it was the size of a large orange. Parker assumed that it had been placed there by Ellie or one of her other colleagues as a gift. She made a mental note to ask them about it later.

Her eyes kept glancing towards the pot over the next couple of hours as curiosity got the better of her. Parker saw markings engraved on it, she couldn't resist the temptation anymore and took a few minutes to inspect it further. Parker picked it up and saw the engravings were, in fact, ornate pictures of a bird, snake, goat, horse, bull, eye, tree and what looked like the scales of justice. Above the images was the word 'ABRAXAS'.

Strangely, as she turned the pot in her hands, the symbols disappeared, and so had the word. Despite how delicately she was holding the pot, it started to crumble in her hands and soon turned to dust, which ran through her fingers and disappeared entirely as it fell onto the desk. She stared at it open-mouthed, then looked around to see if anyone else had seen what she had.

Suddenly, a piercing alarm sounded through the building, she assumed at first that it was a fire alarm, but no one was rushing to leave. Parker walked over to Ellie's desk, to ask her what was going on. She seemed to have a better understanding, as she wasn't panicking. "What is it? What's that alarm? Should we evacuate?" Parker asked concerned.

Ellie calmly responded, "We can't leave, I've only experienced that alarm once before. Everything is on lockdown. Didn't you read your booklet from HR?"

"Yes. Mostly. I skimmed some of it," Parker admitted sheepishly, "apparently this alarm was something I missed."

Jaxon asked everyone to return to their desks and to wait until everything was resolved. Parker sat there for about thirty minutes when the elevator doors opened. Two large imposing men exited and walked towards Jaxon, who after a brief interaction pointed at Parker.

One had dark brown hair with a red tint, it was long and wavy, almost to his shoulders. He wasn't as bulky as the man next to him, but he was obviously very toned. The man walking alongside him was slightly bigger in size and had tight brown curls with dark brown eyes. His eyes had laughter lines as if he was usually smiling; however, he wasn't smiling now. They both wore an all-black outfit, a simple V-neck T-shirt and cargo trousers.

Parker's eyes widened, what had she done? She looked like a deer caught in headlights as they approached. "Come with us." The smaller man ordered. Before she could protest, he had taken her arm in a gentle yet firm manner and started leading her towards the elevator. Through the rush of blood in her ears, Parker could hear Ellie's voice coming closer, demanding answers.

The larger man turned to address Ellie before rejoining his partner. Parker was ushered into the elevator and shorty pressed the button to the first subfloor. She smirked at her nickname for the unknown man. She found that giving people random nicknames was a good way to vent her frustration, even though he was still considerably taller than her.

Parker tried to talk to them several times, but neither answered. She kept reminding herself that everything would be fine; she hadn't done anything wrong – yet. If they kept insisting on treating her this way, she may start cracking heads together. Parker was confident that they had collected the wrong person and that this would all be cleared up shortly. She also knew that Ellie had seen what had happened; she wouldn't let them keep her here, she hoped.

The elevator came to a halt as they arrived at their intended floor. At least she would see what was down here, but would she want to? They all stepped out into a long, well-lit corridor. Parker started to feel claustrophobic, there were no windows, and she began to panic.

"Just take deep breaths." The larger one mumbled to Parker, clearly concerned but wanting to maintain his aloof persona.

She was fed up with being pushed around, bullied and frightened. Nothing anyone had done so far had implied that they would hurt her. Greg and Leo taught Rachel self-defence so that she could protect herself. These weren't the bad guys; they were clearly just doing their job. Soon she would find out what was happening, clear up any confusion and she would be allowed to return to an exciting afternoon of proof-reading spreadsheets. On second thought, maybe she would prefer to stay down here.

There were numerous offshoots of corridors leading from the main one. Eventually, they turned right, took the second left and a door on the left-hand side was opened. She was ushered into a minimally adorned room and directed towards a chair. She had seen enough police dramas to know an interrogation room when she saw it. It even had the cliché one-way mirror.

After she had been seated, the men left her alone with her thoughts. Her only choice was to sit and wait for someone to return. Hopefully, the next person would listen to her. She spent the time remembering old crime shows and secret agent films, her imagination was running wild. Was she about to see a real-life reenactment of good cop, bad cop? Parker then mused that the bigger one would have to play good cop for it to work.

She had already briefly considered climbing on the table, dislodging a ceiling tile and crawling through an air vent, before climbing up a convenient ladder within the ducts. Then she would make her way to the outside and leave triumphantly. If it wasn't for her lack of physical ability and awful sense of direction, she thought that maybe she could have pulled it off.

Approximately half an hour later, the larger man returned, placed a sealed bottle of water in front of her and left. That was considerate she thought sarcastically; the problem was that if she drank the bottle of water, she would need to pee soon and she assumed prisoners weren't allowed bathroom breaks.

Out of curiosity and a little boredom, she examined the bottle. Parker wasn't going to drink it, but she wanted to know if it had been tampered with. The cap looked sealed, and she couldn't see any puncture marks. She completed the test by squeezing it to check for leaks, the water inside also looked normal.

Parker concluded that it was indeed probably just water, and they weren't trying to drug or poison her. Although, she still wasn't sure why they would want to do either of these things to her. Her imagination was clearly getting the better of her.

At least another hour passed, or maybe it was only ten minutes. She had visually inspected every inch of the room several times, it didn't take long. The floor was concrete, the walls were concrete, the ceiling appeared to be made of suspended tiles and there was a mirror on the wall to her left.

At first, she ignored the mirror. Then Parker decided to stare at the mirror and sing every nursery rhyme she could remember, as enthusiastically as possible. Parker knew that it was a random choice, but she didn't want them to see her scared or cowering, she was too proud and stubborn for that. If nothing else, it would certainly confuse her captors.

After exhausting her limited repertoire of nursery rhymes, she briefly considered a rousing rendition of show tunes. Before she could start on the Phantom of the Opera, the door creaked open and the same two men entered. She had wondered if Damon would grace her with his presence, but clearly he was too busy and Parker too unimportant.

They sat down in chairs across from her, both looking far too big for the furniture. Parker waited for them to speak. It looked like shorty was going to be the one to do the talking, "Why did you come to work for Minos Industries?"

"I didn't have much choice. I witnessed something I shouldn't, but surely you already know that. Why am I here?"

"How long have you been a part of the supernatural world?"

"Greg knows. He was the one who told me about it, ask him. I'm not sure why I'm here, but I think that there has been a mistake. If you can tell me what it is you think I have done, I can explain why you are wrong."

"How long have you known Deimos?"

"Who?"

"Deimos Minos."

"I'm confused, isn't Minos Damon's surname? Is that a relative of his?"

"Who have you told that you work for this company?"

"I told my parents, my sister and her children. I also told my friend. Maybe my mum told my aunt. I think she wanted to brag that I got a job here when my cousin couldn't."

"Why did your cousin try and get a job here?"

"The benefits? I don't really know as I haven't spoken to her in months."

"Where have you hidden it?"

"I'm sorry, hidden what?"

"You were seen with it this afternoon, don't lie."

"I'm not lying, and I hate being accused of it. I don't know what you are talking about. If you speak to me like an adult and not some errant child, maybe I can understand what has happened and how I can help."

"You were seen with a small clay pot this morning."

"Oh, that?" Parker was taken aback that all of this was for a little clay pot she'd accidentally destroyed. "I found it on my desk. I assumed that one of my colleagues had left it for me as a gift. I was going to ask them about it at lunch. Why? Was it special? I'm really sorry that I broke it. It was an accident." Parker said sheepishly, it had looked old and maybe she was too heavy-handed.

The two men looked at her whilst frowning and then at each other, each looking slightly pale. They seemed to be having a silent conversation between them, "What do you mean, you broke it?" The bigger man said, leaning forward.

"I'm sorry," Parker apologised again. "I didn't mean to. I picked it up to look at the pictures and it just disintegrated in my hands. I'm sorry I broke it. It was an accident, and I will pay for another one." Parker couldn't help apologising repeatedly, but she did feel bad that all this commotion was due to her clumsiness.

They both looked at the mirror, seemingly to wait for instruction. Two knocks sounded on the glass, they rose simultaneously and exited the room. Parker sighed. At least she now knew what this was all about. How a little pot had caused such drama she didn't know. She would happily pay for a replacement. If it was a valuable antique, they would need to be happy with a payment plan, as her savings were minimal.

She was beginning to get bored of waiting. The door opened again and Damon walked in, with the larger man from before, "Can you please tell me the names of the men I have been speaking with? I need to know the names for when I file my complaint with HR and moan about them later," Parker spat in a frustrated tone to Damon, whilst glaring at the unnamed male. She stopped short of sticking her tongue out at him.

"Sure, Cadmus and Zoticus. Also known as Cad and Zack, this one's Zack." And gestured towards the man on his left. Zack raised one eyebrow at being thrown under the bus.

"I suppose you have more questions. I promised to pay for it, even if I need to make payments. I didn't do it on purpose. Besides, I don't know why it was on my desk in the first place if I wasn't supposed to touch it." Parker responded grumpily.

"Tell me again how it came to be on your desk." Damon requested whilst looking directly into her eyes, she felt like she couldn't look away.

Parker really did want them to believe her, "I don't know how it arrived on my desk; it was there when I arrived at work. I didn't say anything, as I thought that it was a gift from someone. I was going to ask the others about it on my first break. I didn't realise that it was that important."

"Can you describe it to me?" Damon was eyeing her sceptically, he carefully lowered himself into one of the chairs as it groaned under his weight.

"I think so, it wasn't very big. It had a word on it; abracadabra, abacus or abrax. I don't know what it means though. It also had some pictures on it, some animals, like a bird, goat, bull and some others." Parker paused, wracking her brain trying to remember the word. She finally got her eureka moment, "Abraxas!" She exclaimed triumphantly. "What was weird, was that as I was turning it to look at them, all the images had disappeared by the next rotation. That's when it crumbled." Parker continued to get frustrated, "I am not a thief. Why would I want to steal a little clay pot?"

Damon rose and Zack followed, "I have some things that I need to check out. I just need you to stay a little longer. Zack will bring you anything you need and just let him know if you need to use the bathroom." He turned away, before stopping and looking back over his shoulder, "One final request. Please, no more singing." And grinned before walking out.

Zach started chuckling as he left. "A more comfortable seat!" Parker shouted after them as they left.

She sat back and folded her arms in a huff. Hopefully, she would be let go soon. Five minutes later, Zach returned carrying a padded chair. "Sorry, it's the best I could find. It won't be much longer though. Boss needs to show that he's doing his due diligence before letting you go. He doesn't really think that you're involved with the theft. If I could please ask a favour? Tell Ellie that we treated you well. If she thinks that we hurt you in any way, we won't hear the end of it." Zack smiled cheekily at Parker and placed the chair in the corner. He waited to see if she needed a bathroom break before leaving.

Parker began thinking about what Zack had said. The clay pot had been stolen from somewhere. But why if someone stole the pot, would they put it on her desk? Maybe to frame her? But why? She would unquestionably be ranting to Ellie about this later today, maybe this was all her own fault. She had been hoping for a more exciting day after all.

Parker lifted her left hand to push a stray hair out of her eyes when she noticed a mark on her wrist. She pushed her sleeve up further to examine it and saw a circular design with the same symbols that she saw on the pot. She immediately licked her finger and tried to wipe it off, to no avail.

She started rubbing it harder until it hurt, "Zack!" She shouted as loudly as she could, trying not to freak out.

He burst through the door seconds later, "What is it? Are you alright?" He was scanning the room for the cause of her sudden outburst.

"Look!" She showed him her wrist. He looked at the mark and took her by the hand, leading her out of the room. She had to jog to keep up with his strides and they ended up in a larger, more comfortable room. It had a TV on one wall, a couple of worn sofas and a fridge. Damon was talking to Cad on the sofa.

Damon glanced up as they entered and sent a confused look to Zack, "Look at this," Zack insisted, whilst pushing her wrist towards Damon. He took her hand in his, it was pleasantly warm and gentle. He spent several minutes looking at the mark and frowning. He took out his phone and took a photo, He obviously didn't know what was happening either.

Parker was more concerned about it being permanent. Her mum would kill her if she thought that she had gotten a tattoo. Damon came to a decision, he asked Parker to take a seat. "I will," She replied, "But first I need to use the little girls' room." Zack guided her to the bathroom.

She didn't know what she would have done if he had tried to enter with her, but luckily for his own health, he stayed outside. When she was washing her hands, she added extra soap to her wrist and tried to scrub it off, but it stubbornly stayed put.

They returned to the conference room, where she chose a seat far away from the others. Parker wanted the men to know that she wasn't happy with any of them and their heavy-handedness. "When are you going to accept that I'm not some devious supervillain who is out to get you all?"

Damon didn't react, Zack laughed and replied, "But you would make a great supervillain, the nursery rhyme torturer." Parker didn't hold back this time and did stick her tongue out at him; she didn't think her singing was that bad. Cad just smiled and shrugged innocently.

"I have decided that there is absolutely no evidence to refute your claims. Quite frankly, your life up to now has been normal. Nothing that stands out in any way." Damon stated, almost disappointedly.

Parker turned her glare on Damon. If looks could kill, he would have exploded into a million pieces. She hated her life being summed up as boring. If this was his way of apologising, he was awful at it.

"So," he continued, ignoring her death glare, "This is clearly something that cannot be ignored. Between the inexplicable break-in, the vision and now the mark, the universe is speaking to us. If we have learnt nothing else, it is that you must always listen when the universe is shouting at you."

"Does this mean that you are finally going to quit treating me like a criminal?" Parker asked, still enraged.

"Yes, I'm going to tell you the whole story. However, there is one little, tiny piece of business we need to attend to. Ellie has been creating havoc upstairs. Well, you can see for yourself."

Damon rose, followed by Zack and Cad. Damon held the door open for Parker; her death glare was starting to soften. He directed her back to the elevators; her sense of direction was awful. She didn't think that she would have ever found her way out of this labyrinth of corridors and doors.

All four of them stepped inside, it was a tight squeeze and she found herself pressed up against the front of Zack's body. He sent her a light-hearted grin and winked; she couldn't help but laugh. It didn't feel sleazy, he was clearly teasing her. Damon immediately moved them around, so that she was no longer pressed against Zack's body and placed her in front of him.

The button for the twenty-second floor was pressed and up they went. Parker was enormously pleased that she was once again above ground. She felt claustrophobic in those catacombs and she was craving natural light and fresh air.

When the elevator doors finally opened, they were once again on the top floor. They all squeezed out, grateful to have some space. It wasn't a small elevator, these were just large men. She saw the same lady sitting at the desk as before, she smiled curiously at them as they walked across the room. Damon addressed her, "Thank you for looking after them Patricia, it has been an eventful day."

"You can say that again Mr Minos. They have refused beverages; I have offered three times."

"I've asked you before Patricia, please call me Damon." He said in a tone that Parker had not yet heard him use, it was gentle and full of affection. She just smiled warmly at him and returned to typing on her computer.

Damon led the way to his office, followed by Parker and then the others. She heard raised voices coming from the room. As the door opened, Parker was rushed by Ellie who immediately hugged her and glared at Damon. "Are you alright? I can't believe they treated you like that. What did they do to you?" And she pulled Parker away from the men.

"I'm fine, honestly. There was clearly some confusion and other than subjecting me to a few hours of boredom, they didn't hurt me at all. It was no worse than a day in Admin, really. You already know that though, they are just heavy-handed sometimes." And sent Damon a scathing look.

"Hello Marion, it's been a while. Lovely to see you, as always." Damon said to someone behind Ellie, in an extremely polite and respectful tone. Parker looked over Ellie's shoulder and saw a very tall and beautiful woman. She had jet-black hair which fell to her waist in perfectly styled curls. She was wearing an electric blue blouse, with a black pencil skirt and high heels.

The woman was currently giving Damon an unimpressed look, then she turned towards Parker. Her face changed completely from a stern woman who wouldn't be disagreed with, to a warm and welcoming mum. As soon as her face brightened, she realised who she looked like, "Ellie's mum?" Parker queried.

"Yes dear, how did you know?"

"She looks so much like you; the family resemblance is clear."

"Oh, I do like you. Ellie, you have a great choice of friends." Ellie beamed, pleased.

Marion turned her gaze upon Damon, "Don't think that I have forgotten about you, Mr Minos. I hope that you don't make a habit of bullying young girls and whisking them away suddenly?" Parker couldn't believe it when Damon actually looked embarrassed.

"There were extenuating circumstances. I am willing to include you in the following conversation if you can ensure that it doesn't leave this room. You are a very respected member of our community and I do value your counsel."

This appeared to appease Marion, she nodded and went to take a seat. She took one of the single armchairs, Damon took the other which left the three-seater sofa for the four of them. Cad waved his arm towards Zack, Ellie and Parker, indicating that they should take the seat. He then left and returned a few minutes later carrying an additional chair, he made it look effortless, even though its frame was made from solid wood.

Damon began, "I'm not sure how much everyone knows, so I will start at the beginning and tell the full story. Some of you know that the nymphs used to have visions. They were a regular occurrence and we grew to rely on them. They helped to hide and protect us, letting us know when to move on or when we were in danger. They also provided us with knowledge which we used to help others; we couldn't prevent foretold floods, but we could be there to help.

"We have always had a difficult relationship with humans. Many have despised us for our powers, due to their jealousy and fearing what they couldn't understand or control. In an effort to provide a full unbiased picture and full disclosure, I'll acknowledge some of our ancestors haven't always treated humans well either. However, there have been others like King Minos and Ariadne who have helped to protect us.

"Over time the visions reduced. At first, we thought that it was due to our closer proximity to humans. Some of the nymphs chose to exile themselves from the rest of humanity and live in the wild. However, this didn't prevent the decline in the power of precognition.

"Nothing anyone did changed the outcome and we knew that inevitably this ability would soon be lost. About seventy years ago, we thought that the power had already died out, but a young girl walked into a council meeting and foretold of a prophecy. When she spoke the last word, she collapsed, and from her there emanated a bright light.

"A powerful wind stirred the room, papers were flying everywhere. When the wind finally abated, a clay pot was sat in the middle of the council chamber. It was only the size of a large fist, but we knew that it was extremely important. On inspection, the pot was inscribed with a word, along with images representing the different supernatural lines.

"It was decided then and there that this prophecy was too important for us to accidentally influence. So, the prophecy was written down and it was locked away with the pot in a vault. There was an agreement between the council members, to never tell anyone else about the prophecy.

"The young girl came around several days later and didn't remember anything. She must have travelled miles to get to that meeting, but she had no recollection of her journey. It is now almost seventy years to the day. Ellie received a vision, which told us no more than a human woman should attend a party. I believe that Ellie has shared this vision with you Marion." And looked to her for confirmation.

Marion nodded and Damon continued, "As you may have realised from today's events, the pot and prophecy were stored in a vault beneath Minos Industries. That specific area of the vault has not been accessed in seventy years. Yet somehow, that pot not only ended up on Parker's desk, but it also disintegrated after she held it.

"We don't know how the pot left the vault. At this moment we are unsure whether Deimos had something to do with it or if the pot itself was trying to fulfil the prophecy. We can't rule anything out, so we intend to investigate. In addition to the pot disintegrating, Parker has developed a tattoo on her wrist."

Ellie and Marion looked at her quizzically, so she showed them both the new mark. Neither appeared to recognise the design, Marion sat back in her chair and began frowning in thought. Damon finished, "So, Marion and Ellie, you may now understand why we reacted the way we did today. We had to rule out the possibility that Parker was working with Deimos and stole the pot."

Parker spoke up, "I'm sorry to interject, but who is Deimos? Tweedle Dee over here," And pointed at Cad, who just raised an eyebrow, "Mentioned his name earlier when interrogating me. He said that his name was Deimos Minos?"

Zack started chuckling, realising that he must be Tweedle Dum.

Damon wasn't as amused, he clearly hated discussing this person Deimos, "He is my uncle. We have different opinions on how to lead the supernatural community. My father left the company in my hands when he retired with my mum to Scotland. My uncle wasn't happy as he wanted to have control, but there is a reason that he has never had a say in company affairs.

"He believes that supernaturals are superior to humans. He, like a few others believe that humans are the problem and that we should force them to accept our rule. He doesn't seem to understand, that we are most prosperous when we work alongside humans. When we started losing our powers like precognition, it gave him more ammo to use in his campaign to overthrow me and my men." Damon looked truly saddened by this information.

"There is one more thing," Damon said, "It isn't just the visions that have dwindled. Other supernaturals have noticed a decline in their abilities. It is random, some seem to have kept their full powers while others are a shadow of their former selves. The minotaurs have kept their abilities thus far, but we don't know when we will be affected too. Our hope is that this last prophecy is the key to returning our full powers and it seems like Parker may be the key to fulfilling the prophecy."

Parker sat silently, absorbing it all. So, he thought that this 'plain' and 'boring' human could be important to saving his high and mighty ass, she thought smugly. Before realising that she didn't want to be responsible for all supernaturals and she turned slightly pale. "I have decided that if Parker is going to be the key somehow, we should prepare her for whatever may come. As of tomorrow, she will be spending more time with me and the other minotaurs."

He then spoke directly to Parker, "I hope you won't miss your current job too much; you won't be returning to it for the foreseeable. I will ask Patricia to inform your manager. Cad is our IT expert, he will make sure that all of the relevant information and programs have been put onto your phone." That was the best news she had heard in days, no more admin! She then belatedly wondered what 'spending more time' with them would entail, but she would worry about that later.

They all left Damon's office; Marion gave Parker a hug before she left and made her promise to contact her if she ever needed anything. Ellie immediately drove Parker home so that they could have a full discussion about everything. "What happened after they dragged me away kicking and screaming?" Parker jokingly asked.

"It's not funny! I was really worried about you. No one would give me any answers, so I did the only thing that I could think of. I called my mum." Ellie said soberly.

"Why your mum? Although, she did seem scary at first."

"Well, I don't really talk about it much, but my mum is highly respected in the supernatural community. She has done a lot for us all and helped to protect our secrets by obtaining a senior position at a media company. She is also on the board of two charities that help homeless and abused children. She often rallies the supernatural communities to provide support where we can. Damon doesn't owe her anything and doesn't answer to her, but I know that he holds her in high regard. He is a good guy, deep, deep down." She said laughing.

"I guess I will have first-hand experience of that starting tomorrow. I'm assuming that they will let me know what the plan is, at some point." And shrugged.

Parker and Ellie settled in for the night, watching the latest murder mystery series about a detective with mystery-solving aunts. They also binged on pizza and cookie dough ice cream; comfort food fixes everything. It was late when Ellie finally returned home, with a promise from Parker to let her know if she needed a lift in the morning.

CHAPTER 7

A shrill sound pierced through the darkness. Parker nearly fell out of the bed in her panic. It was pitch black in her room, apart from her phone on the bedside table which was fully lit and seemed to be screaming. She snatched it up and stared at it in confused disgust. It was an alarm, but why would it be going off at half past five?

She turned it off as soon as her mind had cleared and flopped back onto the bed. Parker crawled under the sheets and shut her eyes. A couple of minutes later, the phone started blasting out a heavy metal track that she wasn't familiar with. Heavy metal really wasn't her type of music and was even less palatable at that ungodly hour.

Parker flew up and grabbed her phone again, this alarm was titled 'GET UP!!!'. She turned it off and checked the alarm settings on her phone. Parker noticed that these two alarms were set for every day of the week. What sort of sadist would do this and why?

Then she remembered that Cad had been tasked with updating her phone with contacts and necessary information. She was praying that this was just a cruel joke, and they surely couldn't expect her to get up at half past five every day.

Her phone received a text message: *In case you were wondering, you need to get up and get to the office by 06:15. I will be waiting for you in reception. Don't be late - C.*

Well, she was wide awake now anyway. She grumbled and dragged her tired body out of bed, calculating how many hours of sleep she had managed. It was five; her minimum number of hours to function was at least seven and a half. Even then, she wouldn't trust anything clever to pass her lips.

She wasn't sure what was to be expected of her, so after showering she wore a sensible outfit of smart black jeans with a loose-fitting shirt. Parker tied her hair up in a ponytail, it was the most utilitarian style for all situations. If she wasn't dressed correctly, then it would be their fault for not preparing her.

Parker fired off a message to Ellie: *Sorry if this wakes you, but I won't be needing a lift today. They want me in the office by 6:15!!! x.*

She pulled on her black ballet pumps and shuffled her way to the car. There was no traffic at this time of the morning, so she went to the drive-through at the coffee shop and grabbed a Mocha. Parker wasn't a big fan of coffee; but when chocolate was added, it was palatable enough, and she desperately needed the caffeine. She spent the rest of her drive to the office plotting sufficient revenge on Cad for his cruel surprise.

The car park was almost empty, so she grabbed a space near the doors. She glanced at the clock, ten minutes past six. Parker was early and had no intention of rushing into the building. She dragged her feet, whilst huddled around her precious caffeine. Parker mooched up to the doors, expecting them to slide open and when they remained steadfast, she almost walked straight into them.

She started hoping that Cad wasn't going to be late. Parker peered through the glass to see if there was any movement, but it was still dark outside and the lights inside were off. Luckily, it was only a few seconds later that she saw a bright light, as he exited the elevator and walked towards the doors.

Parker was glad that he hadn't seen her almost faceplant the glass. He entered a code, the doors slid open, and the internal lights flashed into existence. She hustled inside quickly and he locked the doors after her. She had never seen it this quiet, it felt eerie but somehow exhilarating. He glimpsed at her drink and enquired, "Didn't you bring one for me too?"

"People who wake me up at half past five in the morning, don't deserve one." Parker glared at him icily.

He just smiled, "We did tell you that you would be spending the day with us, our day starts at five. So really, I let you have a lie in." And grinned annoyingly at her.

Cad entered the elevator and pressed the button for the twentieth floor. She was starting to feel more alive as the caffeine took effect. They exited into a massive workout space, with every kind of gym equipment that you could ever dream of. There was also a boxing ring and a large, matted area.

Parker began to wonder why he would have brought her to this floor. Maybe Cad had to collect something or meet someone. He walked her to a large locker room at the rear, with showers and cubicles. One of the walls housed floor-to-ceiling shelves, they contained training clothes of every size. They also varied in style, she assumed that it matched the training being undertaken. Beyond the cubicles were about twenty large lockers, "Get changed." Cad directed.

"Get changed, please. I see that you have the same issue with manners as Damon. Besides, why do I need to get changed?"

"You won't be able to move in what you're wearing, so you need to get changed," And then added as if in mocking afterthought, "Please." Parker rolled her eyes, unimpressed. "Pick an outfit in your size and change in one of the cubicles. You can use any of the lockers, but no one here will take any of your stuff."

Parker knew that she was going to hate whatever happened next. She had admitted to herself though, that after Friday night's attack, she had wanted to be more capable of defending herself. So, without grumbling too much, she selected her outfit and proceeded to the cubicles.

A few minutes later she emerged. Parker stood in front of a large mirror and checked that everything fit, ensuring it covered all of her more intimate areas. She was wearing a black, fitted tank top and baggy jogging bottoms; they were more flattering than she had expected. She placed her things in a locker, mostly so that she didn't lose anything.

Cad came over when he saw that she was ready and

subconsciously looked towards her wrist, as it was now on display. He guided her over to the mats where calming music was being played, they were next to the wall of windows. "The first thing that we are going to do is assess you, your flexibility, balance and concentration. I want you to follow my directions."

He moved onto a pre-laid yoga mat, she copied him and stood on the one next to his. Parker was feeling quite pessimistic. She had always been clumsy but was willing to give it a go. At least he didn't expect her to run.

They started with the easier poses, warrior one and two, cobra, downward-facing dog and the tree pose, which was quite problematic for her as she kept tipping over. "You aren't currently holding your weight in the right place; you are putting your weight onto your heels." Cad then helped adjust her pose until it was correct. He was very patient with her, supporting and guiding her.

When satisfied, Cad took her through some of the more complex positions, eagle, boat and half-moon poses. These, Parker considered a disaster. She fell over on every attempt, which wasn't helped by her laughing constantly at her epic failures. Her favourite was the corpse pose, where she just lay flat on the floor and relaxed her whole body.

"So, how did I do sensei?" Parker asked, not expecting a glowing report.

"Wrong discipline, I believe the Yoga equivalent is a Yogi. I didn't expect you to be able to achieve all of these poses today, I just needed to assess you. I believe that you are already quite flexible, which can be enhanced by training. Your balance is your weakness, but that can also be worked on. You may ache more than you realise later."

Parker wasn't convinced that a few stretches would cause her to ache but had been proven wrong before. She was only twenty-eight but found that she didn't have the endurance she had benefitted from in her early twenties. It was probably due to the limited exercise, she loved to go for walks but hated sweating. Cad continued, "It's up to you whether you want to stay in this outfit or get changed. Usually, when we finish working out, we just throw the clothes in the laundry basket near the showers."

Parker chose to stay in the outfit; who knew what they were going to throw at her today? If it made a mess, she wouldn't be ruining her own clothes. Cad also stayed in his yoga attire and handed her a bottle of water. Yoga was surprisingly thirsty work. The gym area was still unexpectedly empty, but it was only eight o'clock.

As they were leaving, a couple of the security team were entering. Another one of the perks of working at Minos Industries, Parker mused. They travelled to the second floor, which, Parker discovered, housed a bright and welcoming medical centre.

They had spent a lot of time and effort preventing it from feeling cold and clinical, with an orange and yellow colour scheme. Her gaze was drawn to a large man with a similar presence to the minotaurs she had already met. He was propped up on a hospital bed, with his arms crossed in a petulant manner. Damon had his back to them and was beside the bed talking. Cad walked over, "What happened this time?" And nodded towards the male.

Damon turned to look at Cad and noticed Parker, "The usual, he tried to take on Leo when sparring and Leo tried to throw him through a wall, leaving an Adam-shaped imprint. They are lucky that the whole wall didn't come down with the force. The doc just wants to check that he doesn't have brain damage."

"You mean, more brain damage than usual?" And grinned at the male, who smirked in response.

"Parker, this is Adamantios-" Damon started.

"Adam." The male interrupted grumpily.

"As I was saying. This is Adamantios, but he prefers to go by Adam. The modern name helps us to fit in better. We like to keep the old traditions but blend them with the new. Adam, this is Parker. Adam is one of the minotaurs. Once he has fully recovered, you will spend time with him also."

He didn't have to explain to Adam who Parker was, he already knew. She took a few moments to observe Adam. Parker couldn't assess his height as he was lying down, but he had the same build as Cad. He had short dark hair and a close-trimmed beard. His clothing was the same as those in the training room. Maybe there was a second training area, as she hadn't seen Leo or Adam earlier.

Damon left Cad chatting with Adam and guided Parker to a quiet corner of the room, "How did this morning's session go?" Damon asked, he was genuinely interested.

"I don't think that balance is where my strength lies, but he did say I'm really flexible," Parker responded proudly. Damon raised one eyebrow and smiled; Parker blushed as she recognised the innuendo.

Instead of torturing her further, he continued with the conversation. "In addition to spending time with my team; there are some things that I will ask of you that are compulsory. Other things will be completely your choice. The next item on your agenda is one of the latter, but I do think it will be beneficial."

He then led Parker into a room which looked like a doctor's office, Parker's palms began to get clammy. A middle-aged woman sat typing on her computer. He directed Parker to take one of the seats in the room, he took another. The woman looked up as they entered and smiled warmly at them both.

She was wearing a white lab coat over her clothes, "This is Dr Stanton. I brought you here so that we can discuss running some tests. This is new to us all, but I wanted to take advantage of our technology to gather as much data as possible. This is of course optional, as it is your body."

"Hi Parker, Damon informed me about what happened yesterday. I would like to explain the types of things we would test, with your permission of course. One of the first items on the agenda would be a blood test. We don't know how it will affect you long-term, or if it has changed you already. The blood test will allow us to compare your sample against other humans."

She then turned her seat towards Parker, "We can also then take further samples over varying periods of time, to compare to the control and study any changes. There would be other tests, including a health check. Being completely open with you, I would love to be able to study any effects the artifact has on your body. There is so much that we could learn, and it may aid us in helping all supernaturals. However, as Damon said, we wouldn't force you. This is completely your choice, and we will respect that."

Parker considered their request. She hadn't thought about what the artifact could be doing to her body. However, she hated going to the doctors and no one liked blood tests.

Parker could see the benefits but had some stipulations, "Alright. If I were to agree, there would have to be conditions in place. No implants, digital or boob. No tracking devices. No mad-scientist-type experiments that ask 'could we' without asking 'should we' first. No colonoscopy. No getting naked. No electric shock treatment. All tests must be discussed with me first and must be authorised by me, no one else."

Parker delivered her offer with a deadpan expression but was droll enough that Dr Stanton let out a slight chuckle. Damon let out a bark of laughter, before poorly concealing it with a cough. They both agreed to her terms, "I suppose there's no time like the present, right Damon?" Dr Stanton said eagerly.

Parker sighed, there was no point in delaying it. Damon left the room and the doctor started on Parker's medical history. She didn't suffer from any medical conditions and wasn't on any medication, other than the contraceptive injection every few months. She had no allergies, that she was aware of.

Dr Stanton took her blood pressure first, noting that it was a little high. Parker bit her lip to stop herself from making a sarcastic comment in response. Why wouldn't it be high after the week she'd had? But Parker explained it away with the bucket of coffee that she'd recently consumed, which seemed to placate the doctor.

The blood test followed. Parker was pleasantly surprised that Dr Stanton was gentle and clearly well-practiced as it didn't hurt nearly as badly as she feared. She did wonder if that was purely for her benefit though, would she be as gentle with the larger, grumpier patients like Adam?

The tests continued over the next few hours, urine analysis, height and weight measured, her finger pricked to check her cholesterol and blood sugar. They then tested her lung capacity and attached her to tubes and wires whilst on a running machine.

Parker knew that this was going to be incredibly embarrassing, but that wasn't enough of a reason to refuse the test. She was right. It wasn't long until she was sweating profusely, and her face had turned a concerning shade of red.

Finally, the tests ended and she left the doctor's office. Adam had disappeared, but she could see Damon talking to another gentleman. He seemed to sense her gaze and looked towards her. Parker started to approach, to find out what other plans were in store for her. When suddenly, she felt faint. The room started to spin and before she could hit the floor, she felt arms wrap around her. Darkness followed.

When Parker regained consciousness, she could hear voices and was being carried somewhere. She looked up at a familiar face, Damon. His face was etched with concern and he carried her into a private room. The covers were drawn back, and Damon gently placed her onto the bed. Parker was mortified and avoided making eye contact.

Her hands shook as she tried to work out what had happened. Suddenly it clicked, she had skipped breakfast this morning. She was so focused on wearing the right clothes and getting caffeine, that she forgot breakfast entirely. Then her morning was filled with physical exertion. She begged silently to be swallowed up by the mattress.

Dr Stanton came rushing into the room to check on her. Parker explained in a very small voice what had happened. Instead of people being annoyed with her stupidity, they set about arranging for a high-energy meal to be brought to her in the bed.

She still hadn't looked at Damon. Parker was expecting his face to display annoyance. She was embarrassed enough that he had carried her, especially with the extra pounds that she was carrying.

Eventually, she couldn't avoid him any longer and looked him in the eyes. He was watching her, but not with annoyance. He looked concerned. A young girl entered the room with a tray of food. It contained a protein bar, poached eggs, and a banana.

Parker hated to be rude but couldn't imagine eating anything worse. She picked up the protein bar and began to nibble. Damon's expression changed to amusement, "Not to your liking?" Parker shrugged and smiled apologetically.

When the young girl re-entered, Parker cheekily asked, "Can I have one of those brownies I can smell instead? They smell amazing! And I have never been able to refuse a chocolate brownie."

The girl looked at Parker confused, "What brownies? I'm sorry, we don't have any brownies here." She smiled politely before leaving the room.

Parker looked forlornly at Damon who sniffed. He furrowed his brow and without speaking, turned, and swiftly exited the room. Maybe she had been a bit overly presumptuous to request someone else's snack. Five minutes later he reappeared holding one of the irresistible brownies and placed it in front of her. Parker's face lit up with delight and she thanked him before taking a huge bite.

It was as good as it smelled. Once she had finished, she sat back feeling satisfied. Damon had been staring at her the entire time she had been eating. Finally, he spoke, "The brownies were on the floor above us. Your colleague Pam brought them in for the team. She was more than happy for you to have one. She also wanted me to pass on the message that she hopes you feel better soon. How did you manage to smell them?"

"Well, obviously someone else had one and brought it

down here with them." Parker rationalised.

Damon left the room again without responding. Parker was wondering when she would be allowed to leave the bed, surely someone would be by soon that she could ask. A long time passed before Damon re-entered. "I have double-checked with Pam, she only handed out three brownies. I then spoke to those three individuals, who confirmed that they had eaten them at their desks. Following that, I spoke to every individual on this floor to check whether they had brought in their own brownie or similar, no one had."

Parker didn't reply. She didn't know what to say. If this was because of the pot, it was a bizarre side effect. Dr Stanton returned and confirmed that she was allowed to leave if she felt better. Damon explained to the doctor that he believed Parker had developed a heightened sense of smell, updating her on the brownie incident. "We will of course have to experiment with your sense of smell. What can you currently smell?" Damon asked.

Parker closed her eyes, concentrated, and inhaled, "I can smell the fabric softener on these sheets, and I can smell your aftershave."

"Anything else? Take your time." Damon replied softly. Parker inhaled once more and tried to identify any other smells, but she couldn't. She shook her head. "That's interesting, maybe you don't have control of it yet. Or maybe it only appears when you need it to. Like when your body required energy, it found you sugar." Damon mused.

Parker threw her legs over the side of the bed and suddenly realised that she hadn't thanked him for catching her, "By the way, thank you for catching me. That speed came in handy and it's lucky that your extra strength helped you to lift me." She said awkwardly and blushed.

"Anytime," Damon replied and offered her a hand off the bed. She jumped down and Damon advised that she could go home for the day. He told her to get some rest, as they were expecting her in reception at quarter past six again the following day. Parker scowled at another early morning but vowed that she would eat breakfast in future.

When she arrived home, she remembered that she was still in her workout gear. Ellie was sitting on her doorstep waiting for her. As soon as she saw Parker pull up, she took out her phone and sent a text grinning. Parker was suspicious, so enquired who the message was to. Ellie gleefully informed her that Damon had asked for confirmation when Parker arrived home safely.

Parker rolled her eyes and told Ellie that it was just because of her fainting episode. Ellie became worried and immediately wanted the full details, along with a rundown of the other events of the day. Parker hadn't been told not to tell anyone, so after they were both situated with a hot drink, she replayed her eventful day.

After the story had finished, Ellie responded, "I'm slightly jealous, not of the tests and needles. But I am jealous of how much more exciting your life is getting compared to mine. I don't think I've ever been carried by a strong, hunk of a man." Parker laughed at Ellie's description of Damon.

"It may be time for me to make a change," Ellie stated, having come to a decision. "I'm going to leave the exciting world of admin." And they both laughed.

"What do you want to do?" Parker asked.

"I've actually been thinking about it for a while, I am a 'people person'. So, I've been thinking I want to do something in customer relations. Or maybe get involved with the consultation element of the company. What do you think?"

"Selfishly, I don't want you to leave Minos Industries. So provided you're staying with the company, I think it's a great idea."

"I will have a look at internal vacancies first. I'm not sure if you have noticed, but I'm a little quirky. I don't know if other companies will be as accepting of my little eccentricities."

Parker tried to keep a straight face and appear sympathetic. "Promise me you will never change. For anyone."

Which elicited goofy smiles between them.

They had an early dinner, Parker cooked them a chicken and pasta dish. Ellie explained how the office gossip had gone crazy regarding what Parker had done and where she had been taken the previous day. The excitement had reached fever pitch when Damon had entered the department earlier that day, to request a brownie for Parker.

Parker couldn't stop laughing when Ellie relayed one of the more outlandish theories about a secret office romance. She was slightly concerned that people thought she had done something she shouldn't, so took more comfort from people speculating that she was a romantic interest of Damon's, rather than a criminal.

They agreed that the following night would be spent hanging out at Ellie's house. She was going to cook fajitas for them both. Parker wanted to get to bed as early as possible that night so that she would be well prepared for whatever excitement was in store for her the following day. She was in bed by nine o'clock and then lay awake for the next hour thinking about the day's events before eventually succumbing to exhaustion.

CHAPTER 8

Parker was at least prepared for today's alarm, but it didn't mean that she hated it any less. She bundled her hair up into a ponytail again and pulled on a fitted blue blouse with a black flowing skirt. She was aware that she may have to change into casual attire at some point in the day, but they had that in stock, unlike professional work attire in her size.

Parker had washed and dried the workout gear from the previous day, she didn't like the idea of someone else cleaning up after her. She packed the clothes up, ready to return them. Parker poured herself a large bowl of cereal, learning from yesterday's mistake. She also grabbed a larger-than-usual bag and stocked up on snacks.

The one benefit of being at work this early was that the roads were virtually empty and she arrived in record time. Cad was once again the person to meet her in reception and beat her to the doors. They slid open as Parker approached and he advised that they were going to start the day with more Yoga.

Parker was feeling a little stiff after yesterday's session but she had enjoyed it, which surprised her. Before starting, Cad brought out a breakfast bar and handed it to Parker. Damon had unfortunately told the others about her incident. Parker politely refused; she couldn't be too annoyed as he was just trying to look out for her.

Parker changed into the workout clothes that she had brought with her, and they began the session. They repeated the same beginner poses as yesterday and he added a couple of new ones. She needed less guidance and support today, but she still found the more complex ones too difficult.

Parker wanted to find out more about Cad, especially if she was going to be spending a lot more time with him. She sat down on the mat and faced him, "How long have you worked with Damon and the team?"

"For about twenty-five years. I grew up with all of them, so I have known him for longer than that." Parker thought that he was joking, they both looked around thirty.

She doubted that they had been working together aged five, "No, really. How long?"

Cad suddenly understood the misunderstanding, "I'm assuming that means that no one has advised you about our extended life span? Damon and I may look thirty, but I'm forty-nine and Damon is fifty-one."

"No, everyone seems to have omitted that little piece of information. How old can you get? Are you immortal?" Parker asked fascinated.

Cad explained, "We aren't immortal and before you ask, yes, we can die. We just have a longer than average life span. Some supernaturals have celebrated their three-hundredth birthday. Historically, all supernaturals have enjoyed a longer life; however, this is one of our powers that is beginning to dwindle."

"Does that mean that you avoid dating humans? I can imagine that it would be difficult dating or marrying a person that ages a lot quicker than you do."

She had often thought how lonely life would be if a person was truly immortal. "Well actually, it never used to be a problem. We have an ancient ritual for when a supernatural decides to tie themselves to another person. Once the rite has been completed, the two people are bonded together forever, not literally of course.

"The powers that cause us to exist bind the two so that the human enjoys an extended life span. The problem is that this can only happen once. If they make a mistake and attach themselves to the wrong person, they can't repeat it, even if they meet the right person later.

"This has led to most supernaturals only dating within the supernatural lines. The other person already has an extended life and if a mistake is made, they haven't wasted their one shot. Just to add another layer of complication, the ancient ritual has failed the last two times it has been attempted. Whether they were true soul mates or not, we don't know."

"When were the last attempts made? Has it only recently started failing?"

Parker was trying to see if there was a correlation between the visions dwindling and the rites failing. "One of them happened about eighty years ago and the other only a couple of years ago." She was shocked at how few of the rites were undertaken and believed that they really must be concerned if they weren't even attempting it. Or maybe the supernaturals just generally avoided dating humans. "Would you like to see where we conduct our research into these changes?" Cad asked Parker, as she was clearly enthralled by their problem.

"Yes please, absolutely!" Parker responded enthusiastically.

Cad took her down to subfloor two. He had to scan his ID card in the elevator for it to grant them access. When she realised where the research was undertaken, she wasn't as enthusiastic to see it. She expected this floor to feel just as claustrophobic as subfloor one. However, it couldn't have been more opposite.

It was brightly lit, and she realised that there were windows strategically placed along one side of the building. The building must be on a slope she mused, as they looked out over water. Parker started thinking that there must have been windows in the maze on the floor above too. Or maybe they were blocked, to enhance the labyrinthian ambience?

Finally, she would sate her curiosity about the research conducted. Her mind unhelpfully reminded her of what curiosity did to the cat. The room was open plan, with a couple of closed-off testing areas at the far end. There were large desks spread throughout the room, and powerful lights hung overhead.

Each desk's contents appeared to vary slightly with a mix of microscopes, Bunsen burners, beakers, and computers. There was also a large sink at the end of each desk. It reminded her of school science lessons but a lot more sophisticated. Most of the people were too engrossed in their research to look up, but a couple lifted their heads to observe the newcomers.

A woman started strutting towards them from the middle of the room, they waited for her to approach. "Hello Cad, it's nice to see you in my area. You don't visit often enough." She said smiling, with barely a glimpse towards Parker. Parker surmised that they either had a romantic history or this lady wanted one.

"Danielle, this is Parker. I'm just showing her around, she was curious about the type of research we conduct here." Danielle finally looked towards Parker; she didn't seem very impressed. Parker felt a bit taken aback by her rudeness. She was clearly jealous that she was with Cad, but this seemed presumptuous and unprofessional. "Do you happen to know if Beth is free?" Cad continued, ignoring her attitude.

"Whatever it is Cad, I can help you," Danielle replied in a sickly-sweet tone.

Parker felt embarrassed by her behaviour on behalf of women everywhere. "No thank you. It's alright, I think I can see her." With that, he continued further into the room with Parker.

Cad greeted a lady with rows of braids plaited tightly to her scalp, which were then swept into a large bun at the back of her head. The braids had streaks of pink running through their entire length. She had dark brown skin and was wearing a closed lab coat, but a hot pink skirt poked out of the bottom as she walked.

Parker wondered whether she was a gorgon due to the braids, but it felt very stereotypical and rude to assume. "Beth, always great to see you. It's been too long since my last visit." Cad said warmly. He clearly respected this woman. "Parker, I'd like to introduce you to Beth, she runs this department. Beth, I'm showing her around and would love for you to give us a tour if you aren't too busy?"

"I'm always busy, but I may be able to squeeze a quick tour in." Beth smiled in response. She guided them around the researchers and explained that they were conducting research to enhance their abilities. The department was originally created by Leander, Damon's father. He was concerned that the lines were losing their abilities. He wondered whether they could replicate them with technological devices instead.

Beth also divulged that another reason for the department was that Damon's mum is human. Leander wanted her to have additional abilities at her disposal, so she could protect herself. "Would you like to see the prototypes and where they are created?" She asked Parker.

"Yes please." She replied without any hesitation.

Beth guided them past the desks and testing area. There was a whole other section that Parker hadn't seen from the entrance. They walked through a small passageway, with a door on either side, "We insisted on this separation," Beth explained, "The noises coming from the other side were a bit too loud, so we added noise cancelling materials between us."

This floor appeared to be a lot bigger than the above-ground floors. This new section was enormous, but what really stood out was the size of the men in the room. If there was one extremely tall well-built male, he would be noticeable. However, they were all tall and well-built.

There were numerous workstations throughout the room, creating all sorts of miniature devices. The large men all appeared to be deep in concentration. She saw that they were all using visual aids such as glasses, magnifying glasses or a large viewing device with multiple inserts. She looked up at Cad with a questioning expression, "cyclops." He simply stated, "Has anyone given you the lowdown yet?"

Parker simply shook her head. "They have quite a straightforward origin. There used to exist a supernatural line where the men were larger and stronger than the average man, but they were also extremely skilled creators. The negative being that they all had extremely poor eyesight. So, they used their skills and devised a magnifying device to wear on their face, which enabled them to see.

"The device was a wonder of the times. When people saw these large men with magnifying devices on their faces, they understood them to be one-eyed giants. The word 'cyclops' means 'round-eyes'. People tended to avoid them as much as possible and over time they joined the other supernaturals in hiding."

Beth had been waiting patiently for Cad to finish his story, before leading them further into the room. Parker was shown a nose clip that was supposed to enhance smell, contact lenses that enhanced the vision of the user and a hearing aid that enabled the user to hear over long distances.

Beth explained that the research department did most of the research and design, and then the cyclops used their skills to manufacture the devices. The difficulty was that the equipment still had to work alongside human capability. It was entirely possible to create a device that enabled a human to lift a car with their arm, but then the rest of the body would suffer the strain and weight. They were still trying to resolve this conundrum, without the human having to wear a cumbersome full-body suit.

Parker's stomach started to grumble in an embarrassingly loud way. They all laughed at the bizarre sounds emanating. It was midday and after they thanked Beth for her tour, they went to get lunch in the canteen. Parker sent Ellie a quick message, asking if she was free to join.

Ellie showed up about five minutes after they sat down. They all chose the chilli con carne for lunch. Cad had a double portion and a slice of cheesecake. "What have you been up to this morning? I bet it was more exciting than what I've been doing." Ellie asked.

Parker looked to Cad to check what she was allowed to say, "Damon is fine with Ellie being kept in the loop, he knows how much you confide in her. However, I would advise waiting until tonight to talk about what you saw. We have some rivals that would like to gather as much information about our projects as possible."

Parker obligingly changed the subject, "Have you had any luck going through the vacancies?"

"There are a couple that I may be interested in. I will print out the job descriptions and we can look through them tonight at mine if that's alright? I really would like your opinion." Ellie updated Parker on the old team's gossip, Cad was enraptured by the drama. Before they knew it, the lunch break was over.

After lunch, Cad took her to his department. The entire fifth floor of the office block was dedicated to IT. They had a bank of servers to the right-hand side and several rows of computer desks to the left. There were large rooms to the rear of the floor.

Cad seemed proud of his department, it was obvious in his tone when talking about it to Parker. He started to explain what each section covered: software programming, installations, configuring computer systems, diagnostics, solving hardware faults and security systems. There was clearly a mix of personalities within the team; there were varying hair colours, styles and T-shirt designs. A large percentage were wearing headphones.

A couple of the smaller rooms at the end were meeting rooms. Then there was a large room filled with bean bag chairs, a football table, a pinball machine and a pool table. She looked up at Cad, "Admin doesn't have any of this."

"I'll let you use it whenever you want, as long as you don't tell." He responded playfully and guided her to the next room. There was a small break room with a coffee machine, table and chairs.

Cad took her into one of the meeting rooms, "Did you want anything? A drink? If you can wait here, I have some equipment that I need to set you up with." Parker requested a bottle of water and pulled out a couple of her own snacks while she waited.

When Cad returned, he was holding a selection of small items and her water, "We don't quite have the same equipment as secret agents, but we try." And he grinned, "I'm going to explain to you what each item does, you can then decide what you are willing to keep on you."

"The first item is this bracelet." It was made out of plaited black leather and it held two silver beads. "The beads act as an emergency beacon. When you squeeze them together and hold them for three seconds, an SOS will be sent to Minos Industries. We'll know your location immediately. This is a passive item as it will only be activated when squeezed, it doesn't send out your location automatically. That is where this item comes in."

He placed a silver pendant necklace on the table, "This item contains a tracker. If we chose to look, we would know where you are at a moment's notice." Cad then placed a sim card onto the table, "Your number is already assigned to this sim, you just need to swap it over. It can connect to every network, ensuring that you'll never lose signal. It also has unlimited credit, so if there is an emergency you can always contact someone."

Parker considered the tracking devices, she was happy with the bracelet as she still had her privacy. However, she wasn't sure that she was alright with them knowing where she was at all times. It wasn't that she ever went anywhere that she would need to hide, but it felt a bit too 'Big Brother'.

"Can't you also track me via the sim card?" Parker enquired.

"Yes, but you can turn off the location as you would normally through your settings. It's really an extra precaution if you needed it or lose one of the items."

"Thank you for these. I can't promise that I will wear the necklace, but I really appreciate you looking out for me."

"No problem," Cad smiled, "Do you want to give the bracelet a go and I'll show you what happens at our end?"

Parker immediately put the bracelet on her wrist. It was always a bit fiddly to put a clasp bracelet on one-handed, but it only took a second. She then examined the beads and squeezed them together for longer than Cad advised, just to make sure that it had worked.

Parker followed him out of the room and noticed the monitors hanging from the ceiling throughout. They flashed up an SOS sign. Cad advised the team that it was a drill, before jumping on a free computer. Cad opened a program which detailed who the bracelet belonged to, along with their current location. It also gave options as to the action required: emergency services, clean up, security, response team or M Team.

"What is M Team?" Parker asked.

"It's the seven of us in the senior team, including Damon. It gives the receiver the option to escalate, in case of a major emergency."

"What exactly are you expecting to happen where all this would be needed?" Parker thought that it was all very exciting, but why would they need to have all these systems in place?

Cad responded, "Unfortunately, we have enemies. There are different rules to the human world and sometimes there are clashes. We police ourselves; the humans would eventually notice if a prisoner never aged. We also need to ensure that our secret isn't discovered, so this team helps with deleting videos and removing evidence."

"Alright, so let's get down to the important stuff. Exploding pens? Poison lipstick? Camera sunglasses? A hidden taser in a watch?" Parker asked only half-jokingly.

Cad began laughing, "Sorry, secret agent Parker. You don't get those until you have stamped off your first three missions on your reward card."

After they had covered the equipment, Parker asked Cad if she could have a go on the pinball machine before they left. She had never played on a real pinball machine and was desperate to have a go. Parker and Cad took it in turns. Cad started out vastly superior, however, Parker soon started to improve.

They had been playing for over thirty minutes, time was flying by. She was on a roll, about to beat Cad's highest score, when someone cleared their throat behind them. Parker spun around like a naughty child with her hand in the cookie jar. Damon leaned against the doorframe, watching the two of them. By the time Parker turned back to the game, the ball had dropped. She cursed before covering her mouth apologetically.

"Cad is just testing my reflexes." Parker grinned at Damon and Cad chuckled. Instead of querying their day's progress, Damon walked over and took Parker's place. Parker and Cad observed his game, flicking glances between each other, both surprised that he was playing. She was torn between wanting to be better than him and wanting him to do well.

His score kept rising higher and higher, smashing Cad's score. She glimpsed up at Cad who looked visibly deflated. Parker decided to fight a little dirty, "I'm starting to feel a little faint." Damon immediately turned to look at Parker to assess her state. He was distracted just long enough for the ball to fall.

Damon narrowed his eyes and the other two burst out laughing. "Fine, it's annoying when someone ruins your score." Damon reluctantly admitted.

"At least we can call it even," Parker replied still smiling.

"I wanted to see how you were progressing on day two. No destruction of priceless artifacts or fainting spells I hope." Damon teased Parker.

She rolled her eyes before responding, "I think it's going well. No fainting spells and I've been given a tour of the research department. It's all fascinating. I find it amazing that all of this has been kept a secret for so long. Also, Cad has stocked me up with his latest gadgets. If I ever get lost whilst travelling, I know who to call!"

Damon nodded whilst being updated by Cad. They were also discussing other non-supernatural business, which didn't hold Parker's interest. Eventually, they confirmed that Parker was done for the day and that she could be excused. They would see her tomorrow, bright and early.

Parker had managed to clock off before Ellie, so instead of waiting, she went home to battle through some of her more boring chores. It was dull but passed the time and soon enough it was time to head over to Ellie's. She decided to walk, seeing as it was a pleasant evening.

Ellie had only just arrived home when Parker knocked on the door. She took a seat at the kitchen bar so that they could chat whilst Ellie cooked. Ellie passed her the printouts of the new job descriptions. One of the roles was to work with their supply chain, the other was in project management.

Whilst Ellie continued cooking, Parker took the time to read through the information. The supply chain role included coordinating with contractors and suppliers, ensuring competencies, monitoring stock levels etc. The project management role included planning and organising, quality checking, working within a team, ensuring time frames were on track and expectations met etc. "The supply chain role is within the maintenance branch and the project management position is in the property branch," Ellie explained.

Parker gave her opinion and advised Ellie to apply for both. That way she could ask questions and see if she was interested in the job. They sat down to watch a movie; Ellie had persuaded Parker to try a romantic comedy. Each sat under a blanket with a bowl of popcorn. They talked the whole way through about the various male characters and what they would have done differently in that situation if that ever happened in real life.

Parker was aware that she was up early again in the morning, so she made her farewells straight after the movie had finished. It was already dark and the street lights were on, she was always careful when walking alone. Parker zipped up her coat and promised Ellie to message her when she arrived home.

The streets were quiet, it was serene and peaceful. Parker had only been walking for a minute when she heard a noise behind her. She quickly glanced around and saw a man standing under one of the street lights. She couldn't make out anything more than his shape, he seemed larger than average.

She was trying to convince herself that he just happened to be out and to not be paranoid, but she still sped up. He began to walk slowly in her direction. Parker tried to look like she wasn't panicking, but she couldn't return to Ellie's as she would have to pass by him. She was only a minute from home at this point, so she kept her eye on the man as she hustled along.

Parker considered pressing the beads on the bracelet, but she wasn't even sure that the man was following her. It may just be a gentleman out for some fresh air. He started to speed up but luckily Parker was only a couple of houses away from home. She didn't care if she looked stupid and she ran to the door, with her keys already in hand.

The door was opened in record time and she slammed it shut behind her, slamming home the deadbolts. She then rushed around downstairs and shut all the curtains. She made sure that all the doors and windows were locked, her pulse racing. Parker called Ellie, she wanted to speak to someone to calm her nerves.

She tried to pretend that everything was alright, but Ellie immediately knew that there was something wrong by the tone of her voice. "What's wrong? Are you alright?" Ellie asked concerned.

"I'm not sure. I may just be paranoid, but I think that there was a man following me when I left yours. He just stood there, watching me. It felt like he was waiting for me. I think he followed me home."

"Lock your doors and windows," Ellie advised, affirming Parker had already done the right thing. "I'll sort it. Call me back immediately if anything happens and I will be there." Ellie hung up the phone. Parker sat on the sofa in silence, she didn't want to turn on the TV as it would hide any sounds from outside. She was trying to calm herself down and was taking deep breaths.

Suddenly, there was a loud knock at the door. Parker almost jumped out of her skin and froze, "Parker, open up. It's Leo and Damon." She hurried to the door and opened it so that they could enter. Damon spoke, "Ellie called us, she told us what happened. Leo is going to have a look around outside. If anyone has been here, he will know."

Parker immediately felt safer as Leo went to look around

outside, although she was still concerned about him being out there alone. Damon correctly read her expression, "He will be fine, not much can take down Leo."

"I'm sorry. I was probably just being paranoid. I just got a really creepy vibe from him, it felt like he was watching me. It was probably just a person out for a stroll."

"Well, it doesn't hurt to check. Ellie did the right thing by calling us." Damon reassured her.

Parker made hot drinks and they sat down, waiting for Leo to return. Damon frowned at her, "You really shouldn't walk around alone at night, there are some bad people out there."

"I thought it would be fine. Ellie only lives a couple of minutes away and I don't walk through any isolated or unlit areas." Leo returned and they both turned to hear his report.

"There was definitely someone out there but I think they left when they saw us arrive. They are certainly not out there now. I can see recent male footprints in the lawn by your windows. The impressions are quite deep, which would imply a larger individual." Parker felt sick. Why would there be someone out there watching her? At least he was gone now.

"Are you alright staying here tonight, or do you want to go somewhere else?" Damon asked with concern.

Leaving was tempting, but she felt that if she left tonight, it would be extra hard to return, "I want to stay here. I will double check all of the doors and windows and I will wear Cad's bracelet to bed."

"Alright. I will have a word with a couple of your neighbours before we leave, just to advise them of a suspicious individual skulking around the area. It's always a benefit to have extra eyes looking out."

"Thank you, I really appreciate it. Thanks for coming out and looking around Leo."

Leo nodded in response, "Also if he saw us arrive, he now knows you have friends you can call. He knows that you aren't alone."

Leo did a final tour of the house, to check that the doors

and windows hadn't been tampered with. Once he returned and confirmed that it was safe, they left.

Parker went to bed in a large T-shirt and joggers. She felt better than if she was wearing anything skimpy. Before climbing into bed, she wedged a chair against her bedroom door. It was probably overkill, but it made her feel safer. She must have been more tired than she realised, as against all probabilities, she fell asleep almost as soon as her head hit the pillow.

CHAPTER 9

Parker felt much happier in the morning than she had the night before. Things were always scarier at night. It was still dark outside but she proceeded to get ready for the day. She settled on a long-sleeved, red, fitted top and black jeans.

She had breakfast with a cup of tea before grabbing her things. Parker hesitated as she went to open the front door and instead, glimpsed out of the window first. The sun was beginning to rise and she couldn't see anything out of the ordinary.

She remained acutely aware of her surroundings and felt jittery out in the open as she locked her door and made her way to the car. Parker hurriedly locked her car doors once she'd climbed inside and set off for work. After parking in what was quickly becoming her usual spot, she made her way to the sliding doors.

They opened and she expected to see Cad, however, Adam stood there waiting for her. He had been watching her through the window, ensuring that she arrived safely. "Damon informed the team about what happened last night. He wants you to be able to protect yourself. So, I'm going to teach you self-defence." He didn't sound very excited about his new role, but he turned and led her towards the elevators.

They entered the twentieth-floor gym and Parker quickly changed into fresh workout attire. "Before we start with the physical aspects of self-defence, we need to cover strategies for survival. First, you need to trust your instincts. Last night your instincts were telling you that he wasn't safe. You probably tried to put it down to paranoia, but it's better to be safe than sorry.

"Second, don't put yourself in a dangerous situation. If someone makes you uncomfortable, avoid them. Walk away, cross the street, or simply do not allow yourself to be alone with them.

"Third, don't make yourself a target. Be aware of your surroundings. Don't walk along with your head down staring at your phone or with headphones blaring.

"Keep a safe distance from the individual, don't let them get too close if you can avoid it. Sound confident if approached. Don't put yourself in the role of victim, show them that you aren't a pushover. If your attacker manages to get you onto the ground, don't panic. I will teach you moves that you can use in that position.

"Finally, don't pause. This isn't a fair fight. Do everything you can to ensure they stay down, and that you can get away safely. Do you have any questions?"

Parker understood the importance of what he was saying, so she was trying to focus as much as possible, "No questions yet, but I should probably tell you that I'm not the most graceful. I can be quite clumsy."

Adam nodded, "Cad has provided me with his evaluation. Let's begin." Before they started practising, Adam advised that they needed to warm up. First came arm and leg stretches, followed by other full-body stretches. Some were similar to the Yoga poses she had been learning with Cad. Jumping jacks, burpees and mountain climbers followed. Parker's face was starting to get flushed and inwardly cursed Adam for the burpees.

Once Adam was confident that she was sufficiently warmed up, he advised that he would be teaching her Krav Maga, "It is an extremely practical and effective form of self-defence. As a female, you are automatically at a disadvantage due to your size. This style enables you to build on your natural instincts. We will repeat these moves until they become second nature."

Adam assumed no prior experience and started with the absolute basics, beginning with how to open hand strike. Then came instructions on how to use the side of the wrist to intercept any attack and to knock them back. After came the one move that Parker already had in her very limited repertoire, the traditional knee to the groin.

When grabbed by the arm or bag, Adam instructed her how to use the attacker's momentum against them. Finally, he taught her how to fight back from the ground. Initially by using one or both of her feet to kick them backwards.

Adam encouraged her to try out each of the moves using her full force. Parker held back, as she had never hit anyone before and she was worried about hurting him. "I don't want to hurt you," Parker explained after Adam asked her why she was holding back.

He simply laughed, "The first time you saw me I had just finished sparring with Leo. You've seen Leo? You won't hurt me, I promise."

Parker was already feeling physically exhausted but was determined to try her best, especially after last night's scare. Whilst practising the wrist block move for the hundredth time, she decided that she was going to give it everything she had. She blocked his wrist and with all her strength, used the other hand to open-hand strike his face.

Her palm connected perfectly with his nose and he let out a quiet 'oof' sound. Parker was delighted at her progress. Her delight immediately turned to panic, as he was holding his nose and frowning, "Oh no, have I hurt you?!"

Adam removed his hand and began laughing, "Sorry, I couldn't resist. That was a good one though, I definitely felt that!"

Parker tried to give him a disapproving glare but it failed as she was too pleased by his compliment. "This is only the start, but we need you to master these moves first. I will arrange exercise sessions for you as we need to raise your fitness levels." Parker quickly turned dismayed, she was dreading that part. However, she admitted to herself that she felt absolutely exhausted after this training session.

As she looked around, she realised that there were now a lot more people in the gym than when they started. Parker was glad that she hadn't noticed others had entered, as she would have felt more self-conscious. It was lunchtime, so she shuffled her aching body to the canteen.

Parker treated herself to a burger and fries as she was ravenous and justified that she had earned it. Parker ate alone as Ellie had already taken her lunch break and Adam had 'things to do'. She occupied herself by sending messages to her family and Julia, keeping up to date with their lives and reassuring them that she was still fine.

Strict instructions had been provided to go to the seventeenth floor after her lunch and she was told that there would be someone waiting for her. She exited the elevator and stepped out into an enormous library. There was a large, open space in the middle, underneath an impressive double-vaulted ceiling, with an intricate mural of tree branches and vines painted on it.

From where she stood, she could see the second-floor wooden bookcases, the ends of which were carved into ornate Grecian columns. A wooden railing framed the edge of the floor above. Every bookcase looked like it was an antique. Parker was in love.

She couldn't wait to explore, her inner bookworm was screaming but she was supposed to be meeting someone. After a few minutes of waiting with no one appearing, she convinced herself that it couldn't hurt to have a little browse nearby and that they could easily find her.

Parker walked through the centre first, then sauntered up to the nearest bookcase. The books in this section covered non-fiction, 'Africa' followed by the 'Americas and Oceania'. They covered a wide range, including books which appeared to be very old and delicate.

They also had publications as recent as the previous month. Parker was impressed at how up-to-date they were. She kept browsing; non-fiction wasn't really her thing, she much preferred fiction. Towards the end were large wooden desks, with the same intricate carvings as the bookcases. There were several people sat around the tables, all of them with their heads buried in books.

Parker located a spiral staircase leading to the upper section. She was keen to see the books they had available upstairs, so she worked her way up the spiral. She was wondering whether all employees had access to the library, or whether it was a privilege granted to a select few.

The upper floor covered fiction. The view was just as spectacular, she could see people milling around downstairs. She had a better view of the painting on the ceiling, the detail that was now visible from this distance was breathtaking. Some of the vines held tiny flowers that were dotted around. If she hadn't known better, she would have believed them to be real.

There were areas upstairs that held additional desks and groupings of chairs. Parker saw a section covering urban fantasy and couldn't resist browsing the titles. She was engrossed in the blurb on the back of a particularly interesting book when she was tapped on the shoulder.

Parker jumped in surprise and spun around, clutching the book to her chest. She found herself staring at someone else's chest and looked up. A gentleman over six feet tall stood in front of her and looked down at her smiling. He had unruly dark brown curls which fell towards his face and perfectly framed clear blue eyes.

Parker was pretty sure that this was the person she was supposed to be meeting. "I'm sorry, I didn't mean to make you jump. I'm also sorry that I was late to meet you. I was caught up in my research and didn't realise the time. I hope you haven't been waiting too long."

"Don't worry, I have been enjoying myself looking at all these wonderful books. This library is stunning, can anyone come and read here? How do you check books out?" Parker's enthusiasm may have gotten her slightly side-tracked from her initial purpose in coming to this floor.

The man didn't seem to mind and appeared to thrive off her appreciation, "Yes, it is amazing. I should probably introduce myself before we proceed, I'm Seth. I'm one of the senior team."

"Just Seth? Almost everyone else has a much more complicated name than that."

"Well deduced. My name is slightly more complicated than that. Sophocles is my full name, so you can see why I go by Seth. To answer your earlier questions, anyone can come and read these books. Not all books can be checked out, it usually depends on their age and scarcity. The older ones can't leave the building for fear of damage. I will show you how to check them out, we do it all online."

"How can you be sure that people don't steal the more valuable books?" Parker enquired.

"We have a good security system, but the people who work here are usually very honest and respect the books. I am actually going to show you to a different area, which I think will demonstrate the strength of our security." Seth explained.

He then began to lead Parker back down the spiral staircase. She looked longingly at the books and made a promise to them that she would return as soon as she could. They walked back to the elevator, pressed the call button and waited a few minutes for it to arrive.

When they boarded, Seth swiped his ID card and pressed the button for the third subfloor. Parker was intrigued as to what they were going to find at the very bottom of the building and eagerly anticipated the doors opening. It took longer than usual to get to the bottom, due to the number of people entering and exiting the elevator.

When they finally arrived and the door opened, they disembarked into a short corridor. At the other end was a giant set of steel doors, with a digital display on the right-hand side. Seth placed his palm onto the screen, then placed his face in front of an eye-level camera. After a couple of seconds, a light flashed green and the door opened to reveal another library. The only appreciable difference that Parker could see was that this one also contained glass cases down the centre of the room.

The same style of bookcase as before filled the vast room. Parker looked quizzically at Seth who smiled down at her, "This is our second library. This one is only accessible to a select few. In this library, we store the historical texts of our ancestors. We have tried to obtain every historical artefact and document relating to our lineage and preserve it here."

Parker walked to one of the glass display cabinets in the centre which held a bow and eight arrows. There was a label beneath, 'Bow and arrows of Heracles'. Parker was speechless and moved on to the next display. On a small plinth stood a golden cup labelled 'Golden Goblet of Heracles'.

She then rushed to the next display and there lay a wooden staff labelled 'Staff of Tiresias'. Parker wasn't familiar with this artifact and her innate curiosity immediately wanted to understand its origins.

Seth caught up with Parker, "I have brought you here because my contribution to your development is to broaden your knowledge of our lineage. I also intend to use your fresh perspective to help us to understand the prophecy further. Follow me."

Seth walked over to a glass case separated from the rest, it had extra security measures surrounding it. There was a parchment displayed along with an empty pillow. The case was labelled, 'Prophecy of Daphnis'. Parker looked closely at the parchment, which was written in a language that she didn't understand. A plaque underneath bore the translation:

When the seven women of man are born and
their heart's true desires are met,
Restored will be the powers of those who in their ways are set.

"Can I take a picture of that translation?" Parker asked, "I have a feeling that it will be important."

"We still don't want it known by the wider populace, so we would prefer that it isn't mentioned outside of this room. Writing it down on a piece of paper or photographing it would be too dangerous. It would be best if you simply memorised it." Parker nodded and committed the plaque to memory.

"I am currently reviewing previous prophecies, what they referred to, how they came to fruition and how they were interpreted. During ancient times prophecies were commonplace, so our ancestors were a lot more experienced with interpretation. I am hoping that by studying the previous prophecies and visions, they can guide us to understand this one.

"There is one complication, it is slow going as the texts are not in English. Our research department and manufacturing team created an augmented reality device that automatically translates from ancient Greek by simply placing the device over the top of the page." Seth explained.

"Speaking of translations, has anyone considered why 'ABRAXAS' wasn't written in ancient Greek?" Parker enquired.

Impressed by her astute observation, Seth provided his opinion, "We considered that briefly. Either the pot's magic gave you the ability to briefly read ancient Greek or the pot updated its own appearance to match the language of the recipient."

Parker was eager to begin her own research. Seth guided her towards four ornate wooden desks and comfortable chairs. He indicated that she should choose a desk and get comfortable, he then left for a few minutes.

When he returned, he held several storage tubs, which she assumed contained parchments, and a computer tablet. Seth gave a brief overview of how to use the tablet, it was very straightforward. Parker desperately wanted to start. She couldn't believe that she would look at texts that hadn't been seen by anyone outside of a select few in hundreds, maybe thousands of years.

She carefully withdrew a delicate parchment from its storage container and began scanning the document. Even translated, it wasn't the simplest of texts. Seth provided her with paper and a pen to make notes, but he made it clear that any notes must be locked away and never leave the library with her.

Parker cross-referenced the prophecies and visions against texts written by the scholars of the time. She detailed how each line spoken by a nymph was fulfilled. Unfortunately, due to the deterioration of some of the parchments, she was unable to interpret and analyse every line.

After an hour, Parker needed a bathroom break. Security made it difficult for her to leave the room and re-enter, so she made sure that she had met all her needs before returning. She bought snacks and a drink from the canteen. Seth had to accompany her, as she wouldn't have been able to return to the floor without him.

"I don't suppose that my access will be changed at any point, to give me access to all of these secure facilities you're taking me to?" Parker asked as she hurriedly finished her drink and snacks before entering the room. Parker didn't think that Seth would appreciate grubby fingers and crumbs on the ancient texts.

Seth gave her a side glance as they were returning through the corridor. "Not just yet."

They spent the rest of the afternoon reading through various documents. Parker was thoroughly loving it. It was also a nice respite from her punishing training regime, as her body was starting to ache. They were both deep in quiet concentration when the door whooshed open and in walked Cad.

"Damon and I were starting to get worried about you, Seth. You never showed up for our meeting, so I said that I would come looking for you." Parker and Seth both glimpsed at the clock on the desk, it was after six o'clock. They had both been so absorbed that they had completely lost track of time. Parker rubbed her eyes which were feeling the strain from the intense concentration.

"Sorry Cad, you know how I get. Is Damon annoyed? Did I miss anything important?"

"No, he isn't annoyed, we've known you long enough," he grinned, "We were just going through the usual agenda, problems we have had with Deimos. He wanted your update on

Parker. He also wanted to make sure you weren't late for dinner."

Parker raised her eyebrows, she was a bit irked to be discussed like an object. "What's the update on me?" She goaded.

Cad smiled, he had been baiting her for a rise, "My update is that I've been missing my Yoga partner." And he winked.

Parker laughed, "Yes, I can imagine having someone around as naturally gifted at Yoga as me is a boon."

They gathered up their things and locked everything away. Parker said, "I'd better be going, I wouldn't want to get home too late. Ellie is at her mum's tonight, so it's a quiet night in."

Cad glanced at Seth before asking Parker, "Do you want to come for dinner with us? Zack's cooking."

She didn't want to be invited because they felt sorry for her, so was planning on politely declining. "Thank you, but-"

Cad interrupted, stopping her refusal in its tracks. "We won't take no for an answer, you've already said that you have no plans. I'll come with you in your car, that way I can direct you." Parker felt slightly railroaded but decided to go along with it. She would finally get to find out more about this mysterious group of men.

Once outside the building, Parker and Cad climbed in her car as Seth locked up. She was feeling slightly nervous about gate-crashing the meal but couldn't deny her curiosity. Ellie would be jealous that she was having such an exciting evening.

Cad gave directions as Parker drove for about twenty minutes. Eventually, they drove up a residential street. The houses were all extremely large, but very different from one another in style. Every house was set back from the street and looked very secure, surrounded by high walls and large gates.

The first house on the street was only just visible through a metal barred gate, it was all sharp angles and large glass windows. Parker was too busy concentrating on where she was going to really stop and study the homes.

They pulled up to a large wooden gate, with an intercom mounted on a pole next to the driver's window. She lowered the window and Cad reached over Parker to announce himself. The gates swung silently open and she drove through. She pulled up behind the four cars already parked out front.

Parker chuckled as her car looked extremely out of place, she spotted a Porsche, Bentley, Rolls-Royce and a Range Rover. They were all black apart from the pillar box red Porsche. Her old compact wasn't quite in the same league but she didn't mind. Her car held many happy memories of freedom and always got her where she needed to go.

They climbed out and Seth pulled up behind her a few seconds later, in a black Land Rover. The house was impressive, it looked like a modernised country estate with black framed windows. There was a porch with two columns at the entrance and the entire property had a warm welcoming glow emanating from the windows.

Cad approached the door first and knocked. A minute later someone opened it and they stepped inside. Parker couldn't see past Cad's broad back to see who it was as she followed him into the hallway.

The hall was expansive, with a large sweeping staircase up to the second floor. She stood on warm, dark wooden flooring, under an impressive chandelier and the walls were painted a light beige. There were a couple of chairs placed on one side.

As Cad stepped to the side to remove his coat, Damon made eye contact with Parker. "Parker?" He asked confused and looked towards Cad for clarification.

"She was working late with Seth and said she didn't have plans, so I asked her to come along."

"Well Zack has cooked enough food to feed an army of Leo's, so come on in Parker. Welcome to my home."

"Your home? I thought that as Zack was the one cooking, it was his house." Parker queried.

"Zack prefers cooking away from home so that he doesn't have to do the washing up afterwards." Damon smiled.

"Sorry if I'm intruding, Cad insisted."

"No, of course not. Come on through." Parker followed

them into the living room where the others were already sitting waiting, currently engaged in conversation. The room was centred around a large granite fireplace. Adam and Greg were sitting on one of the sofas and Leo filled a loveseat opposite them.

They were surprised to see her enter, she felt very awkward to be the centre of attention. "Parker's going to join us for dinner tonight. She was hard at work researching with Seth, so it seemed only fair." Cad explained.

She was ushered over to the two-seater sofa by Seth and he sat down next to her, leaving Cad to squeeze in between Adam and Greg on the other sofa. She couldn't help but laugh at the sight of them, so she offered to switch places. "No, don't worry about them." Seth interjected smiling, "We've always been close." And laughed along with Parker.

Damon entered the room and glanced around at the available seating, he opted to stand next to the fireplace. "How have you been getting on with the research?"

Seth indicated that Parker should answer, so she gave her report, "It's extremely complicated and there is so much to go through. Each prophecy can be interpreted in so many ways, that you aren't entirely sure what it's referring to until you can equate it to an event in retrospect. Which makes me think that it could be confirmation bias.

"Maybe these prophecies didn't really mean anything, and we have just attributed events to them, then shoehorned it to fit. I would need to do a lot more research on the previous prophecies and visions to form any meaningful conclusion."

The men all listened intently to what Parker was saying. She was pleased that they valued her opinion. Parker, like most women, had experienced enough misogynistic men in her life that she appreciated those who respected a woman's contribution.

Seth joined in, "I think that it was a good idea to get an outside opinion. I feel like we have been going over these documents for so long that we have become blind to them."

Damon nodded in contemplation. "We should update Parker's ID access. To continue her training efficiently, there are several places that she will need admittance to." Parker was pleased, she finally felt like they were beginning to trust and respect her.

"Dinner's ready!" Zack called from somewhere else in the house. They all rose and the three on the sofa prised themselves apart. Parker followed the others into the dining room. In the centre was a vast, chunky wooden table, perfectly polished to enhance the grain.

They all took a seat. She was between Leo and Greg, across the table from her sat Damon. Zack started bringing dishes through from the kitchen with help from Adam and he shot her a grin before returning to fetch the next dish.

Several platters held skewers of chicken, pork, roasted vegetables and halloumi. The table was also filled with pitta bread, salad, hummus, garlic yoghurt and bowls of lemon rice. Parker's mouth was watering from the incredible smell, "This looks amazing." And she smiled in appreciation at Zack.

"Let's hope you think it tastes as good as it looks. Dig in everyone."

Without a pause, they began to fill their plates. Parker had thought that she had been greedy until she saw the others overflowing plates. Her stomach growled, reminding her that lunch was hours ago.

The only sound was from them all eating, the food taking priority over conversation. Parker finished eating a while before the others and sat back sated. It had been just as good as it looked. She took the extra time to study the room and saw there were framed black and white photographs hung on one of the walls.

Parker observed the same few individuals repeated in the prints. A slightly older couple with their arms around a young boy, he had dark unruly hair which fell over his eyes. Then the same couple smiling happily at a restaurant and another with them on their wedding day. There were a couple of pictures which contained the individuals that sat around her, they all looked happy.

When Parker brought her gaze back to the table, she saw Damon watching her, "The couple are my parents."

"They look like lovely people," Parker replied politely.

"They are. They moved to Scotland a few years ago. My dad decided to pass the company down to me, he wanted to start enjoying life away from the stress and responsibility. My mum has always loved Scotland, with the mountains and lochs."

"Of course, he only left it to Damon because he knew that we were here to look after him. I was always his favourite." Zack chirped in with a grin and a wink and they all laughed.

After dinner, they all helped to carry the empty plates into the kitchen. It was exactly how Parker had envisioned, sleek and modern. The floor was covered in dark grey slate tiles, with a dark grey granite countertop and pale grey cupboards. There was an impressively sized island in the centre, with a generous double sink on top.

They continued back into the living room, "I think you may need to buy some bigger sofas, Damon." Zack noted as everyone started taking seats. Damon handed out drinks, this was clearly a regular occurrence as he knew everyone's preferences. There had been a slight re-arrangement of seats, with Zack and Seth carrying in some of the dining chairs from the other room. Damon ended up sitting next to Parker on the two-seater sofa.

Parker refused an alcoholic drink, knowing she still needed to drive home. Damon provided her with a soda instead, she sat back and snuggled into the comfy sofa. She enjoyed listening to them talk. They were clearly comfortable with each other, as intermittent teasing would occur with good humour.

She felt safe and content amongst these men. It had been a long day and her eyes began to droop. Parker didn't want to be the first to leave, so tried to remain alert. The next thing she knew, she opened her eyes and was alone in the room, still on the sofa, with a knitted blanket covering her.

Parker sat bolt upright and checked the time, it was midnight. She wasn't sure what to do, should she try and leave? She stood and began creeping around downstairs, hoping that someone was still up. She let out a sigh of relief as she saw a light coming from a room she hadn't yet explored.

She followed the light and peered through the crack in the door. The room was a study, filled with books along the back wall. "Come in, Parker." Damon softly spoke, he had heard her moving around with his enhanced hearing.

Parker pushed the door fully open and padded inside, only just realising that someone had removed her shoes whilst she slept. The desk was an identical copy to the one in his office at work. "Sorry, we didn't want to wake you and I didn't think you would appreciate waking up later in a strange bed."

"It would have been quite disorientating. Thank you for the blanket, I've had some long days this week and it's not even Friday."

He just smiled in response and then asked, "How have you been doing this week? I know that I have been pretty hard on you."

"I'm coping at the minute. I may have a breakdown at some point but for now, I'm fine." Parker joked, then said earnestly, "I do appreciate the support the team is giving me. They have all been really patient."

"They are good men. We have been through a lot. I'd trust them with my life." Damon replied earnestly.

"I suppose I should get going, I may be able to fit in a couple of hours of sleep before my early morning start."

"Come in at nine tomorrow, it won't do anyone any good if you are too tired to function. I'll let the team know that you will be in late."

Parker could have cried with relief, she felt so tired and her body still ached from the self-defence training. "That would be amazing, thank you. I'll head off now so that I can make the most of it." Damon nodded and stood to show her out.

Damon walked Parker to her car and buzzed the gate

open. She saw him in her rear-view mirror, framed in the illuminated doorway, watching her leave.

She arrived home, hustled inside and ensured that all the doors and windows were locked before she undressed in record time.

As Parker picked up her phone to change the following morning's alarm, she saw a message: *Did you get home safely? – D.*

She smiled at his concern and fired back a quick message: *Yes, thank you. My house is all locked up. Looking forward to getting some sleep. – P.*

As soon as her head hit the pillow, she was asleep.

CHAPTER 10

Parker woke naturally before eight o'clock, with light streaming through the slatted blinds. She felt refreshed with renewed energy and dressed quickly into a comfortable, long-sleeved, navy top and jeans.

The problem with starting at nine o'clock was the inevitable rush hour traffic. It took her three times longer to get to work. When she arrived, her favourite spot was taken and she was forced to park at the far end of the car park. It was worth it for the extra rest though.

She walked into the foyer with the other staff members and looked around to see if there was anyone waiting for her. After a few minutes, Parker realised how suspicious she looked hanging around in reception. The security guards kept glancing over at her. Parker elected to take the elevator to the top floor to see who was around.

Parker proceeded through security and pressed the button for the twenty-second floor. She scanned her ID and held her breath, unsure if her new access had been granted yet but she was relieved to see it flash green. Once again, the other people on the elevator were looking at her inquisitively when they saw her intended floor. Parker was getting used to sly looks.

Unsurprisingly, Parker was the only person left on the elevator by the time she reached her destination. As the doors opened in the familiar foyer, Parker strode over to Patricia, who was on the phone. Parker left a polite distance until she had finished her conversation, "Hello Patricia, it's nice to see you again."

"Good morning Parker, it's lovely to see you too. How can I

help you?" She enquired. Parker explained her predicament and asked if she knew whom she was supposed to be with today, if any of them.

"Have a seat and leave it with me, I'll find out what your schedule is today," Patricia said kindly. Parker wasn't going to worry about it and relaxed in a chair. She belatedly thought that she could have just messaged them all. Their numbers were in her phone but she didn't want to bother everyone.

Half an hour later, she was enjoying a hot chocolate and a magazine courtesy of Patricia when all seven of them walked in. She thought that they had been dealing with something important from the look on their faces. Seth and Leo looked towards Parker and nodded in acknowledgement before they turned to get Damon's attention.

Damon's mind was clearly lost in thought and Leo had to call him twice to alert him to Parker's presence before it registered and Damon turned to address her. He beckoned for her to follow them and they all proceeded into his office. Parker returned the magazine to Patricia and thanked her for the hot chocolate, before carrying the remainder of her drink into Damon's office.

She took a seat with the others as Damon paced the room, "Greg, please update Parker." Damon ordered.

"We received news this morning of a break-in at one of our facilities. Thankfully no one was injured, but they seem to have escaped with some of our research. The research stolen included some of your personal information, results from your blood test and initial exam." Greg explained apologetically to Parker.

Damon looked to Parker for her reaction, he was expecting fury. "I'm sorry Parker, I never thought that someone would be able to breach our security system. I hope this doesn't damage your confidence and trust in us." He continued to pace.

Parker considered the information taken and the predicament they were in, "Do you think that they broke in specifically to obtain my records?"

"The majority of what was stolen was in relation to you,

so we believe so, yes," Greg replied, the air was thick with tension.

Parker carefully pondered this information, "So that's where you have all been this morning? Do you know who was behind it?"

"Yes, and yes. We received the call first thing this morning so went straight over. It is uncorroborated at the moment, but we are positive that we know who is behind the break-in and the incident at your home the other night. Deimos." Greg explained, and she could see Leo cracking his knuckles out of the corner of her eye.

Parker felt the need to speak up, "I just want to interject. I don't blame any of you, so there is no need to apologise, Damon. You can't be blamed for someone else's actions and I appreciate you telling me. If you had hidden it and I had found out at a later point, that would have destroyed the mutual trust between us."

Damon's shoulders seemed to lose some of their tension, he was still angry at the incident but relieved at Parker's understanding. "Do you know why Deimos wants my information?" Parker continued.

"He is aware of the prophecy. He has ways of gathering data from us that we haven't been able to prevent. We think that he has moles within the company, which we have been unsuccessful in flushing out."

Damon sighed and slumped into his chair. He let himself look tired for the briefest of moments but then on a sharp intake of breath, got straight to work and started issuing orders. Cad was to organise and review the camera footage over the last week, to see if they could see anyone scoping out the facility. Seth was to continue with the research, as it was still a priority. Greg was to organise a full review and stress test of their security system, with strict instructions to isolate and rectify any flaws he identified.

Zack was tasked with interviewing the on-shift security guards to find out whether they saw anything important and to assess whether they required further training. Adam was to investigate the employees working at the facility, to try and establish whether any of them could be the elusive mole.

Leo was tasked with continuing Parker's training; it was apparently also a priority. Parker felt guilty that she was taking up a valuable resource, but eased her conscience by internally vowing to assist them as much as possible. They all dispersed from the room and Parker had to jog after Leo, who was taking large strides on his way down to the gym.

She changed into workout gear and Leo informed her that they were going to work on improving her fitness. Usually, she would have griped and moaned but it didn't feel appropriate against the backdrop of the morning's news.

They started with something Leo described as a 'simple' warm-up, but had Parker already cursing under her breath; squats, crab-walks and lunges. He then directed her to one of the treadmills and Leo programmed a gentle, walking pace. He gradually increased the speed and gradient until Parker was panting and her face was turning red.

She tried her hardest not to let Leo see how hard she was finding it; she knew that her fitness levels were not where they should be. He sensed her starting to falter and slowed the machine down before risking injury. She flopped onto the floor when it stopped, she didn't care about how she looked as her legs had started to go wobbly.

Leo was looking down at her with an amused smile on his face, "Shall we move onto a bit of strength training?" Parker nodded but still held up her forefinger, indicating that she was going to need a minute. He brought her a bottle of water before moving onto a chest press machine.

Leo instructed a scheme of eight to twelve reps and with each set Parker managed all twelve reps on, Leo increased the weight, to assess her ability. She was happier with this type of training and completed a good number of sets before Leo moved her in front of a barbell. Leo demonstrated how to correctly perform a deadlift, Parker then took over and found it significantly harder than Leo had made it look. Even so, she was determined to not give in and was soon lifting sixty kilograms for 5 reps.

They continued with the deadlifts for a while, before moving on to the leg-focused weight training machines. Leo informed her that she was using a leg abduction machine, then a leg extension machine. They finished with a row, Leo took the rowing machine next to her and they began to row in sync.

Parker smiled when she saw Leo on the rower, he dwarfed the machine. She soon stopped smiling when she saw the power he was exhibiting, she was in awe. This was the first time that she had seen any of them display their strength and it looked like he was holding a lot back.

They continued for a while, she was happy with her progress and didn't feel like she had embarrassed herself too much. The problem with exercising in the gym at this time of day was that there were quite a few others also working out. People kept looking at them, most not even bothering to try and hide their stares. "Leo, do you usually work out here? People keep staring at us and I'm trying to convince myself that it isn't because I'm doing badly."

Leo hadn't spoken much in addition to the guidance but it was a comfortable quiet and never felt awkward. "No, we have a separate gym. I know that you are aware of our strength, we have to use specialised equipment, or we'd likely break it on first use. Also, our gym has reinforced floors and walls. It can sometimes get a little bit unpredictable when we spar and train. I don't usually care what people think. When you're as big as I am, being stared at is a regular occurrence."

Parker nodded in understanding, "I'm guessing you also aren't usually seen training with a human."

"Wait, you're human?!" Leo replied in mock surprise. Parker burst out laughing and Leo joined in, causing more people to stare at them captivated.

"I guessed that you didn't train on this floor, as I haven't seen an Adam-shaped face print on any walls." Leo continued laughing with Parker.

They completed a cool-down exercise, stretching all of the various muscles. Parker thanked Leo for taking the time out of his day to spend with her. He simply nodded in response. His session was over, and he informed her that she should choose any of the activities from the week to focus on. He recommended she choose one of the less physical options, like research.

As Leo strode away, she checked her phone. Ellie wanted to know if she was free for lunch. Happily, Parker confirmed her availability and arranged to meet her in forty minutes by the fountain outside, so that they could go out for lunch instead of frequenting the canteen. Before she could meet Ellie, she needed to shower and change, her outfit was no longer as fresh as before the workout.

She climbed into the shower: towels, shampoo, conditioner and body wash were all provided. Parker stood for quite a while, just letting the water cascade down her body. The water pressure was amazing and it felt great on her muscles. She knew from past experience that she was going to hurt later. Hair dryers were also provided next to a row of mirrors, they really had everything covered.

Parker exited the building and couldn't spot Ellie waiting for her, so she sat next to the fountain. It was a beautifully sunny day so she closed her eyes and tipped her head backwards, enjoying the warmth on her face. A couple of minutes later she heard her name being called and Ellie was skipping towards her.

Parker took the time to enjoy Ellie's outfit, she was wearing a shirt with a picture of two giraffes on the front and the arms were giraffe print. She was also wearing a beige, flared knee-length skirt, with a sloth pattern and lace-up boots. Parker wished that she had the confidence to wear whatever she liked. She had tried a more casual look in the past and she looked like a homeless person.

They walked over to a local bistro, which served French cuisine and opted to sit outside. Ellie ordered a goat's cheese, tomato and basil tart while Parker ordered a truffle and camembert beef burger with a side salad. They both ordered alcohol-free cocktails, Ellie had a Passion Fruitini and Parker had a virgin Mojito.

Whilst waiting, they discussed Ellie's progress with the job search. She had already attended the interview for the project management role, with the other scheduled for Monday afternoon. She was intrigued by the role and liked how the interviewer had pitched it. It was a definite candidate and she believed that she had interviewed well.

Parker was making Ellie laugh, detailing her mornings embarrassments. The talking barely paused as they ate, each taking it in turns so that they didn't run over their lunch hour. A shadow fell over the table, Parker glanced up expecting it to be the waiter with the bill. However, it was a well-built gentleman with thick dark hair peppered with greys.

He was clean-shaven, with dark brown eyes and he wore a tailored suit. The gentleman smiled before taking a seat next to them. Parker and Ellie looked at each other in confusion. They each wondered whether the other knew this presumptuous stranger, he appeared to be in his forties but it was difficult to gauge.

"Hello, ladies." He said with a wide smile. He seemed friendly, but they both felt uneasy.

"Can we help you?" Ellie asked.

"I was walking past and saw two lovely young ladies, I just wanted to stop by and enjoy a few minutes of your time."

Parker didn't want to appear too rude, so politely responded, "Thank you, but we really need to be going. We are just waiting on the bill, as we need to return to work."

"That's fine, I will keep you company whilst you wait. What are your names?" Parker was awful at lying and couldn't think of two fake names.

It turns out Ellie wasn't much better at crafting a lie but at least she came up with two names quickly, "Kate and Winifred."

He seemed to know that she was lying, as he raised an eyebrow. "What lovely names. I own a club about an hour from here and would love it if you could both attend tonight. VIP entry, of course, Champagne would be included." He slid a card across to Parker, but it was face down. Parker just smiled in a noncommittal way and took the card to prevent an awkward interaction. She glanced at the waiter who was heading their way.

As soon as the bill was laid on the table, she took cash out of her purse and placed it on top. Parker saw that Ellie was about to remove her credit card from her purse and placed the cash down before she was able to. Clearly, Ellie had forgotten that her real name was printed on the card.

Parker and Ellie hastily grabbed their things, they said polite goodbyes and swiftly started walking back to the office. Parker kept glimpsing back to ensure that they weren't being followed, but the man had remained at their table. She was probably just feeling paranoid but after her training session with Adam, she was going to trust her gut instincts.

Minos Industries came into view and they both let out a sigh of relief. Ellie began to laugh, "What a weirdo, who does that? Who sits down at someone else's table without even asking? So arrogant, I thought he was going to try and sell us something at first." Parker was curious as to which club the man had owned, so removed the business card from her bag.

She stopped in her tracks. The name on the card was 'Deimos Minos' and the nightclub was 'Club Minos'. Parker felt the blood drain from her face and the bottom dropped out of her stomach. Ellie looked at her in concern, "What's the matter? Parker, are you alright? What's wrong?" Parker just handed her the business card.

She was shocked but hadn't reacted as strongly as Parker. Ellie wasn't aware of this morning's theft of her information by the man who just sat across from her. "We need to tell the guys immediately," Ellie stated as she strode into the building, dragging Parker along with her, who was still stunned.

They went straight to the elevators, passed security and pressed the button to the top floor. Patricia was at her desk, Ellie explained that it was urgent and they needed to speak to Damon immediately. Patricia replied that he was currently in a meeting but that it should be over shortly. They both agreed that it could wait a few minutes and they sat on the sofas whilst Parker composed herself.

Less than five minutes later, Damon's office door opened and a tall blonde exited. She was stunning, wearing a fitted green dress that hugged every curve and high heels. Her hair was perfectly styled and the curls trailed down her back. She walked confidently through the room without looking at them and exited via the elevators.

Parker felt a pang of jealousy before being confused by her reaction. She didn't think of Damon in that way. He stood at the door and was looking straight at Parker, he gestured for them to come into his office.

They both walked through his door and Ellie handed Damon the business card. He briefly looked at it, then crumpled it in his fist. Damon was trying to contain his anger. Parker saw his eyes briefly flash red before quickly cooling back to brilliant blue. "What happened?" he growled.

Parker explained about their lunch date and how they hadn't realised who he was until they were almost back at the office. He walked over to the window and gazed out; it was several minutes before he turned back around, "Are you both alright?"

"Yes, he didn't hurt us. We assumed that he was just a pushy flirt at first. I was shocked but I'm alright now. We should have realised due to his size but I'm becoming accustomed to being around enormous men," Parker responded having calmed down.

Ellie sounded concerned when she added, "Honestly Damon, I'm just really worried about Parker. First, there was someone following her home, now Deimos or one of his followers is stalking us when we leave the office. How else could he have known where we were? It's the first time we have been to that place."

"Yes, I think you're right to be concerned."

Damon explained the events of the morning to Ellie, she looked towards Parker. Ellie's face was clearly asking why she hadn't been told about this earlier at lunch. Parker offered the explanation without being asked, "I didn't want to worry you, they are looking into it already. He didn't really get anything of value."

Ellie looked even more worried after the latest revelation, "What do you think he's capable of? Is Parker safe?"

"He won't hurt her, if anything he will want her on his side. However, I can't guess what his master plan is."

"She needs permanent protection; she obviously isn't safe from him. Parker should move in with me." Ellie decided.

Damon appeared to consider her statement before responding, "I don't want to put you in danger, Ellie, maybe she should move in with one of us."

Parker was beginning to get frustrated as they were talking about her instead of to her. She bit back her anger, as it would have been directed at the wrong people. They were just trying to keep her safe, "As it is my life, I will be the one making that decision. I will not be moving in with you, Ellie or any of your team, Damon. I have already been made to move once and I won't be doing it again. End of discussion." Parker stated in a tone that brooked no argument.

Neither of them looked happy but it was clear she wasn't going to be swayed. Damon thought it through and said, "We'll have to put extra security precautions in place. A security system is going to be installed in and around your home before you sleep there tonight. Also, you will not be allowed to take lunches anywhere other than our building, he is watching you. When you go out anywhere, do not go alone. Hopefully, he is less likely to try anything if you are with someone."

Parker still wasn't happy with her diminishing freedom but she was a practical person and knew that it didn't make sense to argue.

Damon picked up his phone and dashed off a few messages. They each took a seat until the arrangements had

THE ABRAXAS PROPHECY

been sorted. Cad and Leo arrived and were charged with installing the security systems at her home. Damon explained to them what had happened and they left with a curt nod and determined expressions.

Parker welled up with emotion, they all seemed so concerned about her and she really appreciated it. "What can I do?" Parker enquired.

Damon responded, "If you can concentrate, it would be useful for you to continue with the research. I would advise spending the next couple of hours researching, then heading home. Cad and Leo should have made good progress with the security setup by then, they will talk you through how it works."

Ellie, feeling that she could do no more there, returned to her job after giving Parker a reassuring hug. Parker headed down to the second subfloor, her ID instantly granting her access. She smiled as she was finally starting to feel a part of the team.

Seth had explained on their last visit how to navigate the library to locate the most relevant texts, so Parker continued from where she had left off and set an alarm on her phone for two hours' time. She had been working her way through the prophecies of the Oracle of Delphi, otherwise known as the Pythia.

The latest prophecy she was researching appeared to support the supernatural council's decision, that the prophecy should be kept a secret for fear of influencing a negative outcome. The Pythia had foretold that a King's son would grow up and kill his father. To prevent this, the King ordered one of his knights to kill his son. The knight couldn't bring himself to kill the child, so hid him away.

When the child grew up, he learnt of his father's betrayal and swore revenge, ultimately murdering his father and fulfilling the prophecy. If the King had not acted as a result of the prophecy, the son would have never desired revenge and murdered his father, the King.

Another prophecy seemed to support Parker's view that they were so ambiguous, that they could be applicable to a multitude of outcomes.

> *'Though all else shall be taken, Zeus, the all-seeing,
> grants that the wooden wall only shall not fail.'*

The Athenians then argued amongst themselves what could be meant by 'the wooden wall'. In the end, they decided that it meant the wooden fleet of ships they were sending to war. As they won the war, they confirmed that this was exactly what the Pythia meant. However, it could have easily been any other wooden object or a literal wooden wall that they were unaware of.

Parker loved this part of her training. The information held in this room was vast. She just hoped that they didn't revoke her access in the future. Maybe she could get a more permanent role after her training finished, working with these documents. Her phone alarm snapped her out of her future daydreaming with a jump. She couldn't believe that it had been two hours already. There was no signal down here, so she didn't even have the usual alerts from her phone to disturb her.

She put away her research, making sure that it was all safely back in the correct places before taking the elevator back up. As she entered the foyer, she sent a quick message to Ellie: *Heading back home now. Will let you know when I get back x.*

Almost immediately she received a response: *Glad you're OK. I'll be waiting for your message x.*

Parker nearly put her phone away, but then decided she should message Damon too: *I am just leaving the office. I have continued with the research. No breakthroughs yet. Heading straight back home now – P.*

He was doing so much for her, that she felt like she should keep him in the loop directly. It took her a couple of minutes to reach her car as it was parked at the other end of the car park. She kept reciting Adam's advice on the best way to protect yourself.

Parker was aware of her surroundings and walked confidently with her head held high. Her head quickly shot towards any slight movement to assess danger. She had a fleeting thought that she was overreacting, but then she dismissed it as quickly as it entered her thoughts, it was better to overreact than not. Overreacting would help to keep her safe.

Her trip home was uneventful, Parker almost detoured to pick up some groceries but decided that could wait. She had promised Damon and Ellie that she wouldn't go anywhere alone, this was going to get old fast. Parker pulled up outside her house, she couldn't see either of the guys at first glance.

She exited her car and headed towards her front door. It was locked so she tried her key. Her key wouldn't turn, she double-checked that it was in fact her house. Parker then tried turning the key again, in the middle of her second attempt the door opened.

Leo stood in the open doorway, her keys still uselessly dangling from the lock. She had to wait until he completely stepped back before entering, as he more than filled the doorway. "You may have already noticed that we changed the locks to a more secure, skeleton key-proof lock. We will give you a new set of keys before we leave, the back door has also had a new lock installed. We still need to install a video doorbell, so if anyone approaches the front of your house you will be immediately notified. There are discreet security cameras on every side of the house and the back garden."

Leo then turned Parker around so she was facing the front door again. Partially hidden by a plant was an alarm.

"The alarm code is a random number. We avoid birthdays because they are too obvious. We have set yours to 5934, if there is an emergency press 4395. The alarm will be switched off. So, if someone is forcing you to turn it off, they will be unaware that a silent alert has been sent through to us. Cad has added extra lighting in your garden, it appears to be purely decorative, but it prevents dark spots where someone could hide."

Leo explained all the changes and downloaded the app required on her phone. "We have hard-wired the security system but it also has a battery backup that can last for forty-eight hours. The system will use your Wi-Fi but will switch to mobile data if needed. Do you have any questions?"

"No, I think you have covered everything thank you. I really want to thank you both for your help, are you guys free for dinner? If you are, Pizza? My treat." Parker offered.

Leo grinned, clearly the route to his heart was through his stomach. "I'm always free for pizza. I'll go and check with Cad." Both guys were free and happily accepted her offer. Six large meat feast pizzas later and they were all watching a classic eighties action film.

Parker loved eighties films and was convinced that she had been born in the wrong era. She had enjoyed the evening. Cad and Leo spent the entire movie verbalising their opinions on how realistic, or not, the fight scenes were. Parker didn't mind as she had watched it before and she liked listening to the banter between them.

At some point during the night, Parker had received a message from Damon. She had only noticed after the two men had left at midnight: *No official training this weekend but keep practising at home. I have visitors this weekend. It's important that you meet them. 4pm tomorrow at my home. Don't hesitate to contact me if you need to. Keep safe – D.*

Parker set her security alarm, turned off her morning alarm and retreated to her bed.

CHAPTER 11

Parker woke to a drizzly and cold Saturday morning. She decided to make the most of staying indoors and downloaded a book. She chose the book that she had been torn away from in the library by Seth and grabbed a fleecy blanket. Parker sank into a comfy armchair that overlooked the garden and was thankful for it; her body was aching from the previous day's exercise.

As the rain fell more heavily and cascaded down her windows, she became really immersed in her book. The only time that she paused was to make a hot chocolate and to rearrange herself to be even more cocooned.

One o'clock came and went and reluctantly she focused on needing to be at Damon's house. Parker set the book down, acknowledging that she hadn't practised any of her training yet. She knew that she probably wouldn't get any time for it later, so had a quick Yoga session before showering.

Parker studied her selection of clothes and tried to settle on an outfit. On the one hand, it was a Saturday afternoon but on the other, he had told her that she was meeting important visitors. She chose the same black skater dress that she wore to the neighbourhood party, it was comfortable yet flattering.

She added extra product to her hair after showering, as she was concerned that it would frizz wildly from the rain. Parker accented her outfit with some simple, silver jewellery and gathered her money, phone and ID into her purse.

Parker grabbed her umbrella, not wanting to get drenched. She dashed to her car after setting the alarm and locking the door. She heard her phone notification acknowledging that there had been motion recorded at her front door and she smiled. The traffic was heavier than usual due to the rain. She was singing along to her playlist as she drove, she loved belting out tunes in the car.

Parker arrived at Damon's house with a couple of minutes to spare. She lowered her window a tiny amount to avoid the rain pouring in. After announcing herself at the intercom, the gates opened. Today the driveway was empty, there was a garage at the far side and she assumed that's where Damon's car was kept.

She parked just outside the door and readied the umbrella to protect herself. She swiftly made her way to the shelter of the porch. Right on cue, Damon opened the door, clearly waiting since her intercom buzz. He was dressed casually in navy jeans and a fitted T-shirt.

Parker spent a second too long admiring Damon's body before composing herself and smiling brightly into his face. He looked amused and welcomed her inside. She had been wondering who the important visitors were. There were far too many people from the supernatural community that she was unaware of for her to make an educated guess. Parker left her umbrella in the porch. She removed her shoes, as she didn't want to traipse water throughout his pristine house.

Damon guided her into the living room, where a man and woman were sitting on the loveseat. They rose as she entered. They seemed familiar to Parker but she couldn't place them. The man looked like he was assessing her, but the woman smiled at her warmly.

"Parker, this is Leander and Rose. My parents." Damon announced. Parker's eyes widened for the briefest of moments but she composed herself quickly. She held her hand out towards them and Leander grasped it firmly to shake. Rose ignored the hand and embraced her in a hug instead. Damon's mum had a kind face, framed by short brown hair.

They both looked like they were in their late forties but Parker knew better. Rose was wearing a white blouse with a green flowing skirt. Leander looked a lot like Damon, they had the same hair and eyes. He was also built like Damon and dwarfed his wife. Leander and Damon were also wearing very similar outfits, but Leander's T-shirt wasn't quite as fitted.

"My parents are visiting from Scotland for a few days. They are aware of the major developments with the prophecy and we wanted to take the opportunity for them to meet you." Damon explained.

Parker smiled, "It's very nice to meet you both. This has all been a bit of a whirlwind for me. I didn't even know that supernaturals existed last month."

Rose replied on behalf of the couple, "From what my son tells us, you are handling it quite impressively considering the circumstances. You should be proud of yourself, it's a lot to take in. I should know, I also didn't know they existed until I met Leander."

"I remember hearing that you're also human. How did the two of you meet?" Parker asked inquisitively. They all took seats before Rose continued. Leander and Rose returned to the loveseat, Damon and Parker chose the other sofa.

"It was a different time back then; women were still fighting for the right to vote. I wanted to make a difference and attended my first rally. It was on my way home that I was stopped by a group of drunken men. They saw my wooden placard and it angered them. I was pulled into an alleyway, where they surrounded me. I was so afraid of what they were going to do.

"A man rushed in and pulled me behind him. He took on all four of them easily but I was so scared for him. That day I was made aware and shown the power of the supernatural world. He barely even broke a sweat dealing with them. He then walked me home and explained all about the different supernatural lines. Leander told me about his ancestry, I was enthralled. Over the next few months, he visited me regularly and many years later, here we are."

She then looked affectionately towards her husband. "We wanted to meet you, as you could be the linchpin to the entire prophecy. Its awakening is our best hope for the survival of the lines."

Parker couldn't reply to her statement. She didn't know how she could influence the prophecy and hoped that she wouldn't let everyone down. Leander spoke, "My son has placed a lot of faith in you. Bringing you into our secret isn't a decision made lightly."

She could see the similarities between Damon and his father through Leander's attitude. They were both slow to trust and it was clear that trust needed to be earned. She could understand why, they both cared deeply about their people and took their responsibilities very seriously.

Drinks and snacks were offered by Damon, they each accepted a hot drink. Parker found that she quickly warmed to Rose, she was kind and friendly, such that Parker began to converse like she had known her for years. Leander also started to open up to her, taking comfort from his wife's ease around Parker. Damon brought out the hot drinks and a tray of snacks. There was a knock at the door.

Damon's parents looked at him questioningly but he shook his head with a perplexed look set on his brow, indicating that he hadn't invited anyone else. He stood and went to answer the door. When he returned, the blonde woman from the previous day followed him in. She was wearing a fitted royal blue dress, which enhanced every asset. Parker was grateful that she hadn't worn jeans.

The newcomer rushed to his parents and hugged his mum. It may have just been Parker projecting but they didn't seem pleased by her interruption. "Parker, this is Acantha." Damon introduced the woman with no emotion in his voice. Parker was trying to understand the relationships between the group.

Acantha smiled coldly at Parker, there was no warmth in her green eyes. "Hello Parker. I have heard lots about you." Her tone sounded like she hadn't been impressed by what she'd heard. She looked towards Damon and her face transformed effortlessly into a beaming and much warmer smile, "When I heard that your parents were here Damon, I just had to stop by to see them."

He didn't return her smile. Parker thought that he looked irritated by her arrival. "Parker, you're probably wondering about me and Damon, we've known each other forever. We just can't keep away from each other." Acantha said whilst leaning into Damon's arm.

Parker just nodded at her awkwardly. She wasn't sure what this little display was about but she seemed to be staking her claim on Damon. Acantha requested a negroni from Damon, she clearly had no intention of leaving. Parker thought the extremely bitter cocktail suited Acantha's behaviour and so, amused, she sat back on the sofa to observe the interactions between the four.

She seemed to be gushing over his parents. Acantha kept alternating between complimenting them and talking about her own accomplishments. Rose was smiling politely during the conversation and Leander just made non-committal noises, which left Acantha to carry the entire conversation.

Parker had sat on the two-seater sofa. Acantha chose to sit on the empty three-seater. When Damon returned, he handed Acantha her drink, picked his own back up off the table and sat down next to Parker. Rose hid her amused smile behind her own cup. Acantha started glaring daggers at Parker as if she had done the unforgivable.

Leander covered up his laugh with a cough and what followed was an awkwardly long silence. Parker wasn't sure why Damon had sat next to her when Acantha clearly wanted him with her. She assumed that he was also fed up with her open flirting and was pushing back.

Acantha gathered herself and fell back into her friendly persona, "Parker, I've heard that you're spending a lot of time with Damon and his team. I was just wondering what you could be contributing. You are an outsider, aren't you?" She didn't seem to realise that she had alienated the room further by implying that humans were inferior. She had clearly forgotten that Rose was a human.

Parker wasn't fazed by the supposed offence. She didn't feel like she had anything to prove to this woman and was definitely not ashamed of being human, "Yes, I have been working with the team a lot. They have all been so welcoming. I'm definitely the one getting the better end of the deal." She smiled at Damon.

Leander finally spoke, "Damon, don't we have dinner plans shortly?"

"Yes," Damon replied a little too enthusiastically, thankful for the lifeline. "We will need to leave within the next ten minutes."

Parker picked up her bag, "It was lovely to meet you all."

"We've reserved the table for four people. Parker, you're coming too." Leander smiled at her, then glanced towards Acantha.

Acantha smiled, "I'm sure that we can ask the restaurant to change the reservation to five, we will have a fantastic time catching up." Everyone was too polite, so no one refused her self-imposed offer.

They collected their coats and bags. Parker slipped her boots back on. It had stopped raining, so umbrellas weren't required but Parker remembered to grab hers from the porch. Acantha was getting a lift with Damon as she had been dropped off. Parker began walking to her car, she was going to follow them to the restaurant. Damon's car was a sleek all-black Range Rover, and while large, it was still crowded with his parents and Acantha in it and she was planning on going straight home afterwards.

It was a short drive before the two cars pulled up outside an Italian restaurant and the whole dinner party walked in together. They were seated in a private area towards the rear, it was bustling and the food smelled mouth-watering. Acantha chose the seat next to Damon and Parker sat across from him, with his mum next to Parker and dad at the head of the table.

The waiter was very efficient and took their drinks order shortly after being seated. They were all browsing the menu, Parker almost chose Spaghetti Bolognese but didn't want to risk the inevitable mess. She decided on a Chicken Penne Pasta with a small glass of white wine.

As they were viewing the menu, Acantha kept leaning into Damon and asking his opinion on certain dishes. He didn't appear to notice her attempts at gaining his affection or her pushing her body closer, he was more interested in the menu options.

They gave the waiter their orders and proceeded to talk about the trip that Leander and Rose were currently enjoying. The visit to Damon was en route to their next destination. Parker joined in the conversation, "Damon told me that you moved to Scotland for the scenery, I have visited Scotland a couple of times myself. It's absolutely stunning, I stayed near Loch Lomond on my last holiday and toured the area. Some of the scenery easily rivals the Rocky Mountains."

"We love Loch Lomond and The Trossachs National Park. We viewed a property there when we first decided to relocate. But after we saw our current home, there was no competition. We now live near Lochgilphead on the west coast. We bought a lovely piece of land." Rose said with a fondness in her tone.

Their meals arrived, everyone had chosen various forms of pasta dish. Leander and Damon also had a couple of sides each. There was a brief pause in the conversation as they ate, the food was as good as it smelled. Acantha was the first to break the silence, "What do you think of my hair Damon? I've been growing it out since we were last together, I thought you would like it."

Damon glanced up, clearly oblivious to the change. "Yes, it's nice. I tend to prefer red-heads though." He then returned to his food. Acantha's face turned scarlet and she stabbed a piece of chicken forcefully whilst looking at Parker, oblivious to the sniggers Leander and Rose gave each other.

The remainder of the meal passed by uneventfully.

Acantha had toned down her advancements on Damon. Parker ignored the death glares being thrown her way and focused on the other members at the table. "How long are you going to be staying with Damon?" Parker enquired.

"We'll be leaving tomorrow evening; we have a late-night flight to catch. We don't want to intrude on Damon too much but we love getting to see him," Rose replied, whilst looking proudly at her son.

"You know that I love your visits, you are always welcome to stay with me," Damon said smiling.

Leander insisted on paying for the meal. There was a little bit of resistance from Damon but he finally accepted the inevitable. They made their way outside and Parker thanked them for a wonderful meal. Rose hugged Parker, "It was lovely to meet you, make sure the boys aren't too tough on you!"

Parker laughed at someone referring to the seven huge men she'd been working with lately as 'boys', before turning her attention to Leander. She felt like he had warmed up to her as he also hugged her goodbye. Parker was pleasantly surprised and felt like she had started to earn his trust too.

Acantha hugged Leander and Rose. She then went across to embrace Damon, who responded with an awkward one-armed pat on her back. As Parker was climbing into her car Damon walked over, "Message me when you get back safely, there's no point in taking any risks." Parker smiled and nodded in confirmation. The roads were quiet as she drove and she continued singing along with Freddie Mercury.

Parker arrived home, let herself in, turned off the alarm and then locked the door behind her. She remembered after noting the absence of a doorbell notification that she had silenced her phone before meeting Damon's parents. She rummaged in her bag and pulled out her phone, there had been one more motion notification whilst she was out.

When she replayed the video she saw a black flash across the screen but then nothing. It was probably a trick of the light but she decided to send it to Cad anyway. It was better to be safe than sorry. After sending the video over, she sent Damon a quick message: *I'm safe at home, the alarm is on and the doors are locked. Your parents are lovely, it was great meeting them. I know that your father is going to be sceptical about my sudden arrival into your lives, but I hope that my winning personality has won him over - P.*

Parker was grinning as she wrote the last sentence.

A message appeared from Ellie on her phone: *Hey, I was supposed to go on a spa day with one of my sisters tomorrow but she has cancelled. Do you want to come with me? x.*

Spas weren't usually Parker's thing, but her body would probably welcome the rejuvenation after this week: *I would love to come, I can drive. What time shall I pick you up? x.*

Almost immediately she received the response: *9:30. See you tomorrow! x.*

Parker decided to take advantage of an early night and went upstairs. She completed her usual routine and snuggled under her sheets. It took her a little while to fall asleep, she kept thinking back to the meal. Finally, she drifted off. Her night was less than restful, as it was filled with dreams of Acantha and her death glares. One dream had Acantha chasing her down a dark corridor. Damon was at the other end and she was desperately trying to reach him before Acantha caught her.

When Parker opened her eyes, she didn't feel as refreshed as she should have. It was already eight o'clock, so she showered and shaved before pulling on loose clothing. She probably wouldn't be wearing it for very long anyway, as they would be changing into robes and slippers at the spa.

Parker grabbed a light breakfast, then packed a bag with her essentials and a swimsuit. She found that she was really looking forward to a pamper day and arrived at Ellie's earlier than requested. Parker sent a quick message to tell her that she was outside and turned the radio up to sing along.

Parker was particularly enjoying being a hero, just for one day, when her passenger door opened and she jumped, startled. Ellie laughed at her reaction as she climbed in, then proceeded to scold her for not paying enough attention to her surroundings. Ellie provided backing vocals, in between directions.

Ellie had also chosen loose clothing but her outfit was bright orange. It took about forty minutes to get to their destination, where they parked up and Ellie took the lead. After they had checked in and locked away their belongings, they changed and proceeded to the pool, deciding to swim a few laps before the first of the treatments.

After swimming, they indulged in the hot tub, it felt amazing on Parker's sore body. She felt like her body ached even more today from the exercise. Parker updated Ellie with the events over the last couple of days. She was careful not to mention anything supernatural, as they had to raise their voices to be heard over the sound of the jets.

She told her about the new security system at her house and the pizza night. Parker then moved on to the previous day's excitement. Ellie was surprised that Damon had introduced her to his parents, "You do realise that meeting someone's parents is a major step in any relationship."

"Yes, but we don't have a relationship, remember?" And they both began laughing. Parker was building up to the next interesting part, where his ex-girlfriend had shown up unannounced.

"What?!" Ellie exclaimed, "Tell me everything."

Parker then explained that it was the blonde they saw leaving Damon's office on Friday. She regaled the awkward interactions between the individuals and how Acantha had unknowingly insulted Damon's mum. She relayed her comment about Parker being an 'outsider' and therefore having little to contribute to the team.

Ellie was alternating between getting angry at Acantha's audacity and laughing at the awkward moments. "Don't you think that Damon's actions were interesting though? I mean, I get that he isn't interested in Acantha anymore but he seemed to be sending you some interesting vibes."

Parker just rolled her eyes, "He really doesn't see me that

way. He was just using me to try and prove his point with Acantha." Ellie didn't seem convinced but she let it drop.

They had a couple of treatments booked after lunch, a mud wrap followed by pedicures. A manicure was tempting, but if her life continued like the last week, they wouldn't last a single day at work. Ellie suggested they use the sauna. Parker wasn't great with heat but was willing to give it a go. The sauna was a small room with a couple of women already sitting inside, so Parker and Ellie sat on an empty bench to the right. The wave of heat when they entered was intense and Parker needed a moment to catch her breath.

Parker sat back and relaxed with her eyes closed. Ellie was chatting about her sisters and what each of them was up to. Eventually, she was starting to feel too hot and needed a break. She exited the sauna and checked the time. Twenty minutes until their lunch slot, so Parker jumped back in the pool to cool off.

The water was freezing cold after the intense heat and it took her breath away. Ellie stood at the side of the pool, laughing at Parker's expression. "Stop laughing at me, it's your turn now!" Parker called to Ellie, who rose to the challenge, jumping in herself. When she emerged, she had the same expression as Parker and they laughed at each other.

Getting out, they pulled on their borrowed, fluffy white robes and wrapped the ties tightly around their waists before slipping on the little, single-use flip-flops and shuffling towards the restaurant. They told the waiter their names for the reservation and were directed towards a two-seater table. The menu looked great but it only offered healthy options.

They both chose smoked salmon for a starter. Parker had a wild mushroom linguine and Ellie had a beetroot and feta cheese salad. The waiter also brought a bottle of Champagne to the table. Parker looked towards Ellie, as they hadn't ordered it. "I'm sorry, we haven't ordered any alcohol," Ellie explained.

The waiter smiled and responded, "It was ordered via a phone call, a gentleman paid for the bottle and requested that we bring it to you at your table. One of you must have a very romantic partner, it's our best bottle."

Parker didn't want to show her alarm to the waiter, "Yes, we both have wonderful partners, did he leave a name?" The waiter left the bottle and offered to check for them. When he left, Parker and Ellie looked at each other in confusion. They then began speculating who could have sent it. The only people that knew they were here were Ellie's family members and it seemed like an odd thing for them to have done.

The waiter returned, "He didn't leave a name, but I checked the credit card that it was paid on for you, Mr D Minos."

They thanked the waiter and Ellie asked, "Did you tell Damon that we were coming here? That's very forward of him. Clearly, he does like you." And she smiled.

Parker was frowning, "There is another D Minos, and it isn't Damon."

Ellie stopped smiling and also began to frown, "Do you really think that it was Deimos? How would he know that we are here? He must still have people following us."

"There is one way to know for sure. When we leave, I will ask Damon if he did it. If he didn't, I will let him know what happened. We are perfectly safe here and are surrounded by witnesses. If it is Deimos, it's probably some childish mind game that he's playing. Let's not worry about it and enjoy the rest of the afternoon." Parker then passed the bottle of champagne to a young couple. She wasn't going to enjoy it and thought that someone might as well.

Following lunch, they proceeded to their mud wrap and both went into the same room. The women applying the treatment were extremely friendly while still maintaining a calm ambience as they entered the room. Soft music played in the background and the room was warm. The smell of eucalyptus gently filled the room.

They each received a full body exfoliation. It was a bit rough, but not too unpleasant. Once they had exfoliated every inch of their bodies, they moved on to applying dead sea mud.

It was a bizarre feeling and Parker had to stop herself from scratching, as it was extremely tickly in places.

Once they were left alone, Parker set about trying her hardest to make Ellie laugh as neither was supposed to move. Eventually, the two women returned and removed the mud, the crack lines at the corners of the Parker and Ellie's faces, the only giveaway. The final part of the treatment involved them applying an all-over body lotion. It felt absolutely amazing. Parker had never been a spa person, but after today she was a total convert.

They continued onto the pedicures, which were located at the other end of the facility. The room was large and had several rows of chairs, half of which were currently occupied. They were directed to two chairs next to a window, where they could sit side by side. They slipped off the flip-flops and their feet were placed into a foot spa; they were provided with magazines to pass the time.

Parker was given a beauty magazine, whilst Ellie had a bridal magazine. Parker loved browsing the photos, to see how they had been styled in new and interesting ways, likening the makeup artistry to a craft project. Ellie kept pointing out the dresses that she loved, versus the ones that she wouldn't be caught dead wearing. The conversation reminded Parker of something, "I've been meaning to ask, what's the latest at the rumour mill at work? Am I still the hot topic or am I old news?"

"Now that you mention it, there have been some interesting ones lately. No one actually believes them but it helps to pass the time. There was a lot of gossip when they saw you with Leo in the gym. My favourite theory was from Stephen, who surmised that you had been dating Damon in secret. Then you moved onto Leo as you like bigger men." Ellie followed it with a wiggle of her eyebrows and began laughing uncontrollably. Parker joined in laughing, mostly at Ellie's current breathless state.

When the ladies returned, she removed one of Parker's feet from the spa. She cut and filed her nails before moving onto her other foot. Exfoliation then occurred, followed by a massage. Her feet felt amazing, this was going to have to become a regular treat. Finally, they each had to choose a nail polish colour.

Parker chose a dark shade of red as it complimented her skin tone. Ellie chose an orange polish, to match her car. A UV lamp was used to speed up the drying process and to increase its longevity. They slipped their flip-flops back on. This treatment was planned later in the day, as they didn't want to ruin all of that hard work in the pool.

They finished their day in the conservatory. It had comfortable seating, an amazing view of the gardens and a café which offered cakes and drinks. They both indulged in a cake. Ellie settled on a carrot cake, matching her toes to her confection, while Parker chose a chocolate fudge cake. After sitting there relaxing for an hour, they finally got up to leave. They reluctantly changed out of their robes and into their clothes. Parker retrieved her phone from the locker and checked for messages as they walked back to her car.

There were a couple of missed calls and Damon had messaged: *Call me when you get a chance – D.*

Parker decided to wait until she arrived home, as she didn't have handsfree in her car and she didn't want to be distracted whilst driving, but it bugged her the entire way as she wanted to know what Damon wanted.

She finally dropped Ellie off, thanked her for a wonderful day and returned home. Parker followed her usual routine of turning off the alarm, locking the door behind her and removing her shoes before calling Damon. The phone rang a few times but then went to voicemail, she didn't bother leaving a message as he would know why she called.

Parker was well aware that she had skipped her training for the day, but she rationalised that the guys would never know. As she looked around her living room, she noticed that the floor needed a hoover. She brought out the vacuum and gave it a quick once over.

She zoomed around the downstairs, hoovering as fast yet

thoroughly as possible whilst singing "I want to break free," by Queen. When she turned off the hoover, she heard a knocking at the door. She rushed over, aware that they may have been standing there knocking for a while. She peeped through the window, it was Damon.

She opened the door and welcomed him in, not sure why he had decided to visit. "Have your parents left for the airport already?" Parker queried.

"They should be setting off now. I explained that I needed to check in on you, so they offered to get a taxi to the airport."

"Check in on me? Why?"

"Cad showed me his analysis of your video. Someone visited your house. The speed of their movement confirms that they are supernatural. Even with slowing it down, we couldn't see a face but due to the size and body shape it appears to have been a woman. Our theory is that it was one of Deimos' followers and they are keeping an eye on you.

"I wanted to check that you were safe as you haven't been answering our calls. I also wanted the outside of the property to be searched for clues but the others have tonight off and I didn't want to bother them."

Parker nodded whilst frowning, "I do need to check something with you. I'm positive that the answer is 'no' but I didn't want to worry Ellie. Did you send a bottle of Champagne to a spa today?"

"No. I didn't even know that you were spending the day at a spa. Why would you have thought that I'd sent it?"

"Because the waiter checked who had ordered it and the card that paid for the bottle was under the name of Mr D Minos."

Damon swore in frustration. "I don't think that you will take me up on this request, but I must ask. Will you move in with one of us, so that you aren't alone?"

"No. Besides, you can't be with me all the time. He hasn't hurt me, he is just being a stalker and a pest at the minute. I will keep attending my training, Adam has been teaching me some great self-defence moves."

Damon nodded, resigned to her refusal. "I will go and have a look around outside, lock the door behind me." He then walked out of her front door; she sat on a barstool awaiting his return. Damon knocked on the door twenty minutes later, "As I thought, nothing is out there. I've surveyed the entire perimeter of your property but I think they left when they spotted the camera."

"I really do appreciate you coming out here to help me. I know that this mess has pulled you away from spending time with your parents." Parker placed her hand on his arm and smiled up at him, she wanted him to really feel her gratitude.

His face started out tight and full of tension but his face softened as he looked down at her. He offered her a small smile in acknowledgement and said, "I know." They locked eyes for several moments until Parker looked down and away.

Damon continued, "If you do go away with Ellie or anyone and don't have access to your phone, just let me know. We do worry about you but we want to respect your privacy as much as possible." Before Parker could respond he made his way to the door, pulling it shut behind him.

Parker locked the door, set the alarm and made her way up to bed. It was still early but she planned to finish the night with a good book and her bed was a favourite place to read. She thought back to her interaction with Damon and Ellie's comments from earlier. She thought that there may have been a moment between them but discarded her thoughts and focused on reading her book instead.

CHAPTER 12

Parker woke before her alarm. She had slept like a log, waking up in the exact same position as she fell asleep. Clearly, the spa day was exactly what her body and mind needed. She tied her hair up in a ponytail and chose black jeans and a forest green, fitted shirt. Parker quickly rushed around to attend to all of her plants before breakfast, remembering that they were due for watering. She grabbed a couple of slices of toast before heading out.

Cad was already waiting for Parker in the foyer, as they had a morning Yoga session scheduled. Once she had changed into workout gear, they tried some more advanced positions to those of her previous sessions. She was gaining confidence and her balance was improving. She only fell over twelve times, as opposed to the twenty last time.

She stayed in her workout gear and Cad passed her over to Leo's care. Parker continued her fitness training. She hadn't improved in the slightest from her last attempt. Parker was depressed that real life wasn't like in films, where they had a training montage and were fully trained in five minutes. Today's session wasn't as intense as her last, as she was due to swap to Adam's training afterwards and they didn't want her too exhausted.

Parker insisted on a break after Leo's training. She needed water, a bathroom break and sugar. Adam was sitting on the mats, waiting for her. She walked up and offered him one of her chocolate bars, which he accepted eagerly. It was her way of apologising for the delay. After a warm-up, he made her practice the moves he'd already taught her, over and over, perfecting her forms. She didn't manage to land another direct hit but was unquestionably improving.

Adam showed her another barrage of self-defence moves, which included a selection of; punches and strikes, kicks, defending against punches and kicks, knee strikes, grappling and ground techniques. He chose a couple of moves out of each category to start with, but Parker was recalling the speed of the supernatural caught on her doorbell camera.

"Adam, I really appreciate you taking time out of your day to teach me how to defend myself, but, do I really stand a chance against one of you guys?"

Adam paused for a moment, studying her face. "Honestly, in a fair fight you probably wouldn't stand a chance. Our strength and speed are far greater than yours, however, you have two very important things going for you. One, the supernatural lines underestimate humans and they will underestimate you. Their arrogance will benefit you and give you the upper hand.

"The second thing going for you is the type of training you're undertaking. This isn't boxing, this isn't teaching you how to fight with honour or rules. I am teaching you how to survive, defend yourself at all costs and get away to safety."

Parker nodded, "Fair enough, thank you, Adam."

He smiled down at her, "No problem." Parker felt determination flow through her, which brought with it an extra boost of energy. She kicked harder than ever before and threw everything she had at Adam. He was impressed with her display as they continued. Adam then ran through a scenario where he was the attacker, allowing her to practice the moves as if someone was trying to attack her.

She backed off, not letting him get too close. When he kept coming at her and tried to strike with his hand towards her face, she used her right hand to knock his arm, changing the trajectory so it missed. He then regrouped and aimed a kick at her legs. She turned ninety degrees so that the kick slid past her and she used the opportunity to follow through with her own punch whilst he was unprepared. The hit connected and Adam grinned, proud of his student.

Adam provided feedback on her stance and they repeated the role play. He swept her feet out from under her and she tucked her head into her chest, softening the fall by hitting her hands on the mat. This break-fall prevented her head from connecting with the floor.

Parker used her left foot to push her hips off the ground and raised her right foot, kicking Adam in the chest as he began to lean in. She hit him squarely in the chest and he stumbled slightly, it felt like kicking a brick wall. Parker then took the opportunity to scramble away and stand up. She was panting with the exertion.

Parker was really pleased with herself. She was doing far better than she ever believed she could. Adam also seemed happy with her progress. He had her practice more kicks from the ground position. Funnily, he wasn't as keen for her to practice the groin kick on him. She started to struggle as her energy reserves were depleted, she had been through a lot of exertion this morning and it was showing.

"I know that you are getting tired, but this is the most important time for you to continue practising. The people attacking you won't wait for you to be in your peak physical condition. You may be sick, they don't care. I need to ensure that even when you are at your worst, you can still protect yourself." Parker nodded solemnly. They continued practising for a further twenty minutes until he finally took pity on her.

"I'll take you out for lunch, and then we'll continue your training in a different facility," Adam informed her. She had a quick shower and changed out of her workout clothes. Parker followed Adam down to the car park. She proceeded to her own car with the intention of waiting for Adam to collect his and then she would follow him. He arrived a few minutes later, driving the Bentley she saw outside Damon's.

Parker mused that the guys must have their own private parking, as she would have noticed a Bentley in their car park. He was easy to follow, he indicated early when making a turn and ensured that there was enough space for them to both pull out before proceeding.

He took her to a small, family-run pizza restaurant. Adam ordered a ham and pineapple pizza along with two, three-cheese pizzas. Parker decided on the chicken and sweetcorn option. They ate in companionable silence, the waitress kept checking if they needed anything. However, she was only interested in Adam's response.

She barely glimpsed at Parker but Adam appeared to be oblivious to her flirting. Parker was always surprised by the audacity of some people. They weren't a couple but the waitress didn't know that. Adam paid the bill and they continued on to the afternoon's excitement.

He turned through a five-bar gate and onto a large piece of land, surrounded by barbed wire fences and security cameras. They drove up to a large metal barn and pulled up outside. Parker looked at Adam for guidance, "We thought you might like to switch up your training and have a bit of fun. I am teaching you evasive driving this afternoon. You are mainly alone whilst travelling, so this could be a potential weak point. It is both fun and practical." Parker beamed; she was excited to start.

Adam led her inside the building, it looked like a giant aeroplane hangar. To the far left there were some old, beat-up cars. There were also giant storage containers on the right, which she couldn't see inside. He headed straight for the cars, "Alright, pick one and I will take you around our outside course." Parker perused the cars, before picking a bright yellow Volkswagen Beetle, thinking of Ellie's. He had opened the side door, at the far end of the building.

Adam began in the driver's seat and drove through the side door, out into a training area. He started with an open section of track and demonstrated a J-Turn. This allowed her to quickly change direction if someone was blocking the road. Once he had performed the manoeuvre a couple of times, they swapped seats.

Parker had been observing his every move and was eager

to give it a go. It didn't work the first few times and she ended up on the grass. Adam was patient and they kept trying until she performed it correctly. Parker beamed a giant smile the first time she managed it, then proceeded to repeat it several more times until Adam was confident that she could perform it in a high-stress situation.

Parker stayed in the driver's seat, whilst Adam assessed her ability to drive accurately in reverse. She was able to navigate in reverse competently but then Adam had her doing it at a greater speed. A couple of times she almost flew off the track but mostly kept to the road.

Adam then escalated it further, playing rock music at full blast through the radio, setting off an alarm on his phone and shouting random things at her. Parker's number of mistakes grew exponentially and she almost rolled the car. Adam had proven his point; she would need to ensure that all these new techniques were second nature to her, so she could complete them from muscle memory alone and remain calm in any stressful situation.

Next, she had to manoeuvre around cones on the track that Adam had laid out, whilst maintaining a set speed. She hit a couple on her first attempt. Then when she improved, he raised the speed. When Parker managed to master the faster speed with the current set of cones, he moved them.

Adam was very supportive but pushed her to explore her limits. He told her that she should learn how to break through a barricade and taught her where to align your car for the most impact. Parker thought that it was great fun, partly because it wasn't her car that she was crashing.

He explained that they were going to play a game of cat and mouse, he was going to switch vehicles and try to tag her. As Adam revved his car behind her, Parker's heart began to race. She pushed the accelerator to the floor and sped off. She wanted to last as long as possible. Parker saw Adam's vehicle leave the starting line and the chase was on. Her adrenaline was causing her to push the car faster than she had previously. The Beetle squealed around the first corner and she flew through the cone course.

He was beginning to gain on her but she didn't let it psyche her out. Parker concentrated on navigating the course but within a short space of time, Adam's car tapped her bumper lightly. She pulled over, "That was so exhilarating, my heart is pounding!" She excitedly told Adam.

He smiled at her, "You were doing brilliantly, want to go again?" Parker grinned and leapt back in the car. They made their way back to the starting line and she set off. Her aim was to make it further than last time before he tagged her car.

She pushed the car as fast as it would go, it was clearly unhappy and began to sound like it was ingesting itself. Parker was ecstatic as she had gained a good distance on Adam, it was probably due to him having a slower car. She didn't care and pushed it faster and faster.

Parker hit a sharp corner and the whole car lost its grip on the track. She hurtled to the left and the car started to roll. Parker felt like she was in a washing machine, flipping over and over. When it finally stopped, she took a second to get her bearings.

The car had fallen a short distance down a slope and the driver's door wedged against a tree. The Beetle was crumpled at the front. She was desperate to get out and began to panic. She crawled over to the passenger seat and shoved at the passenger door with all her might, it flew open.

Parker crawled out the door and slumped on the grass nearby, gulping in fresh air and safety. Adam's head popped up from over the top of the slope and he scrambled down to her before she could blink. His face was etched with concern, scanning her from head to toe, "I'm so sorry Parker, I shouldn't have pushed you this far. You were just doing so well that I thought you would be fine."

Parker was still shaking and trying to get her breath but she gave him a wobbly smile, "I'm fine, nothing is broken, besides my pride. I probably just have a couple of small bruises." Adam made a quick phone call, then stood to look at the car. He spent a long time looking at the passenger door. Parker decided to lie down on the grass, she was still feeling shaky but surprised at the lack of pain she currently felt. Especially when she saw the state of the car she had just exited.

Approximately ten minutes later Adam called out, "We're here!" After about a minute, she heard someone approaching and a face appeared over her.

"Are you alright? Are you hurt? Can you move? Do you need us to call an ambulance?" Damon hurriedly asked with a concerned look on his face. He reached out to take her hand as he knelt next to her.

Parker smiled up at him and used his hand to help her sit up. "It's ok, I'm fine. I was lucky, I'm a little stiff, but nothing worse than I've felt after one of Adam's sparring sessions." And she smiled across at Adam, wanting him to know that she didn't blame him.

At the mention of Adam's name, Damon's face darkened, "You are supposed to be teaching her how to protect herself, not putting her in danger."

Adam bowed his head and looked at the floor like a scolded schoolboy, "Sorry, Damon."

Parker couldn't stand it, "Don't have a go at Adam, he did nothing wrong. I chose to push myself beyond my limits. I appreciate your concern Damon but please don't blame Adam. If you're angry with him, you have to be angry with me too." And she took Damon's hand, squeezing it a little to reassure him that she was genuinely alright. His face softened once again as he looked at her. Damon nodded once to confirm that he had heard her.

Adam called over to them, "Damon, you need to see this." Damon rose and walked over to the car. Parker couldn't hear their conversation but could see that Adam was explaining something to him. She decided that it wasn't worth the effort to stand up, to find out what they were discussing.

Eventually, they walked back over to where Parker was sitting. "It's annoying as I was doing so well, I had left Adam in the dust," Parker said, grinning at the two men.

Damon rolled his eyes whilst smiling, before asking, "Do you need me to carry you to my car?" Parker felt a spurt of energy as she leapt up faster than she believed possible. There was no way she was going to let him carry her, again. Although, her body then immediately screamed at her, the muscles in her back and legs hurt. With the adrenaline reducing, the muscle pain was beginning to set in, with a vengeance.

They both noticed her wince and frowned at each other, "Let's just take it slowly then. I'll drive you home, Adam will make sure your car gets returned." Parker was happy to let them take care of her and it felt like hours until they reached Damon's car. She sighed in relief, as she finally sat in the passenger seat.

Even lifting her feet was uncomfortable, so Damon helped to manoeuvre her into the car and shut the door. The car was incredibly comfortable with a cream leather interior. She had to admit that she was slightly jealous.

Damon climbed into the driver's side and pulled away slowly. Parker felt every lump and bump in the road. She couldn't wait to take some painkillers and go to bed when she got home. "Other than the accident, how have you been getting on today?" Damon enquired, hoping to distract her from the discomfort.

"I think it's been a good day. I can definitely tell I'm improving, I just hope that I'm meeting your expectations."

"Yes, we're all really impressed with your dedication. No one expected you to be an instant expert at everything. Things take time, we have all been there."

"Well, they are great teachers."

"I just want to check one final time before I take you home, do you need medical assistance?"

"No, I promise. I'm not seeing double, no headache. It's just my body that aches all over but I'm happy with that. I saw the car, I'm lucky that I just have a couple of extra bruises. Please don't blame Adam, he has been so wonderful to me that I couldn't bear it if you were angry with him."

"Don't worry, I don't need to be angry with him. He is blaming himself enough right now."

When they finally arrived at Parker's house, Damon jumped out and strode around to the passenger door to help her out of the car. Parker had a moment of thinking he was being extremely chivalrous before a wince of pain snapped her out of it. He opened her front door and led her inside. She directed him to her bathroom medicine cabinet, where her painkillers were kept. He left the room for five minutes before returning with a glass of water and tablets.

She thanked him and took them both. "I have set a hot bath running, you should really soak before bed." A bath sounded wonderful. He helped her upstairs and she paused as she reached her bedroom. How was she going to manage getting undressed and into the bath?

"Maybe I don't need a bath. A good night's sleep will probably be as good."

Damon chuckled as he identified her concern, "I will help you but I will be a complete gentleman. If it makes you more comfortable, I will keep my eyes closed the entire time." Parker considered his offer, her body ached so much that she was willing to try anything. She finally agreed to his terms, he had already filled the bath with hot water and bubbles after all.

"Eyes shut time," she instructed Damon. He was trying to hide his smile but obediently closed them. He knelt in front of her and removed her shoes and socks first. He slowly trailed his hands up the outside of her legs, she froze and held her breath.

Damon moved his fingers along the waist of her jeans and popped open the button, before lowering the zip. He gently pulled down the jeans from her hips and helped her to step out of them. Parker was grateful that his eyes were shut, as she was enjoying this far more than she felt she should.

He stood and unbuttoned her shirt, carefully not touching her skin any more than necessary. He didn't want to take advantage of her vulnerable state. Damon slipped the shirt down her arms and it fell to the floor. He placed his hands on her shoulders, stepped closer and trailed his hands down her back to the bra clasp.

Parker kept her gaze on his face the entire time, it was a unique opportunity to really examine him up close. As his hands caressed her back, she saw beautifully thick eyelashes and a powerful jaw. Her gaze paused on his lips, they looked soft and inviting, parted slightly in concentration. She had to restrain herself from leaning into him.

Her clasp popped open, and her bra fell away, leaving her chest bare. She shivered in response, once again being grateful that his eyes were closed. He moved down to her black lace briefs, hooking his fingers on each side and sliding them down to the floor. She could feel his breath on her stomach and it gave her goosebumps as she tried not to visibly shiver again.

He helped her lift each foot to fully remove her knickers. Parker stood very still as he knelt in front of her, barely breathing. Damon paused; the moment seemed to last an eternity and yet all too brief for each of them. Ripping them both out of their longing, he suddenly stood and led her to the bath.

Damon had to use every ounce of his self-restraint, the temptation to open his eyes or embrace her was all-consuming. Having his eyes shut enhanced his other senses, he could smell her skin as he knelt in front of her. He could hear her intake of breath as he touched a sensitive area. But he couldn't let the first time he truly touched her to be when she was injured and vulnerable.

He guided her to the bath, checking that she was safely lowered before leaving the room. Speaking to the door, he said, "I'm going to sit on the other side of the door and check on you periodically. I want to ensure that you don't have a concussion but I will leave you in peace to relax." Parker's response was a barely audible sigh as she smiled and reclined in the bath, the heat of the water felt amazing on her battered body.

Closing her eyes, she tried to empty her thoughts. She almost drifted off when she heard, "Are you still alright?"

Parker smiled, "Yes, it feels wonderful in here. I'm so glad that you convinced me to take a bath."

"I've been in your position once or twice before, often following a spar with Leo. Is the water still warm enough for you?"

"Yes, thank you. I will want to get out in the next ten minutes if that's alright with you?"

"Of course, just let me know and I will grab you a towel."

"I will, can you please also grab me a night dress? It's probably the easiest item of clothing to wear." Parker was cursing the old cotton night dress in her drawer but she hadn't expected Damon to see it.

As the water started to cool she called Damon into the room, reminding him to shut his eyes. He entered holding a large bath towel. Parker had already released the plug to drain the water with her toes. Damon placed the towel on the side next to the sink and helped her to stand.

He then wrapped her gently in the towel and lifted her out of the bath. Damon helped to dry her, moved her into the bedroom and slipped the nightdress over her head. As soon as the nightgown had covered her, he opened his eyes. Damon tucked Parker into her bed, raising the sheets under her arms.

Parker thanked Damon again. The bath helped but she was still extremely stiff and it hurt to move. He checked his phone and left the room for a few minutes; she heard a doorbell alert on her phone. Damon then returned with a selection of food dishes. He scattered them across the bed, he seemed to have bought something from every cuisine.

She saw a meat feast pizza, noodles, fried chicken, fries, tacos, a cheeseburger, jerk chicken and samosas. Parker immediately began to laugh, "How many people have you invited into my bedroom for dinner?"

"I wasn't sure what you liked and I didn't want to disturb you whilst you were relaxing, so I arranged for the full selection. Besides, I'm sure the two of us can work through this." Damon grinned.

Parker immediately reached for the jerk chicken, it was

one of her favourites, even though she often struggled with the spice level. She also pulled the fries next to her. Damon grabbed the pizza and tacos. They ate in companionable silence for a short time, she was getting incredibly full so she sat back on the bed.

"There is something that I need to discuss with you." Damon started. Parker tensed anticipating bad news. "It's not bad news but I didn't want you bombarded straight after the accident. Do you remember opening the passenger car door?"

"Yes, my door was blocked. I felt trapped and wanted to get out, so I pushed as hard as I could until it opened. Why?"

"The entire frame of the door deformed where you pushed it open. Your powers are beginning to show. Our theory is that they manifest when you need them most. We were born with our abilities so they come naturally to us. You will need to learn to wield them at will."

Parker nodded, "I'll do whatever is required."

"We can continue this discussion another day. Tonight, you need to rest. I just wanted to make sure that you knew what had happened."

Damon wanted to distract her for now, to allow her to focus on healing. He retrieved a brown bag hidden out of sight on the floor. From it, he drew out a chocolate brownie. "Too full for a brownie?" He asked playfully.

"There's no such thing as too full for a brownie." And she reached for it. Damon gave it up immediately, fearing her wrath if denied.

It tasted amazing and Parker sighed appreciatively. Damon chuckled at her pleasure in such a simple item. He continued eating the food on the bed, surprisingly for Parker, the noodles were the only item remaining. Damon cleared the empty wrappers away and put the noodles in the fridge.

The painkillers were finally starting to kick in and Parker began to get drowsy. Damon softly said, "If it's alright with you, I'll sleep in your spare room tonight. That way if you need anything, you can just shout for me." She was too tired to protest and snuggled under the sheets, not even waiting for Damon to leave the room. Which meant that she didn't realise that he sat peacefully for a while, watching her as she slept.

Early the following morning, Damon gently woke Parker, "I have to leave for an important meeting but I have left some more painkillers and water on the table next to you. Rest, there's no training scheduled and I will check in on you later." Parker had barely woken to acknowledge his statement, before turning over and falling back asleep again.

CHAPTER 13

Parker was still slightly stiff when she woke but felt significantly better than the night before. She checked the time; it was nearly midday and the sun was streaming past the blinds. Parker decided that she had earned the right to get up slowly. There was no point in rushing as she wasn't expected anywhere. She shuffled into the shower, the extra heat would help chase away any lingering aches.

After showering and blow-drying her hair, Parker pulled on her jeans and a black T-shirt. She decanted the noodles from the fridge onto a plate and slung them in the microwave. Once warmed, Parker took the noodles, sat in an armchair and watched daytime television as she ate. She was surprised at how good the noodles tasted and made a mental note to ask Damon where they were from.

Midway through the morning, she noticed a voicemail on her phone. Parker was vaguely surprised that she hadn't heard her phone ring but this thought was clouded as soon as she heard Ellie's voice, *'Hey Parker. Sorry to disturb you, but can you come and collect me from Richmond? My car broke down and I'm scared of being here alone. My phone's battery is flat, so I'm calling you from a payphone.'* She stood up as quickly as she was able.

Parker began to worry and searched online for Richmond, she identified a small group of houses a few miles away. She grabbed her purse and keys, locked up the house and set off in her car. Parker tried several times to call the payphone number back. The call wasn't going through, which made her drive even faster.

Luckily Richmond was very small, so it should be easy for

Parker to find the payphone. The whole place was eerily empty, so there was no one around to ask for directions. It took her about five minutes of searching when she spotted it. On a bench near to the payphone sat Ellie, with her face in her hands. Parker pulled up nearby but Ellie didn't look up. She left the car and began to walk closer.

Parker called her name a couple of times but received no response. Her entire body was screaming at her that something was wrong and she stopped in her tracks. At first, she thought that she was just concerned for Ellie but then the feeling intensified. Ellie lifted her face and removed her hands. It wasn't Ellie. Parker's heart raced. Realising her mistake, she took an instinctive step backwards.

A hand touched her on the shoulder and Adam's training rushed into her head. She spun, knocking his hand away and without flinching, kneed him in the groin. The man fell to the ground groaning. Parker used the pause to assess her surroundings. Seemingly out of nowhere, there were now five bearing down on Parker, including the fake Ellie and the one writhing on the ground.

She was surrounded and in front of her stood Deimos, "Hello Kate, or should I say Parker?" He said in a cheery tone as if they were old friends. He didn't even acknowledge the man still lying on the floor. Parker felt a flash of pride at how she had effectively incapacitated him. The three men were all wearing black suits, the only difference was that the henchmen were wearing white shirts and Deimos' was black.

"What do you want?" Parker asked in an emotionless tone, she hated playing games.

"I just want to spend some time with you. I haven't had a chance, with Damon and his minions slobbering over you."

"Well thank you for thinking that I'm worth spending time with but I really should get going now." And she motioned to side-step.

"I really must insist that you accept my offer. I want to show you my side of things. It's only fair." He then indicated to two of his men to flank her, Parker was resigned to going with him. There were too many of them and they were faster than her if she tried to run. Too strong for her if she tried to fight back and she didn't want to face what was coming injured.

Parker was guided to a black car with blacked-out rear windows. They took her bag, phone and keys, then forced her into the middle rear seat. She was sandwiched between two men, one being the man she had kneed. Deimos took the passenger side front and another man drove.

She didn't know what had happened to the fake Ellie but Parker wished severe period cramps on her, every day for the rest of her life. Deimos turned in his seat to face Parker and spoke, still maintaining the friendly persona, "I am really sorry about the subterfuge. I know that you are close to Ellie, but we didn't want to risk harming her. Our little Rebecca has always been great at imitation."

Parker now had the name of the evil little witch who tricked her. She also heard the implied threat to Ellie in his voice. She sat in silence, gathering her thoughts and trying to think of how to get out of this.

Deimos became bored with her lack of response and turned back to face the road. They drove through unfamiliar towns. She kept making mental notes of the road signs, hoping that she would be able to use the information.

She began to fiddle with her bracelet, suddenly realising that she could use it to get help. Parker checked that no one was watching her, before pressing the beads together for over ten seconds. This was one time when she wasn't going to take any chances.

A minute later, Deimos retrieved his phone out of his back pocket and appeared to be messaging someone. He turned to the side and looked at Parker regretfully, "I'm disappointed in you Parker, please hand over all of your jewellery." She paused for a second, but she knew that she didn't have a choice and slowly removed it.

She was trying to delay it for as long as possible,

pretending to struggle to release the clasp. Parker then handed the jewellery to the henchman on her left, he proceeded to throw it out of the car window. She felt slightly deflated at the thought of the jewellery lying useless at the edge of the road but at least they knew that she was in trouble.

Damon was right, they had a mole in the company. Parker made a mental note to tell Damon what had happened, it may help him to narrow down the search. She thought back to the individuals in the IT department, there was a high probability that it was one of them.

They were driving further away from the residential and built-up areas, out into the countryside. They drove up a single-track dirt road, to an open field with an aeroplane hangar in the centre. There was a runway to the left and to the right was a helicopter. Her stomach sank.

They drove towards the helicopter and pulled up nearby. They all exited the car and Parker followed obediently. She knew that she had no other choice but to play along for now. Parker was trying to remember as many details about her journey as possible.

The helicopter was jet black and had sliding doors, Deimos climbed up the steps first. The pilot was already onboard and Parker followed between two henchmen. The steps automatically retracted and Parker took a second to look around.

There were six seats in total for passengers, two rows of three seats, facing each other. They were made of light brown leather, with dark brown seatbelts that she was strapped into. Deimos sat facing forward, Parker sat between the two men facing Deimos.

"I'm sorry, Parker," said Deimos with not even a trace of sorrow in his voice, "But I need to take precautions. Please put this on." And he handed her a blindfold, it was extremely soft and not uncomfortable. As she slipped it over her eyes, she tried to think positively. She wouldn't be able to see where they were going but she could estimate a length of time.

Parker heard a mumbling between the men and a couple

of minutes later, she felt a scratch on her neck. She raised her hand but didn't feel anything. Her hand and head suddenly felt very heavy. She shook her head, to try and clear the fuzzy feeling. Parker realised that the scratch must have been an injection, she didn't have the time to feel anger before she passed out.

Parker stretched out her arms above her head and rolled onto her side before pulling the sheets up higher. She still felt drowsy and didn't want to train today. It took another couple of minutes before she regained her senses and sat bolt upright in the bed.

This was not her room. The cover and sheets were pure white, spread out across a vast four-poster bed. She cursed Deimos for drugging her but she wasn't surprised that he would resort to this sort of tactic. She had the briefest inkling that it wasn't planned, given the largely pointless blindfold but she didn't dwell on the thought. Before jumping out of bed, Parker wanted to take stock of her surroundings.

The room was very minimal; there was a small table with a vase of flowers on top, and a wooden wardrobe sat in the far corner, next to a partially opened door. It was the second door leading off the room and it appeared to lead to a bathroom. The pleasant floral aroma and vibrant flowers were in contrast to the coldness of the room.

Parker concluded that the shut door was her way out. The whole room was decorated in various shades of white. Parker suddenly panicked and lifted the sheets, she let out a sigh of relief as she was still in her own clothes. The only items missing were her shoes and jewellery.

She clambered out of the bed and walked towards the window. There was a large open lawn to the rear. The building seemed very old and she mused that she could be in a castle. Unfortunately, that didn't narrow down her location, as they weren't unique to any one area.

Parker didn't expect to see anything in the wardrobe but opened it anyway out of curiosity. He had been planning this, as she saw a range of clothing in her size, including underwear. Parker also put this out of her mind, as it began to creep her out.

She proceeded to the bathroom, she hoped that there was something in there that she could use. There wasn't. It didn't even have a glass mirror, instead, there was a silver film on the wall for her to view her reflection. The barest of essentials were left next to the sink. Parker tried to see if there were any cameras before she used the facilities, but sometimes you didn't have a choice.

Parker heard a knock at the bedroom door moments before a key was inserted in the lock and opened. She exited the bathroom and faced the man that she had kneed in the groin. He didn't look pleased to be there but delivered the message that Deimos was awaiting her presence and to follow him.

Parker wanted to know what the rest of the building looked like, so followed without protest. She was right, it was a castle. Tapestries hung on the walls and Parker took her time walking in order to study them. She was looking for clues as to her whereabouts, but alas couldn't find anything obvious. Parker walked along the corridor after the man, they then descended a beautiful flight of stone stairs with an ornate bannister.

He led her to a large wooden door and pushed it open, ushering her inside. She stepped through and saw a large table, it could have easily fit sixteen large people. Deimos sat at one end and gestured for her to sit at the other, where a place had been set.

Parker's stomach began to rumble. She decided that there was no point in weakening herself by not eating and took her seat at the table. When Deimos spoke, he didn't raise his voice, the room's acoustics helped it to travel. "I should probably apologise for drugging you but I wanted to take every precaution possible. So, you can't really blame me." And he attempted a friendly smile.

Unfortunately, when someone has kidnapped and drugged you, a friendly smile doesn't quite cut it as an apology. "Should I be on the lookout for additional drugging attempts?"

"Oh no my dear, there is no need for drugs now. You won't be able to leave until I allow it." Parker didn't feel like his statement warranted a response, denying it or becoming angry wouldn't help the situation.

Several people entered the room and hustled about their roles in efficient silence. One placed a starter in front of her, another lit a candelabra in the centre of the table. She glanced at her plate, it was goats' cheese on ciabatta with chopped hazelnuts. One server poured her a glass of white wine and another placed a glass of water on the table. Parker waited for Deimos to begin eating and then followed suit. Eating was preferable to talking to him. Yet, she was hoping to find out his motives. Why did he want her?

After they both finished and the plates had been cleared, there was an awkward silence before the next dish. Parker, who would have enjoyed the starter if not for the company, opted to fill the silence. "Why am I here?"

"I told you. I want to spend time with you. I feel like Damon and his minions have been brainwashing you, persuading you that their way is the only and righteous way. I want an opportunity to show you my way, that's only fair."

Parker thought that he sounded like a spoiled child but as he hadn't physically hurt her yet, she wasn't going to antagonise him. After all, he could talk as much as he liked. It would help her to bide her time until Damon saved her. Parker was convinced that he would come for her.

The main course was placed in front of them, it looked amazing. Sliced lamb loin with rosemary and a lemon and herb risotto. Once again, she waited for Deimos to start eating as she didn't want him watching her.

She really enjoyed the meal, forgetting for a moment the man who sat across from her. His chef really was brilliant. Parker decided that she might as well enjoy the good food whilst she could. Who knew when he was going to turn and Parker already had the impression that Deimos wasn't a stable or rational man.

"Do you like your room? It has one of the best views over

the lawn. I'm hoping you enjoy your stay here."

"The room is pleasant and I appreciate the view. It's difficult to truly relax in a place where you are being held hostage."

"I sincerely hope that in time, you won't feel like you are a hostage and instead will choose to stay here." He was smiling at her in an overly familiar way and Parker thought that he must be delusional. Why would she ever want to stay with someone who stalked, kidnapped and drugged her? But she merely gave a non-committal shrug.

The plates were cleared again and a glass of ice wine was placed in front of her. The final course was French, raspberry macarons. They paired with the wine perfectly. She had been secretly dreading that a brownie would be placed down in front of her, afraid that it would mar her memory of Damon's sweet gesture.

They once again ate in silence. Deimos also clearly enjoyed the meal. She was surprised that his portion sizes matched her own. She pondered the reason for this, as the other minotaurs she had met could easily eat three times that amount. Parker deduced that it could be another game he was playing, pretending to be just like her and distancing himself further from Damon and the others.

"If you are feeling up to it, I would like you to join me for a drink in the drawing room." He stood, not waiting for an answer. Parker was still feeling the effects of the drug and she just wanted to sleep but she got the impression that joining him wasn't optional. Parker stood and followed Deimos, she wasn't quite sure what a drawing room was and assumed that it was a castle thing.

She realised as she followed him that they were walking into a living room. There were two double sofas facing each other, flanking a roaring fireplace. Parker waited for Deimos to sit before choosing the opposite sofa, he smirked but remained seated.

He sat watching her for a few minutes until a woman

brought in two crystal glasses with a brown liquid and set one in front of each of them. Deimos took a slow appreciative sip before starting, "Leander and I were close brothers, only a couple of years apart. It's a rare thing for a minotaur to produce more than one son. I'm not sure if you're aware but a minotaur usually can only have male offspring. My brother and I are the only current case that I am aware of where a minotaur had two children."

Parker hadn't known this and Deimos read that from her face, "As I told you before, they haven't told you everything. I can fill in those gaps for you." He appeared to be waiting for Parker to react but continued when he didn't get the response he desired.

"We grew up together and had a great life. It all changed when our parents were killed by humans. They were caught up in an armed robbery. They could have saved themselves but chose to keep our secret instead. Their final act was to protect supernaturals from humans. They shouldn't have had to make that choice. If we weren't in hiding, they would still be alive today. If humans understood our capabilities and feared us more, my parents would still be here today."

Parker felt like Deimos had reconciled this in his mind numerous times. It felt like he was trying to elicit her sympathy and understanding. However, she could feel his hatred of humans shining through.

"After their death, Leander didn't react the same way I did. He still believed that we needed to be hidden from humans. He mourned our parents but he didn't feel my anger. We couldn't relate to each other anymore and worked on our own separate goals. We both developed a network of followers who believe in our causes and Leander passed this down to his son. Unfortunately, they have managed to brainwash people. Encouraging the belief that secrecy is a necessity, with the threat of being destroyed if exposed."

Deimos paused for dramatic effect. "I believe that we are vastly superior in every way to humans. We are smarter, faster, stronger and have abilities humans can only dream of. I believe that our fear of humans is keeping us suppressed. Our abilities are dwindling because we aren't embracing our true selves. You are part of this now. You can help us to achieve our potential and fulfil the prophecy. I need you on our side."

Parker didn't want to risk encouraging him but couldn't help but ask, "Why haven't you exposed your powers to humans then? You clearly have your own followers, what's stopping you from just doing it?"

He smiled at her engagement, "I want to. I want to announce to the world that we exist and are ready to rule. However, I need greater numbers for it to work. If Damon's followers don't stand with me, we could be wiped out as the humans far outnumber us. My calculations support my theory that if we can get the majority of supernaturals to support us, we will rule within a year."

Parker believed that Deimos had forgotten that she was human. Due to her role in the prophecy, he had clearly chosen to label her as a supernatural. She didn't know what to say, so kept silent. Deimos was studying her face, "I know that I have given you a lot of information, so I will let you retire for the evening. Think about what I have said."

He then nodded at someone behind her and a man appeared at her side. Parker felt dismissed and rose from the seat. Following the henchman out of the room, without glimpsing back. Her drink still sat on the table untouched.

She entered the bedroom and heard the door shut and lock behind her. The drugs still in her system were causing her eyes to droop as soon as she saw the bed. Parker checked the wardrobe for nightwear, there were silky night dresses and lacey camisoles and short sets.

She didn't feel comfortable being that exposed, so she searched for a more comfortable option. She settled on a pair of black leggings and a long cotton T-shirt. Parker wanted a shower but couldn't allow herself to be that vulnerable. There was no chair to wedge under the door handle.

Parker looked out of the window again, trying to see something in the distance that would give her a location clue.

She was hoping to see the lights from a Church or building but total darkness greeted her. There were lights strategically placed around the garden but there was nothing beyond.

Parker knew that an escape was a long shot but she had to try, she wasn't going to give up yet. She was focusing on the fact that she hadn't been hurt and he was trying to win her over with amazing food.

She climbed into the bed. There was a draft so she pulled up the sheets. Parker was thinking over what Deimos had told her. He was obviously hoping that by providing her the details of his parent's death she would soften to him. She understood the anger as it was natural to want to blame someone, but he had twisted it into hatred instead of allowing himself to heal.

His conviction and hatred of humans scared her. She would never want someone like him in a position of power. Parker had dated someone in her past who was an expert in manipulation. He twisted situations to control her and made her feel guilty. She had learnt from her experience and vowed never to let it happen again.

One positive that emerged from the toxic relationship, was that she was more adept at deciphering agendas. She could read Deimos easily; he was trying to provide her with extra information and details about supernaturals so she doubted Damon's openness. However, she wasn't that easy to manipulate.

She lay in bed, listening to the sounds of the night. Footsteps were heard along the corridor. Parker tensed, concerned they would enter. As they continued past she wondered who else had a bedroom on this corridor, was Deimos in the room next to her?

She was wracking her brain trying to think of ways to escape. They started out quite comically, she would hide under the bed, waiting for the door to open. A henchman would enter and believe she was missing. Parker would then slip out the door unseen and exit through another bedroom, which conveniently had a sturdy trellis under the window. This would end in her commando rolling behind bushes until she managed to escape.

Parker chuckled to herself, she had always had a fertile imagination. She decided to shelve that plan and would bide her time, thinking of a better idea. Parker was wondering how Damon was going to find her, the SOS from her bracelet would have been sent from a random location.

They would trace the bracelet and she wouldn't be there. Even if they could follow the tracks to the aeroplane hangar, the helicopter couldn't be followed. She was regretting the rule about no implants. It began to grate on her that she was waiting for a man to save her, she hated the idea that she was a damsel in distress.

Parker was amazed that she hadn't fallen asleep yet as she was so tired. She let herself relax into the bed, as she wanted to face the new day energised.

Within seconds of shutting her eyes, she was asleep. She dreamt about Damon; he was searching for her in a hedge maze but every time she thought he was close, he hit a dead end. Parker was calling for him. Each time she called he seemed to be getting further and further away.

She couldn't chase after him, as she was held to the floor with vines. They twirled up her legs, strangling her the more she struggled. Waking up sweating, Parker realised that she had become tangled in the sheets. Parker straightened the bed back out and immediately fell back asleep. She didn't remember the dream in the morning.

CHAPTER 14

Parker woke with a start. Her bed sheets lay in a crumpled heap on the floor. It hadn't been the best night's sleep she had ever had but it wasn't the bed's fault. She felt grimy and decided to have a shower, regardless of there being no guarantee of privacy. After moving the vase off the table onto the floor, she placed the table in front of the door. It wouldn't stop anyone from entering but hopefully, it would give her fair warning if they did.

The shower had poor water pressure and it caused her to spend longer than she would have liked getting clean. She wrapped a towel around herself and hurriedly dressed. The clothes all felt familiar and she tossed on another pair of jeans, twinned with a red shirt. Parker walked over to the window. There was a small window seat which she chose to sit on. It was a beautiful day and she could see people walking around the grounds. Parker spent what seemed like hours sitting there, just watching people coming and going.

A knock sounded at the door and it opened before Parker could reply. She turned her head in order to see the visitor enter. A thug she hadn't met before entered and careered straight into the side table. Parker took great pleasure in watching him stumble over and then try to regain composure. Besides the embarrassed red cheeks, he was entirely nondescript and she would have struggled to pull him from a line-up with the others. "Deimos has urgent business to attend this morning, so he has kindly arranged for you to spend time enjoying the garden. He wanted me to remind you that you will be constantly monitored, so there's no point in attempting an escape."

Parker jumped up out of the seat. Just because someone told her that attempting to escape was pointless, didn't mean she was going to accept defeat at face value. Parker was still going to seize the opportunity and survey any possible escape routes.

They left the room and once again, Parker followed a henchman along the corridor and down the stairs. He turned and walked through the large entrance hall. They proceeded down a corridor and through a large wooden door, which opened to the outside. He returned her shoes, which she quickly slipped on.

Parker instantly felt better being outside in the fresh air. "You can wander anywhere within the walls. If you even think about escaping, it won't end well for you." She rolled her eyes and walked into the garden without dignifying him with an answer.

In front of her was a perfectly manicured garden, with symmetrical topiarised hedges on either side. Parker began to walk along the path, through the hedges. Her aim was to get as far away from the castle as possible, at least then she could have the illusion of privacy. She continued following the path, enjoying the feeling of stretching her legs.

Parker decided that if she could find a good spot, she would practise her Yoga. It would be more difficult in jeans but it was better than nothing. The plan was that it would help to keep her calm and centred.

The gardens were extensive, she walked through an arch and came across a path lined with statues. Parker took her time to study them, they all had a Grecian theme. There was a deep arch covered in vines ahead of her. When she emerged through the other side, there was a pond with a wooden bridge crossing it. Parker stood in the middle of the bridge, leaning on the rail and staring into the water. She could see fish swimming around.

Parker spent a while enjoying the tranquillity of the water. She tried to inconspicuously glance around and spot someone watching her, but they were either good at not being seen, or not there. As she hadn't yet come to the end of the grounds, she continued to explore.

This area appeared to be more natural, as the path meandered into a woodland area. After a few minutes of walking, she spotted a good area to practice her Yoga. When Damon finally rescued her, or she escaped, she could tell the guys that she had kept up with her training. Parker felt more in tune with nature in these surroundings and she performed almost all the poses perfectly.

Following her Yoga, she continued on her walk. Realising that she had completely forgotten to have breakfast, she made a fortunate turn and found herself in an orchard. She was in luck, there were still apples on the trees and Parker picked one. This would have been a wonderful weekend away, if not for the circumstances. The apple was perfectly ripe and she was trying to spot whether there were any other fruit trees.

There was a wall to her right as she walked. It was starting to get a little warm but there was adequate shade. She hadn't noticed any weaknesses in the wall. Parker made sure that she didn't look at it too long, as she didn't want her walk cut short.

A few minutes later she came across some ruins, Parker excitedly began exploring them. She was interested in learning what the building might have been. She started imagining what it used to be and concluded that it was probably a chapel or some sort of outbuilding. Parker made a mental note to ask Deimos about the castle's history.

As she began thinking about the castle, she turned to face it. Parker begrudgingly admitted that it was probably time to return. The castle was a faded white and more modern than the interior indicated. The roof was dark grey and on one side were two pointed turrets. It looked tired but still beautiful. A female came walking towards Parker, so she paused. She was wearing the female version of the male's attire, a black suit and white shirt.

"Deimos has requested your company for lunch, he will

expect you in the dining room in ten minutes." She then turned and stomped back to the castle, not waiting for Parker. Whilst she walked back, she was pondering whether she should try and befriend one of the henchmen or women. The idea didn't hold much promise, as none of them wanted to acknowledge her.

As she walked to the door, it opened, and a henchman guided her to the dining room. She was guided to the same seat as the previous evening. Parker was studying the room while waiting. Previously, when Deimos was sitting across from her, she didn't have an opportunity to take it all in. There were paintings of countryside views along the walls and underfoot was an enormous, dark red rug, with repeating patterns in a border around the edge.

Deimos entered her side view and sat across from her at the table, "I hope that you enjoyed your morning walk around my gardens. Have you had an opportunity to think about what I told you?"

"I loved the walk. Your gardens are very impressive. I found the ruins by the far wall. Do you know what they used to be?"

Deimos looked unimpressed that she was more interested in the gardens than the important decision she was faced with. "They are the ruins of a chapel I believe." He made it clear from his tone that he wasn't interested in discussing it further.

A woman arrived with lunch; she placed Deimos' down first. The plate held a bacon, tomato and avocado open sandwich. They ate in silence. Parker finished several awkward minutes after Deimos. "In case you are still holding out hope, I just want you to know that Damon isn't going to save you. They are running about like headless chickens. They have no idea where you are." Parker sat in silence, there was nothing for her to say.

He was intently studying her face, her lack of reaction was getting him more riled up. "Don't you know how important it is that the prophecy is fulfilled? I am the only one who truly understands what is at stake. I can lead us to a future where we prosper and thrive. Haven't I treated you well? You could be by my side whilst I rule." His voice was rising as he uttered each word.

Parker wasn't sure how to handle this, she wasn't going to be able to lie convincingly. He wanted her decision, and she wasn't going to do anything to aid this megalomaniac in his cause. She took a breath and told him the truth, "Your hatred scares me and I won't support your vision in any way. It is wrong to rule by force. I don't believe that anyone is superior to anyone else, we all have things to contribute. Your parents' death was a tragedy, but you need to let go of your anger."

Deimos was looking down at the table as she spoke. When his face rose, she saw a cold and cruel monster staring back at her, "I tried to be nice. I tried to make you understand. Everything that happens to you now, is a result of your choice."

A thug roughly grabbed her arm and forced her to stand, she hadn't even heard him approach. He marched her out of the room, gripping her arm tightly. Determined to not show fear or give him the satisfaction of her struggling, she did not resist. She was still hoping that he underestimated her and that there might be an opportunity.

Parker was taken through a door, led down stone steps and into a dungeon. There were numerous cells and she was taken to one at the far side. She was roughly shoved inside and the door slammed behind her. It was colder than the rest of the castle.

Parker inspected the room. There was a coarse, threadbare blanket dumped in one corner and a bucket in the other. The walls were made of solid stone and there was a tiny window looking up to the sky. It would let in the cold and rain but it was worth it to see the outside. The window made it bearable.

Parker folded the blanket to try and create a bit of padding and sat down on it. She hadn't noticed anyone else in the other cells but wanted to double-check, "Hello? Is there anyone else down here?" She waited several seconds before trying again louder, "Hello?!" Silence met her.

Parker considered her options, she could either have a meltdown and cry, or she could take the opportunity to try and encourage her powers to appear. Still not wanting to admit to being a damsel in distress just yet, she chose the latter and tried to expunge all negativity from her mind.

Before trying to summon her powers, she checked every nook and cranny of the cell for cameras. She didn't want to inadvertently help Deimos, by doing exactly what he wanted of her. She wasn't sure whether telepathy was one of her powers but she thought that would be a good one to start with.

Parker imagined the castle in her mind, every tiny detail that she could remember. She then thought of Damon and wished with everything she had, that she could send him the image. She thought of the castle, then Damon. Imagining her thoughts being pushed into his mind.

After a pause she switched to Ellie, she had a special connection with Parker. Ellie was the one who first had a vision of Parker, so she switched to projecting the vision of the castle to her instead. Parker tried for what seemed like ages, before moving on to her next idea. After all, she wasn't going anywhere for a while. Parker had a moment of frustration. Even though it was the most important item on her agenda, she wouldn't know if it worked until a lot later.

Parker thought about the powers she had already displayed, smell wouldn't help at all. If anything, it would just tease her with the delights that Deimos was enjoying. The strength was too difficult to demonstrate on a small scale, especially with the objects at hand and she didn't want to alert Deimos to her abilities.

She thought about the powers that she was aware of, the harpies' power of conversing with birds would be useful about now. She started focusing on calling birds to the window, imagining as many types of birds as possible. Parker always felt like ravens seemed like an intelligent bird, so she started there.

The only way that Parker could measure the time passing was by the sky through the window, it was starting to get dark.

She asked out loud to no one in particular, "No three-course meal tonight?" And chuckled.

Her positivity and keeping herself busy were working. Her spirits were still high, but she didn't know how long it would last. She wasn't going to be able to sleep yet, so tried calling to ravens in her mind. Parker was glad that no one knew what she was doing, she sounded crazy.

Parker kept trying to communicate with birds for the next hour but nothing appeared at the window. She considered another Yoga session but instead called it a day and tried to get some sleep.

The lack of hygiene options in the room was the worst part of her incarceration and she hated not being able to shower or brush her teeth. She unfolded the blanket and considered her choices. She could fold it in half and sleep on it or lay it over her and lie on the hard floor. Parker decided that lying on it was the better option, as it would limit the cold from the floor.

She angled herself so that she could look out of the window as she lay, wondering what Damon and his team were doing. Parker hoped that he realised there was a mole, based on the jewellery being detected after she activated it. Otherwise, the mole could update Deimos with every move he makes. If that happened, she would never be rescued. However, she knew that Damon's team were really smart, so one of the guys would work it out.

It was surprisingly pleasant lying in the quiet. She started to pick up the sounds from outside, crickets chirping and foxes barking. Parker closed her eyes and pretended that she was camping under the night sky. She lay awake for an indeterminate amount of time, before falling asleep.

A loud noise echoed through the cell and Parker was jerked awake. She sat up and looked around for the source. Deimos stood outside the cell door with a metal bar, he had a cruel smile on his face. "Have you rethought your answer to my offer after spending a night down here? You still have the choice to join me and you can enjoy every luxury I possess."

Parker paused, looked him straight in the eyes and responded, "Yes, I have spent time considering your offer. I am even more certain than before, that someone like you should never be given power."

The smile dropped from his face and he looked at her with disgust, "We will see how you feel after your stomach churns from hunger and your lips crack with thirst." With that parting shot, he turned and left, leaving her alone once again. She was beginning to get a little thirsty, lunch seemed a like very long time ago. Parker was trying not to panic and decided to concentrate on encouraging her powers to emerge.

She held on for as long as she was able but eventually had to use the bucket. Parker spent a very long time trying to call birds in her mind, then decided to stand under the window and call to them as loud as she dared, "Raven, please come to me. If you do, I will give you all the food you could ever want when I leave here." Parker tried variations on the plea, to no avail. She had been at it for a very long time and decided to switch to Yoga, hoping that it would keep her body from seizing up.

The day dragged on, seemingly forever. She couldn't stop the negative thoughts from intruding. What if no one rescued her? What if they simply gave up? What if her powers deserted her and Deimos decided that she was no longer useful? She could put up with uncomfortable conditions but she didn't think she could withstand physical pain.

Parker decided to nap as much as possible. Whilst she was asleep, she could ignore her dry mouth and a rumbling stomach. She lay down and let a single tear cascade down her cheek before she hastily wiped it away. Parker had always been stubborn and she wouldn't let him win.

The day continued with her trying to project her thoughts to Ellie and Damon, trying to call birds and trying to stay positive. Night fell and she was sat against one of the walls, with her knees pulled up to her chest.

Parker was extremely thirsty and uncomfortable; she was

desperate for anything to drink. She feared that if this continued for another day, she would cave to Deimos' demands. Her mind drifted towards water, refreshing and cold. A glass full of water and ice with condensation on the outside. She knew she was torturing herself but she couldn't help it.

Her hand felt wet on the stone floor. Parker glimpsed down, she was sure that she was starting to hallucinate. She wondered whether this was what happened to people lost in the desert, a mirage. She investigated the water and saw a small trickle from one of the bricks, midway up the wall. It then disappeared through a crack at the bottom of the wall.

Parker stared at it for several minutes, before deciding that she had nothing to lose and drank from the water. It was the best thing she had ever tasted. When her thirst was quenched, she sat back happily. Parker began to consider where the water had come from and decided to inspect it further but the water had dried up.

After a few seconds, she grinned happily. It wasn't a power that she had been trying to summon but it was what her body truly needed. She felt an extra burst of optimism and lay down on the blanket to sleep. Parker's dreams were about escaping. She did start to acknowledge that she was especially excited about seeing Damon in particular.

Midway through the night, an annoying noise woke her, it wouldn't stop. She saw a shadow at the window, whilst furiously trying to blink her eyes into focus. Parker stood and walked closer, she saw a jet-black bird. It was trying to fly through the window. Finally, it tucked its wings against its body, lowered its body to the ground and shuffled through. It fluttered down to the floor in front of Parker, she was concerned that someone may see it.

She sat back in the corner with a gap between her and the wall, then draped the blanket over her. This created a space where the bird could sit without being seen. Parker held out her hand towards the bird and he slowly walked closer. He nudged her hand with his head and she gently stroked his feathers.

They looked at each other for a couple of minutes before Parker tried to communicate, "Can you understand me?" The bird cocked its head to one side and she felt a brush against her mind. Parker immediately switched to non-verbal communication and tried to clear her muddled thoughts and open her mind to this bird.

She felt a sense of confusion but an eagerness to help her. Parker focused on images that she thought would guide him. She brought up a clear picture of the castle, the cell in which she was held, a clear image of Rachel and then the Minos Industries' building.

Rachel was a harpy and so would also be able to communicate with the bird. She concentrated on the pictures in sequence several times, before the bird appeared to nod and flew up to the window. He repeated the process of tucking in his wings, lowering himself and shuffling through the window. Then, with one look back at Parker, he was gone.

She prayed that he would be able to find Rachel. It could be a long distance that he would need to travel, but she was feeling very optimistic and proud of herself. Parker was finally gaining control of her powers. She just wished that the guys had focused on the types of powers held by the different supernatural lines.

Parker didn't sleep much the remainder of the night, she was too excited. Every time she heard a slight noise outside her eyes shot open, hoping to see the bird. She knew it wasn't rational, as he was hopefully far away by now. Parker began to feel thirsty and focused on the trickle of water, it appeared after a few minutes. She then relieved herself in the bucket, the lack of food had one positive outcome. Parker only had to use the bucket to relieve her bladder.

Halfway through the morning, she heard a commotion. She sat up and relaxed against the far wall. Parker tried to straighten out her clothes and hair, to make herself look as calm and unfazed as possible. Deimos appeared at the door, he looked down at her and was visibly shocked to see her looking as she did.

He obviously expected her to be severely dehydrated, but she still looked fresh-faced. "Ready to change your mind yet?" He asked in an abrupt tone.

Parker lazily glanced up at him, "No thank you." His face turned red and a flash of crimson darted across his eyes. She was worried about pushing him into doing something stupid out of impulse but there wasn't anything she could do.

Parker just hoped that he would continue to leave her isolated in the cell but it didn't go that way. Deimos stood to the side and a man entered the room. He was tall and slim with a scar running down his face. Parker gritted her teeth, she knew what happened next was going to push her to her limits.

He pulled her up to stand and then slapped her across her face. She glared at him defiantly, he then slapped her again splitting her lip. The second blow stung much more than the first. A third slap landed and it knocked her staggering to the ground.

As she lay on the cold hard floor, he kicked her in her upper left leg four times and finally kicked her in her stomach. Parker had to resist fighting back, as she knew that she would only be hurt worse in retaliation. She curled into the foetal position and kept thinking of the raven.

The blows stopped and after a few seconds, she felt a sharp pain in her arm. They were taking her blood but she couldn't stop them. This continued for a couple of minutes as Parker lay there defenceless, only hearing the rush of blood in her ears. Retreating footsteps echoed, the door was closed and locked. She didn't dare move until she could no longer hear their footsteps.

Parker was in a lot of pain. Her cheek throbbed and she placed it against the cold stone wall for some relief. She had been afraid that in the face of physical pain, she would crumble and she had just proven to herself that she was stronger than she first imagined. Deimos thought that this would break her but it had the opposite effect.

After the wall had finally taken the heat out of her cheek, she stood and walked around the cell slowly. Where he kicked her on the leg, it pulsed with pain. Parker was concerned that it was going to seize up, which she didn't want to happen. She may need to run at a moments notice.

Parker sat in the corner of the room, she didn't like the vulnerability of lying down. She had never been hit before, beyond fights with her sister as a child. At the thought of her family, she hoped that they were unaware of what was happening. She didn't want them to worry, as there was nothing that they could do. Parker started thinking about whether the raven would have made it to Rachel, the benefit was that he could fly in a straight line. However, she had no idea how far that was.

There was no way that she could practice Yoga in her current state, so she tried to manipulate the trickle of water that she could now call on command. It appeared that calling and dismissing the trickle was the only thing that she could do. It wouldn't bend, change in flow or vary in any way. Parker wasn't disheartened as she still appreciated the fresh water.

She wanted a bird to appear so that it could keep her company. No other birds had visited her, no matter how hard she tried. Parker wiled away the day thinking of a name for the raven. She seemed to remember from her research that ravens were linked to Apollo, so she settled on that for his name. Apollo suited him. Of course, she would have to fact-check herself when she finally escaped.

Parker eventually fell asleep sitting up. She had a vivid dream of Damon. He was standing around a table with the others from his team, they were all staring at a map. He kept running his hands through his hair and pacing, even Zack looked serious. The dream then turned more surreal.

Deimos stood behind her and as hard and as fast as she ran, he was always just behind her. It was like trying to run through water but Deimos wasn't suffering the same constraint as he walked towards her. Parker finally leapt forward and Ellie was calling her name in the distance, her family were all there. She panicked as she didn't want them to be involved, so changed direction and fell into a swimming pool full of crocodiles.

Parker jumped awake but couldn't remember anything other than crocodiles. She was stiff and sore sat against the wall and lay down to stretch out. Soon after, she was fast asleep again.

CHAPTER 15

Damon had returned to the office, following a business lunch. He had successfully negotiated a profitable new business venture. Damon sat down at his desk, he needed to read through a new proposal for their property development branch. After making a couple of amendments, he heard his phone ring. Cad was calling, "Hi Cad, everything alright?"

"Parker has sent through an SOS from her bracelet. We're currently tracking her down and should have her location in a couple of minutes. I just thought that you'd want to know."

Damon immediately stood and briskly strode towards the elevator, calling to Patricia as he walked, "Please cancel all my meetings for this afternoon. Something important has come up."

Cad was still on the call, "Alright, we have located the bracelet. I think that there might be a problem, it was moving but it stopped suddenly. It is showing that she is stationary, at the side of a road in the middle of nowhere."

"Send me the location, I will check it out. Let me know if you manage to get hold of her."

Damon ended the call and moments later heard a message notification. Cad had sent through the location. He jumped in his car and headed out, the traffic was terrible and he couldn't help but curse. Damon was getting more concerned as he drove, as no call from Cad came through to report a false alarm.

It should have only taken twenty minutes to arrive but thanks to the traffic, it took thirty. He pulled over to where the bracelet had last sent a signal. After a brief scout of the area, he spotted her jewellery in the dirt. It had been damaged beyond repair. Damon immediately called Cad and began scanning the area for further evidence.

"She isn't here. Alert the team that she has been taken. I will continue along this road, hopefully I will either find her or a clue. Can you look to see if there is anything on this road that I should check out?" Cad confirmed that they would investigate it and send him any relevant data.

Damon felt sick. He was surprised by how hard this was hitting him. As he scanned the area for footprints or any other signs of life, he kept thinking about the last time he saw her. She had looked so vulnerable when he left her in the bed, she was adorable when half asleep. He knew that he had to find her.

He tried to search as quickly and thoroughly as possible, trying to be methodical and not give into frantic panic. He knew that the more time he wasted, the farther away she would be getting from him. Damon climbed back into the car and set off along the road, scanning for any clues. Cad began to call again, "Talk to me." Damon directed.

"There's a private airstrip a few miles down the road. We can't see anything else that they could've been heading for."

"Understood." Damon hung up and concentrated on looking for the airstrip. Eventually, it came into view, his heart was pounding. He was usually calm and collected but this had really thrown him. He turned down a single-track road and drove straight up to the hangar. He jumped out of the car and tried the door, which was locked. Damon gave it a little shove with his shoulder and it flew open. A man was sitting at a desk, he looked up at Damon in surprise.

"I need to ask you some questions. Did you see a red-headed woman come through here?" The man was clearly uncomfortable.

"I'm sorry, this is a private airfield. I am not at liberty to discuss our client's movements."

Damon frowned and closed the distance between them. "I'm sorry, you seem to be under the impression that you have a choice. Did a red-headed woman come through here today?"

The man was clearly scared, intimidated by Damon's large and threatening presence. "I haven't seen a woman," Then continued following Damon's expression, "But there was a group of people that came through here an hour or so ago. They left in a helicopter."

"Where were they going?" Damon demanded. It wasn't a question.

"I don't know. I was paid to ensure that a space was allocated for a helicopter to land and take off. I didn't ask where they were coming from, or where they were going."

"Are you required to file a flight plan? Show it to me".

The man stammered, "No flight plan. They paid in cash to keep it off record. I swear I don't know anything!"

Damon couldn't believe what he was hearing. After inspecting his face for a minute, Damon decided that he was telling the truth. However, just to make sure, Damon was going to send Nicola out here for a little word with him. It didn't hurt to double-check and he wouldn't forgive himself if it turned out that he had missed something important.

Damon called Cad back as he climbed into the car, he answered on the first ring, "Did you find out anything?"

"No. There was a man there, but he said that he didn't see anything. Send Nicola out. If there's anything that he's hiding, she'll get it out of him. They left in a helicopter and haven't filed a flight plan. Go online and check the forums for UFO sightings. I'm heading back to the office, I'll come straight to your department. Assemble the team."

All sorts of scenarios were flying through Damon's head but he forced himself to think logically. There was no doubt that it was Deimos who had kidnapped Parker. He wouldn't want to harm her, as he needed her. Parker was strong, Adam had taught her self-defence and he hoped that she was able to use it.

The return drive was quicker, as the traffic abated. He stormed straight to the IT department. Damon walked through to the meeting room, where he saw the other minotaurs had gathered. They all looked concerned, even Zack wasn't smiling.

"Greg and Leo, interview the neighbours. Find out if they saw anything suspicious, or anything at all. We need as much information as possible."

Cad shut the door behind Damon, "I think the mole is in my department. The timings are too coincidental. The SOS came through and under a minute later the signal stopped and the jewellery ditched. Parker is smart, she wouldn't have used them if she was being watched. This leads to one conclusion, the mole informed Deimos of the SOS."

The team looked grave, no one wanted to believe that there was a mole in the department. Cad detailed his plan of weeding them out. It involved checking phone logs and reviewing active screen time. Leo and Greg left, promising to report back any news.

Cad had been typing away on his computer and brought up Parker's voicemail account. They sat and listened to Ellie's message. Damon nodded at Adam, who immediately called Ellie. He updated her on the situation and listened to the response. After hanging up, Adam explained, "Ellie said that she didn't make that call and that she doesn't know anything about it. She's worried and wants to help, so will be heading into the office."

Damon was angry that one of their IT staff had colluded in Parker's kidnapping. He was glad that Cad was going to deal with it, as he didn't think that he would be able to hold back. "Zack, Adam, Seth and I will investigate each one of Deimos' properties. I don't know who we can trust and we can't risk Parker's life by trusting the wrong person. From now on, only our immediate team and Ellie are allowed to know what we're doing."

Seth responded, "I can obtain a list of all companies that he owns or is related to in any way. It may take some time; it will allow you three to start investigating the obvious ones immediately and I'll keep adding to the list."

Damon nodded and turned to Zack and Adam, "Make sure that you report back to Seth as soon as you unearth anything.

I don't want anyone else going missing. Seth, please report any findings directly to me." Seth pulled out his laptop and began searching for associated companies. Damon began pacing the room, he hated feeling useless. He immediately relocated everyone to the top floor, where the security was tighter.

About fifteen minutes later, Ellie rushed through the door and into Damon's office. "What do we know? Is she alright? How can I help?" Ellie asked concerned.

"We know that she was kidnapped and taken via a helicopter somewhere. We don't know the destination yet. She managed to send us an SOS but the kidnappers found out and discarded the jewellery. We are positive that Deimos is behind this.

"There's a mole in our IT department, so don't talk to anyone about this. Cad will be weeding them out and dealing with them. I know that you want to help, so you can work with Seth. He is creating a list of Deimos' properties and land. I'm about to head out to help with the search. We need to ensure that everyone is kept updated."

Ellie nodded, she was determined to help. Whether that be research or kicking someone's ass. They walked to Seth's office. Adam and Zack had already left to search the first properties they'd identified. "What do you have for me?" Damon asked.

"Adam went to search his club and Zack has gone to a building that we believe is a research facility. I'll send a location to your phone. It's listed as storage."

Damon immediately turned and began walking to his car. He was too focused on the search for Parker to pay attention to the people around him. He was clearly visibly determined as everyone avoided his path as he exited the building. Damon stopped by his house en route to grab additional clothing, suitable for whatever he may find. The location on his phone was nearly a two-hour drive, it was frustrating but couldn't be helped.

He was trying to remain calm but his worry for Parker

was starting to become all-consuming and he was struggling to think clearly. He began to realise that he had real feelings for Parker, beyond that of a colleague or just an attractive woman. After an hour, he received a call from Seth. Nicola had visited the man at the airfield. She hadn't found out anything more from him. He was telling the truth.

Damon sighed, he was hoping to get something extra from him. Almost immediately after hanging up with Seth, Greg called. He and Leo had spoken to every one of Parker's neighbours. Two of them had seen her leave. They saw that she was rushing but she was alone as she drove off. From this, Greg inferred that Parker must have been ambushed where the voicemail had sent her.

He commanded Greg, "Please go to the destination detailed in the voicemail with Leo, try to find any clues or witnesses. If you can't find her car there, file a stolen car report with the police." Damon was hoping that the police could use their resources to locate it. He didn't hold out any hope of a clue in the car but had been taught by his father to always be thorough.

Damon was a mile away from the storage facility, he located a local supermarket and parked his car amongst the others. He then pulled on a black turtleneck sweater, to pair with his black jeans and trainers. Damon silenced his phone and walked calmly until he was behind the supermarket, then he began jogging. There was woodland surrounding the facility and he used his enhanced senses to scour his surroundings. He was looking for cameras and listening for sounds of movement.

He heard a couple of rabbits, a fox and several birds on his jog. He slowed as he glimpsed it in the distance, it was starting to get dark. His vision wasn't inhibited but the men guarding the facility would be at a disadvantage. The building looked like a warehouse, with a large roller door at the front and a small, single pedestrian door at the rear.

Damon didn't want Deimos to know that he had been there, the objective was to get in and get out without being seen.

He observed the rotation pattern of the guards. There were only two of them and he could tell that they were regular security guards, not professionals.

He timed their routes and identified a two-minute window where no one was manning the rear door. They did have a security camera but it was pointing away from the building and didn't cover the door. He would have to use his advanced speed to ensure that he wouldn't be noticed.

He waited for the opportune time, then sprinted for the door at top speed. He was prepared to force it open but it was unlocked. Damon glanced inside before stepping in and pulling the door shut behind him. The warehouse held several rows of storage units. He would have to open each door to see what each contained. Damon was careful and listened prior to opening each door.

Junk, junk and more junk, Damon thought. Old furniture and random items were contained within each unit. He kept his hopes up until the very last one, which turned out to be empty. Damon rested his forehead against the door and closed his eyes, sighing. He took a second to push away his disappointment and made his way back to the door.

Damon waited at the door and used his advanced hearing to identify when the guard had passed, before slipping out and sprinting for the woods. He returned to jogging, as it was less suspicious than a sprint. When he could see the lights of the supermarket in the distance, he retrieved his phone and called Seth.

"Strike a line through the storage unit, it was just junk. She isn't there. Anything from the others?"

"Adam and Zack have both searched their first facilities and are on their way to their second. So far, no one has found anything to indicate where she is."

"Send me the locations of those closest to me." Damon requested. He spent the remainder of the night and early morning travelling between the different locations that Seth provided.

He sent the rest of the team home at two o'clock in the morning, he wanted them at their peak. Damon couldn't take his own advice, as he felt like stopping to rest was giving up on Parker and letting her down.

Damon travelled to four more locations before returning to the office at ten o'clock in the morning. With each fruitless endeavour, he felt more and more disheartened. He didn't know what he would do if Deimos hurt her. Damon walked back into the office and went straight up to the top floor, resting his forehead on the elevator wall, dejectedly. He allowed himself one private sigh to vent his feeling of hopelessness.

The team were already there, so he called a meeting to catch up. "I have checked several properties but no luck. Seth, how many more do we have on the list?"

"I have four more properties for you to check. They were harder to find, so I'm hoping that means they hold something more valuable."

Damon nodded, then turned to Cad, "The mole?"

"I have him. All of the evidence points to his guilt. I wanted to get your opinion as to the punishment," Cad responded.

Damon paused for a moment, he wanted to make him suffer. However, he was still holding out hope that Parker was fine. "I may change my mind if anything bad happens to Parker but does he live in one of our properties?"

Cad consulted his laptop before responding, "Yes, he lives in the Dogwood community, west of here."

"Brilliant. Organise for our movers to clear out his entire house and put it in a truck. Change the locks. Our contracts are very clear, we have the right to evict any of our tenants without notice. All funds paid by him will be retained and classed as a rental fee. I want him blacklisted with all companies that we have a contact in.

"Once you have organised it all and his home has been emptied, call security to escort him from the building. After he is outside, please inform him that we know what he did. If he attempts to retaliate in any way, we will also review the status of his friends and family's accommodation."

Cad nodded whilst smiling, "I would love to. I don't know if I would be that lenient if it was up to me."

"As I said, I may change my mind if anything bad happens to Parker." Cad then returned to his own office to organise.

The next three days passed by very slowly. They had explored the four remaining facilities and there was no sign of Parker. Two of them were research facilities, one looked like it was preparing for a battle and the final one looked like a giant nuclear fallout shelter. Damon had barely slept, he was exhausted.

The others only went home to rest at night because Damon made it an order. The strain was clear on everyone's faces. Ellie approached Damon on the fifth night, "I want to talk to you." And she led him into his office, aiming for privacy. "You need to rest; you aren't going to be any good to Parker in this condition." Damon smiled at her, he knew that she was also struggling to sleep from worrying.

"I'm alright Ellie, don't worry about me. I know that you're already concerned enough about Parker."

Ellie frowned, "Just this once Damon, I'm going to talk to you like you aren't my boss. You need to sleep. I'm not going to accept your excuses. I need you to save her. I can see how much you care for her and I want you to be at your best." And a single tear fell onto her cheek.

Damon couldn't argue and sighed, "I don't want to let her down. She has been through so much already. I need to save her." He didn't want to tell Ellie what Parker meant to him before he had a chance to tell her first. "I will rest, I promise." Ellie smiled up at him and quickly hugged him before leaving the office.

He couldn't bring himself to leave the building in case something happened. So, he turned into the bedroom directly off his office to sleep. He looked in the mirror and had to admit that he didn't look in peak condition. It was already two o'clock in the morning. Damon fell asleep within a few minutes of lying down, he had never operated on such little sleep in his whole life.

Seven hours later his eyes opened, he had been having strange dreams of castles. He immediately felt guilty for indulging in sleep when Parker was still missing and pushed the dreams aside. Damon climbed out of bed and went on the hunt for progress. He opened his office door, Patricia turned her head and walked towards him with a foil-wrapped package. She handed it to him before returning to her desk.

He could hear noise coming from Seth's office, so he headed in that direction. Ellie was slumped in a chair next to Seth, sipping from a takeaway coffee cup. Seth glanced up and shook his head at Damon, "No updates. I can't find any other properties. We tried thinking up variations of his name but it hasn't worked."

Ellie looked towards Damon, hoping that he would have a solution but he sighed as he had run out of ideas. He examined the foil package that Patricia had handed him, it was a sausage and egg baguette. He smiled and ate it within a minute, whilst listening to Ellie and Seth talk about search criteria.

There was a commotion at the elevator and he could hear Patricia's concerned voice. Damon heard his name being called, so he walked out to investigate the commotion. Ellie had followed him out and spoke before Damon could, "Rachel? What are you doing up here? And why do you have a raven on your shoulder?"

Rachel's face was lit up with excitement and a tinge of worry. "I don't know if you'll believe me but I've had a message from Parker." The trio all shared sideways glances at each other before silently shepherding Rachel into Seth's office and bustling her into a chair.

"Tell me everything. From start to finish." Damon ordered.

"I was just about to enter the office and start my shift when I heard a bird squawking above me. I glanced up and this raven was swooping straight at me. I put my hands up to protect myself but he landed in front of me. He was staring intently at me and I saw a sequence of pictures in my head. I saw a very clear image of Parker, then a castle, followed by an image of Parker in a cell. Then I saw my own face and the Minos Industries building."

Ellie was grinning, "She did it!" The raven sat peacefully on Rachel's shoulder whilst the story was being told. Damon felt a slight relief. They finally had a lead but they still needed to find the location. Ellie continued, "Is the castle a faded white colour, with a dark grey roof and two pointed turrets to one side?"

Everyone looked at her and Rachel nodded, "I dreamt of it a few nights ago. I didn't realise that it was Parker trying to send me a message. This is great, I think that I can draw it with Rachel's help." Damon realised that he may also have dreamed of the castle.

Ellie grabbed a pen and paper and started sketching with Rachel's input. Damon said, "Seth, let the team know the update. They should all start preparing for a rescue." Damon was already in black clothing. He knew where they could obtain balaclavas to cover their faces on short notice.

He paced the room until Ellie announced that she was finished. Cad arrived, took a picture of the castle and did an internet image search. The style was analysed by the team, which helped to narrow down an approximate age.

Finally, they managed to narrow their search down and Cad excitedly exclaimed, "I've got it! It's listed under his mother's maiden name. It's in Austria." Damon rushed around him, to see his computer screen. The castle looked almost identical to Ellie's drawing, the computer image looked fresher and less worn. He smiled with relief as they finally had a location.

Damon requested that they relocate to his house to form a plan of attack. He wasn't taking any chances with a second mole. Within an hour, Damon's house held his team along with Ellie. Rachel had played her part, so returned to work, with the promise that she didn't mention it to anyone until Parker was safe.

They assembled in Damon's study, where he had rearranged the furniture to suit their purpose better. Cad had projected a map of the area onto the wall and they were discussing the best approach. After an hour of planning, they were each assigned a role. There was a river near to the castle and Adam knew where they could source a boat. That was going to be their point of entry.

Greg was to take point to scout out the guard situation. Ideally, they would have observed for several nights before breaching, but they couldn't afford to wait. Damon had fabricated a decoy plan, which Adam was going to organise. They needed Deimos to be out of the picture when they breached and Damon was going to play on his arrogance.

Adam was going to organise a backup team to openly try and enter Deimos' hidden research facility. The idea was that he would be both concerned that they had found out about it and smug that they still hadn't managed to find his real hideout. Therefore, he wouldn't be able to resist being there in person to gloat.

Their reconnaissance mission had highlighted an oversight on Damon's part, he could no longer turn a blind eye to Deimos' activities. The research facility needed further investigation as Zack had witnessed a large inventory of medical equipment being offloaded but they had to make a sacrifice and risk its relocation to save Parker.

The real plan was that they were going to infiltrate the castle three hours after darkness fell, when their enhanced sight gave them a natural advantage. Damon requested that everyone study and commit to their part of the plan, before meeting again at the Minos' company jet. Ellie was to remain in Damon's home, with Damon promising her an update as soon as everyone was safe.

The plane touched down in a small airfield just outside Vienna. The team disembarked and jumped into two cars Adam had arranged, which took them to his local contact's boat. They were wearing all black clothes and donned the balaclavas once they were aboard. Not far from the castle, they killed the engine and drifted under momentum. They were going as slowly as possible, to not cause any unnecessary noise.

Greg's reconnaissance had identified where the guards were located. Each of them had been assigned a group to immobilise. The aim was to get in and out without permanently injuring anyone. They finally pulled up to the agreed spot and tied the boat to a branch. Seth was to remain in the boat to ensure that their escape route wasn't compromised. After climbing out, they jumped over the wall and silently headed off on their individual missions.

CHAPTER 16

Parker forced her eyelids open; she was fed up. Her body hurt and she didn't want to be in a cell anymore. She wanted to talk to Ellie, to be comforted by someone. Parker wanted a moment where she didn't have to be strong.

She had been holding back the tears. She feared Deimos walking in and seeing weakness, betrayed by red, puffy eyes. Parker couldn't let him think he was winning. She was trying to convince herself that things couldn't get worse. He wouldn't want to permanently injure her because he needed her. He also couldn't let her die for the same reason.

Although she tried not to be afraid, she was starting to worry that Deimos and his friend would return. She knew that she would survive it but she was already hurt. Parker was struggling to concentrate sufficiently to work on her powers, the starvation was getting to her. Her stomach hurt externally from the kick and internally from the hunger pains.

She wasn't even sure anymore how long she had been in this cell, it could have been anywhere from two days to three weeks. Her energy was leaving her and water wasn't sustaining her, especially with the blood loss. Parker forced herself to her feet, she was determined to be ready to leave when Damon came for her. She couldn't let herself give up.

The next few days were a blur. Deimos' friend turned up again and repeated the beating and taking her blood, he took a lot more this time. Once again, Deimos asked whether she had changed her mind but she refused to give in. If he treated a person he needed this way, how would he treat the humans he hated? Parker could barely leave the floor anymore. It felt like a cycle of painful consciousness and restless sleep.

She heard two sets of footprints approaching the cell. The only time that two footsteps were heard, was when Deimos and his friend visited her. The only difference was that it was dark outside the window, maybe they were amping up their torture.

Parker didn't bother lifting her head to acknowledge them. They would complete their sickening tasks and leave again. It took them longer than usual to open the door, she felt a hand touch her arm. It was dark and she couldn't see them, she just waited for the pain. "Parker, are you alright?"

She raised her head to face them but it made her dizzy. The hand tightened and she heard an urgent whisper, "We need to get her out of here. Now!" Parker felt arms lift her and she groaned with the pain. "Shhh, it's alright. We're here now." Parker was struggling to understand what was happening, she was skirting consciousness. Two men were whispering in hurried, hushed tones. Parker feared that this was another of Deimos' little games.

"I've cleared the two guards at the gate. Greg has ensured that the three in the house are out of action and Leo has taken out the six perimeter guards. Seth is waiting in the boat." She was held tightly against their body but their hands were gentle. Parker blinked and they were past the castle walls, she must have blacked out.

She tried to focus on the men surrounding her, they were wearing all black, including black balaclavas. Parker felt like she knew these men but her mind was struggling. It was taking everything she had to remain conscious.

Another blink and they were running through a thick forest. She was being jostled quite harshly and passed out from the pain. When Parker next opened her eyes, she was cradled in a lap and they were on a boat. A hand began to stroke her hair gently, she tried to look into their face but it was still so dark and her eyes were struggling to focus.

As she was determinedly staring at their face, the moon emerged from behind a cloud and the light shone into his eyes.

Parker let a single tear fall, she would know those piercing blue eyes anywhere. He had come for her, she sighed and relaxed into him. Parker allowed herself to let go, she didn't need to be strong anymore and she slipped into slumber.

Parker woke in an unfamiliar room and began to panic. She was afraid that she had imagined the rescue. Parker looked around but wasn't strong enough to lift herself up. She felt a tug on her hand, a cannula had been inserted and it was linked to a saline drip.

There were other wires attached to her and a monitor to her right showing her heartbeat. She was in a bedroom, not a hospital. It was decorated in warm tones of yellow, red, brown, and orange. The room was the complete opposite of the one in Deimos' castle.

The door handle turned and the heart monitor blipped angrily as Parker tensed. Ellie entered, she was looking down at her phone and walked to a chair by her bedside. Parker was so happy to see her. It wasn't until Ellie sat down and placed her phone beside her, that she looked up. Parker noticed that she looked tired and not her usual bubbly self.

Ellie's face lit up as soon as she realised that Parker's eyes were open. She immediately jumped up and went to hug her. Ellie stopped herself at the last second, realising that it may not be the best idea, "You're back with us! I'm so happy you're alright. I was so afraid." Parker attempted to respond but realised that her throat was too dry, all that came out was a croak.

"I'll be right back." And Ellie swiftly left the room. Parker hadn't imagined it, they had come for her. Ellie returned with a glass of water and a straw, following her was Damon. Ellie held the glass to Parker's lips and she took a drink, she was incredibly grateful for the water.

Parker tested her voice, it was no longer a croak but it still sounded weak. "Thank you." Both Damon and Ellie smiled back at her. Ellie's was a lot more enthusiastic but she could see that

Damon's held true warmth.

He spoke first, "There's a lot we need to discuss, but it'll wait until you've recovered. It's important you know you're safe here, you're in my home. Just let me know if there's anything you need or want."

"Can you please open the curtains and window? I want to be able to see outside." Parker whispered, which ended with a pained cough. Ellie rushed over to the window, fulfilling her request. Parker was so grateful to be in a comfortable bed and not in that dark dungeon.

"I'll be right back," Damon advised, "Now that you are awake, we want to try and get a small amount of food into your stomach. It'll help you to rebuild your strength." Damon left the room and Ellie pulled the chair to the side of the bed closer.

She sat before speaking, "We've all been so worried about you. As soon as you went missing, the whole team began searching. Damon has barely slept. I have so many questions, but they'll wait."

There was a sudden commotion at the window and in flew a black raven, "Apollo!" Parker whisper shouted as her voice was hoarse. The bird flew and landed on her knee, she tried to raise her right hand but couldn't. Apollo seemed to sense her struggle and hopped down next to her hand. Parker managed to stroke him gently for a few seconds before letting her hand drop.

"That's amazing," Ellie whispered, not wanting to disturb the moment. Parker focused on Apollo and sent thoughts of gratitude to the bird, who then nodded and perched back on the windowsill. "You are making it really difficult to not ask questions but I promised Damon."

Parker smiled, once she started the story it would take a while to relay and she didn't think that her voice would last. Damon returned with a bowl. Parker noticed his attire, he was wearing black joggers and a light blue T-shirt. Ellie stood, she was wearing a lot more colour, a green pinafore dress with orange tights. It was these simple familiar things, that made everything alright.

"I need to go and tell people that you're alright, I'll be back soon." Ellie squeezed her hand, before walking out of the room.

Damon sat on the side of the bed with the bowl in hand, "It's vegetable soup. You can only have a small portion, as we don't want your stomach to rebel."

"Wait, I need to tell you. There's a mole in your IT department." Parker rushed out urgently.

"Shhh. We know. Don't worry. I told you that it can all wait. Don't worry about anything and focus on getting better. Now, open." And he grinned, before pushing a couple more pillows behind her back. Parker conceded that she wouldn't be able to feed herself yet and opened her mouth when the spoon met her lips.

She ate in silence. The soup was simple but exactly what she needed. Once she finished, Parker glanced over at Apollo who appeared to be standing sentry at the window. "Could you please do me a favour? Is there anything that you could bring up to feed Apollo?" and nodded towards the bird.

Damon smiled, "He has already been well cared for, don't worry. I'll be asking you about him at some point but not just yet." He then rose with the empty bowl and returned downstairs. A few minutes later he appeared, with a plate that held a selection of food. Damon placed it on the windowsill, next to the bird. Apollo strutted over and sample-pecked at a couple of different items before tucking in.

"How are you feeling?" Damon asked with his brow furrowed in concern.

Her stomach had started to cramp as it began to process the food but she didn't want to complain. "I'm fine, so much better now I'm out of that cell." Damon clearly didn't believe her and his face darkened as she mentioned her prison.

Parker's blinks were getting longer, she still felt so tired but had been fighting it. She was afraid that she would fall asleep and wake up back at the castle. "It's alright Parker, get some rest. You'll be sleeping a lot whilst you recover."

She didn't want to show her fear and couldn't look at him

when she whispered, "Please don't leave me."

"I won't. I'll be here when you wake, I promise." He then took her hand in his and sat in the chair, he shuffled into a reclined position and lay his head on the back. Parker smiled and almost instantly fell asleep.

When she next woke, it was dark outside the windows. Damon was still sitting in the chair next to her, he was concentrating on his phone and typing away. He hadn't realised that she was alert and she spent the time inspecting his face. Damon looked tired and worn, he had a darkness under his eyes that wasn't there before.

He was incredibly handsome and his appeal had grown the more she had gotten to know him. Damon finally glanced up and noticed her watching him. He smiled and lay the phone down beside him. "Shouldn't you be getting some rest too?" Parker asked.

"I have been resting," he lied, unconvincingly.

"Come on, this bed is big enough for the two of us. You need to get some rest and this bed is super comfortable. I won't bite." Parker grinned.

"I don't want to disturb you and moving you will probably cause you unnecessary pain," Damon responded, still sitting in the chair.

Parker took a moment to think it through, "Honestly, it isn't just for you. Having a warm body next to me helps to remind me when my eyes are closed, that I'm not in that cell. I'm sure I will get over it but for now, I would love that extra comfort." Parker knew that she was fighting dirty and Damon couldn't refuse her request when it was phrased like that. Not that it was a lie, she really would feel so much safer with Damon next to her.

He immediately stood and removed the heart rate monitor pads, she was no longer at risk. He then gently scooted her across the bed and lay down beside her. Even though it was a large bed, his body touched along the length of hers due to his width.

She suddenly felt a wave of security and comfort wash over her. If she had been able to move without extreme discomfort, she would have snuggled further into him. Parker hoped that this would force Damon to rest.

Parker fell into a deep and contented sleep. When she finally woke, she felt fully refreshed. Damon was still next to her and he was sleeping soundly. She really needed to go to the bathroom but wasn't sure how to do that without help. Her discomfort woke Damon, who smiled at her before sitting up in the bed. "I really need to go to the bathroom, is there someone who can give me a hand?"

"I can see if Ellie is downstairs if that would make you more comfortable?"

"Yes please, that would be great." He then rose and left the room. When he finally returned, it was with Ellie and Dr Stanton.

Both of them helped Parker to the bathroom, where she was finally able to use the toilet. Dr Stanton began an examination. Parker explained where she had been hit and Dr Stanton assessed the areas for damage. Dr Stanton determined that she had severe bruising but nothing was broken or fractured.

She removed the saline drip and prescribed bed rest but with frequent small walks, to increase her mobility again. Parker requested that they help her with a shower, she wanted to wash off the stench of the dungeon. Dr Stanton didn't recommend such a big exertion but acquiesced as she understood the emotional desire.

Parker was assisted back into bed following the shower and she thanked Dr Stanton for her aid. Damon had exited the room when she visited the bathroom, so only Ellie remained after Dr Stanton left, "How is your throat feeling?"

"It's a lot better already. The soup worked wonders but I'm starting to get really hungry again." As if on cue, Damon walked back through the door with a tray. He placed it across her lap, there was a banana, fish and eggs.

"I'm not expecting you to eat all of this, your stomach is still getting used to food. But I thought that you could pick and choose what you fancied. I promise that once you are back to yourself, I'll get you as many brownies as you want." And he smiled.

"Deal," Parker responded smiling. She had been getting more strength back in her limbs and used her fork to feed herself the fish, followed by the eggs. Her stomach began to cramp, so she left the banana and pushed the tray further down her legs. Fruit juice had been provided with the meal and she sat back to enjoy it.

Drinking something other than water felt like a luxury. Parker glimpsed at the window, Apollo was missing. She wondered whether he had left now that he knew she was alright. Parker felt a wave of sadness, she would miss him.

Damon asked, "Are you up to having more visitors? The guys want to see you for themselves, to make sure you're really alright."

Parker beamed, "Of course, call them up." One by one the men filed through the door; the room began to feel very small.

She had begun to develop real friendships with them all and was so grateful for their help. Her emotions bubbled over and she began to cry, she then began laughing at herself for crying. Seth and Leo gave her a confused look before Zack explained that they were happy tears. "Thank you so much, everyone, I don't think I'll ever be able to thank you enough or repay you."

Parker received awkward grunts in response and after a few comments along the theme of, "Get better soon," they all filed back out. The room felt a lot bigger without the huge men occupying it.

Parker was left with Ellie and Damon once again. The excitement of the day was starting to tire her out and Damon was too astute to miss it. He advised that she rest, they would be downstairs. She was left alone to have a nap, she started to relax again and heard a noise at the window.

Apollo had returned, he flew over and landed on the bed next to her. Parker experienced a feeling of happiness radiating from him, she sent her own feelings of gratitude and happiness in return. He shook out his feathers before settling down on the sheets. Parker fell asleep easily, knowing that she had good people and Apollo protecting her.

A short time later, Parker woke from her power nap. She thought back to her experience, she was going to focus on the positive that came from it. Parker had a lot to update Damon and the team on. Apollo ruffled his feathers and flew back to the window as the door opened, Damon stepped through. He had taken the opportunity to shower and change, as his hair was still wet.

"Did you want to stretch your legs?" Damon hadn't even finished the question before Parker had flung back the covers.

"Yes!" He chuckled and walked over to the bed. He assisted her with sitting and swinging her legs around. Damon then took her arm and helped to steady her as she stood.

Parker was feeling a lot stronger and began to walk across to the window, she was still craving the outdoors. "Is there any chance that I can go outside?"

"I'm sure we can make it happen." He then steered her towards the door instead and down the stairs she had seen on her first visit. Damon led her away from the front door, through the kitchen and out into the garden.

It had taken a while to get out into the garden and she was starting to struggle. He sat her down on an Adirondack chair which she relaxed into and sighed in contentment. Damon pulled up another and sat down beside her.

He held out the banana to her and Parker smiled at his thoughtfulness. She ate it whilst looking out into his garden. It was expansive and framed with a secure wooden fence. Trees and shrubs were skilfully arranged throughout, drawing the eye down the centre and providing several points of interest.

"Are you ready to talk?" Damon asked carefully, not wanting to push her.

"Yes, there's a lot I need to tell you. Do you want me to start?"

"That's probably for the best. We've figured out some of it but there's a lot we don't know." Parker explained how they had managed to kidnap her, by playing on her concern for Ellie. She explained her theory of the mole in the IT department. Then she led onto Deimos' attempts to sway her to his side. The story about his parents and the meals.

Parker peppered the story with her own insights and feelings but was careful to brush over the details of the beatings, not wanting to relive it. She was explaining about her incarceration when she was cut off suddenly by a loud crack. Damon had squeezed his hand on the chair arm and the wood had splintered.

Focusing on the positives, she told him about how she had remained strong and tried to continue with her lessons, even in the cell. Parker also relayed how she had tried to access her powers and used the water to sustain her. Finally, she explained about communicating with Apollo and trying to hold out hope, waiting for Damon to rescue her.

Damon hadn't spoken at all during her story, allowing her to explain it freely. He just nodded to show support and understanding as she spoke. "I'll need you to describe the man who beat you in great detail to me." Parker nodded in confirmation, she wouldn't lose sleep over him receiving his comeuppance.

"I can't tell you how proud I am of you, Parker. We were all so worried about you and we feared what he would do. You've made us all proud." Damon then proceeded to fill in the gaps of what she had missed, "We were at the office when your bracelet SOS came through. We began tracking your jewellery but suddenly the signal stopped moving. I tracked it down but as you know it had been tossed by the side of the road. We immediately began investigating, interviewing your neighbours to see if anyone knew what had happened. They saw you leave and drive away but they said that you were alone.

"Cad managed to hack into your phone and we retrieved the voicemail. We were immediately concerned for Ellie but she didn't know anything about it. It was obvious that Deimos was behind it but we had no evidence." Damon paused and dashed back into the house to collect a blanket. He draped it over Parker, before sitting back down and continuing.

"We spent every waking moment trying to find you and we quickly realised that the mole was in our IT department. He has since been dealt with. The only ones I could trust were the other minotaurs, they're all fond of you and wanted to help in any way they could.

"We began investigating every one of Deimos' properties but our efforts were fruitless. Ellie also spent a lot of time working with us, barely taking a moment to rest. Honestly, we were getting desperate, but then a miracle happened.

"Rachel came rushing into the building one day and sped up to my office with a raven in tow. She told us that the raven had been waiting for her outside, to pass on a message. As soon as she described the images, Ellie said that she had been dreaming of the same castle but had dismissed it.

"What you don't realise Parker, is that Harpies lost the ability to communicate with birds hundreds of years ago. You and Rachel are the only ones we are aware of who have access to the ability. Seth believes that this is your role in the prophecy coming active, waking up the old powers." It was as if he knew that he was being talked about and Apollo flew onto her lap.

She smiled affectionately at him and stroked his feathers, as he settled on her blanket. "As you can see, you have re-established a bond that was lost. When we had the mental pictures to guide us, Ellie painted the image and it allowed us all to search for the castle.

"It didn't take long once we had a lead for us to locate the castle, you were in Austria. We'd missed it because it was registered under his mother's maiden name. Then came the part where we put our rescue mission into action. I planned for a raid on one of his research facilities, he thinks that we don't know about it. We knew that he was overconfident in his hiding of you and would want to be at the research facility personally, to gloat that you weren't there.

"However, I sent a backup team to the research facility whilst the other minotaurs and I snuck in to rescue you. We've been working together for so long, that it was easy to infiltrate as a team.

"We didn't want to permanently injure anyone, so the brief was to temporarily incapacitate, Leo's speciality," he smirked. "Of course, that may have changed had we known your condition before we found you."

Parker reached out and squeezed his hand, wanting to convey both her gratitude and reassurance that she was alright. They had made it in time. Damon turned his hand over and returned the gesture. "I really want to focus on bringing my powers to the surface. I think that they'll be the biggest deterrent, to him trying to manipulate me again." Parker explained.

"Yes, but I have my own request. Please stay here with me. I don't think I'll be able to function whilst worrying about you." Damon pleaded whilst looking Parker in the eyes, she smiled at him. His gaze dropped to her lips, he leaned forward and kissed her gently.

Parker leaned into the kiss, not wanting it to end. It was as good as she had imagined and she grabbed onto his T-shirt. They abruptly pulled apart as Apollo ruffled his feathers between them. A door opened and they heard a tray rattle towards them, Apollo had given Parker advanced warning. She blushed and Damon responded with a genuine smile, his eyes twinkled with amusement. He held onto her hand as Zack came into view.

"Hi, Sleepyhead! I thought you might want a snack or drink out here. We all want you back at your peak." The words were light-hearted but the way he studied her showed his genuine concern. She knew why they were all so worried. When

Parker visited the bathroom and looked in the mirror, her face looked pale and gaunt. She had a black eye where she had been hit and a split lip. Her usual extra few pounds had vanished but she didn't look better for it.

She made an extra effort to show them that she had survived the ordeal and was out the other side. "Yes, I'd heard that you were all completely lost without me." And grinned back at Zack. Her response had a bit of the tension easing in his shoulders.

"Are you going to sit out here with us? I'm not yet ready to go back inside. If that's alright Damon? I understand if you have things to do."

He smiled at her and squeezed her hand, "Nothing important. We can stay out here as long as you want to."

"You may regret that, we could be camping out in these chairs."

"I'll bring the hot chocolates!" Zack chirped up from behind and they all began laughing. Zack had also brought out some snacks for Apollo, who left her lap as soon as he was called. Damon had held her hand the entire time, it was a comfort to Parker as he made her feel safe.

Zack pulled up a chair and sat on the opposite side of her to Damon. They sat in companionable silence and it wasn't long before Parker drifted off. She woke as she was being carried carefully up the stairs. Parker looked up into Damon's face, he was carrying her incredibly gently and lay her on the bed before tucking her in.

She saw that it was dark outside. She must have been asleep for a while before he started to move her. Parker began to drift off and Damon motioned to leave, "Stay with me." Parker requested. He turned around and lay on top of the sheets next to her. She turned her body into him and fell into a peaceful sleep.

CHAPTER 17

Parker woke refreshed, she was alone in the bed but she wasn't surprised. Damon had an entire company to run, he couldn't spend all his time with her. A tray sat on a table next to the bed with more eggs and a wider selection of fruit. She picked up the bowl of strawberries and began to eat. The only way that they could have tasted better, was if they were covered in chocolate.

Parker wanted to try and regain some independence by visiting the bathroom alone and after putting the empty fruit bowl back, she swung her legs off the side of the bed. She gingerly put her feet on the floor and started to stand on her own, it went better than she had hoped. Parker shuffled carefully around the outside of the room so that she could lean on the furniture but she made it to the bathroom without issue.

Parker used the facilities and as she washed her hands, looked at herself in the mirror. Her face looked less hollow and was starting to get back a healthy glow. "Are you alright?" Parker heard Ellie call through the door.

"Yes, I'm fine. I'll be out in a minute." She took one final look in the mirror before making her way back into the bedroom.

Ellie was smiling, trying to mask her concern. "I'm fine, I'm taking it slow. I just needed the bathroom and wanted to see if I could do it by myself," Parker explained.

Ellie wanted to rush over and help but restrained herself, "I want to hear about your new abilities. I couldn't believe it when I found out that you had managed to project into my mind. I didn't even realise that was something supernaturals could do."

"I didn't know either to be honest but because I didn't know, I gave it a shot. I was thinking that I should learn about every supernatural ability, past and present."

Parker sat on the edge of the bed, "Do you think Damon would mind if we caught up in a different room? Or even outside? I've had enough of staring at the same four walls."

"It's getting a little cold outside but Damon has a great little snug downstairs where one wall is floor-to-ceiling windows. It even has a cute little fireplace." Parker stood, eager to explore.

Ellie linked arms with her and they slowly made their way downstairs. The house appeared to be empty. As they walked past Damon's study, she heard his voice through the door. As it was only one-sided, she assumed that he was on a call. There was a door at the end of the corridor, which Ellie opened.

The room looked incredibly comfortable and cosy, it held a two-seater sofa and an armchair. A small coffee table stood in the middle of the room and a fireplace sat on the opposite wall to the door. Ellie sat in the armchair and Parker arranged herself in the seat closest to the fire. "I suppose Damon has told you what happened to me?"

"Yes, he explained how they managed to get you alone. I hate that they used me to get to you."

"That's alright, they know how close we are. I was always going to help you. The evil little witch who pretended to be you was called Rebecca. I can't describe her as she was dressed and styled to look like you."

Parker saw Apollo at the base of the window, he was tapping on the glass. Ellie quickly stood to let him in, he flew over to Parker and perched on the seat next to her. Parker suddenly had an image of a man at the far end of the garden, he wasn't familiar and Apollo radiated unease.

Parker stood up as quickly as she was able and hurried back to Damon's study with Ellie following close behind. She pushed the door open without knocking, Damon looked up with his ear still to his phone. "Apollo saw a strange man towards the back of your garden, I don't recognise him."

"I've got to go," Damon said into the phone before running past her and out the door. They walked back to the little room and Parker sent a message to Apollo, to keep an eye on Damon and to report back.

Ellie once again opened the window following Parker's request and he flew into the garden. "Leave the window open. I've asked Apollo to keep an eye on Damon. Do you think he'll be alright?"

"I'll go and see if there's anyone else here that I can send after him, don't leave this room." Ellie quickly exited. Parker sat on the edge of her seat, nervously staring out of the window, hoping to see Damon return. A few minutes later Ellie returned, "I found Adam arriving through the front door and directed him to go after Damon."

Parker finally relaxed a little, she had confidence that the two of them could take on almost anything. Parker decided to continue with her story, it would help to pass the time and distract her until the two men returned.

She told Ellie about them taking her jewellery after she had sent the SOS, highlighting the mole in the company. Parker explained about the room and his attempts to entice her to his cause. She put a humorous slant on her time in the cell, focusing on her failed attempts to use her powers and skirting over the darker elements.

Ellie wasn't fooled but didn't call her out on it. "How did you know about the Harpies' connection with birds? Did you realise that they haven't had access to this power for hundreds of years?"

"On that work night out, Rachel told me about it. She omitted that they'd lost the power. It seemed like a useful one to try and I'm very grateful it worked. I tried to use other powers, but I wasn't able to do more than cause a trickle of water. However, when you have been denied water, it's the most wonderful ability in the world."

Parker had felt a sense of triumph when she had learned that abilities were starting to awaken. She had felt like a fraud that was letting everyone down before, but now she felt like she could make a difference.

Damon walked back into the room with Apollo on his shoulder, he stayed near the door. The raven immediately flew back to Parker and perched beside her on sentry duty. "There was a man snooping around. He was hiding but Apollo helped to direct us to his location before he could really do anything. As soon as he heard us heading towards him, he ran. Unfortunately, he had a head start so we lost him near the lake. He may have been a harpy."

Apollo had been projecting images as Damon talked, it was an amazing ability. Parker picked him up off the seat and gave him a gentle cuddle. She realised that she was going to have to start carrying around snacks for him.

Damon walked over to the fireplace and fiddled with it until it was roaring. Parker hadn't realised until the fire was lit that she had goosebumps all over her arms. Damon had noticed and was still looking after her.

Adam walked in with a couple of hot chocolates for her and Ellie, he had even added marshmallows. They were both speechless, there was an entirely different side to these gruff and grizzly men. Parker thanked him and he nodded in response before leaving.

Even Damon was surprised that Adam had made them the drinks, "They're still worried about you, they all want to do anything they can. I guess that includes making you a drink, although it would have been nice if he'd made me one too." And all three of them laughed.

"I'll leave you two alone, I'm going to organise stepping up my own security. I've never really needed it before. But if I want to be able to provide people with a safe house, I need to ensure that it really is safe. I also wanted to ask if you are up for a meal with the guys and Ellie tonight. Don't worry if you aren't, it can wait. Zack keeps offering to cook a meal for you and obviously, the whole team wants to take him up on his offer."

Ellie and Parker laughed, "I would love to have a meal with everyone. Please tell Zack that I will bring a minotaur-worthy appetite."

Damon left the room and they picked up their hot chocolates, they were rich and creamy, with plenty of chocolate. She could get used to being doted on but she was still eager to get her energy back. Parker sent her thoughts of affection towards Apollo, which he returned. She was grateful that he was sticking with her.

"What's happened between you and Damon?" Ellie asked, noticing a difference in the way they were acting around each other. Parker didn't want to kiss and tell, especially with him being in the same house but her smile betrayed her.

She was honest with Ellie, "I'm not sure. We had a couple of moments but I'm not sure how he feels. I guess we'll see if anything progresses, or whether it's a result of all the excitement. If Acantha is his type, then I'm definitely not."

"I haven't had a chance to tell you, I found out some information about Acantha. It turns out that they did date for about a year, back when they were younger. He split up with her and she didn't take it at all well. I heard through the grapevine, that she is more interested in his status than him.

"She has tried numerous times to get back together and they did a few years ago. However, it only lasted a couple of months before she left him for someone she thought was rich. Turned out that he was faking it and she dumped him as soon as she found out. Unsurprisingly, she tried to return to Damon but he wasn't interested. I think she found out that he was spending a lot of time with you and got her heckles up."

"I'm surprised that Damon was interested in her in the first place, although, she is very beautiful and well put-together."

"You're so much more beautiful than she is. The difference is that her beauty is purely superficial."

Parker smiled but didn't believe that she was more beautiful. "What time is it? I'm still wearing the same outfit I went to bed in. It would be nice to have a shower and get changed before dinner. Would you help me?" And Parker exaggeratedly batted her eyelashes at Ellie, who laughed in response.

"Actually, do I even have any clothes here? I haven't really given it a thought before now," Parker asked.

"Luckily for you, I thought of that before I drove over here yesterday. I brought a selection of your usual choices. Three pairs of jeans, three T-shirts, three blouses, a shirt, your sexiest underwear and socks."

Parker laughed, "Why did you think I would want my sexiest underwear?"

"You never know, it's better to have it and not need it. Besides, you are sleeping under the same roof as Damon," she said and wiggled her eyebrows, making Parker grin. "We have a few hours before anyone arrives, so we can relax here for a bit longer unless you want to stretch your legs?"

"Stretching my legs would be brilliant, I want to keep building on my strength. I already feel so much stronger than yesterday."

They rose. Parker sent an update to Apollo, letting him know that they were leaving the room. He showed her an image of the outside and flew out of the window. Parker shut it after him and proceeded out of the room with Ellie.

It wasn't the most exciting walk, as they were just exploring the downstairs of Damon's house. They then proceeded upstairs, the doors were all shut. Parker reluctantly refrained from snooping in them, it didn't seem right. Over the next couple of hours, Ellie helped Parker to shower, dry her hair and get dressed in her jeans and blouse.

Parker had realised that the jeans were loose on her. It wasn't enough to be worried that they were going to fall down but she did wish she had a belt. Getting ready could have been completed in half the time but they spent a lot of time getting distracted and joking with each other. Ellie then topped up her own makeup and checked her hair, concerned that the steam from the shower had caused it to frizz.

Parker sat down for ten minutes, not wanting to overexert herself. When they finally returned downstairs, all of the guys had arrived. Cad handed her a glass of water, apparently, she wasn't allowed alcohol yet. Parker didn't care, she was enjoying spending time with everyone. They moved into the dining room, this time Damon sat next to Parker and Greg was to her left. Ellie sat across from her and the others filled out the other spaces.

Zack had cooked four large lasagnas. There were bowls of salad, plates of garlic bread, roasted carrots, broccoli, and asparagus to accompany it. It all looked amazing but Parker resisted taking more than she would be able to eat. Her stomach was almost back to normal but not quite.

Everyone was laughing and joking as they ate but she kept noticing concerned glances toward her. As the meal progressed and they saw how well she was improving, everyone relaxed around her. They sat around talking after Cad and Greg cleared the table and the topic of Deimos came up. Damon placed his hand on her leg, she covered his hand with hers and squeezed reassuringly.

The problem was that she could tell everyone that she was alright but they would have to see it for themselves. Parker said, "I would have loved to see his face when he discovered I was missing. If he was trying to get me onboard using food, he should have hired Zack." She winked at him and they all started laughing.

She did get tired but had kept up with everyone else. They all began to filter out, until it was just Damon and Parker remaining, "I have a little surprise for you." He stated before leaving the room. Parker raised her eyebrow, she was intrigued.

When he returned, he was holding something behind his back. Still hiding it, he took her hand and led her back into the cosy room from earlier. They sat on the sofa together and he showed her what he had been hiding. A chocolate brownie, she began to laugh and impulsively kissed him.

He kissed her back, bringing his free hand up to cradle the

back of her head. She used her hands to hold onto him as the kiss deepened, one on his arm, the other clutching his T-shirt. As they parted, they were staring intently into each other's eyes.

Parker was breathing heavily, she had held her breath through the entire kiss. He smiled and brought the brownie up to her lips. She returned the smile and took a bite. Parker had made up her mind as to what she wanted. It wasn't the brownie.

Parker stood, took his hand and led him upstairs. Her heart was pounding with excitement. She had a fleeting worry of rejection but quickly dismissed it. As she was about to walk into her room, he took the lead and pulled her further along the hall. He opened the door next to hers, it was decorated in shades of grey. The bed was larger than hers and had dark grey, cotton sheets. She was finally seeing Damon's bedroom.

He turned to face her and replicated the moment from the night he undressed her. However, this time he kept his eyes open. He began to unbutton her blouse, keeping eye contact with her. Her lips parted, she wanted to kiss him again but held still.

Parker wanted to see what he would do next. After her blouse was unbuttoned, he slid it off her shoulders and down her arms. Damon lowered his head and kissed along her neck, down to her shoulders. Parker angled her head to give him access, closing her eyes, lost in pleasure.

Parker had to grasp his arms to not lose her balance. She enjoyed the feeling of his muscles through his T-shirt and pushed her chest towards him. She began tugging on the bottom of his T-shirt, she wanted to feel his skin against hers. He swiftly ripped it off over his head and returned to kissing her neck. He began trailing kisses down her body, lightly skimming over her bra. Kissing her stomach before unbuttoning her jeans and pulling them down her legs.

Parker shivered as she stood there in her matching bra and thong, she was grateful for Ellie's forward thinking. He trailed his hands over her behind and down her legs, inhaling as he pushed his face closer to her stomach.

Damon removed her bra, sliding the straps down her

arms. He glided her thong down her legs, exposing her completely. He stood and lifted her in one fluid, effortless motion, carrying her to the bed. Damon stood back, he wanted to enjoy her laid out in front of him. She ignored her insecurities, all she wanted at that moment was Damon.

Parker beckoned him with her finger, he unbuttoned his jeans and slid them along with his boxers to the floor. She couldn't take her eyes off him. He was standing, stripped bare, in every sense, for her and he looked magnificent. Without breaking eye contact, he knelt on the bed and crawled on top of her. She grabbed a fistful of his hair and forced him to lower for a kiss. It was passionate and his lips were as soft as she remembered.

Despite Parker's reluctance to let go, he reared back. Kissing her chin, moving down to her chest. He was careful to kiss every inch of her breasts, spending extra time on each nipple. Parker was at boiling point, she couldn't wait any longer. She pulled him up her body and wrapped her legs around him. In one thrust, they were joined.

Parker began raking her nails down his back, she had never felt like this before. She never wanted the moment to end but it soon became too much. They climaxed together and he lay on top of her, both panting.

He lifted his head to check that she was alright and smiled when he saw her grinning. They both needed a shower. Damon insisted that they shower together so that he was there to assist if necessary. Parker didn't believe his motives were purely selfless. He was grinning the entire time he was saying it, Parker couldn't help but find it adorable.

Damon took the sponge and body wash from her hands and took over. She was slightly nervous that she was still too sensitive but he was incredibly gentle with her. Parker offered to return the gesture but after noticing the playful glint in her eye, he decided it could wait for another time.

After drying off, he took her hand and guided her back to the bed. They climbed under the sheets and Parker pushed her back into his body. He turned on his side and held her close as they spooned. Her mind went into overdrive with thoughts: What did this mean? Were they together now? Would this change anything?

Finally, she forced herself to push them all out of her head. She replaced them with thinking about the feel of his arms as they wrapped around her and the warmth of his body pressed against her. She was genuinely happy.

When Parker woke the next day, she was alone in his bed. She was disappointed but told herself that it may not have meant anything to Damon. Parker stole one of the sheets, wrapped it around herself and walked back to her own room.

She then proceeded to get dressed in jeans and a T-shirt. Her stomach was rumbling from hunger, so she made her way downstairs. In the kitchen was Acantha, Parker's mood deflated. Damon was sat on a barstool and she stood between Damon's legs. When he turned towards Parker, he had her lipstick on his lips. He abruptly stood up but it was too late.

Parker's stomach dropped and she felt her face pale. However, she didn't want to show either of them that it had bothered her. She forced herself to slap a smile on her face and walked towards the fridge. Taking the time that it took to grab something to eat to centre herself. After all, he hadn't promised that they were exclusive.

She knew that Acantha had been hanging around but she wasn't the type of woman to share. Parker wanted to go home, she didn't want to be here anymore. She didn't think that they would let her go home alone, so she decided to move to Ellie's house.

"Great to see you again Acantha, how have you been?" She asked as pleasantly as possible.

"I'm wonderful, thank you. I'm just enjoying my visit with Damon." And she gave a sickly-sweet smile.

"Damon, I've decided that I would like to move in with Ellie. I think I'll be more comfortable there. I would contact her myself but I never got my phone back after the kidnapping." Parker informed him. Damon looked stunned.

"Kidnapping? That's exciting, I guess that's what happened to your face. So glad you're back." Acantha's tone strongly implied that she wished she hadn't returned. Parker didn't particularly care, it wasn't her problem. She could keep Damon.

Without waiting for a response from Damon, she went upstairs and began packing her things. She opened the window, trying to spot Apollo. After a few seconds he came flying towards her and landed on the windowsill. She sent images of Ellie's car and Ellie's house to him, so that he knew what was happening. He sensed her hurt and began rubbing his beak on her hand before turning and flying back out of the window.

Ellie had arrived by the time Parker was ready, so she walked downstairs and towards the front door, "Thank you for taking me in Damon and looking after me. Once I have a new phone, I'll send you my number and we can arrange for me to continue my training." Damon was still looking at her baffled.

She turned before waiting for a response and threw her bag onto the back seat. Ellie was looking at her puzzled, "I'll tell you when we get back to your house." And Ellie began the drive home.

Parker wasn't sure what hurt worse, being physically kicked in the stomach or the pain she now felt from Damon's actions. Parker was annoyed that she had fallen so hard, so quickly. Ellie kept giving her side glances but Parker wasn't ready to explain. When they arrived back at Ellie's home, Parker grabbed her bag and they both walked inside, locking the door behind them.

Ellie couldn't wait any longer, "I'm worried about you, are you alright?"

Parker sighed. She wouldn't break down, "Yes, I'm absolutely fine. I'm just foolish. I thought that Damon and I were starting something. We were intimate last night but this morning when I went downstairs, Acantha was in between his legs and he had her lipstick all over his mouth."

"I can't believe it. I didn't think Damon was like that. What a scum bag. You can stay here as long as you like."

"I genuinely do need to get a new phone though. I never got my old one back and I don't know what happened to it. I would also love to have a lazy day with you, binging old movies and eating junk food."

Ellie grinned, "That, I can definitely do!" and she immediately turned on the television. A few seconds later, her phone began to ring, it was Damon. After a glance towards Parker, she ignored the call. She grabbed a couple of blankets from the cupboard, threw some popcorn in the microwave and raided her chocolate stash. They picked an easy-watching romantic comedy and they had the lazy day Parker had wished for. Ellie kindly ignored the odd tear that fell down Parker's cheeks and the numerous missed calls.

CHAPTER 18

Parker woke disoriented, she was in a different bed again and was beginning to get fed up with it. She wanted to wake up in her own bed for once. Parker and Ellie had talked long into the night and they had come up with a plan. Once Parker managed to tap into her abilities, she would be able to demonstrate to Deimos that he should back off.

Damon had sent her a message on Ellie's phone last night: *I hope that you're alright, let me know if you need anything - D x.*

Parker rolled her eyes in frustration. It was her fault for thinking that he would choose her when he could have Acantha. She asked Ellie to reply: *Thanks, I want to continue with my training. I need to work on enhancing my powers. Deimos needs to realise that I'm not someone to mess with. – P.*

She was hoping that Damon got her subtle dig, he should also not mess with her. Parker dressed from her limited clothing selection and headed into the garden with Ellie. They had talked it through last night. The guys had tried to help her but Ellie wanted to give it a go. Her garden was beautiful and had a small stream running through it, which was fascinating because it appeared out of nowhere and disappeared into nowhere.

"I'm not as powerful as some of my single ancestral line friends but I can access both water and forest abilities. I'm hoping that I'll be able to relate to you better, as you also have more than one strain of ability running through you." Parker simply nodded and they sat in the middle of her lawn. They sat facing each other, next to the stream. "You've already proven that you can call water, so we'll start there."

Apollo flew overhead and landed on a rock next to the

stream, watching them. "I want you to close your eyes and try to sense the water. You have seen the water with your eyes. Next, I want you to hear the water, trickling as it flows." Parker closed her eyes. There were a lot of background noises, cars driving along the road at the front of the house and children laughing as they played a few houses down.

She tuned out the distractions and listened to the water. After a few minutes, Ellie asked her to keep her eyes shut and lightly place her hand in the water, feeling it trickle through her fingers, "I want you to imagine the water rising, up your hand and twirling around your elbow."

Parker concentrated and felt the water begin to rise to her wrist. She was unable to manipulate it further but opened her eyes in surprised excitement. Ellie was grinning, "I knew it. The guys have been training you based on their own powers but they haven't been trying to encourage the ones they're unfamiliar with."

They spent the next couple of hours working with the stream, trying to manipulate it and bend it to her will. Parker made great initial strides. She could now divert the water. She directed it to the tree that Ellie had indicated. Ellie set her increasingly more complicated challenges.

It sometimes took a few tries but she was determined, "Alright, time for a break." Ellie announced, standing up. "Did you remember to grab breakfast this morning?"

Parker also stood and shook her head, "No, I wasn't hungry and I was eager to start training with you."

They both went indoors. Ellie had a large new plant in her living room. Selected especially for its thick branches, for Apollo to perch on. He was going to be spoilt going forward, Parker felt so lucky that he chose her. She knew that he was constantly aware of their surroundings, he wanted to keep her safe.

Ellie began grabbing snacks out of the fridge, there were croissants, muffins, and a selection of fruit. Parker found a couple of plates and placed them on the counter before helping herself to a bit of everything. They sat on the breakfast bar together and discussed where Ellie thought her training should go. Parker had been doing so well with water that they were going to continue working with it. Changing the sources of water she worked with, as well as increasing the scale.

"I'm so sorry Ellie, I forgot to ask how your job interview went."

Ellie began laughing, "That's alright, you've had one or two other things on your mind. I didn't go to the second one, I couldn't focus on an interview when you were still missing."

"I'm sure that they'll understand though, can't you reschedule?"

"Probably, but it isn't the most important thing to me at the minute." Parker gave her a quick side hug in thanks and continued eating.

"I want to take you to my mum's house this afternoon. Don't worry, she's on holiday at the minute so it'll just be us. It's not actually her house that I am interested in, she has an indoor pool and hot tub out the back of her house."

"I'm assuming that you aren't planning a relaxing swim and soak?" Parker asked sarcastically.

"No, it gives us a large body of water that we can practice with, whilst also being completely private. I don't think that Damon would be happy if we practised with the duck pond in the park."

Parker packed a bag with a change of clothes and one of Ellie's spare swimsuits. After Ellie had grabbed various items from around the house, they climbed into her car. She couldn't see Apollo but could sense him nearby. Their bond had been growing every day they spent together. Parker was beginning to understand his feelings and motivations on a deeper level.

It took about an hour to get to Marion's house and they passed the time singing along with the radio. They had a very similar taste in music and loved a karaoke-friendly track. They pulled up outside a very beautiful building, with a high-pitched roof to the left and wooden cladding on the front. The left-hand side with the pitched roof had full-height windows.

Ellie parked to the right, next to the garage. They walked around to the back garden and Ellie unlocked the pool house, "Have you told your mum that we're here? I don't want to intrude."

"Yes, she was happy to help in any way. She started offering to teach you herself but I saved you from that trauma." Ellie laughed.

They began by removing their shoes and socks and dangled their feet in the water. Ellie demonstrated what she wanted Parker to do. She sent small jets of water into the air from the pool. Ellie retrieved the random items she had collected from her home and explained to Parker that once she was able to create the jets, she would throw the items for her to use as target practice.

Parker spent the next hour attempting to shoot jets into the air. To start with, they were weak and barely left the water. She placed her hands into the water, to feel more linked. Once she'd improved the connection, the jets shot higher into the air and with more concentrated force.

Ellie began throwing the items for Parker to hit. They were both having great fun. Ellie kept retrieving the items, by causing small waves to bring them towards her before throwing them again. "You're doing so well Parker! You've exceeded all my expectations and I can't wait to show the guys what you can do." She then glimpsed at Parker mischievously, "There is a very difficult thing to do with water, did you want to give it a go?" Parker didn't even wait to hear what it was before agreeing.

Ellie moved towards the steps and walked into the water fully clothed, becoming entirely submerged. She then walked back out of the pool but was bone dry. Parker was shocked and had to close her mouth, "It involves a lot of concentration, you need to focus on a large amount of water. Imagine it being repelled from your skin."

Parker couldn't wait to try it and she walked around to the steps. Concentrating on the water being repelled, she slowly walked into the pool. It appeared that she was managing it until her foot slipped on the bottom.

Suddenly she was drenched and spluttering, she climbed back up the steps looking like a drowned rat. Ellie couldn't breathe she was laughing so hard. Parker attempted to give her an annoyed glare but found the situation too comical and burst out laughing too.

She then changed out of her wet clothes into her swimsuit and Ellie followed her lead. Parker began swimming laps, it was easier on her body than other forms of exercise. Ellie moved through the water like a fish, she was underwater for a long time.

Parker wasn't concerned, as she could see glimpses of her as she glided along the bottom. It felt like several minutes had passed when Ellie popped up out of the water. She rushed out excitedly, "I can't believe I just did that, Parker. I've never done that before. When I was under the water I didn't need to breathe. Even full water nymphs lost that ability years ago. I did it!" Ellie was beaming.

The next couple of hours were spent practising in the pool. Ellie kept timing herself to see how long she could stay underwater. It didn't appear that she had a limit. Parker tried to use her abilities to push herself through the water faster. It took quite a while for it to work and by then she was getting tired, "It's starting to get dark out Ellie and I'm starving. We should probably get going."

"Yes, you're right. I just can't get enough of my enhanced ability. I keep wondering what else I can do now." She proceeded to climb out of the pool and Parker copied her. They showered off and changed into their dry clothes.

When Ellie checked her phone, she had numerous missed calls and messages. Damon had been trying to call her, he had also sent messages: *Hi Ellie, are you and Parker alright?* - D

They escalated in concern as the hours passed. Ellie pressed the call button. Parker could only hear her side of the call. "Hi, Damon. Yes, we are both fine. We're at my mum's house. We've been working on Parker's water-based powers. Yes. Yes.

Alright, we'll be back in about an hour. Yes, bye.'

She then turned to Parker and updated her as they walked to the car, "Damon is going to meet us at my house, he wants to talk to you." Parker sighed, it was inevitable. He was probably going to want to talk about this morning. She wished they could just forget it ever happened. There was no point in overthinking or hiding from it though, they would have to talk at some point.

Ellie locked everything back up and they walked towards the car, Parker felt uneasy. Things looked worse at night, every shadow could be a person hiding. She sent a query to Apollo, who relayed a feeling of safety. She knew that he would let her know if he had seen anyone.

The drive home was uneventful. Parker wasn't in the mood for singing along to the radio, so Ellie filled the void with random topics. Parker was grateful to her for filling the silence, it stopped her from focusing on Damon.

Damon was already outside Ellie's house when they arrived, he exited his car and followed them inside. He turned to Parker, "I was worried when we didn't get a response from Ellie. I was concerned that something had happened to you." Ellie stated that she had to put her laundry away in her bedroom, so she would be a while. She then swiftly left.

"I'm fine Damon, we were just at Ellie's mum's house."

He ran his hand through his hair, looking flustered, "I'm not sure what happened Parker, I'm so sorry. I thought that you wanted last night to happen but I shouldn't have taken advantage of you when you weren't fully healed. I clearly scared you. How can I fix things between us?"

Parker was looking at him confused, "What are you talking about? I was a full participant last night. What we did wasn't the problem."

"Then what was it? I just don't understand and I care about you too much to let you go easily." Parker brushed away the tears that were forming in her eyes. He was saying all the right things but she knew what she saw.

"I saw you the next morning Damon. I saw you with

Acantha." Damon frowned, then suddenly looked at her with understanding.

"I messed it all up, I'm sorry. It's not what you think though."

"Explain it to me then." She demanded.

"I left you in bed sleeping, you looked so content and I didn't want to wake you. A few minutes after I went downstairs, Acantha turned up. She kissed me before I could stop her and told me that she wanted us to get back together. I pushed her away immediately but she strolled into the kitchen and kept leaning into me. I was about to tell her about us, to show that I wasn't interested. When you appeared downstairs and she backed off, I thought it was finally clear to her.

"I thought it would have been obvious to you that I wanted you, not her. I didn't want to tell you what had happened. I was worried that you would think that the kiss was reciprocated. I'm normally a very intelligent man but when it comes to you, all coherent thought goes out of the window." Damon looked at her so earnestly that she wanted to believe him.

She walked away and took a moment to remember that morning. Acantha was standing between his legs, he had the lipstick on his mouth. However, she never actually saw them kiss. Parker had only met her properly twice but knew that it was well within her character to twist a situation. Her attitude and comments were supposed to imply they were together but she never actually said it.

"Alright, I believe you. Don't make me regret it, Damon." He immediately began to smile, as if a great weight had been lifted from his shoulders. Damon walked towards her and kissed her like he had been away from her for years. She couldn't resist and kissed him back just as passionately. She knew him, she knew who he was. He was honourable and trustworthy. Acantha wasn't going to stop this wonderful thing that she had with Damon.

When they finally parted, he guided her to the sofa, "OK,

now that we are back on the same page, I have some things to give you." He then handed her a new mobile phone, "This is pre-programmed with all our numbers and your old numbers. It's a new number though. We don't want to make it too easy for Deimos to harass you."

Damon then removed a case with different items of jewellery, "Honestly, I wish that the first time I gave you jewellery, it didn't have a practical purpose. I promise I'll make it worth the wait though."

He handed her an identical necklace and bracelet to the ones she lost. Damon also pulled out a pair of flesh-coloured stud earrings, "These also have a tracker in them. If you press either one for three seconds, an alert will come through directly to me. No one other than myself and my team know about these.

"They are flesh-coloured so that no one will realise you're wearing them. The alert will go straight through to me. If I do not acknowledge it for any reason within ten minutes, it will then be sent to the rest of my team. This means that if we have any other moles, they'll be in the dark."

She smiled at Damon as she took the items, how could she have doubted him when he had been so focused on keeping her safe and happy? "I won't push you to move back into my house but please consider it. I feel like I can protect you better there. Also, I like you being with me for purely selfish reasons." Parker smiled, then realised that she wanted to update him with her progress.

"I really do appreciate you protecting me but I'm hoping that I'll be able to protect myself." She then told him about what she and Ellie had spent the day practising. Parker proudly told him how she was now able to manipulate water, she also told him about Ellie's levelling up of her own powers.

Damon was looking at her with admiration and pride, she began to blush. "Ellie had a theory that you had all been teaching me with your own abilities in mind. However, she can help with my other abilities."

He nodded, "Ellie is right. Our abilities are physical and we have focused on them because that's what we know."

"I would actually like to go back to my own home at some point, even if it's only to water the plants that must be long dead by now and to access my clothes."

He nodded, "I can come with you?" Suddenly, her stomach gave an embarrassingly loud growl and they both chuckled.

"I probably need to get something to eat first."

"Would you like to go out for dinner? I can ask Ellie if she would like to come too." Parker nodded enthusiastically, she liked that he had included Ellie in his offer.

Ellie made up a random excuse as to why she couldn't attend, which was obviously because she wanted them to have alone time, so Parker went upstairs to talk to her before they left. "Are you sure you don't want to come with us? You won't be interrupting anything."

"That's alright, I don't mind being a third wheel usually. But you two are still new, you should enjoy this time together." Parker hugged her, before borrowing a jacket and heading out with Damon.

She climbed into his car and relaxed in the seat, "Where are we going?" She asked curiously.

"It's a surprise, I've called in a favour." Parker began to get nervous, she was dressed casually in jeans and a shirt. However, if Damon didn't care, neither did she. He drove her to a built-up area but then kept going to the outskirts. They couldn't park outside the restaurant, so they ended up parking near a river and walking along it.

Damon directed Parker to a small Greek restaurant. Instead of going through the main entrance, he led her around to the back door. After knocking twice, it opened and in the doorway was a beautiful, middle-aged woman. She was wearing chef's clothes and looked at Damon affectionately. They were ushered inside and led through the kitchen. She could see the main room to her left, it was full of people, extremely loud and vibrant.

They were led into a tiny room that could barely house a

curved bench seat and table. Two places were set. After they sat down, Damon introduced the woman, "Parker, this is Esme. She is a long-time family friend."

"It's lovely to meet you Esme, I hope we haven't put you out."

"Of course not. I would do anything for Damon and his family. His mum and I have been friends for a very long time. They are partners in my restaurant and they were the ones that encouraged me to follow my dream. My best server will be looking after you tonight but let me know if there's anything I can do to make your experience any more special." Esme then gave a little wave as she left the room.

Almost as soon as Esme left, a woman entered, "Good evening, I'm Janice and will be your server tonight," She then handed them the menus, "Can I get you any drinks to start?" Damon requested a beer and Parker chose a cola. They were sat next to each other, so they kept touching subconsciously. Parker felt so relaxed and comfortable with Damon, she wanted to be physically connected to him in some way all the time.

The food all sounded delicious and she struggled to narrow down her options, "Have you decided what you want?" She asked Damon, "Because I'm really struggling to decide."

He smiled, "I know the solution. If you're happy with it, I will order a selection. That way you can try a bit of everything."

"Sounds perfect to me." When the server returned, Damon ordered Souvla, Kalamari, Dolmades, Sheftalia, Pastitsio and Pagidakia. Parker couldn't wait to see what arrived. They passed the time talking about their childhoods. Damon was an only child who had grown up with the other minotaurs. Parker had grown up with a sister, their childhoods were drastically different. However, they both came from very loving families and had parents who adored each other.

Damon shared, "My parents argue, they disagree and they bicker. I love how they challenge each other. I think it pushes them both to be the best that they can be. They love each other so much that they would be lost without each other. Growing up I wanted to find someone who meant that much to me." He looked into Parker's eyes as he finished speaking and squeezed her hand.

Parker's stomach was doing somersaults. Looking into his eyes, she knew that he could be the one for her. They leaned towards each other and they shared a slow, lingering kiss. Breaking the moment, the waitress walked back into the room carrying six plates of food. Parker pulled away, she began to get embarrassed that they had been walked in on during an intimate moment but Damon squeezed her hand and diverted her attention.

The plates held lamb, pork, potatoes, pasta, stuffed vine leaves and squid. They didn't have their own individual plates, they just switched between them. Parker had been avoiding the squid, it wasn't her usual choice. Damon held a piece of Kalamari out in front of her face, daring her to try it. Parker didn't want to back down from the challenge, so she did. The chewy texture wasn't to her liking but it had soaked up the lemon and garlic sauce, which she enjoyed.

Damon once again kept eating after she had finished. She smiled as he had been holding back, to ensure that she had first choice. She placed her hand on his leg and filled in the silence with small talk whilst he ate. Parker had even told him about her childhood pet, Gizmo the hamster and his penchant for escaping.

Esme popped into the room to ensure they had been enjoying their meal and they both expressed their love of her cooking. She couldn't stay, as the restaurant was full and the kitchen was hectic. Parker had eaten plenty and refused the option of dessert. Damon paid the bill and after thanking and hugging Esme, they left the restaurant.

Parker was quite full, so opted for a slower walk back along the river to their car. They were walking holding hands, she felt like it was a perfect evening. Her thought immediately jinxed it. Damon stopped and pulled her back, seconds before four men stepped out from the shadows. One of them was

Deimos, in his usual black suit and shirt.

Damon squeezed her hand before releasing it, "It's been a long time Deimos, how can we help you?" If he felt nervous with the odds, he didn't let it show.

Deimos responded, "Although I wish it had been longer, it can't always be helped. You really should learn to share your toys."

Parker took offence at being called a toy. She was conflicted as to whether she should let Damon handle it or stand up for herself. Before she could think of a scathing retort, Deimos' henchmen took several steps towards them. Parker glimpsed at Damon, he had grown in height and his eyes glowed red as he angrily faced Deimos.

Parker was worried for Damon, it was one against four. She couldn't let him fight alone and she was getting angrier. How dare Deimos think that he had the right to kidnap and torture her? Whilst they were focused on Damon, she glimpsed at the river beside them. She used her anger and channelled it towards the water, demanding that it heed her command.

Before the first henchman reached Damon, he was hit in the chest with a strong jet of water, knocking him head over heels backwards. The others no longer thought of her as the weak link and one changed course to head for her instead of Damon. This meant that they each faced one individual, with Deimos hanging back.

Parker didn't want to give him a chance to hit her or even get close, so she focused hard and sent a giant tentacle of water shooting up and out of the river. It wrapped around him and dragged him into the cold, dark water beside them, leaving only a few bubbles behind. It caused the one currently fighting Damon to falter, his distraction immediately gave Damon the upper hand and he knocked him out cold with one powerful blow.

Deimos was left standing across from them, Parker stepped towards him, "I am not a toy. I will never bow to your commands. I would suggest that you leave us alone or I will cause every drop of water in your body to flood your lungs until you suffocate."

Deimos paused for a second, he then bowed sarcastically and walked away. Leaving two henchmen unconscious on the floor and a third drowning in the river. Damon turned Parker towards him, his eyes were still glowing. Parker grinned excitedly, "I'm not actually sure if I can do the lung thing but he doesn't know that."

Damon kissed her forcefully, she reciprocated in kind as adrenaline coursed through her. Damon reluctantly prised himself away, he didn't trust Deimos. However, after Parker's display, he doubted that he would return for her. Deimos clearly wanted someone he could control and that wasn't Parker.

Parker had noticed that his eyes had returned to his usual beautiful blue colour. She wanted nothing more than to return with him to his house. Whilst they were finishing their walk to the car, she messaged Ellie letting her know that she wouldn't be home that night and to lock the doors.

"Damon, can you arrange for a security system to be set up at Ellie's? I worry about her, especially as Deimos knows what she means to me."

"Of course. I will check with her first, as I don't want to be on the receiving end of her or her mother's wrath. But we should be able to get it set up tomorrow."

They both climbed in the car, "Let's go back to yours." Parker dictated. She would worry about her clothes later. She was far from ready to move into Damon's but for tonight she wanted to be with him.

"You were breathtaking tonight. Every day you surprise me, Parker. I can't wait to see what you'll do next." She placed her hand on his thigh as he drove and relaxed into the seat. Today had exhausted her, the adrenaline was beginning to wear off and she started to doze.

Parker woke as Damon was carrying her through his house to his bedroom. She snuggled into his chest and had no intention of moving. He lowered her gently to the bed, removed her jeans and tucked her under the covers. She rose in the bed, as this wasn't how she had imagined the night ending. Damon smiled at her and kissed her on the forehead whilst he undressed.

He climbed in beside her and pulled her towards him, tucking her rear into his front. Parker would have loved to initiate more between them but she was exhausted. Between the last few weeks and her extensive use of her powers, she could hardly keep her eyes open. He had his arms wrapped around her and she fell asleep, safe within his arms.

CHAPTER 19

Parker was woken by movement behind her. Damon was climbing out of the bed but she noticed that it was still dark outside, "Where are you going?"

"I need to go into work today. I have important meetings all morning and wanted to fit training in first." Damon whispered in response.

Parker mumbled, "What day is it? I don't have a clue at the minute what day of the week it is."

"It's Monday, I've told Ellie that you take priority. That means that if she schedules in training with you, she should consider it an extension of her job. Get some more sleep."

Parker didn't need to be told twice and snuggled back under the sheets. She was asleep before Damon had even left the room, so she didn't react when he laid a gentle kiss on her forehead before leaving.

When she woke for the second time, the light was streaming through the windows. She could still smell Damon in the sheets and smiled contentedly. Parker rose and went downstairs. She began to wonder how she would get home. On the kitchen island was a breakfast platter of avocados, pancakes, croissants, toast, jam, waffles, and a fruit selection. She shook her head, exasperatedly. He had forgotten that she couldn't eat as much as he could.

Next to the platter was a set of keys and a note, *'These keys are for you. If you decide to leave, I have organised a company car for you, it should be in the driveway.'* She wasn't sure how she felt about being given a set of keys to his house. After a brief pause, she decided that his actions had made it clear how serious he was about her. Parker smiled, realising that she was serious about him too.

Parker had taken a selection off the platter, heated up the waffles and placed them on her plate. Just as she was about to take a bite, there was a knock at the door. She wouldn't usually answer someone else's door, but Damon had advised that a car would be delivered for her.

Parker opened the door and Acantha stood there in a beautifully fitted red suit. Acantha's smile quickly changed to a scowl when she saw who had answered the door. Parker was feeling extremely self-conscious, as she was in the same clothes that she wore the day before. Deliberately clipped, Parker said, "Acantha. Can I help you with something?"

"Hello Parker, I came by to see Damon. I'm surprised that you're here. Are you helping him around the house?"

Acantha narrowed her eyes at Parker before sneering at her creased clothing. "No. Why? Is that why you're here?" Parker replied innocently, she didn't feel threatened by Acantha.

"Is Damon here?" She replied, clearly frustrated that Parker hadn't risen to her insult.

"No, I'm sorry. He's at work, I'll be sure to tell him that you stopped by though." Parker had decided to take the high road, she wasn't going to stoop to Acantha's level.

"Yes, please do. Tell him that I really enjoyed our kiss the other morning."

Parker smiled at Acantha's attempt to rile her, "I will let him know. Your feedback is very important to us." She said with a perfect monotone voice, mimicking an automated response to a survey.

Acantha turned red, "He'll never be happy with an outsider." She then turned and strode away, Parker shut the door behind her.

Regardless of her outward appearance, she was irate. Parker replayed the interaction in her mind and was proud of her responses. It was too easy to resort to name-calling or petty retorts. Parker wasn't going to provide details of their private life to this gold-digging woman but she would ensure that Damon knew that she had stopped by.

She quickly sent a message: *Morning Damon, I hope your day is going well. Just wanted to let you know that Acantha stopped by to see you. She wanted me to let you know that she enjoyed your kiss, I told her that I'm sure you will appreciate her feedback. I don't think that she's gotten the hint yet. Anyway, thank you for breakfast. I will probably go home today, I need to change into new clothes Xx.*

She saw belatedly that the keys to the company car had been posted through the door in a white envelope. Parker scooped them up from the floor, returned to the kitchen and finished her breakfast. Unfortunately, the waffles were cold again but she didn't bother heating them for a second time. After finishing, she gathered the platter, wrapped it back up and placed it in the fridge.

Parker locked the door behind her and walked over to the company car. It was a brand-new Mercedes-Benz C-Class AMG in electric blue. After spending this much time in new cars, her old compact was looking a little tired in comparison. As she drove home, she was wondering what had happened to her car. No one had mentioned it but surely Deimos would have had to get rid of it.

The heated seats that she was currently enjoying made a persuasive argument for buying a new car anyway. Her car still had the original CD player, while this one had a sleek infotainment system and exhausts that barked.

Parker had decided that once everything had calmed down, it was time to indulge. She deserved it. She pulled up outside her house, her car wasn't there either. Parker suddenly realised that she had lost her house key when Deimos took her belongings.

It was a long shot but she looked through the set of keys Damon had given her and found a familiar one. Luckily for her, Damon had thought of everything. The key wasn't exactly the same, he'd had the locks changed in case Deimos still had her old key.

Cad had already paired her new phone to the video doorbell, so she received a notification. She dismissed it before deciding on her agenda. Parker wanted to shower, brush her teeth and change into a fresh set of clothes. She wanted to change it up slightly, so threw on a dress instead of jeans.

She then attended to her plants, they weren't looking very healthy, so she made a mental note to ask Ellie for her green thumb assistance. Parker didn't want to be stuck anywhere without her necessities again, so she prepared an overnight bag with several outfit choices. It made her feel proactive and ready for whatever may come.

Parker sent Ellie a message: *I'm back at mine. I'm pretty sure that Deimos will back off after my display last night. I need to update you on everything but I'm going to move back into mine for now. Thank you for putting up with me x.*

She received a response within a couple of minutes: *I'm at work at the minute but we need to have a catch-up. I'll pop by after I finish x.*

Her phone vibrated and a message appeared from Damon: *I'm sorry that you had to put up with her again. I hope that she's finally got the message. I've had an interesting morning and think we should meet up. Are you free to pop into the office? I have a gap this afternoon. I think that we've found out more about the prophecy – D xx.*

Parker responded: *Yes, I've had a chance to get myself sorted. I'll head into work shortly – P xx.*

Before she set off, she wanted a catch up with her mum. Parker called her and she answered on the second ring. "Parker, have you got a new number? Thank you for asking Ellie to message me with updates but it would have been nice to hear from you directly." Parker made a mental note to thank Ellie for messaging her mum and preventing her from worrying. She was aware that she couldn't tell her about the supernatural world but that didn't stop her from updating her mum about Damon.

"Sorry mum, I've just been busy with work. Also, it

took me a while to decide on a new phone." Parker then listened to the updates from her mum. Most prominent in the conversation, was that her parents had booked a twenty-one-day cruise around the Mediterranean. Once her mum had run out of updates, Parker told her about Damon. If it did get more serious, she didn't want to blindside her parents later. Her mum took the news very well and was pleased her daughter had found someone.

Once the call ended, Parker put her overnight bag into the boot of the company car and set off to the office. It wasn't until she walked into the foyer, that she remembered her ID was still in her old car. She walked over to reception and explained her predicament. The woman behind the desk was quite stroppy and gave her a long lecture about being careless and unprepared. Parker was getting fed up with being told off and decided to cut it short, "When Damon Minos asked me to come straight in for an important meeting, it just slipped my mind."

It worked. Within a few seconds, she had a new ID hanging around her neck. She hated name-dropping but the receptionist was verging on rudeness. Parker proceeded up to the top floor and walked over to Patricia. They warmly greeted each other and Parker advised her that she was supposed to be meeting Damon when he was free. Patricia had been informed of her appointment and advised that his last meeting would be over shortly. She handed Parker a magazine and offered her a drink.

Parker declined the drink and thanked her for the magazine. She didn't get a chance to even glance at it when Damon opened his door and strode across to Parker. He embraced her and kissed her chastely on the lips. Damon then took her hand and led her back to his office. Parker returned the magazine on the way and gave Patricia a parting smile.

Once the door clicked shut behind Parker, Damon turned and gave her a more intense kiss. Her back was to the door and his body was pressed against hers. Parker was lost to the kiss, her hands were grabbing his arms, keeping him close.

When Damon finally stepped back, he apologised, "Sorry, I wasn't planning on kissing you like that but when I saw you out there, I couldn't help myself. You are so beautiful." Parker blushed before grinning. Damon had a playful smile on his lips. They crossed the office to sit on the sofa, angled towards each other.

"I wanted you to come in, as we have noticed some big changes. I was sparring with Leo this morning and he could barely touch me. My abilities appear to have levelled up and I can only link it to our new relationship. We have a new Leo-shaped hole in our training wall. Amusingly it's right next to the Adam-shaped dent. I'm thinking of getting them framed. It was a first for Leo and probably did him good, it will encourage him to not get complacent."

"Ellie also appears to have gained new abilities. When we were training, she could stay underwater indefinitely." Parker explained.

Damon nodded, his brow furrowed in thought before he continued, "I have discussed it with the others, we've all heard rumours of one or two powers returning to different lines. So far it seems to be those that you have been linked with. However, only my abilities have levelled up. I don't want to pressure you but we think it's because of your feelings for me."

Parker didn't respond as she was deep in thought, she did care for Damon. Did she love him? Did he love her? She wasn't ready to have that conversation yet. "It's an interesting theory, do you think that Deimos knows that? Has he interpreted the prophecy to mean that the man or woman the seven women fall in love with will gain an extra boost in power?"

"Honestly, I'm not sure. At first, I thought that he merely wanted the women to be on his side due to their access to every power. Who knows what that maniac is thinking?"

They leant back on the sofa, contemplating that point. Trying to get inside Deimos' head as to what his larger plan was. Parker concluded that thinking too hard about Deimos' schemes was making her head hurt and changed the subject, "Thank you for sending the car for me, I'm thinking I may have to treat myself to a new one. Between your car and the company car, I'm getting a bit jealous."

"I think you're right to change the topic, we aren't going to solve Deimos in one afternoon. Regarding the car, it's not a problem. You can use the company car for as long as you want it. And I'm sorry again for you having to deal with Acantha. I can have another conversation with her if you want?"

"Honestly, I don't think there's a point. Time away from her will be a more powerful statement."

Damon nodded, "You're probably right. She always shows up at the most inopportune times."

Parker laughed, "You can say that again."

They spent a bit of time enjoying each other's company, he updated her on the morning's meetings. Parker mentioned to Damon that Ellie was looking for a new challenge within the company. She didn't want him to give her unfair advantages over others but wondered if he knew of a role that would be better suited to her. She was asking him as a boyfriend, not the boss. As she mulled over the term 'boyfriend', she wasn't exactly sure how they were supposed to reference each other.

"I'm going to break the unwritten rule and just ask you, Damon, what are we to each other?"

Damon smiled and gave her a brief kiss, "I know what I would like to call you but for now, shall we stick to partner? Girlfriend sounds so childish." Parker laughed, she knew exactly what he meant. She was grateful for his upfront response. Parker had always hated the games and politics of dating. She liked to know where she stood from the beginning.

"Are you coming over to mine tonight? Or I can come over to yours? Unless you aren't free of course." Damon blustered.

"Ellie is coming over to mine after work for a catch-up but you can come over later?"

"Sounds perfect." And he kissed her again. Each kiss took Parker's breath away. She didn't want to leave but needed to get home before Ellie arrived.

Parker waved goodbye to Patricia before heading back down in the elevator. She stopped by the admin department, hoping to see Rachel. Parker walked to her desk and paused as she was on the phone. She hovered, waiting for the call to end. As she stood there she glanced around the department, nothing had changed apart from a new person at her old desk.

Rachel's call had finally finished and she turned around in her seat. Parker hugged her before standing back, "I was in the office and wanted to say thank you. If it wasn't for your help, I would probably still be stuck in that awful cell."

"I was just happy I could help. I was shocked at first when the raven visited. I know that I told you that one of our powers was a connection to birds but I have never experienced it. It felt amazing like a part of my soul had been restored. I have told others in my line, our hopes have been renewed."

She then hugged Parker again, "I've been working on communicating with other birds. I managed a very basic connection but nothing like with the raven you sent."

"He seems to have stuck around, I named him Apollo. He really is wonderful, we can meet up and the two of us can work together to try to call another bird. Maybe Apollo can help."

"That would be amazing, just let me know when you're free." Parker gave Rachel her new number and promised to message her.

Parker saw that Ellie was still working. She was on the phone, so Parker headed out. She would be seeing her shortly anyway. After stepping outside, Parker felt a wave of reassurance and a familiar presence. She glanced around and saw Apollo flying overhead. She made a mental note to spend some extra time working with him, trying to enhance their bond.

Parker didn't feel the same anxiety and fear that previous walks to her car had caused. She was feeling more formidable and had her side-kick Apollo there too. Parker was aware that her fridge was mostly empty so swung by a store on the way home. She didn't want to stock up with too much perishable food, so bought a selection of freezer and cupboard essentials.

Ellie had pulled up a few seconds before Parker. She walked over to help unload her groceries. As soon as Ellie saw the state of the neglected plants, she went into forest nymph mode. She flitted between the different plants, providing water, trimming off dead leaves, moving them around and adding plant food.

When she had finished, Parker had a hot drink waiting for her at the breakfast bar. They sat down together and Parker started by thanking her for messaging her mum. "That's alright, I know you're close. I didn't want her to worry, I also knew that it would be difficult to explain after the fact. Especially with you not being able to tell her about us."

Parker nodded, "It has been hard not telling her everything but I've gotten around it by telling her everything else. She knows about you and Damon."

"Oh really, what does she know about Damon?" Ellie replied whilst smirking. They both began laughing.

"Well as you may have realised, we are back together. He explained what had happened with Acantha and I believe him. My trust is based on what I know of him and what I know of her."

"I'm glad, I've never seen him act this way around anyone else."

Parker then shared her latest run-in with Acantha. Ellie kept shaking her head in disbelief, "I don't think I could have responded as placidly as you. I would have had to get in some vicious digs of my own and rubbed in the fact that I was the one sharing his bed, not her."

"It was really tempting but I just wanted her to get the hint and go away."

Ellie nodded, "I can understand that. Let's just hope that she gets the message this time."

"The night before was an interesting one too. Damon took me out to this amazing Greek restaurant and we had a private room in the back." Parker then proceeded to tell her about the food and Esme. "Then came the walk home, which started out great. Then Deimos showed up."

"Are you alright? Did he hurt either of you?" Ellie asked concerned.

"No, don't worry. There were four of them including Deimos. Clearly, he is afraid of Damon. We know that he didn't see me as a threat but still brought three henchmen to face Damon. Luckily for me, we were next to the river and I began to concentrate like you taught me. You would have been so proud, I started with one of the jets and knocked one of his minions off his feet. He hit the floor so hard with his head, that he was completely knocked out.

"Then one redirected towards me. So, I created a giant tentacle from the water and grabbed him, dragging him into the river. Damon finished off the last henchman with a fist to the face, simple but extremely effective. Deimos conceded defeat and left."

Ellie looked shocked and proud at the same time, "Do you think he'll leave you alone now?"

"I hope so. We think that he'll try to move on to one of the other six women the prophecy alludes to. We just need to make sure that we find them first so that we can protect them from him."

"How are we going to find them?" Ellie queried.

"Absolutely no idea," Parker said flatly. They speculated for a while as to how the other women could be found but ended up not reaching a workable outcome.

Parker had been considering the stream in Ellie's garden and had asked if she would be able to create her own. Ellie had promised that they would work on it together the next time she was around. However, she didn't have time that evening as she had a date. Ellie told Parker that she had been seeing someone but that it was still very new and casual. She had a date planned with them after her catchup with Parker, so she had to run home to get changed.

Once Ellie had left, Parker washed up their cups and straightened out her living area. She heard her phone notification that there was someone at the door and simultaneously, she heard a knock. Parker opened the door to see Damon, Apollo flew in behind him, landing on a purpose-bought tree branch sculpture. Parker had seen it online and knew that it would be perfect for him to sit on.

He arrived with a bottle of white wine, a bouquet of deep red roses and a paper bag holding two brownies. After welcoming him with a kiss, she put the flowers in a vase and poured the wine into two glasses. Damon sat on the sofa whilst she was pouring the wine and she carried the glasses and bottle to the table in front of him. She then tucked herself into his body and asked what kind of film he wanted to watch, "I'll follow your lead, what do you suggest?"

After a brief consideration, she chose a film adaptation of a classic murder mystery and snuggled further into his side. They had both read the book so they knew who the killer was but they were intrigued as to how it had been adapted to film. Damon admitted that her touch was distracting and they spent the middle section of the film kissing, learning each other's moves and preferences.

Parker retrieved snacks from the kitchen and they spent the rest of the evening watching films and kissing. It meant that they missed large chunks of the films, but neither cared. It was already getting late by the time they retired upstairs, Parker felt that Damon's large presence made her cosy room feel positively small.

They both prepared for bed and Parker was tempted to put on her old cotton night dress again, just to tease him but she settled for a green silk chemise. As she turned to face Damon after getting changed, she saw him watching her.

He was staring at her intently as he sat on the bed. She sashayed towards him, putting an extra sway to her hips. He grinned and she pushed him backwards onto the bed, straddling him as she took charge. Parker liked the feeling of control. She kissed him sensually on the mouth. Teasing him and pushing him back down when he tried to rise and kiss her back.

After a couple of minutes of her being in control, Damon

growled in frustration and flipped her over onto her back with him between her legs. Parker pouted at the change of position but couldn't dwell on it as Damon pinned her hands above her head with one strong arm and then kissed her as hard and passionately as he had been wanting to, but she had denied him.

He caressed her body, sliding his hands over the silk. She was breathing deeply, wanting more. They couldn't get enough of each other, "I love you, Parker." Damon then kissed along her neck and collarbone, she grabbed his arms and pulled him back up to her face. Wrapping her legs around him she tried to pull his body closer, keeping eye contact the whole time. He resisted for a moment, before giving into her request and burying himself in her.

She felt overpoweringly connected to Damon and the pleasure was intense, she never wanted the moment to end. Time seemed to stand still and nothing else in the world mattered but them. They reached their final climax as one and Damon collapsed slightly to the side of her body, ensuring that she wasn't crushed by his mass. As Parker regained her senses, she thought back to Damon's statement, he loved her. She smiled contentedly and considered her own feelings.

Damon finally rose and Parker walked on wobbly legs to the bathroom. She had a quick clean-up, before choosing a different chemise and returning to bed. Damon climbed in behind her and tucked them both under the sheets.

Parker wasn't sure of her feelings yet. Did she love him? She knew that she cared for him a great deal and that she had strong feelings for him but wanted to be sure before telling him. At that moment she realised that she truly did love him. 'I love you too, Damon,' she whispered before falling asleep.

CHAPTER 20

The next two weeks passed without incident, Parker and Damon spent almost every night together. Most of their nights were spent at Damon's, "I would like to meet your family at some point, if you're alright with that?" Damon admitted.

"That would be great. I'll organise a barbeque or something so that you can meet them all in one go. It'll be like ripping off a band-aid." Parker laughed.

A few days later, Parker informed Damon, "I have spoken to my parents and sister about meeting you, they are free this coming weekend."

"Brilliant. I can do either day, whatever works for them."

"Let's schedule it for Sunday afternoon then. The kids usually attend clubs on a Saturday, this way they don't have to miss them."

Damon had offered to take food but Parker explained that her dad loved a barbeque and would have everything covered. Parker was feeling nervous, she wanted Damon to like her family. She also wanted her family to get on well with Damon.

When Sunday arrived, Parker wore jeans and a T-shirt and Damon followed suit. Begrudgingly, Parker had to admit that he wore it better. Damon followed her directions and pulled up outside her parent's bungalow. They had downsized a few years before once Parker and Cassie had left home.

It was painted a fresh cream colour and had rose bushes under the windows. Her brother-in-law was already parked out the front. Parker took a deep breath, before exiting the car. Damon took her hand as they walked towards the front door. As per their usual custom, Parker didn't knock before entering.

She turned right as they entered the hall, through a doorway and into the living room. Cassie took her husband's hand and pulled him towards them. "Welcome. I'm Cassie and this is Jake, my husband. Our four boys are currently running around in the garden. Mum and Dad bought them a new game, so they are having a great time."

"It's very nice to meet you, I'm Damon. I've heard a lot about you from Parker." He then shook Jake's hand.

Parker and Cassie left the two men talking about generic man stuff. They walked into the kitchen, to find their mum busily preparing the sides, "Hi Mum, can I help?" Parker offered.

"Hi dear. No thank you, it's all in hand. I just need to take a couple of items out of the oven, and I'm finished." She paused and then whispered, "So, where is he?" After noticing that Parker was alone.

"He's talking to Jake in the living room," Parker responded. As if summoned by their names, the two men strolled into the kitchen.

Damon walked up to her mum and smiled, "It's great to finally meet you, Deanna." Parker wasn't used to hearing her mum's name during get-togethers. She was always just Mum or Grandma. Her mum's face lit up, she dusted her hands off on her apron and walked towards Damon.

She placed her hand on his arm and replied, "It's wonderful to meet you too Damon. Would you like a drink?"

After drinks had been handed out to everyone, they filed out into the garden. The boys were looking at Damon suspiciously. They had always adored Auntie Parker, so they began sizing him up. Damon spent a while chatting to her dad. They started by discussing various barbeque techniques and the difference between cooking with gas and coal barbeques. Parker was watching him affectionately, he was making a great impression on her family.

They soon all had plates in hand and were sat in various mismatched garden chairs. Realising she had been initially tense and worried as to how this would pan out, Parker relaxed.

She was starting to enjoy herself. After he had finished eating, Damon joined the boys in their latest game. They were playing dodgeball. She was wondering how Damon would handle it. Would he be able to play human? Would he be too competitive to allow them to hit him?

She needn't have worried, Damon was amazing with the boys. They were still young and he tailored his response to the child. Malcolm was the oldest aged eight, Charlie came second at six, James had just turned five and Liam was three. When Liam threw the ball at Damon, he allowed it to hit him in the leg.

Damon fell to the floor with an exaggerated imaginary injury, Liam was in hysterics laughing. The boys then proceeded to pile on top of him. Parker was laughing, she didn't think that it was possible to love him more than in that moment.

After a few hours of chatting and nibbling on food, they made their excuses and said goodbye. She knew that it was a success when halfway through the afternoon, Liam fell asleep on Damon's lap. Parker promised her parents that they would be back to visit again soon.

The next week was uneventful. Parker hadn't forgotten her promise and arranged for a session with Rachel, to work on their powers. She had scheduled it for a Saturday morning. Rachel was eager, so Parker didn't want to delay it longer than necessary.

Parker had arranged for it to be at her house, as she didn't feel right organising it at someone else's home. She ensured that she was there first thing, to carry out any cleaning that may be required.

Rachel knocked on her door and Parker's phone notified her of a guest. Parker invited Rachel inside and offered her a drink, "I'm alright thank you. I have just finished an espresso. If I have any more caffeine, I'll be bouncing off the walls." They both chuckled. Parker then led her into the garden, where she had laid out a blanket and some cushions.

Rachel had come dressed in comfortable loungewear, she

thought that it may help her to relax and focus. They both sat with their backs to her house, facing into the garden. Parker had already placed trays of bird seed around the blanket, to encourage them into the garden.

Parker wasn't sure which of her actions in the cell caused Apollo to appear, so she repeated the entire process from the beginning. As in the cell, first, she called out to them. Following that, she closed her eyes and projected her thoughts, willing them to appear. Apollo flew down and landed in her lap, Parker laughed, "It wasn't you I was trying to call this time." And she tickled his head affectionately. He appeared to nod in response and settled next to her on the blanket.

Rachel copied her actions almost exactly. She tried speaking to the birds and tried to project her thoughts. They waited a few minutes but no bird appeared. Parker suggested that they both close their eyes and project their thoughts. She hadn't tried this before but was hoping that combining their thoughts would amplify them.

"Is there a specific type of bird that you feel an affinity with?" Parker asked.

Rachel paused and considered her answer, "I have always loved robins, I think they're beautiful."

"Alright, let's try and focus on calling a robin. Imagine one in your mind and focus."

They both closed their eyes again, imagining a robin. It couldn't have been longer than ten minutes before Parker heard a twittering in front of them. Opening her eyes she saw a robin on the edge of the blanket, staring at them curiously. Parker quietly explained how she initially bonded with Apollo and Rachel followed her lead.

Parker silently observed the interaction, whilst stroking Apollo's feathers. It took a while, but eventually, the robin hopped onto Rachel's knee. She stroked him gently and he appeared to nuzzle into her hand. Rachel looked at Parker with delight, "She's wonderful!"

"Don't be disheartened if she doesn't choose to stay. I

wasn't sure what Apollo was going to do at first, I think he took pity on me." Parker grinned.

"I completely understand. I think that one of the reasons we lost our ability to communicate with birds, is that we started to take them for granted. I'm just so thankful that I've been given this opportunity, I won't waste it. Thank you, Parker."

"It's the least I can do," she responded smiling. She was glad that she had been able to help her.

Parker felt like this was the least she could do, she owed Rachel for her rescue. "There is one thing though," Rachel continued, "You may be inundated with requests from other harpies, we are all desperate to reclaim our lost abilities. I'm not sure about the others but I've always felt like a part of me was missing."

Parker wanted to help as many people as possible but she was concerned that it would become a full-time job. Would all those who approached her use the power for good? She knew how it could be used for nefarious means, like spying on people. Deimos would want to have access to this ability. Parker decided to cross that bridge when she came to it.

Rachel and Parker spent the morning in the garden. Rachel had been bonding with the robin and Parker was playing with Apollo, "I suppose it's time that I head home, I just hope this little lady follows me there." Parker rose and walked her to the door. They hugged and she promised that she would be there to try again if it didn't work out with the robin.

Damon had messaged her whilst she had been outside: *Are you free tonight? - D Xx*

Parker replied: *Yes, what do you have in mind? - P Xx*

A few minutes later she received a response: *A night in, just the two of us at my house. 6pm – D xx*

Parker smiled, she loved spending time with Damon. She then called Ellie to ask if she was free. She was eager to cultivate a stream in her garden. Parker had tried to do it solo but she just ended up soaked with a swampy garden. Ellie promised that she would be around within the hour and would be bringing lunch.

Ellie turned up with a selection of tacos and they both tucked in as soon as she arrived, "No one wants to work on an empty stomach." Ellie grinned. They hadn't been spending as much time together lately, as Parker had been with Damon most nights and Ellie had been with her current love interest. Parker still hadn't met him but Ellie kept promising that it would happen soon. She wanted to decide whether she was serious about him first.

They lounged on the same blanket that Parker and Rachel sat on in the morning and Ellie took the lead. She explained the theory behind creating the stream. They had to call the water, direct it, then release the water at the other end. They also had to insert a fixed command, so that it would continue indefinitely. Parker was excited to have a stream and had decided exactly where she wanted it. She liked the idea that she would have access to a source of water, it brought her a sense of calm.

It took a lot longer than Parker had expected, Ellie explained that it sometimes took hours. However, she was hoping that it was quicker than that, due to the two of them working together. By the time it was finally established, Parker had a numb bottom. The cushions had started out being useful but after hours of being sat there, she was incredibly stiff.

Ellie was raving to Parker about her new job, she was assisting Patricia and the senior team. Her job seemed to fit with her personality. There was always something new, she ran errands, helped to organise their meetings, engaged with other departments and worked closely with Patricia.

Parker was happy to hear that Ellie was so content in her new role. She had ensured that Ellie knew that she had asked Damon's opinion, on where he thought she would thrive. It was clear that it wasn't a case of favouritism, as Damon had assigned Patricia the task of recruiting and interviewing. Ellie was the best person for the job and was promoted on her own merit.

Time got away from them both and Parker had to rush Ellie out of the door, as she wanted to shower and change before meeting Damon. Even though it was a quiet night in, she wanted to put a bit of effort into her outfit. She wore a red strappy dress with black tights and added extra makeup, to accentuate her eyes.

She climbed into the company car after locking up. Parker knew that she couldn't keep it forever but she enjoyed driving it so much. She told herself that she would keep it for one more week before returning it. After that, she would have to decide what she was going to do about getting a new car.

Parker pulled up outside Damon's, it was a beautifully clear evening. The stars illuminated her path to the front door where she let herself in. She could smell roasted lamb and her mouth began to water.

Damon appeared from the kitchen and smiled as he saw her. He had also put effort into his outfit tonight. He was wearing black jeans with a black shirt. The shirt sleeves had been rolled up to his elbows and the top two buttons of the shirt were undone.

They met each other in the middle and embraced, when they parted Damon spoke, "You look gorgeous."

Parker smiled, then replied, "You don't look too bad yourself, Mr Minos." And she winked at him before they both laughed, "Dinner smells wonderful, did you cook?" Parker enquired.

"Yes. It's almost done, come with me." He then led her towards the rear of his house, Parker was wondering where they were heading.

Damon took her through the back door and out into his garden. He had completely covered the rear in stunning flowers. A deep red rose arch had been placed across the path. He had even sourced a patio heater, to ensure that she was warm enough.

There was a small wooden table and two chairs. Two places were set, and the candles placed in the centre were emitting a soft glow. He had considered everything, the gentle lighting ensured that the stars weren't drowned out by a harsh light.

He guided her to one of the chairs, leaned over her and kissed her briefly. Parker was grinning from ear to ear, no one had ever gone to this much effort for her before. She was planning on enjoying every moment of it and was feeling very loved. He brought back a glass of white wine for her to drink whilst she waited. Parker relaxed and looked up at the stars, she could identify one or two constellations but soon exhausted her knowledge.

Damon placed their plates down on the table, he had cooked a roast lamb dinner. Parker was really touched by the effort he had put in, she squeezed his hand, "I love you."

He smiled, "I love you too." They began eating, she was really impressed with his cooking skills. She was going to persuade him to cook more often.

Apollo had visited briefly to steal some food before leaving again. She sensed him settling in a tree nearby, happily eating his hoard. Once dinner had finished, Parker sat back and gazed out over the garden. Damon cleared the plates and when he returned, they sat in comfortable silence.

"Has anyone explained to you about our ancient rites? Where two individuals bind themselves together?"

"Yes, Cad briefly mentioned it when he was explaining about supernaturals."

"That's good. Throughout our history, supernaturals have been able to bind themselves to a human. There is a ritual and when completed, the human's life extends to match that of the supernatural. It was a gift bestowed on us from the beginning and one we cherish. The decision is never taken lightly, as once bound it can never be undone.

"We are each given one chance at binding. This causes a lot of supernaturals to fear the commitment. As you know from the high divorce rate in our country, people make mistakes. If a human falls for the wrong person, they can divorce and remarry. Supernatural-human relationships can end but they can't then bind themselves to another. The fear is that they then meet their soulmate, they would have to watch them age and die, whilst the supernatural lives the remainder of their lives alone."

"Cad told me that it had been failing, that the last two attempts hadn't worked."

"He is correct, luckily my parent's binding worked. I can't imagine what my dad would have done if my mum had aged before him and he had to live without her. Theirs was one of the last that did work. There's a reason I wanted to discuss this with you. Parker, I love you more than I can ever say. In you, I have found my soulmate, my equal. I know that I want you by my side for the rest of my life. Will you undertake the binding ritual with me?" He had taken her hand in his and looked vulnerable, yet full of hope.

Parker's heart felt like it was bursting in her chest, she was so happy and wanted nothing more than to be with the man in front of her forever, "Yes. Definitely. Yes." And she leapt up from her seat and kissed him whilst straddling his legs.

She had never felt so complete and happy. Damon looked like a giant weight had been lifted from his shoulders, ecstatic that she had agreed to spend their lives together. He was grinning at her and Parker rained kisses down all over his face, whilst laughing. Damon led her across to the Adirondack chairs and she sat in his lap. He kept kissing the top of her head whilst running his hand up and down her back.

Thoughts were flying through Parker's head, would she tell her parents? How would she explain a supernatural ritual to them? How would Ellie react when she told her? Does this mean that she will be moving in with Damon? Is it like marriage where you can take the other person's surname? Is marriage still a possibility?

She had a lot of questions but pushed them aside as she wanted to enjoy the moment. Parker lay against Damon and they looked up at the stars. Damon began pointing out the different constellations and telling the stories behind them.

He then pointed out Taurus, "It's one of the oldest constellations. If you look closely, you'll see that one of his eyes shines brighter than the others. That is a giant red star, called

Aldebaran." After a brief pause, he continued, "Have you heard the story of Andromeda and Perseus?" Parker shook her head.

"Andromeda was the daughter of King Cepheus and Queen Cassiopeia. The Queen boasted to everyone about her daughter's beauty. She also boasted that Andromeda was far more beautiful than the Nereids. When Poseidon heard of her boast, he became angered and vowed vengeance. Poseidon's wife was a Nereid.

"He sent a sea monster called Cetus to destroy her home and the city in which they lived. Poseidon's command was that Andromeda was sacrificed to the creature. Her father, the King, chained her to a rock to be sacrificed. Perseus happened upon Andromeda, he fell in love and decided to rescue her. He then slayed the beast and asked for her hand in marriage. They were then wed.

"It was a happily ever after story, they had eight children together. After their death, they were both turned into constellations. This allowed their love to exist in the heavens eternally." As Damon spoke, he pointed out the constellations for each of the characters, Andromeda, Perseus, King Cepheus, Queen Cassiopeia and Cetus the sea creature.

Parker was disappointed when the story ended, she was enjoying Damon's soothing voice. She began to shiver, so they rose and went inside where it was warm. "Do you think the ritual will work?" Parker asked Damon, it was the one question that wouldn't wait.

"You have shaken things up. I believe that provided we go into this with every fibre of our being, it will work. If it doesn't work, we can always try again. If we are only supposed to have fifty or sixty years together, I will take all I can." Parker's eyes welled up with tears and she kissed Damon lovingly, hoping to convey her feelings through that one act.

"I would like to invite the team over tomorrow, to let them know the good news. Of course, that's only if you are alright with that."

"Yes, I would love to be able to share the news. We have to

invite Ellie too."

"I didn't think that needed saying," Damon replied with a grin.

They moved inside to the living room and spent the next twenty minutes organising the following day via messages, "I almost forgot." Damon stated before leaving the room again, "I did have a backup plan in case you said 'No'." He then held out a plate with a brownie on top.

Parker smiled, taking the plate from him. "How would you have used this to sway me?" She teased.

"Well, I spoke to the company that makes these. I persuaded them to share their recipe with me and I made this one myself. I had to promise to keep their secret recipe to myself. So, the added bonus for you of saying 'yes', is that I can make you these brownies for the rest of our lives together. That is, until you get bored of them." And they both began laughing.

"Don't worry, I won't get fed up with these anytime soon." Parker savoured it. He had made it exactly like the bakery. They spent the rest of the evening discussing the ritual. Damon explained what it entailed and what would be expected of them both. It wasn't as formal as it initially sounded. Provided certain steps were taken, the rest was fluid. Usually, Parker would spend her time searching for information online but she would have to be patient and wait.

Parker was beginning to get tired. Damon never seemed to tire, he was always up before her. She would have liked to have his energy but she also really enjoyed her bed. The only time that he had looked less than perfect, was after she had been kidnapped. His exhausted face and the darkness under his eyes displayed his concern.

They flowed through their usual routine, undertaking the various tasks in turn. She had left a range of clothes at Damon's. It was easier than trying to remember everything, every time she stayed.

They snuggled up together under the sheets, their touches were gentler and more tender than before. Instead of being a passionate desperate affair, each touch was light and careful. Really exploring each other's bodies. The kisses were light and Damon proceeded to kiss every inch of her body lovingly. Parker closed her eyes and focused on how they felt, grabbing onto the sheet beneath her.

He then slowly slid up her body and whilst kissing her, they joined together. It was slow and it made it feel more intense. She could feel every movement. Parker finished moments before Damon, his continuing movements after release were almost too much. He then reached his peak, falling down onto his side and pulling Parker towards him. She fell asleep in his arms.

Her dreams that night were happy, sitting in a flower-filled field with Damon as he played with her hair. Followed by him meeting her family for the first time, which ended in them all doing the macarena. Once again, she didn't remember them in the morning.

CHAPTER 21

The following morning was another lovely day, the sun streamed through the windows around the blinds. Damon had stayed in bed with her, answering and sending work emails on his phone as she slept. Parker liked him being there when she woke and she showed her appreciation with a deep kiss. She then remembered about morning breath and shuffled into the bathroom.

When she returned, she climbed back into bed. Damon put his phone away and kissed her. Parker then settled into him, he had one arm around her and was tickling her arm. They sat there enjoying each other's company, she was in no rush to move.

Damon said, "I hope that I've made it clear how much I love you. You made me the happiest man alive when you agreed to perform the ancient ritual with me. I know that you didn't grow up in our world and have other traditions, so I want to commit to you in every way possible. Will you marry me?" He then produced a ring box, Parker was grinning. He was right, she had grown up in the human world and marriage was important to her.

He opened the box, inside was a stunningly beautiful ring. It had a large red stone surrounded by diamonds, the band was platinum. After kissing him, she allowed him to slip the ring onto her finger. She kissed him again, whispering 'yes' into his mouth. Unfortunately, the ring was slightly large and Parker feared losing it.

Damon placed it back in the box, he was going to get it resized as soon as possible. Parker was disappointed that she couldn't wear it but it was only a symbol and didn't change the fact that they were engaged. They remained in bed for another hour, enjoying each other before forcing themselves to get up.

After dressing they went downstairs, Damon prepared breakfast. She had bacon, eggs, and buttered toast with a cup of tea. They sat next to each other and read the morning papers whilst eating. Parker smiled, they already acted like an old married couple.

"Do you want to come shopping with me? I need to grab some food for the get-together. After hearing you mention a barbeque yesterday, I was thinking we could do that. It's supposed to be good weather today." Damon asked.

"Yes, I'll come with you. I can add my own choices to the trolley."

Before they headed out, Parker wanted to spend some time with Apollo. She felt like he had been slightly neglected in the last couple of weeks. She took a blanket and a hot drink outside. Parker sat in one of the Adirondacks and called Apollo to her.

A couple of minutes later, she saw him flying in from the distance. It did cause Parker to wonder what their communication range was. When Apollo landed on her knee, she queried how far away he was when he heard her call. Apollo sent her an image of a pond in a park.

Parker was familiar with it, the park was a couple of miles away. She made a mental note to test their range later and sent her thoughts to Apollo who nodded. Parker asked him what he had been up to, for the first time his response was more than just brief images.

She saw a video playing in her mind, along with his feelings. He had been hunting for food. Parker experienced his search, followed by the thrill of the chase. Finishing in the capture of an insect and the satisfaction that accompanied it. Parker spent some more time with him, feeding him scraps from the kitchen.

Eventually, she informed him of their plans and stroked

him before returning inside. They headed out in Damon's Range Rover, it had a lot more boot space than hers. He avoided the smaller stores and headed straight for the larger supermarket.

Her standard trip to a supermarket usually consisted of browsing for a long time, followed by spending a lot more than she intended. However, Damon went straight to the butcher's section of the store. He started piling ribs, burgers, chicken, sausages and steaks into the trolley. Parker was shocked at the amount of food he was buying but then remembered who they were going to be catering for.

They headed over to the sides, they bought bread, halloumi, sweetcorn and salad. He picked up extra cheese for the burgers and a large selection of beers. "I already have plenty of wine at home, is there something specific you would like?" Parker nodded and headed over to the soft drinks, adding a couple of bottles of cola to the trolley.

Desserts were next and they bought a selection of pastries. Damon stopped to pick up coal for the barbeque. Rachel spotted Parker whilst shopping and she rushed over and hugged her, "It worked, she decided to stay with me. I've been working with her every day to grow our bond. I couldn't be happier. I decided to call her 'Red'. My sister is jealous, I've tried to sit down with her and combine our powers like you and I did," She whispered that part, "But it just hasn't worked for her. I promised that I would ask if you could help her too. But don't feel pressured, I've told her that you are extremely busy and she understands."

"I'm so glad that it worked for you. I can't promise when just yet but I'm sure I can try for her. I'll be in touch with you to organise." Rachel hugged her once more before leaving.

Damon had stood back during the conversation, once again not used to being ignored. He found the interaction quite amusing and kissed Parker, "You are amazing." She just grinned in response and strutted towards the checkout.

On the drive home, Parker said, "I know that we'll tell everyone about the engagement when they arrive but we also need to tell our family as soon as possible. I'm thinking that we should pop over to my parents one night this week, to share the news."

"Yes, that works. I'll call mine tomorrow, it will be too late once everyone leaves tonight."

Parker couldn't wait to tell her family. She was excited but wanted to do it face-to-face. She began imagining Cassie's reaction, she would want to know their plans immediately. Parker was pleased that she could share that moment with her family.

Her mind then drifted back to the comfort of Damon's car, which reminded her, "Can you come with me at some point in the next couple of weeks to buy a new car? I feel like they will be less likely to try and take advantage of me if you're there."

"Of course. You're more than welcome to keep the company car though. I can see if they have a different one if you don't like it?"

"It's not that, I love the car. I just want to buy my own, I don't want to take advantage."

"What if I wanted to treat you to a car?" Damon replied.

"I would say that's very kind of you, but I am a strong independent woman," And she laughed, "I like the idea of buying my own car. I've been saving a lot of money lately with not having to pay for such a high mortgage."

"Alright, just let me know when and we can go." Damon conceded.

Parker had been thinking about how she had let her training lapse, so as they returned to Damon's she asked, "Do you mind if I take an hour to practice the Yoga Cad taught me? I haven't done it for a while now but I want to keep it up."

"No, of course not. I have a basement with mats that you can use." He then guided her to a nondescript door, it was the only door downstairs that she hadn't explored.

Parker went up to their room and donned her workout gear, she should have just enough time to squeeze in a quick session and shower before the others arrived. After changing she returned to the door.

There was a flight of stone stairs leading down to a basement, she was nervous that it would bring back bad memories of the cell. Parker paused for a minute on the top step, she didn't want those memories to hold her back and she forced herself to descend.

However, it was so brightly lit, that it was the opposite of the dungeon. She proceeded down and one wall was taken up with mirrors, she faced them as it would help her with her alignment.

Her wrist had been irritating her all morning but she had been ignoring it as they had been busy. Now she was wearing a vest top she inspected her wrist, the tattoo had changed. A letter had been emblazoned in the centre of the circle, 'A'. She immediately ran upstairs, yelling, "Damon!".

He almost ran into her in his panic, "What's wrong? Are you alright?" Scanning her from head to toe. Once he saw that she wasn't hurt, he searched the room for a threat.

"I'm fine, the tattoo has changed." She then showed him her wrist, he took it gently in his hands.

After a minute of inspecting it, he voiced his thoughts, "This may mean that your heart's true desire has been met." He repeated the prophecy, "When the seven women of man are born and their heart's true desires are met, restored will be the powers of those who in their ways are set." He then looked up into her eyes, his smile was beaming.

Damon lifted her up and kissed her deeply, before lowering her gently. Parker teasingly rolled her eyes, "Alright, settle down. You already know how I feel about you. I have agreed to the ritual, remember. So, you being my heart's desire shouldn't come as a surprise to you."

"It's nice for it to be confirmed though," Damon stated, still beaming.

Parker enquired, "Should we contact the others to let them know the change?"

"They will all be here within the hour for the barbeque, we

can tell everyone then." Parker was running out of time for Yoga, so went back upstairs and dressed ready for people arriving. She put on a blue-fitted short-sleeved top and grey flowing skirt, before returning downstairs. Parker belatedly felt guilty that she hadn't helped Damon with any of the prep work for the get-together.

He was outside in the garden and had begun warming up the barbeque, the meat was all ready to go. Parker heard the door and went to answer it, Cad and Greg were the first to arrive and she welcomed them inside. Before she could shut the door, the others had all pulled up. Their timing was impeccable.

Everyone was ushered in, including Ellie. They all congregated in the kitchen and Damon cleared his throat to get everyone's attention, "We have asked you all here today as we wanted to share some news with you. Parker has agreed to undertake the ancient rites with me. She has also agreed to be my wife." He grinned, before pulling Parker to his side.

The guys all slapped him on the back and congratulated them both. Zack hugged Damon before hugging Parker, "Welcome to the family." Parker grinned back at Zack.

Damon then interrupted, "Before we continue the hugs, we also need to tell you that we believe Parker's part of the prophecy has been fulfilled. Her tattoo has changed." Parker held out her wrist, whilst everyone inspected the new letter in the centre.

Seth spoke up, "It seems to me that once their heart's desire is met, a letter of 'Abraxas' is inserted in the centre. It's a great indicator for us, we will know how far it is progressing. But I don't think this is the end of Parker's role. There will unquestionably be more to come."

They discussed the prophecy for a few minutes and the possibilities. Ellie said loudly, "Alright, that's enough about the prophecy for now. Let's focus on celebrating Damon and Parker today. Where's the ring?" She walked over and hugged Parker tightly.

Ellie threw her head back, her eyes had turned white. In

a voice that didn't sound like her own, she rasped, "The next of the seven has emerged to fulfil the prophecy." Her head then snapped back to face forward, her eyes were still white and she was mumbling. Several minutes passed and Parker's concern was growing but she didn't know what to do.

Ellie's eyes finally cleared and she began to slump, Leo surged forward and grabbed her before she hit the floor and carried her into the larger living room. He placed her carefully on the sofa and Adam placed a cushion under her head. Parker sat by her side, not wanting to leave her until she came to, "Damon, what do we do?" Parker asked him desperately.

Damon came to stand behind her and placed his hand on her shoulder, "She will be fine. Our ancestors had visions all the time and were never harmed. We just need to be patient, her mind is processing it all. She will wake up once she has made sense of it. I'm going to take the guys out the back, it'll give you some quiet in here. I'll start cooking, people still need feeding and it gives us something to focus on."

Parker sat by Ellie's side over the next hour, Damon brought her a plate of food. She nibbled at it but had lost her appetite. She knew in her head that Ellie was going to be fine, but she still felt sick.

Ellie began to stir and sat up, "Well, this is definitely better than waking up on the floor like last time." She chuckled.

Parker sighed in relief and hugged her, "You had me worried, your eyes went white and you spoke in a completely different voice."

"I wasn't aware of that as I obviously can't see myself when I have a vision. I understand why you would be concerned."

"Are you ready to tell the guys what you saw? Or do you need a moment first?"

"Other than aching slightly, I feel fine. Call them in. We need to act quickly." Parker rushed out of the room, she saw Adam first and asked him to get everyone back in the living room.

Once everyone was seated, Ellie shut her eyes and explained what she saw in her vision, "I started out in a car park, there were oak trees lining the left-hand side. There were maybe spaces for about two hundred cars. It isn't somewhere I have been before. I was facing a large supermarket. The colour scheme was green but I couldn't make out the name. Out in front of the building, there were wooden benches and floral planters.

"I began walking towards the building, children were playing to the far right. I think that there may have been a school or a playground. Outside the building there stood a woman waiting for a taxi, she had a cluster of brown shopping bags around her feet. She had dark brown hair, it's almost black. There was a wave to it and it sat on her shoulders.

"Her skin looked golden like she had a very good tan. I couldn't see her eye colour, it may be green or blue. She was very petite and was wearing a dungaree romper, with a black T-shirt underneath. The woman suddenly grasped her wrist, she looked to be in a small amount of pain. A tattoo matching Parker's appeared. The centre was empty. I had a strong feeling of urgency, we need to get to her fast."

Adam pushed a pen and paper into Ellie's hands, she began sketching a picture of the location and the woman. "How are we going to find her?" Parker enquired.

Damon started pacing, "Once Ellie has finished sketching, we will get the whole of the IT department on the hunt. Hopefully, Ellie has provided enough information to narrow it down for us. We can split the team, half searching for her image online and the other half searching for the location. We need to get to her before Deimos, the feeling of urgency concerns me."

Parker merely nodded, this must be how they felt when they were searching for her. Ellie was sketching as fast as she could, a picture was appearing before her eyes. The woman was beautiful, she looked delicate but had a determined expression on her face.

When Ellie finally finished drawing the woman, Cad took a picture and brought out his laptop. Whilst Ellie moved on to sketching the location, he started a software program running. Trying to match her features with social media profile pictures, Parker imagined that it would be difficult in the age of filters.

It was a long night, Cad contacted as much of his team as possible and requested that they work overtime. Everyone was using every device possible to search for this unknown woman. When the pot and tattoo first appeared, Parker wasn't impressed with the guy's handling of the situation. After all, no one appreciates being called a thief. However, she wasn't left alone and ignorant. This poor woman has had a tattoo branded on her wrist and she has no idea what it was or where it came from.

They weren't sure whether Ellie's vision was of the past, present or future. Parker was finding it hard to focus on the phone screen, she wouldn't know if it was the right woman or not in this condition. Ellie was in a similar situation, the vision had exhausted her.

Damon encouraged them both to get some rest, Parker took his bedroom and Ellie used Parker's old room. She was considering taking some tablets as she had a pounding headache but decided that she would rather shut her eyes and not move again.

Parker was lucky, her headache subsided enough with her eyes shut that she fell asleep almost instantly. She woke when Damon shook her the next morning. "We think that we've located her. The store is two hours from here. I didn't want to leave without telling you."

She sat straight up in bed, "I need to go with you. Just imagine, you and the guys turning up and asking her to go with you. You don't exactly scream harmless. You need me and Ellie with you."

Damon nodded, "I didn't even think of that. Can you hurry getting dressed? We need to leave immediately."

Parker leapt out of bed and rushed her bathroom visit. They were taking three cars, Ellie and Parker joined Damon. Leo, Seth and Cad took the second with Greg, Zack and Adam in the third. They drove in tandem, pushing the speed limit the whole way. Damon briefed Ellie and Parker on what they had found.

"The woman's name is Grace Byrne. It's unclear where she's from originally. She's twenty-six years old and single. Her social media accounts were locked down, so we struggled to get any more information on her. The minimal information we obtained combined with the supermarket image and description gave us the location. I just hope that we get to her before Deimos does."

Parker relaxed in the car and glanced out of the window at the passing scenery. It was going to take two hours to get there, so all she could do was wait. Ellie spoke up from the rear, "Sorry about my vision stealing your limelight from yesterday. We're all extremely happy for you both."

Parker laughed, "It wasn't really your choice. It doesn't matter anyway, things are always hectic around here. Maybe one day it will calm down." Damon placed his hand on her thigh and squeezed reassuringly.

Parker turned the sound up on the radio to fill the silence but they were barely listening to it. They all felt the sense of urgency weighing heavily on them. When they were only a few minutes from the destination, Parker sat forward in her seat. She was staring at the people they were passing, hoping to spot Grace in the crowd.

Damon turned into a car park and her stomach sank, there were police everywhere with flashing lights. An area had been cordoned off. He parked at the far side, near the oak trees. Parker and Ellie exited from the car, they blended in far better than the men. Once they were near the entrance, Parker saw that in the cordoned-off area there were several brown bags strewn over the floor.

They moved closer to try and overhear the police chatter but they weren't discussing the facts of the incident. Ellie and Parker split up, to each try and get as much information as possible. There were a couple of women who were gossiping about the incident, so Parker sidled up to them, "Wow, what's happened? It must be something major to have this many police." The older of the two women glanced at her before excitedly including her in the gossip.

"Apparently, there was a young woman waiting for a taxi and a van pulled up next to her. People heard a disagreement before the sliding door opened and a man pulled her into the back. They sped off with their tyres squealing. All her shopping was just left behind." Parker turned pale and she excused herself as soon as she could, she walked back to Damon's car.

She climbed inside and turned to Damon, "Deimos has Grace."

AUTHOR NOTE

Thank you so much for reading The Abraxas Prophecy and following Parker's journey!

I hope that you enjoyed the story as much as I enjoyed writing it.

For information on future releases, please sign up for my newsletter at **hfpayneauthor.com** or follow me on Instagram **@hf.payne**

If you enjoyed the book, please consider leaving a review. Every review makes a huge difference to an author and it is greatly appreciated.

Thank you for your support.

H.F. Payne

Printed in Great Britain
by Amazon